Strange things happen in The Gulp.

The residents have grown used to it.

The isolated Australian harbour town of Gulpepper is not like other places. Some maps don't even show it. And only outsiders use the full name. Everyone who lives there calls it The Gulp. The place has a habit of swallowing people.

A couple of weed dealers give themselves a real headache.

A young man finds joy in a secret place with the new love of his life.

The children of violent, bigoted parents fight for survival.

One of the world's biggest stars takes time out in Gulpepper's newest Institution.

The return of an old foe threatens the existence of Gulpepper itself.

Five more novellas. Five more descents into darkness.

Welcome to The Gulp, where nothing is as it seems.

PRAISE FOR THE RISE

"At the center of Gulpepper is a blackened heart that pumps fear into each of these new stories. With The Rise, Baxter proves there is far more lore to uncover, and while I'd never spend a minute in this town myself, I sure as hell love reading about the poor souls who do." – *John Durgin, author of The Cursed Among Us and The Envelope*

"In *The Rise*, Alan Baxter returns to Gulpepper, and there's something about this small town that draws you in. Wouldn't want to live there, not sure it's the safest holiday destination either, but I'm still thrilled to set foot on its disturbing streets once again. These five new novellas balance masterfully between heartbreaking, horrific, and out-right action packed. Whether you're a hardened local, or visiting for the first time, any trip to The Gulp is an experience you'll never forget." – *Joanne Anderton, author of Pixerina: A Haunting and The Bone Chime Song*

PRAISE FOR TALES FROM THE GULP

"If you're a fan of one town horror anthologies with a best of 80s vibe (like anything from *Castle Rock* or Josh Malerman's *Goblin*) then you really should get yourself some 'Tales from the Gulp' by Alan Baxter." – *Sarah Pinborough, bestselling author of BEHIND HER EYES*

"...filled with relentless tension." – *Hellnotes*

"Alan Baxter has created a stunning collection of small town horror that perfectly blends tones and themes of The Twilight Zone, Stranger Things, Castle Rock, The X-Files and Twin Peaks – in an irresistible concoction of the weird and macabre, small town horror has never had it so good... An arrestingly brilliant collection of horror that bewitches its reader and pollutes the mind with Baxter's mastery of horror in all its dark shades" – *Ross Jeffery at Storgy Magazine*

"The Gulp delivers on all fronts." – *Jim McLeod at Ginger Nuts of Horror*

"It feels like Baxter has crafted the literary equivalent of a Venus flytrap and, by the time we feel the descent towards our own doom, the trap is already closing..." – *Thomas Joyce at This Is Horror*

"Welcome to The Gulp, a town of eldritch terrors, disturbing mysteries, and pulpy horror at its absolute best. Vividly created and authentically Aussie, these novellas are delicious fun for fans of the genre. Prepare to revel in them, but beware... they will creep into your dreams." – *Joanne Anderton, award-winning author of The Bone Chime Song & Other Stories*

"Kept me turning the pages fast and furious... we get a perfect mix of crime thriller and straight up horror. Baxter is able to mix those two genres seamlessly and create an environment where absolutely nothing seems out of the realm of possibility. Anything can and does happen..." – *Joe Scipione at Horror Bound*

"Fancy some Eldritch nightmares? Then look no further. The Gulp is the perfect combination of weird, brutal and creepy." – *Tammy at Books, Bones & Buffy*

"Alan Baxter has found his Castle Rock. Baxter has time and time again released highwater releases, so to see him elevate his game to yet another level was truly stunning and made me smile. This is a collection with no weak links, no dip in quality or storytelling and with the familiarity of each character and the town itself, one that will surely become a classic release... Baxter has set the bar high in the past, but he easily surpassed it and more. Solid storytelling, real characters and a setting both beautiful and depraved. Baxter hits the ground running here and never lets us get off the thrill ride. We're all the better for it." – *Steve Stred at Kendall Reviews*

"Great structure ... recurring characters and locations ... a bigger picture that is as mesmerizing as it is confusing ... wonderfully weird and dangerous. The Gulp is obviously the start of something glorious!" – *Aiden Merchant*

"I thoroughly enjoyed every page of this book and was sad to see it end. In creating The Gulp, Baxter has created his own playland mash up of Innsmouth and Castle Rock. There are so many more big background stories to be told and so many more inhabitants to learn about. I hope we get to visit The Gulp again soon." – *Brandi the Bibliophile*

"Warped. Twisted. Fabulous. 5 out of 5." – *Leo McBride at Altered Instinct*

"a more than worthy sequel and a phenomenal opportunity for readers to set foot again in this horrifying little town-by-the-sea" – *Brennan LaFaro at Dead Headspace*

"I typically don't find myself liking a sequel to a book/movie but this is not that type of situation at all. Baxter has such an elegant way of intertwining all the stories together that I am just blown away at how talented he is in his craft–one of the best in my opinion."
– *nw.reader*

"It deeply pleases me that Australian horror is alive and well and this incredibly satisfying." – *Flick at Strange Queer Things*

"*The Fall* by Alan Baxter is the incredible follow up to *The Gulp*, and in this collection of five new tales, the twisted web drawing the town further and further into chaos is getting stickier! Horror readers, this is another book by Mr. Baxter that you cannot miss." – *Erica Robyn Reads*

"*The Fall* ratchets the tension from page one, as readers are drawn into the twisted, dark world of Gulpepper. Nothing is as it seems, and Alan Baxter takes no shortcuts, and no prisoners. Inventive, fast-paced and often disturbing, have no fear you'll be treading old ground. Baxter has created a world of bottomless terrors, no two alike yet intricately woven together in a web that tightens around you the further you descend. Highly recommended." – *Laurel Hightower, author of Crossroads and Below*

"Read this book in one sitting. Couldn't stop. Alan Baxter hit it out of the park again with his continuing stories about the sinister and mysterious town of Gulpepper, or The Gulp as town citizens call it." – *Crystal Pegasus*

"With *The Gulp*, Baxter created a stunning setting and entwined stories that creeped me out and had me riveted. With *The Fall*, Baxter manages to keep the setting/town as bonkers as ever, while delivering even BETTER stories than the first. And that's saying something." – *Steve Stred, author of Mastodon*

"The imagery in these stories is off the charts. There are great visuals and complex characters that make you root for them with every turn of the page. Another great effort form Alan Baxter and I hope we get another Gulp book in the future. 5 out of 5." – *Joe Scipione at Horrorbound*

PRAISE FOR ALAN BAXTER

"Baxter delivers the horror goods." – *Paul Tremblay, author of The Cabin at the End of the World*

"Alan Baxter is an accomplished storyteller who ably evokes magic and menace." – *Laird Barron, author of Swift to Chase*

"...if Stephen King and Jim Butcher ever had a love child then it would be Alan Baxter." – *Smash Dragons*

"Step into the ring with Alan Baxter, I dare you. He writes with the grace, precision, and swift brutality of a prizefighter." – *Christopher Golden, NYT bestselling author of Ararat and The Pandora Room*

"Alan Baxter's fiction is dark, disturbing, hard-hitting and heart-breakingly honest. He reflects on worlds known and unknown with compassion, and demonstrates an almost second-sight into human behaviour." – *Kaaron Warren, Shirley Jackson Award-winner and author of The Grief Hole*

"Baxter draws you along a knife's edge of tension from the first page to the last, leaving your heart thumping and sweat on your brow." – *Midwest Book Review*

THE RISE

Another Five Tales From The Gulp

ALAN BAXTER

THE RISE

ISBN-13: 978-0-6450019-8-3

13th DRAGON BOOKS

First Trade Paperback Edition – February 2026

Copyright © 2025 Alan Baxter

Cover Art "Road Through Jerrara" (oil on canvas)

© 2018 Halinka Orszulok

Cover Design © Alan Baxter

Edited by Mallory Wiper

Internal layout by David Wood

All rights reserved

Alan Baxter www.alanbaxter.com.au

ALSO BY ALAN BAXTER

BLOOD COVENANT

SALLOW BEND

RECALL

DEVOURING DARK

HIDDEN CITY

BOUND (Alex Caine Book 1)

OBSIDIAN (Alex Caine Book 2)

ABDUCTION (Alex Caine Book 3)

REALMSHIFT (The Balance Book 1)

MAGESIGN (The Balance Book 2)

SERVED COLD – Short Stories

CROW SHINE – Short Stories

AND FIRE POURED FORTH – Short Stories

THE GULP: Tales From The Gulp 1

THE FALL: Tales From The Gulp 2

THE LEAVES FORGET

THE ROO

THE BOOK CLUB

GHOST OF THE BLACK: A 'Verse Full of Scum

GOLDEN FORTUNE, DRAGON JADE

Co-authored with David Wood

PRIMORDIAL (Sam Aston Investigations Book 1)

OVERLORD (Sam Aston Investigations Book 2)

CROCALYPSE (Sam Aston Investigations Book 3)

SANCTUM (Jake Crowley Adventures 0)

BLOOD CODEX (Jake Crowley Adventures 1)

ANUBIS KEY (Jake Crowley Adventures 2)

REVENANT (Jake Crowley Adventures 3)

DARK RITE

This book is dedicated to

every creepy town

and every creepy resident therein...

Table of Contents

Strange Leaves 21

Sunlight On Clear Water 75

Vitulinum 121

The Gulpepper Institute of Health and Wellbeing 189

The Rise 239

Afterword 315

Acknowledgements 316

About 317

Please note that this book is written in Australian English, using Australian spelling and terminology.

Strange Leaves

Strange Leaves

Adam Campbell and Neil Jones stood looking at the blood-soaked, crumpled form of Ramsey Golden on the stained cement floor. Ramsey's eyes were half-open, rolled back, a crescent of scarlet-tinted white in each. His nose sat crooked, one arm bent awkwardly back. Blood ran in rivulets from either side of his slack mouth. He was very still.

"Have we fucking killed him?" Neil asked.

Adam looked from the broken man on the floor to Neil and back again. "Shit."

"It was only meant to be a warning."

"Well, he won't fucking do it again."

The large workshop unit on the south-west side of Gulpepper, innocuous among the various factories and industries there, was quiet in the depth of the night. Shelves and crates stood around the walls, metal desks scattered with tools filled one end. Weak light from the one overhead fluorescent they'd turned on made stark shadows in the corners. Adam wasn't really sure what his uncle did here for work, but he had a key and it was a good, quiet place for meetings, so that worked for him. He just knew that he wouldn't want to be in his sixties like Uncle Aaron and coming to a shithole like this every day to make a living. What a life that would be. At thirty years old, Adam wasn't exactly setting himself up, but he hadn't needed to take some crappy trade or anything like that either. He didn't like the term 'petty crime' because it was anything but petty, but he did all right for himself on his own terms. Until now. Had he just fucked everything up?

They were alone right now, Adam reassured himself of that. No one had seen them come in, no one had heard the shouts, the beating. So no one would have any idea they had been here. They had time to do something about this.

Neil shook his head, pointed uselessly at the dead man. "Chrissy Carter will skin us alive for this."

"She doesn't need to know."

"Dude, Ramsey was her man. He's worked for Chrissy since forever. He worked for her dad, for fuck's sake. She'll be livid."

Adam turned, pinned Neil with a steely gaze. "She. Doesn't. Need. To. Know."

"So what do we do?"

Adam licked his lips, dragged a palm down over his face as he thought. Neil was right, this was a real fucking mess, but they could sort it. Just a bit of thought, planning, utilise some smarts. They could do this. "Chrissy doesn't know he was dealing us weed on the side. Ramsey told us that, right? That we needed to keep these extra deals from Chrissy?"

"'It stays cheap all the time Chrissy doesn't know' is what he said. He also said that if Chrissy ever did find out, he would deny everything and tell her we must have been stealing from him."

Adam saw the fear in Neil's eyes. He got it, he was scared too. No one got away with crossing Chrissy Carter. She was at least as formidable as her dad before her. In some ways, moreso, because she was so calm all the time. So calculating. Adam had never met a smarter woman, and smart women scared the shit out of him. He shook his head. Focus only on the problem at hand. "Chrissy has no idea Ramsey was skimming her weed and selling cheap to us. Our beef with him was just between the three of us."

"He shouldn't have tried to short us on this deal."

Adam glanced at the bag of weed on the table beside them. The bag that was supposed to contain five ounces of good bud but was at least half grass cuttings from someone's lawn. Did the man think they were idiots? That they wouldn't notice? When the yelling started, Ramsey had made threats and Neil had got scared, started punching. Adam joined in and they got carried away. It was unfortunate, but not their fault. Not really. "You're right. He shouldn't have tried to stiff us."

"So, what now?"

Adam nodded as his mind slowly wrapped itself around the variables. "Okay, so Chrissy has no idea we were working on the side with Ramsey. If Ramsey just disappears, that's very unfortunate, but no one has any way to connect it to us, right? Why would they? Fuck me, this is The Gulp, people go missing around here all the time."

Neil narrowed his eyes. "You're saying we get rid of the body and keep quiet about the whole thing?"

"Exactly that."

"How?"

"How what?"

"How do we get rid of him?"

Adam sucked a breath in through his nose, lips pursed. "Get him in the back of the car and drive up into the hills behind Enden. You know, towards that Eagle Hotel place."

"I heard that burned down."

"Yeah, I heard the same, but that doesn't matter. We don't go that far. Just into the thick bush high up and find a spot that drops off steep from the side of the road. Chuck the body over."

"Just chuck it in the bush?"

"Yeah, it's steep as fuck in places up there. The body will fall down in the trees and shit. If we pick a good spot, it'll roll down what? Fifty metres or more? Weather and animals will take care of it. It'll probably never be found. And if it is, there's nothing to connect it to us anyway, right?"

Neil wrung his hands together, nervous, but nodded. "I've heard stories like that before. People disappearing bodies like that."

"Exactly. It's so steep and thick and wild out there, I bet there's hundreds of dead fuckers rotting away."

"One more won't hurt, eh?" Neil gave a short laugh, some relief pushing through the nerves.

"That's right. But we should hurry." Adam pulled out his phone, checked the time. "It's just after one. We've got a good five hours or so before it starts to get light, but there might be early traffic."

"I dunno, man. It's pretty fucking remote up there."

"Let's not take any chances. Work smart. It's about forty-five minutes to Enden. Maybe the same again to get up high enough on the mountain road? Maybe a bit more?" Adam squinted as he did the maths. It took a moment. "An hour and a half. Maybe two hours."

Neil let out a breath like he'd been straining to work it out too and was relieved Adam had saved him from the pain of it. "Right. So about half two or three when we get there."

"If we're quick now. Grab that tarp."

They worked with the speed of purpose, rolling Ramsey Golden's body up in a dirty blue tarp and dragging it to the side door of the unit. Adam found a bottle of white spirit and spilled it all around on the blood stains, diluting them to run across the cement.

"That'll evaporate pretty quickly. You can't hardly see any blood among all the oil and other marks anyway. That'll do, right?"

"We could torch the place." Neil watched Adam's face for a moment, then said, "What?"

"We're trying to be discreet here, dickhead." Adam gestured at the floor. "You can't see any more blood, so I think that's enough."

"All right, no need to be an arsehole about it."

"Torch my uncle's fucking workshop, what's wrong with you? Help me lift him."

Taking one end each, they hefted Ramsey up then Adam paused. "Wait, better check." He put his end of the corpse down again and slowly opened the door a crack, looked out. The harsh glow of a streetlight lit the road, but the night was still. Adam watched for several seconds anyway, straining to hear. He picked up the distant hum of light traffic down in town, the chitter of fruit bats somewhere nearby, but nothing else.

"Okay, let's go."

They hustled out of the workshop and to Adam's car, a twenty-year-old Toyota Camry that used to be red, held together now by rust, duct tape and hope, parked only a few metres away. Adam threw open the back door of the battered old sedan and they muscled Ramsey Golden onto the back seat and Adam closed the door again.

"Just as well Ramsey didn't drive here," Adam said, checking the street again. "We'd have to worry about his car too."

"He walks everywhere, eh?" Neil said.

"Not any more."

They allowed themselves a moment of relieved laughter, then Adam patted the air with both palms. "Stop fucking around, we're on the clock here." He ran and locked up the workshop, then came back to the car. "Get in."

Adam put in the key and turned it and the old Camry coughed and tried unsuccessfully to turn over.

"This car, mate," Neil said. "You need to retire it."

"Gonna buy me a new one?"

Neil laughed, shook his head.

Adam turned the key again and it coughed a couple of times then roared into life with a nasty sound of metal on metal. Adam winced, cast a daring glance at Neil. Neil raised his hands, said nothing.

They drove through night-darkened streets, sticking to the large roads to make the journey quicker. Heading down Tanning Street to the harbour, they saw the old woman standing on the sea wall, looking out over the water. She was a Gulpepper fixture, always hanging around the harbour. Barely four and half feet tall, wrinkled like she was made entirely of elbow skin, with wild white hair in disarray about her head. She always wore layer after layer of woollen clothes whatever the heat. As far as Adam knew, no one knew her name or where she lived. Most people called her the sea witch, though probably not to her face.

"That old witch gives me the creeps," Neil said.

"She gives everyone the creeps."

"Geoffrey Wong says she was around when he was a kid and she was already that old even then."

"The old guy who runs the newsagent?"

"Yeah."

"He has to be sixty or more."

Neil nodded. "At least."

Adam's face scrunched up as he was forced to do mathematics for the second time in quick succession. "So if she was already old fifty-odd years ago, she'd have to be over a hundred now."

"I guess."

"Geoffrey Wong is bullshitting you. She's old, but not that old, surely?"

Neil shrugged. "Dunno. That's what he said."

Adam turned left onto Gulpepper Street and headed west out of town, quickly swallowed up by the thick bush on either side as houses and farms gave way to old country. When they reached the T-junction, he turned north for Enden and they drove in comfortable silence.

Adam and Neil had known each other since primary school, at first taking solace in each other as year threes when the year sixes beat them up until they graduated to year six themselves and took their turn at thrashing the younger kids. School had taught Adam one thing above all else: take or be taken from. It was a lesson he carried through high school until he dropped out, and on into adult life. While he'd never had an actual job, he'd managed to blag his way through life without too much trouble. True, he'd always pulled Neil along with him, but Neil was the kind of guy who needed help. The fool had even taken on a proper job once or twice. He'd tried to be an apprentice mechanic but hadn't the aptitude for it. He'd even done a stint in the Gulpepper funeral home for a few months, but old Alfred Wilmott, the funeral director, had freaked him out.

"No one should take that much pleasure from working with the dead," Neil had said, in a rare moment of insight. "The man isn't just respectful and professional or anything like that. He's downright fucking gleeful all the time, and never happier than when he's handling a corpse."

So Neil had quit that job too, along with several others over the years. He always came back to Adam and they made their way together, getting by with a little larceny here, a little violence there. But this evening marked a new stage in their relationship.

"Hey, Neil," Adam said, breaking the silence as they drove through the quiet streets of Enden and turned west to head up into the mountains. "You ever killed someone before?"

Neil turned to look over his shoulder at the tarp-wrapped body on the back seat. "No. You?"

"No, first time. Feels weird, right?"

"Weird?"

"Yeah. Shouldn't we be more fucked up about it or something? The way we just laid into him and then his head cracking into the edge of that metal machine and then onto the cement floor."

"Sounded like someone hitting a six with a cricket bat, huh."

A shudder went through Adam at that description, it was strangely accurate. Maybe he was in shock. "Yeah. We fucking killed him, bro."

"Well, we beat him up and he accidentally died. I mean, we didn't plan to kill him, right? And we didn't mean to kill him. Fucker tried to sell us garden waste, dude."

"I suppose. Let's chalk it up to misfortune and forget about it, yeah?"

"Absolutely. Ramsey Golden is a fucking prick anyway. Thinks he's so much better than other people."

"Was."

"What?"

"Was a fucking prick."

"Yeah, right!" Neil laughed. "Let's be honest, we've probably done Gulpepper a favour in the long run."

"True. Well said, m'man. We'll get rid of the body and everyone is better off."

"A public service."

"For the greater good."

"Except we'll need to find a new weed supplier."

"Worry about that later, eh?"

The road got steeper and narrower, the trees on either side tall and ghostly in the night. In several places, hairpin bends made the going slow as they drove higher and higher. Eventually, Adam slowed and started looking out for a good spot. In several places, the metal crash barrier on the side of the road had less than a metre of ground on the other side before it dropped steeply away, the trees hanging on to rocky slopes punctuated with slender gulleys. As they rounded another bend, the drop-off was the steepest Adam had seen yet and he braked to a halt.

Neil snorted, roused from a doze, and sat up. He looked a question at Adam.

"This'll do it," Adam said. "Let's heft him over and fuck off home."

They hadn't seen another car on the winding road since leaving Enden, but Adam pulled over as close to the crash barrier as he could get, just in case anyone else came through. They hopped out into the still-warm summer night and went around to get Ramsey's body out. As Adam dragged it across the seat, the loosely tied tarp came undone and he found himself staring into Ramsey's blood-soaked face.

"Ugh, fuck. Help me, Neil."

The other man came around and got his hands under Ramsey's shoulders as Adam held onto the dead ankles.

"What about the tarp?" Neil asked.

"Fuck it, leave it in the car. We'll throw it away later. Don't want to waste time fucking around with it now in case someone comes. Just chuck him over."

They moved around the back of the car and stood side-on to the crash barrier.

"How do we do this?" Neil asked.

"We wanna lob him out a long way, but gravity should take care of most of it. Swing him once, twice, and let go on three, yeah?"

"Sounds good."

"Okay, let's go."

Both men drew a deep breath and then hauled the corpse back and swung it out over the barrier.

"One!" Adam grunted.

They swung again.

"Two!"

One more swing and Adam shouted, "Three!" and they let go.

Ramsey Golden sailed out into space, arms and legs flopping like a puppet with no one holding the strings, and fell. He went three or four metres out from the edge and crashed to a stop over a gum branch less than two metres below road level with a crunch of dry twigs. A shower of leaves fluttered down. Adam and Neil stared as the body hung there in plain view, even in the darkness of the night, lit only by a half-moon. Ramsey drooped face-down, arms and legs dangling like a sleeping leopard. The branch sagged under the weight, but wasn't anywhere close to breaking.

"Fucking hell," Adam said. He looked at Neil and his friend's face was pale, eyes wide in concern.

"Shit," Neil managed.

Adam looked back at the corpse. "Well that's no fucking good!"

"Do we leave it like that?"

"No, we don't fucking leave it like that! It'll be seen in no time. We need it disappeared." Adam leaned on the barrier to look out over the edge. "If he'd missed that branch he would have gone down for ages, I can't even see the bottom. Fuck!"

"So what do we do?"

"One of us has to go down and knock him loose."

"Fuck that!"

"We can't leave him like that!" Adam heard his voice rise in pitch and volume and sucked in a breath to calm himself. "Seriously, bro. We can't. You go. You're taller than me." He pointed. "See there? Scramble down to that rock and I bet you can reach the end of the branch from there. Yank on it and I reckon the body'll slide off and disappear down below. It'll get lost in the leaves and trunks and rocks and whatever."

"So might I!"

"Nah, you'll be fine. You're in good shape."

"What does that have to do with it? You go! I'm only about two inches taller than you. I bet you can reach the branch too."

Adam held out one hand, his fist closed. Neil looked down at it, then back at Adam.

"Ah, fuck off."

"Come on, it's a fair way to decide."

Neil sighed, ground his teeth. Then he held out one fist too. Adam grinned. Neil always went for scissors the first time, every time. Adam wasn't even sure the man was aware of it himself, but whenever they needed to decide something, it always came down to rock, paper, scissors, and Neil always went scissors, so Adam always won.

Adam bounced his fist in the air. "Rock, paper, scissors, go!" and kept his fist closed.

Neil extended his index and middle finger and grimaced. "Fuck." He looked up. "Fuck, Adam!"

Adam shrugged. "You'll be all right. Just climb down carefully, grab the end of the branch and shake him loose. You'll be down and back in less than two minutes."

Neil stared over the barrier, worrying at his top lip with his bottom teeth. His hands opened and closed a few times.

"You got this," Adam said.

"This is bullshit." Neil climbed over the barrier and held it with one hand while he pressed a foot into the downslope of the mountain. A few small rocks and a shower of dirt tumbled free, but the ground held.

"Stay close to the ground," Adam said. He had all kinds of advice now he knew it wasn't him going down there. If he was honest, he wasn't sure he'd be able to do it. Neil was a dumbass but he was pretty brave too. He wasn't stupid enough to think this manoeuvre wasn't dangerous as hell. "Keep your belly close until you get to that rock to stand on, yeah?"

Neil shook his head, muttering something Adam couldn't hear, but he did as suggested. Almost lying against the steep side, hands and feet splayed wide, he half-crawled and half-slid down the three metres or so but was too far to the left to make the rock.

"Shift to your right!" Adam called out. "About a metre. You're nearly there!"

Neil glanced up and Adam flinched from the look of almost hate in his friend's eyes. Neil was clearly scared out of his mind, his teeth clenched together.

"I will roll you the biggest joint after this, mate! And I'll get the beers in tomorrow, yeah? You're a legend."

Neil shook his head and pushed up from the slope a little to look down under his body and between his legs. He shifted to his right and a flood of loose stones went down below his feet in a mini avalanche. Neil cried out, scrabbling at the rocky slope, eyes wide in panic.

Adam held his breath, and couldn't help thinking that if Neil fell, he'd have to go down himself after all. Imagine all three of them ending up at the bottom of the ravine. Or just him and Neil while Ramsey fucking Golden stayed hanging in that tree for anyone to find. What a bloody irony that would be.

"Fuuuuck!" Neil lurched to the side and yelped in pain as his knee fetched up hard against the rock he'd been aiming for. He threw himself sideways and lay across it, gasping, as dirt and stones and clumps of dried grass tumbled down below him. Neil looked up, blood trickling from a nasty-looking cut over his left cheekbone.

The falling debris slowed and there was a moment of calm. Of quiet. Then Neil started to giggle. Adam's cheeks stretched in a grin, then he was laughing too.

After a moment, Neil gasped and said, "I thought I was going to fucking die then, ya cunt!"

"I'm glad you didn't! Shake that fucker free and get back up here. I reckon crawling back up will be a lot easier than sliding down."

"It better be."

Neil moved up onto his hands and knees, casting a rueful glance at his bloodied fingertips, then slowly rose to his feet. He steadied himself, then turned to look up at the branch with Ramsey Golden lying on it like he was having a nap.

"This fucking guy," Neil said quietly. He reached up, stretched onto tiptoes, and managed to get a grip on the thin end of the branch, gathering a handful of twigs and gum leaves together. The branch was quite long, curving in a graceful arc from the trunk of the tree, bowed under the weight of the corpse.

Adam watched his friend figure out the best movement, looking over the steep drop then back up at the branch. He understood the need to decide on a good course of action, but he was getting nervous about someone driving by. The longer they were here, the more likely they'd get spotted.

"Just give the thing a good shake and he'll slide off!" he called down.

Neil turned to look up at him. "I'll do it in my own time, thanks!"

With the motion of turning, Neil added tension to the branch and it arched a few centimetres downwards. Enough for Ramsey Golden to start sliding.

"Neil, look out!"

Neil turned back, looking up just in time for Ramsey's head to crack into his cheek with a sound like a dry stick snapping. Neil's head whipped back and he let go of the branch, but Ramsey was already free, flopping into Neil and wrapping him in lifeless limbs. Neil shrieked and stumbled backwards, his foot hovering for a moment in the air with no more rock below it, then both Neil and Ramsey were falling, a mess of arms and legs and Neil's shriek rising in pitch and volume until it was a scream that cut off suddenly with a sickening crack. A sound that was most definitely not something wooden.

The two men had vanished down into the darkness where the moonlight didn't reach. Adam listened to the sounds of breaking branches and tumbling rocks for a few more seconds and then everything was still.

He stared into the gloom, mute and paralysed. After several seconds he managed a weak, "Neil?"

Nothing. No sounds but the distant cry of a night bird somewhere across the gully. "Mate? You okay?"

Adam's legs shook, his hands trembled as he gripped, white-knuckled, to the top of the crash barrier.

"Fuck. Neil?" His voice was louder, then he was shouting. "NEIL! Mate! Answer me!"

But he knew his childhood friend was well past answering anyone. Those sounds when they'd been falling, the way Neil's scream had silenced. No, he was gone. Just like Ramsey Golden, Neil Jones was gone forever.

"Shit. Fucking shit."

Adam stood, hands on his head, and turned in a useless circle. He licked his lips, shook his head. That was that, then. There was absolutely nothing he could do about what had happened, and only he knew about it. No other cars had been along the mountain road. In fact, they hadn't seen a soul since leaving Enden. And both Neil and Ramsey were deep in the gully, never to be found.

Adam went back to the car, the tarp still hanging out of the open back door. He gathered it up, rolling it into a tight ball and looped the rope that had come undone back around it. He went to the barrier, looking to be sure there was a good gap between branches, and tossed it down. It started to unfurl as it went, but fell into the shadows and out of sight. Even if that could be seen from the road in daylight, so what? Someone tossing an old tarp, or maybe it just blew loose off the back of a ute or something? Didn't mean anything.

Adam ran back to the car and checked the back seat. In the glow from the interior light he couldn't see any blood on the upholstery. He just had to go. If anyone asked after Ramsey or Neil, well, he didn't know, did he. He hardly ever saw Ramsey, had no reason to. And sure, him and Neil were best buds, but they didn't live in each other's pocket. Yeah, they shared a flat, but each had their own lives to live. He hadn't seen Neil for a while, that's what he'd say.

He closed the back door and climbed into the driver's seat, turned the key. The old Camry coughed and growled, then died.

"This fucking piece of shit car," Adam snarled.

He tried again and once more it coughed, made that metallic grinding as it had before. But it didn't start. Adam imagined being stranded all night, and he tipped his head back and roared "Fuck!" at the uncaring sky.

He sucked in a breath, took a moment to calm his nerves. He patted the steering wheel a couple of times. "I'm sorry. You're not a piece a shit. You're a good car." And it was true to a degree. He'd had the Camry a long time and it had served him well. They'd had adventures together.

He turned the key again, saying, "Please, please, please" as the engine ground and whined. Then it coughed, then kicked, and started.

"Thank you!"

Adam revved the engine a couple of times and it settled into something like a normal rhythm. He made a careful three-point turn on the narrow road and headed back down towards Enden, thinking again on what he would tell people about Neil.

They'd been in Clooney's together the night before, him and Neil, so people would remember that. That's the last time he officially saw Neil, Wednesday night. Soon enough it would be Friday morning. But Thursday morning, yes, Thursday, the day after they'd been at the pub together, Neil had gone away, that's what he'd say. Gone where? "Come on, think, ya bastard!"

Neil's grandparents lived up in Wollongong. That was good. Adam's parents were long separated, his mum moved up to Brisbane and his dad... well, who the fuck gave a shit where his dad had got to by now. Last he knew, the man was working in Canberra, but that was years ago. He could be anywhere by now.

Neil's mum had died of breast cancer several years before and his dad had died in all that weirdness in the Gulp a couple of years back. The night most residents chose not to talk about too much, a kind of mass psychosis that had driven the town to madness. Neil's dad disappeared that night and hadn't been seen since, like many others. But Neil had grandparents, in Wollongong. He'd told Adam about them a few times, kept saying he ought to visit before they died. They'd be in their seventies or something by now.

Yes, there it was. They'd been to Clooney's Wednesday night, then Thursday morning Adam had driven Neil to Enden where he was planning to catch the bus up to Wollongong. Stay with his grandparents for a few days. That's all he knew. All he needed to know. He wasn't Neil's keeper. Adam nodded to himself as he drove. Good. That was simple and easily believable.

And when Neil didn't come back? If people started asking, if Neil wasn't answering his phone? Well, Adam was as confused and worried as everyone else, wasn't he.

It was dead strange indeed. He really hoped Neil was okay. In all honesty, it was entirely likely the poor fucker would hardly be missed by anyone except Adam himself, but if anyone did ask? Well, it was a terrible mystery.

Shit, he was going to miss the dumb fucker. They'd been friends for over twenty years. Adam shook his head and concentrated on driving home. He was so tired, it was after 3 a.m. The last thing he needed now was to fall asleep and wreck the car, maybe kill himself too. A trifecta of deaths for the night.

He opened the window to blast himself with air, got the Foo Fighters yelling at him from the car stereo, and drove for home.

It was nearly 5 a.m. when Adam finally stumbled into their flat. His flat now. And there was another problem. He'd have to find all the rent now Neil was gone. Then again, he'd carried Neil half the time anyway. But with Ramsey Golden out of the picture too, one of their more lucrative income streams was curtailed, so financial constraints were coming in several directions at once. What a massive pain in the arse the whole thing was. But he would have to think about all that later. Adam's eyes were gritty with tiredness. He had a headache and needed to simply collapse. He locked the front door behind himself, walked into his bedroom and fell face first on his bed, fully-clothed, and enjoyed oblivion until nearly 2 p.m. the following day.

He was woken by his phone ringing. Rich Blake calling. Rich was one of Chrissy Carter's men. Chrissy Carter's main man, in fact, the lucky bastard. What did he want? Adam couldn't remember how or why they had each other's number, but they'd done a couple of business deals here and there. Petty stuff. He dragged himself to sitting upright and swiped to answer. "Hello?"

"Adam Campbell, yeah?"

"That's right."

"Rich Blake. You know who I am?"

"Sure, sure. How are you?"

"You sound rough as fuck, mate. You sick?"

"Nah, morning voice. Had a late one and you woke me up."

"Jesus, what were you doing? Partying hard?"

Adam's heart raced and he gave himself a mental slap. He needed to be smart about what he told people. What he told anyone, but especially anyone connected to Chrissy Carter. She was Queen of The Gulp since her father died. He thought fast. Adam had always been good at thinking on his feet. "Nah, nothing so fun. Just got really into a videogame I was playing and had a bottle of decent scotch. Stayed up almost all night."

"Was that fun?"

"Sure, it's a good way to spend time. My flatmate's away, so I was enjoying the peace and quiet." Adam smiled to himself. That was smart, dropping a little tidbit of the Neil story.

"Neil's away?" Rich asked.

Adam frowned. These fucking people knew altogether too much about them. "Yeah. I dropped him in Enden yesterday morning to catch the bus to Wollongong."

"What's in Wollongong?"

"Fuck all, I expect. But his grandparents live there. He went to visit."

"Right, right. That's weird, because I thought you and him were meeting up with Ramsey Golden last night."

A physical shudder went through Adam and he nearly dropped the phone. Suddenly, his headache was back and his mouth was dry as sand. And he desperately needed to piss. "Fuck, my battery is about to cark. Give me two minutes to find the charger, I'll call you right b—"

He stabbed the button to end the call and stared at the phone in disbelief. He really needed to think fast now. He hurried to the bathroom, took a piss long enough to make a horse raise an eyebrow, and downed a glass of water, thinking all the time.

Okay, so Rich—and therefore Chrissy—knew he and Neil were due to meet up with Ramsey the previous night. So Rich was probably ringing to ask if Adam knew where Ramsey was, right? They were missing him. Which meant all Ramsey's talk of skimming from Chrissy was so much bullshit, if Rich knew about it. No way would Rich cross Chrissy. In truth, Adam had always been surprised Ramsey was willing to risk that, but the cheap weed had meant he didn't think about it too hard. Which, in hindsight, was something of an error. He should have known better. Ramsey was pretty smart, certainly too savvy to cross Chrissy Carter as well. Had they been playing him and Neil all along?

He needed to think more on why Ramsey might have been pretending there, obviously with Chrissy's full knowledge, but that could wait. Right now, he needed to account for last night with a new story. His brain raced as he opened the phone and redialled Rich.

"Hello, Adam. Had a moment to have a good think, have you?"

"What, no. Nothing like that." Adam forced a laugh that sounded so fake he winced. "You woke me up, I really needed to piss too. But the phone's plugged in now, so all good. What were you asking about again?"

There was a soft sigh at the other end, then, "You told me Neil went to see his grandparents yesterday morning, and I asked why, considering you were both due to meet up with Ramsey Golden last night."

"Oh, yeah, of course. That's right. Neil got a call from his grandma really early Thursday. Said his grandad was sick, taken a real bad turn. So Neil rushed off to see them. I met with Ramsey on me own."

"Right, I see. So any idea where Ramsey is now?"

"Right now? No. Why would I know where he is?"

"What time did you see him last might?"

Adam paused, sniffed, made like he was thinking about that. "Ah, it was pretty late. Maybe a bit after midnight."

"Thought you said you were up all night playing videogames and drinking scotch."

"Yeah, yeah. I was. I mean, after I saw Ramsey. You know, because Neil wasn't here when I got in."

"As he's at his grandparents' in Wollongong."

"Exactly. Yeah."

"So what time did you leave Ramsey?"

Adam hated feeling like a little worm on a big hook. He decided a little belligerence was required. "What the fuck is this about, Rich? Why is my business of any interest to you?"

"We're just trying to track down a mate, Adam, that's all. No need to get touchy."

"What, you've lost Ramsey have you? Checked behind the couch cushions?"

"You're a jester, aren't you? No, no, just wondering where he's got to. We knew he was meeting with you last night, and he didn't come to work this morning. So I'm thinking maybe you were the last person to see him and perhaps you have an idea of where he might be."

"Nah, sorry. Saw him as planned, bit after midnight. Then I came home. Offered him a lift somewhere, but he declined. You know Ramsey, walks everywhere. We said goodbye and that was that."

"And where was that?"

"My uncle's workshop."

"Up near Turner's Manufacturing there?"

"That's right."

"And what were you two meeting about so late, in such a quiet location?"

"That's our business." Rich was playing with him and that made Adam angry. "Anyway, you know all about the meeting so I'm assuming you know everything else. Stop fucking me about. I said goodbye to Ramsey a bit after midnight and fucked off. That's all there is to it. Can't tell you anything else, sorry. I'm sure he'll turn up. Maybe he's sleeping in as well."

"No, he's not. I'm calling from his place and he's not here."

"Well, I hope you find him. Anything else I can do for you?" Adam's voice was soaked in sarcasm. He knew it was an error to irritate Rich Blake, and by extension, Chrissy Carter, but he was pissed off.

Rich chuckled softly. "No, thanks for your help, Adam. Appreciate it."

The call ended and Adam stared at his phone again. "What the fucking fuck?" he muttered to himself, then went to make a strong coffee.

His mind churned with the implications of the call. Rich, and therefore Chrissy, knew Ramsey was dealing weed to them on the cheap. Which meant what? Adam thought back to the grass cuttings in the bag that had started such horrible events the previous evening. Had Ramsey been stiffing them all along and only now they'd noticed? A couple of times recently Neil and he had both complained about the quality of product, not as strong as they'd hoped. As it used to be. Several of the people they sold on to—mostly teenagers and other young losers around The Gulp—had also made complaints from time to time. But beggars couldn't be choosers and all that. Was Chrissy passing off substandard product through them? That pissed him off even more.

Adam leaned back against the kitchen counter, sipping coffee. He knew Chrissy grew a substantial crop there on Carter's farm, up in the hills on the southern side of town. Was it possible some of it wasn't as good as she'd like?

He went back through into the lounge room and opened the cupboard beneath their sixty-inch Smart TV. His TV. There was no them any more. A wave of what he assumed was grief passed over him, but he needed to put that aside for the moment and focus. He pulled out the bag they'd saved from the last deal with Ramsey. They always sold about eighty per cent of any deal, making a tidy profit from that and keeping the rest of the gear for their own consumption. It was a time-honoured tradition, most dealers ended up dealing to support their own burgeoning habit. With the risks came the rewards.

He held the clear plastic baggie up to the light and squinted at it. It wasn't all bud. Never was. Ramsey admitted early on there would always be a little bit of leaf mixed in because everything was harvested by hand. Adam pursed his lips, wondering at that. He hadn't thought twice about it at the time, but it seemed disingenuous now.

He pulled out his phone and searched for images of marijuana plants. He felt a little stupid, it wasn't something he'd ever really thought too hard about before. Weed came as balls of sticky buds in a plastic bag and he only had the most cursory awareness of what it looked like before that. He was familiar with the classic five-fingered leaf, of course. That was seen everywhere, on t-shirts and hats and posters and a million other things. His quick research showed him similar leaves, long, thin, serrated along each edge, grew out from the bud as it matured atop any given plant, so it was fair to assume some of those leaves would end up in any deal. But...

He held the baggie up again. There were lots of bits and pieces of leaf among the paler, resin-spotted bud, but they were the wrong colour and simply didn't look like the long, serrated leaves in the photos. He scrolled again, saw photos of buds hung up to dry after harvesting, and none had any leaves at all. Just bud. All those long leaves had been pulled away, it seemed.

He put down the phone and shook the bag out onto the coffee table in front of the couch. Carefully separating the contents, he ended up with mostly bud, obviously the good stuff. But about ten percent or so was chopped up leaf that looked more like parsley, only a perhaps a little thicker, a little darker. He took a pinch and sniffed it. The aroma was acrid, somehow acidic. He knew what parsley tasted like, so nibbled a small amount, shoving it around his mouth with the tip of his tongue. It tasted foul, sharp and almost rotten.

With a grunt of disgust, he spat it onto the carpet and took several gulps of coffee to wash the sensation away. That wasn't parsley and it certainly wasn't weed. What the fuck was it? He was pretty sure it wasn't lawn clippings either.

He thought back to the night before, chatting amiably enough with Ramsey while Neil took the bag of their most recent deal. Then Neil frowning, holding the bag up to the one weak fluorescent light.

"What the fuck is in here?" Neil had said.

When Adam thought about it, he remembered a look pass over Ramsey's face just then. Was it concern? Guilt?

"What are you on about?" Ramsey had asked.

Neil had become instantly agitated. "Are you fucking ripping us off? What is this, grass fucking cuttings?"

"Careful what you accuse people of, cunt!" Ramsey had snapped, and then Neil had shoved him and said, "Answer the fucking question!" and then Ramsey had swung at Neil.

That was all it took. There followed a few hectic seconds of brawling before Ramsey slipped or tripped or something and his head clipped that metal corner then *thocked* into the concrete floor and... Yeah, Adam remembered well enough everything that had happened since then.

Perhaps Ramsey had been padding out the bags all along only this time he'd overdone it and Neil noticed. Maybe even Chrissy didn't know that. She obviously knew Ramsey had been dealing to him and Neil, but had she been unaware Ramsey was padding the deals? Maybe keeping some for himself? Perhaps it wasn't entirely untrue that Ramsey was crossing Chrissy. Or maybe Chrissy knew about that part too.

Where was last night's deal?

Adam cast his mind back, remembered panicking,

wrapping Ramsey up, putting him in the car and everything that happened after. The glovebox. He recalled Neil getting into the car and shoving something into the glovebox.

He went down to the street and opened his car. Sure enough, the baggie was there, supposedly packed tight with five ounces of Chrissy's best bud. He tucked it against his body and hurried back inside for a closer look.

The bud was indeed mixed up with a bunch of that other strange leaf. It had been chopped up quite finely and would likely go largely unnoticed as it had done before if there were a little less of it. But there was just enough this time to be a bit more obvious. Adam brushed the other stuff from the table back into its bag and held both up for comparison. One was full and the other nearly empty, but it was immediately apparent the new deal had more of the strange leaf in it.

"Well spotted, Neil," he muttered softly, then lamented the discovery. If Neil hadn't noticed, both he and Ramsey would still be alive.

But what did any of this mean? What was he supposed to do about it? Did he challenge Chrissy? Approach her and ask what the fuck she was cutting her weed with. Or did he go a different angle and see Chrissy to tell her Ramsey was cutting her weed with something else, in case she didn't know?

He let out a humourless laugh. As if anything happened in The Gulp that Chrissy didn't know about. But it was a less confrontational way of approaching the subject. Another thought occurred to him. He could see her and say he'd noticed this extra cut in the weed and perhaps Ramsey had been doing that to other customers as well and one of them had noticed. Maybe they'd been pissed about it and done away with Ramsey.

Adam smiled to himself. That was cunning as fuck. Tell Chrissy exactly what they'd done, but frame it as being a possibility enacted by some other disgruntled third party. Was that swimming a little too close to the edge? He needed to think about it. He needed a joint.

Tucking the new deal away for the moment, he went back to the old one, with less of the strange leaf in it. He rolled a joint, carefully picking out as much of the extra leaf as he could, then sat back to enjoy a smoke. He would certainly be removing it from any future smokes as best he could, but he'd been smoking weed from Ramsey for months. Ramsey had been supplying them for a good couple of years, in fact. No matter. He knew about it now.

It was dark, well into Friday night, when Neil's voice roused him.

"Adammm."

Adam blinked, smacked dry lips together. His mouth felt like a UFC fighters groin guard after five championship rounds. He'd sunk deep into the couch and his neck was stiff. He'd gone a bit too hard on the weed and passed out. He hauled himself up. What was Neil on about now?

Wait, Neil?

Recent events flooded back like a sudden tide and Adam looked around the gloomy lounge room. A shape stood in the doorway, silhouetted by a weak street lamp outside leaking in through his bedroom window.

"Neil?"

"Aaadddamm…"

He scrambled across the couch, pulse throbbing in his throat, and flicked on the standing lamp in the corner. He spun around to see.

Neil stood there, but Neil was fucked up. His right leg was crooked behind him, his foot twisted entirely around so the laces of his grubby trainer rested on the floorboards. His right arm was a bloody mess, hanging limp like seaweed, the skin and flesh on the back of his hand scraped away to reveal a web of thin, white bones. Neil used his left hand to hold his head up by the hair, rocking imbalanced on his one good leg, to look at

Adam with blood-filled eyes. The skin all down the right side of his face had been shredded, torn away in places, muscle glistening through. Adam saw his friend's back teeth through one particularly gaping wound. Neil's nose was crushed to one side, his chin and chest a flood of scarlet.

Still hammered, not thinking straight, Adam pushed back into the couch, driving his heels into the cushions like he could keep going right through the wall and get away from the broken, ruined apparition of his friend. Was this a nightmare?

"Addaammm, I fucking died, bro."

Neil let go of his hair and his head fell, his left cheek flat against his chest, the skin of his neck stretched taut and thinned, no longer connected by any bone. But he stood there still, swaying slightly, a breathy moan leaking from his ruined mouth.

Adam was close to pissing his pants, crammed as far back into the corner of the couch as he could get, staring. Neil put pressure onto his shattered left leg and Adam heard the broken bones grind, heard torn flesh squelch, and Neil took one limping step forward. Then another. He reached up to grasp his blood-soaked, collar-length hair again and hauled his head up, swinging horribly side to side with no connected spine to steady it.

"Addammm, I fucking died."

"I... I know, bro." Adam began to cry. "I'm sorry, man!"

"You killed me."

"Me? It wasn't me. You fell!"

"Your fault. You always cheat."

"Cheat?"

"At rock, paper, scissors."

Adam gaped like a fish a few times, his mind slipping and sliding, trying to gain any kind of purchase on what was happening. "You always go scissors first, Neil. Every time."

Neil limped forward, somehow still able to put

enough weight on his inverted foot to scuff his left foot forward. Inch by inch he came on, pushing the coffee table aside with his knee.

"Fucking killed me, bro."

"It was an accident, Neil! A fucking accident!" Belligerence, Adam's driving emotion, pushed up through his fear. "You fucking started the fight with Ramsey anyway! Everything that happened last night was all your fault."

"Killed me, bro!"

"You killed yourself! *Your* fault!"

Neil limp-dragged forward, his face swinging left and right with his movement as he held onto his hair. "Ramsey cheated us!"

"I know, man. I know. But it's not... it's not lawn clippings, man. It's... something else."

Neil paused, swaying, his eyes rolling randomly in all directions. Adam shook, every muscle tensed as he stared up at his desecrated friend less than a metre from him. Neil lurched forward, bending at the waist to swing his head within inches of Adam's. Adam screamed and blackness surged in from the edges of his vision. Just before unconsciousness swallowed him, he felt Neil land wetly on top of him and his friend wailed, "It's coming!"

It's coming.

What's coming?

The thought rattled around Adam's head as he came to, laying back on the couch. He gasped and jumped up, scrambled around the coffee table to turn on the main light in the room. Everything leapt into brightness but he was alone. No Neil.

Had he dreamed all that? Was it some kind of stoned psychosis?

Then he saw the blood on his arm, smeared in a stripe from wrist to elbow. He ran to the bathroom and looked in the mirror. His Korn t-shirt had bloodstains on it too, and there was a dry, brownish mark across his cheek and lips. He gagged and tore off his clothes, stumbled into the shower. He spent a good ten minutes in the hottest water he could bear, scrubbing himself all over.

He tried not to think about anything while he washed, but when he finally stepped out of the shower into the steamy room, there were marks through the condensation on the mirror.

it's coming

Neil had been there somehow. What was coming? What the hell was happening?

Adam threw his clothes into the washing machine along with everything else in the laundry basket and set it to a hot wash. He ignored the blood trails on the floor where Neil had dragged his ruined foot. Then he dressed in fresh clothes and went into the kitchen. It was nearly 2 a.m. and he'd just got dressed. He had lost all track of time. But having slept in after the night before and then passed out again on the couch, sleep was the last thing on his mind. Nowhere would be open. Even the big cities were likely quiet by this time, but a small country town like Gulpepper was comatose. Clooney's stayed open late on Friday sometimes, but that meant maybe until 1 a.m. Surely it would be closed by now, as would The Victorian. Chrissy owned Clooney's, having inherited it from her dad, so that pub was best avoided anyway until he'd got his head around what was happening and what he might do about it.

Maybe the Vic would be open if there was a party happening or something. Regardless, he needed to get out. He'd walk that way and get his head together.

Adam left his flat and headed west on Noonan Street, crossed Shellhaven and came out onto Tanning. He looked across the road and past the park behind Carlton Beach to watch the low surf breaking on the sand. He drew in a deep breath, savouring the salt air, hoping to gust away the worst of the stoned mugginess still slowing his thoughts. He turned left and headed another block to the Victorian, but it was all dark and closed up, as he'd expected. He kept going, heading for the harbour, thinking he'd walk along the wall, maybe head out onto Spiny Point and the lighthouse, just for the exercise of it.

As he reached the corner with Gulpepper Street and looked across the road to the harbour beyond, he saw the old woman there, standing on the sea wall. Like always, looking out over the water like she expected something, was waiting for something. Or someone. He remembered the conversation with Neil just the night before.

That old witch gives me the creeps.

Geoffrey Wong says she was around when he was a kid and she was already that old.

Was that really possible? Stranger things had happened in The Gulp, no doubt about that. As he stood there wondering, the old woman turned slowly and looked right at him. Adam startled slightly at the sudden, intense scrutiny. He was momentarily paralysed, rooted to the spot. It felt as though she were looking right through him. Then her eyes narrowed and she tipped her head to one side, seemed to be looking past him.

Nervous, but unable to resist, he turned to see what she was looking at. Neil stood there, less than a metre away, broken, bleeding, head hanging flat against his chest. Why didn't that neck skin just split and tear free?

Adam yelped and found his energy, staggered away from his friend. Neil took hold of his hair and lifted his head, swinging his face around to focus on Adam.

"It's coming!"

Adam tried to hold back a scream and managed to squeak out, "What is?" instead.

Neil let go of his hair, his head slapping down against his chest again, and raised his one good arm straight, pointing across the road at... what? The harbour? The sea witch? Charles Head across the harbour and the big hole where Blumenthal Manor used to be before it collapsed into the old smuggler's caves beneath a couple of years before?

Adam turned and saw the old woman still watching.

"Can you see him?" Adam yelled. He turned to point at Neil, but the footpath behind was empty again, as if Neil had never been there. A few spots of blood spattered the pale paving where he'd been standing though. He *had* been there.

Adam turned back and the old woman was walking away, heading towards Spiny Point. "Hey! Wait! Please, wait!"

He went to run after her and there was a screech and the blast of a horn shattered the stillness of the night. Adam cried out, staggered back and tripped on the curb to sit hard on his arse as a white van went past. Adam caught a glimpse of the weird fellow driving, pale as chalk, in his baggy, threadbare jumper and overalls. He drove that van around all over the place, but Adam had no idea who he was or what he got up to. What was he doing hooning around at this time of night, anyway?

Adam got back to his feet, rubbing his bruised tailbone, and looked across the road, but the old witch was nowhere to be seen.

"Damn it."

She had seen Neil, so maybe he wasn't going mad. He really wanted to talk to the sea witch all of a sudden. He had never so much as said hello to her before, but now he *had* to speak to her. He hurried over the road and headed up the footpath towards Spiny Point, looking in every shadow. Where the hell had she gone?

He followed the path, lined evenly with tall, old Norfolk pine trees, inky patches of shadow under each one. But there were street lights too, casting pools of brightness, the chiaroscuro effect disorienting as he ran along. But the entire area was deserted.

He reached the car park at the top of the point, large grassy areas all around it that sloped down until they reached rocky edges and disappeared into the sea. The lighthouse stood tall on the end of the peninsula at the apex of the point. Adam turned in a slow circle. Where had she gone? A footpath looped around the parking area and branched out to the lighthouse. There was nowhere to hide. Nowhere to conceal a person. Unless the old woman was hunkered down in one of the shadowy areas, hoping not to be seen. Or maybe in the lighthouse?

He looked up at it, watched the beam blink as it circled around and around. On dark, foggy nights a person could watch the brilliance slice through the air, sweeping out over the ocean in regular cadence. He'd found it mesmerising as a kid, but it was the kind of thing a person got used to as they grew up. Like how everyone in The Gulp dreamed of things falling from stormy skies, but only the kids ever talked about it. Adults mostly stopped having the dreams apparently. Adam had them only occasionally.

The lighthouse was entirely automated these days, surely. It wasn't like there was some grizzled old keeper, in oilskins and boots, with a thick beard and grumpy demeanour. That was kid's story stuff. Presumably someone came by and serviced it or whatever, kept it clean, but no one lived there. Unless the sea witch did.

Adam walked out along the narrow peninsula, the tide slapping and hissing at the rocks below. When he got to the tall, smooth, white wall of the lighthouse he was reminded again how big it was. Up close, it seemed huge, much wider around the base than it looked from a distance. Even from as close as the car park and grassy areas around it. Adam did a lap and there was only one door, thick, wooden, also painted white. It had a sturdy sliding lock and heavy padlock securing it closed. Adam hefted the padlock and it was solid, salt-encrusted. It looked like it hadn't been opened in quite a while.

He let out a soft laugh. As if the sea witch lived in the fucking lighthouse, what an idiot. But where had she gone? Must have slipped away in the shadows. He desperately wanted to talk to her, but maybe she didn't want talk to him. He'd walk back slowly, keep an eye out. Otherwise, he'd check again the following day. She spent most of her time standing there on the harbour wall, looking out over the ocean. Easier to catch her then, approach without her noticing, give her no chance to scurry away.

He turned to head back and gasped at Neil standing right there.

"Why do you keep fucking doing that!"

Neil lifted his head by the hair and his mouth hung open, eyes rolled back to show only the blood-stained whites. He gasped a couple of deep, slurrying breaths, then his eyes rolled around to focus on Adam. "Coming!"

"What's coming?"

"Preparing them. Using us."

"What are you talking about, Neil?"

Adam had trouble looking at the broken state of his friend, bloody and torn, raw flesh and bone exposed and glistening. Was the poor bastard really there? He shot out one hand, index finger extended, and jabbed Neil in the chest. The man's ribs seemed to flex back and Neil coughed, a warm spray of blood spackling Adam's eyes and mouth. He tasted rotten copper and gagged, staggered back, dragging both palms repeatedly down his face to wipe away the foulness.

"What the fuck is happening, bro?"

"Using us!"

"Who is? Ramsey? He's dead too, you know that!"

Neil began coughing again, blood and something else, something black and viscous, bubbling up, spattering out. Adam backed up further, appalled by the sight and the stench of whatever Neil was expectorating.

"Die!" Neil choked out.

"I know, mate. You died. I'm so sorry."

"No. You. Die!"

"Fucking hell, bro, I'm sorry, okay? Everything about this is fucked up, I—"

"Better if you die!"

Was that sadness in Neil's face? He was crying, tears filling his lower lids, cutting tracks through the blood on his face.

"It's better if I die? What is?"

"Don't let him!"

"Who? Let him what?"

Neil began coughing again, harsher, phlegmier than ever, and pitched forward with the effort. He lost his grip on his hair, face slapping into his chest, then he fell. As he hit the ground, he seemed to ripple and flex. Adam blinked, unable to focus for a moment as Neil squirmed.

"What the actual fuck?" he whispered to himself. Maybe he would try to go to sleep after all, if being awake was this much of a nightmare. He turned for home.

Neil dragged himself back up to his feet and staggered after. Adam winced when he realised.

"Fuck off, mate. Please? Look, I'm really sorry you died, but it's not my fault. I can't do anything about it."

Neil hopped and dragged his ruined leg and kept coming. Adam let out a whine of despair and hurried up, desperate to outpace his broken friend. When he turned into Noonan Street, he glanced back, saw Neil still coming but way behind. He gasped a breath of relief but kept up his pace until he got home. He let himself inside and closed the front door, leaning back against it for a moment.

Neil stood just inside the lounge, head swinging gently as he held his hair to stare at Adam.

"Fuck! Dude, please, just..." Adam rubbed his face. "What do you want?"

"Use you," Neil said wetly. "Better off dead."

"Who will use me? How? Why?" Anger bloomed. "You're not making any fucking sense, ya cunt!"

"I died. You die!"

"Bro, get fucked! Seriously."

Adam stumbled to his room, determined to not speak to Neil any more, not even look at him. He turned out all the lights and climbed into bed, dragged the doona up over his head. But he heard Neil's slushing breath right beside him, smelled the rot even through his bedclothes.

He tried to sleep, but managed nothing better than fitful dozing, constantly aware of the proximity of his dead friend. After an eternity he was startled by banging on his apartment front door. He glanced out from the covers. Had Neil gone? The clock beside his bed said it was a little after 8 a.m. "Who the fuck..?" He twisted out of bed, planted his feet on the floor, and screamed.

Neil still stood there, broken, bleeding. Now his skin was blackening too. As he grabbed his hair and hauled his head up, Adam saw his face seemed to be slowly peeling away from the skull. His lips hung loose, the lower lids bagged away from his eyeballs, purpling and lined with tiny veins. Among the blood on his chin and chest were streaks of the foul-smelling black ichor he had been coughing up the night before.

"Don't!"

Adam frowned, scrambled back across the bed to get out the other side of it. He stood, keeping the bed between them. "Don't what?"

Banging on the front door punctuated the air again, hard, aggressive.

Neil swung his face towards the sound. "Don't!"

"Don't answer the door?"

The banging came again, followed by a shout. "Open up, Campbell. I know you're in there."

It took a moment, then Adam realised who he heard. Rich Blake. Chrissy Carter's guy. He looked back at Neil. "Why?"

Neil coughed, strings of thick, tar-like phlegm looped out and splatted across the bedsheets.

Adam winced. "Dude, shit! That's my fucking bed!"

Neil tried to form words but kept coughing, staggered left and right. Rich kept banging on the door.

"You got thirty seconds before I kick this door in,

Adam!"

"What do I do?" Adam hated the high, panicked tone of his voice.

Neil coughed, spluttered blood and ichor, then tipped forward. He hit the bed with a sound like someone throwing a heavy rock into mud and spread out in a black splash. The stench was appalling and Adam turned his face away and vomited. He spat, dragged an arm across his mouth. A dark patch like a shadow was all Neil had left behind. That and the blood spatters and strings of shining black phlegm. Adam's bed was a ruin.

"Last chance, Campbell!"

If Rich kicked his door in it would only add to Adam's problems, extra grief with the landlord. And the bastard clearly wasn't about to give up and go away.

"I'm coming! Hang on!"

Adam dragged jeans on over his boxers and found a t-shirt, then hurried into the hall. He closed the bedroom door behind him, then opened the front. Rich Blake stood there as casual as hell, like he'd only knocked the once and then waited patiently.

"Knew you were there."

"I was sleeping. You woke me up."

"Good. Well, find some shoes."

"Why? Where are we going?"

"Chrissy wants to see you."

The neighbour's door across the hall opened a crack and Adam cast a hateful glance that way. It clicked quickly closed again. "What does Chrissy want?"

"That's for her to tell you. You really want to keep her waiting?"

"Ugh. Wait a minute."

Adam left the door open but Rich stayed out in the hallway. As Adam pulled on his trainers and grabbed his wallet and phone, Rich said, "This place is a fucking sty."

"Just as well you don't live here then."

Rich grinned. "Neil back yet?"

Adam relived the moments before, the coughing, the warning, the collapse into blackness. "Nah."

"How's he going up there?"

"I don't fucking know. I'm sure he's having a wonderful time."

Rich turned and walked away, heading for the stairs down to the street.

Adam grabbed his keys and closed up. "So I'll follow you in my car then?"

"No, I'll drive you."

"That's okay, I'd rather take my own car and—"

Rich looked back over his shoulder, eyes hard. "I'll drive you."

"Right. Yeah. Okay."

Adam's knees trembled slightly as he followed Rich down and out into the already warm day. A big, bronze Isuzu D-Max crew-cab ute was parked at the curb and Rich opened the passenger door for Adam and walked around to the driver's side.

The journey was short, maybe ten minutes, and they didn't talk on the way. South out of town, past the workshop where all Adam's woes had begun a couple of days before, and then up the road that became a steep, switchback dirt driveway and ended at the natural level plateau that housed Carter's Farm. Looking back, Adam saw Gulpepper laid out below, like one of those weird miniature town tourist attractions. Rich pulled up next to a nice-looking and pretty new Mercedes sedan in the car port and climbed out.

"Follow me."

He led Adam into the farmhouse, through a back door directly into the kitchen. Adam had never been up to the farm before and certainly not in the house. The whole place seemed strangely unprepossessing. He wasn't sure what he had expected now he came to think about it, but maybe he had visions of some Corleone mansion or a faux-Tudor manor or something. But it was just a nice, Federation-style white weatherboard

Australian farmhouse on a completely normal farm. There had been black and white cows behind the white fence in the paddock beside the driveway. Friesians, he remembered they were called, and realised his mind was racing in a panic.

The kitchen was nicely appointed, granite benches, brushed aluminium appliances. It was big too and, in the middle, was a solid-looking oak table with eight chairs around it, three to a side and one at each end. They were well spaced, room for plenty more. At the far end sat Chrissy Carter. She looked up at him and smiled.

"Hello, Adam."

Chrissy was beautiful. Arrestingly so, with long dark hair that tumbled over her shoulders and shined in the sunlight through the picture window over the kitchen sinks. She wore jeans and a tight t-shirt that accentuated her body and Adam worked really hard to look only at her eyes. But her eyes freaked him out. They were large, dark, but seemed to somehow generate their own gravity. They drew against him relentlessly. He sucked in a breath and looked away.

Chrissy Carter was a powerful woman, despite only being around thirty years old. She was the erstwhile Mr Carter's daughter, and lover while he was alive, if the gossip was true. No one doubted the power Mr Carter held over Gulpepper and it was widely accepted that when all that weirdness went down, when everyone lost their minds that strange night, it had been Carter sacrificing himself at Blumenthal Manor that had saved the ones who survived. That had saved Gulpepper. There were all kinds of rumours that went along with it. Adam had given up listening to most of them. Suffice to know weird shit happened in Gulpepper and that night had nearly destroyed everything and everyone. But Carter, with some help, most agreed, had saved it. And it cost him his life. Which meant his daughter had inherited everything. The Gulpepper Inn, that everyone called Clooney's, the farm and, of course, whatever powers her father might have wielded. Mr Carter had run Gulpepper and any people who challenged that in any way had a habit of disappearing. He'd kept the place ticking along nicely though. Now, it was widely agreed, Chrissy had the power and the control, and she was more formidable in every way than her father had ever been.

"I said, 'Hello, Adam.'"

"Chrissy. Ms Carter. Hello." His voice shook as much as his knees.

Chrissy laughed, a light, bright sound. "Will you fucking relax. You can call me Chrissy. Sit down. You're going to be fine. Assuming we can come to an agreement."

"An agreement?"

"Coffees?" Rich asked.

Chrissy smiled at him. "Please. You want one, Adam? It's fresh ground Arabica. An amazing blend."

"Sure. Thanks."

Rich went to a coffee machine, a full barista set-up like a fancy café, and Chrissy turned her attention back to Adam.

"You've caused me a little consternation."

"Sorry about that. What have I done?"

"I think you know."

Adam shook his head, mind racing. How much could she know? He couldn't give himself away and tell her more than she knew. How could he draw her out?

"You can't draw out what I know, Adam. You have no power here."

How the fuck did she do that? Had she just read his mind?

Chrissy sighed. "My father taught me ways of interacting with the universe you couldn't even conceive of, Adam. And I've far surpassed my father's skill since he died. I know everything already. I want *you* to tell me what happened."

"You mean with Ramsey?"

"Of course with Ramsey."

Adam gestured over his shoulder. "Like I already told Rich—"

Chrissy's fury was instant and incandescent. "Don't fuck with me, Adam Campbell." Her voice seemed to resonate more deeply than the room should allow, like it was her speaking here and somewhere else. Somewhere deep and cavernous. Adam's bladder threatened to blow.

Chrissy picked up a tablet that had been lying on the table by her arm and turned its screen to face Adam. She tapped it alive and set a video to playing. It was grainy CCTV footage and Adam realised with dismay that it showed the front and side of his uncle's workshop. It must have come from a building across the street somewhere. In the weak streetlight, he watched low-resolution footage of himself and Neil carrying a tarp-wrapped body to his car, locking up, and driving away.

"Where did you dump the body, Adam?"

He swallowed, his mouth suddenly dry. "In the..." He cleared his throat, tried again. "In the hills behind Enden. High up on the mountain road."

Rich put a cup of coffee before him and another in front of Chrissy. He leaned back against the kitchen bench and sipped his own. Adam picked up the coffee and took a gulp. It was hot but the moisture of it was welcome. And delicious. He looked in surprise at the cup.

"Told you it was good," Chrissy said.

"It's amazing. Best I've ever had."

"Don't get used to it. I don't plan on having you as a guest here very often."

Adam looked up, tried to gauge what that meant. Her eyes! He couldn't cope, like he would fall into them if he looked too long. He returned his gaze to the coffee, sipped again.

"And Neil Jones? He's clearly not in Wollongong." Chrissy tapped one finger on the tablet as she laid it back down. Adam noticed her fingernails were relatively short and painted a deep burgundy. They looked enamelled.

"There was an accident."

"What kind of accident?"

"He fell. When we were getting rid of Ramsey. He fell and went down with him."

"Unfortunate."

"Yeah."

"And what chance is there of either of them being found, do you think?"

"Absolutely zero. It was steep, well into the bush. No one will know they're there."

Chrissy smiled, even white teeth bright. "Good. That's one thing. Now, the other thing."

Adam looked up, waited. The silence grew uncomfortable. "Sure, yeah. Anything."

"Ramsey did good work for us. Had been doing good work for a while. So I have that gap to fill. And you're going to fill it."

"I am?"

"You are. You work for me now. You need to pick up Ramsey's clients around town as well as continuing to supply your own. Time runs short, Adam Campbell, and we need to be ready."

"Ready? For what?"

"Something is coming. To Gulpepper. You don't need to know any more than that. But suffice to say, you're a part of it and you need to up your game. Why did you two idiots kill Ramsey?"

"It was an accident! An argument." He had to ask her. He had to know. "Neil saw that the weed was cut with something else and he challenged Ramsey about it. There was a fight. We didn't mean to kill him!"

Chrissy glanced up and Rich and Rich nodded. "A little too much," he said.

"Cut back just a bit, yeah? But we need to move fast."

"Sure." Rich finished his coffee and put the mug in the sink. "I'll do it now."

"What is it?" Adam asked. "The stuff with the weed?"

"Just a little something to help protect our town."

"Protect? How?"

Chrissy sat forward, elbows on the table. "Okay, here's how it goes. You don't ask any more questions. You're not going to learn anything else. But you'll be absolutely fine if you do as I ask. And I'm asking you to cover Ramsey's work, as you fucking killed him and nearly derailed everything." There was a hint of her rage again, underlying the words, and Adam knew he would do anything and everything she asked of him. "Think you can manage that, Adam?"

"Absolutely."

"Good. She slid a sheet of paper over the table and he picked it up. "Those are the names and numbers of four people Ramsey supplies to. You and Neil were the fifth. Those people, like you, sell the weed on and enjoy the profits. No problem, that's business. That now continues. You make contact with those four, tell them you're taking over for Ramsey as he's had to go away. Overseas, let's say, yeah?"

"What about Bali?"

"Adam, I don't give a flying fuck where, that's up to you. No one gives a shit, they just want their weed. If any of them ask about the quality of the stuff, or complain it's cut with something, you simply tell them that's the local strain we've been perfecting, okay? Because that's true. It's just as good, if not better, than anything else they can get."

Adam licked his lips. "Can I be honest with you?"

"I would remove your balls for anything less."

He swallowed. "Right. Well, the quality has gone down a bit and I've been thinking about that. This other thing in with the bud. It's always been there, but you've started using a bit more, yeah?"

"And?"

"Smokers are noticing. It's affecting the high. So you should go back to however much you were putting in before because the product was really good then. We already lost one customer, me and Neil. Said they were getting their stuff from a guy in Enden now, because it was better. Didn't used to be, but is now."

Chrissy looked up over Adam's shoulder and he turned to see Rich back in the kitchen doorway. "Hear that?" Chrissy asked.

"Yeah. We'll go back to the previous mix. Will it be enough?"

Chrissy shrugged, lips pursed. "It'll have to be, won't it. Let's just hope we have more time than we anticipate."

"You said he's distracted in Monkton right now?"

"For the moment. Let's hope it stays that way for at least a little while."

"Who's distracted?" Adam asked.

"Remember what I told you about asking questions?"

He withered under the force of her gaze and returned his attention to the coffee.

"How long?" Chrissy asked.

"Few hours," Rich said.

"Okay. Adam, Rich is going to drive you home now. Sort your shit out and make contact with those four." She gestured at the paper beside his cup. "Rich will be by again later today with a bunch of product and you need to start where Ramsey left off. Get those people working. Reassure them the stuff is better than it's ever been and don't fucking disappoint me."

"Sure. No problem."

"Good. Fuck off, then."

"Oh. Right." He gulped the last of his coffee and stood, turned to follow Rich again.

"Wait."

Adam looked back and saw Chrissy had stood and was leaning forward, palms on the table, scrutinising him. Her gaze was more intense than ever, he saw tiny sparks of electric blue flickering in her eyes. Her perusal was physical, stroking over his exposed skin like a cold breeze, raising goosebumps on his arms.

"You're carrying someone."

"What?"

"There's an unquietness hanging onto you." She laughed. "Quite a powerful one too. It reeks of anger and blame, but there's something else… maybe concern?" Her eyes seemed to snap back to something more normal and she tipped her head slightly. "Been seeing any ghosts lately?"

Adam swallowed. How could she know that? What did he admit to? "No, I don't think so."

"You don't think so?" She laughed again. "You really don't have an honest bone in your body, do you?"

Adam wasn't sure what to say to that.

"You just better be loyal to me, Adam. I can make pain and regret last a lifetime."

"Oh, don't worry about that. I'm happy to help, however I can. And I can keep my profits of this new arrangement, yeah? Only, especially without Neil pulling his weight, I've got bills."

"Business is business, Adam. We all have to make a living. Just don't stiff me."

"No way. Hey, Ramsey told us he was dealing outside of your knowledge. We thought he was skimming you."

"And you thought that was okay, did you?"

"Oh. Well, no. I mean—"

"What's your point, Adam?"

He waved the slip of paper. "These guys? They know the deal is direct?"

"Tell them whatever you like. I think Ramsey was just having fun at your expense, but it's up to you what you tell your customers now."

"Sure, right. Okay." He turned to leave, then paused again. "Hey, if I was seeing ghosts, are they dangerous? Like, can ghosts hurt you?"

Chrissy smiled. "That really depends on the nature of the ghost, Adam."

He stared for a moment, wondering if he should ask more.

"Fuck off, Adam."

"Right. Okay." He followed Rich out to the ute and Rich drove him back down the hill without a word.

As they headed along Tanning Street, Adam said, "You're pretty new to the Gulp, huh?"

"Been a few years now. Three or so. You were born here?"

"Monkton. Mum moved here when my dad fucked off."

"Right."

"You and Chrissy..."

"What about me and Chrissy?"

"You guys are an item maybe?"

"How is that any business of yours."

Adam patted the air at Rich's steely tone. "Just making conversation, bro."

"Yeah? Well, maybe don't. You and I really have nothing to talk about."

So much for buddying up to this guy. Adam would have to come right out with it. "What are you guys doing?"

"What do you mean?"

"You're putting something in the weed you're selling. And you're clearly doing it for a reason beyond making more money."

"Very perceptive."

"Yeah? So what is it?"

"Remember how I said you and I have nothing to talk about?"

"Yeah."

"That includes this." Rich hit the indicator even though the road behind him was empty and turned left into Noonan Street. He drove up to Adam's building and pulled to the curb, then turned in his seat to pin Adam with a gaze as hard as his tone. "You know the best thing for you to do?"

"What's that?"

"Exactly what Chrissy tells you to. You do precisely as you're told, you keep your head down, and you stop causing trouble. Do you have any idea how much you've fucked things up killing Ramsey? How much you've potentially derailed at a very sensitive time?"

That old belligerence rose up again. "Maybe you guys should have been more careful at padding out the bud, then. Maybe it wouldn't have been noticed. If you think about it, this is all your fault. You're the ones who have been fucking around with our arrangements. Arrangements that had been working smoothly for a long time, I might add."

"We are altering the arrangement. Pray we don't alter it any further."

Adam stared. Everything around him had the sensation of falling apart, cracking into pieces and drifting away. "Just make sure the weed is easy to sell, man. Don't make it so obvious."

"Get the fuck out, Adam. I'll be back this afternoon with the product."

Adam stood on the curb outside his building and watched Rich drive away. Rage boiled in his gut, made worse by his impotence in the face of it. He was not a stupid man and had managed to exist on the fringes of Gulpepper society for a long time without dealing directly with the Carters, Chrissy or her father before her. Adam prided himself on that fact. And now, in the space of a day or so, he was dragged in so deeply he saw no way out. And he had no idea what they were really up to. Fucking Neil, getting all aggro when he'd looked at the last deal they'd been given. Neil started the fight that led to all this.

He turned to go inside and jumped to see Neil standing right behind him.

"Fuck, mate! Why do you keep doing that? You need to fuck off!"

His friend had degraded further still, his skin purpling, eyelids drooping. His eyes seemed to be drying out, shrinking in their obits to reveal meaty, red raw flesh beneath. Adam heard Neil breathing and it was like air being sucked through tar. Neil's mouth worked as he tried to speak, but only thick, black bubbles and a gust of foul air came out. Neil reached forward, his fingers clutching at Adam, the nails yellowing and lifting from the beds.

Adam moved back a moment too late. Neil's ragged fingertips dragged through Adam's t-shirt, clawed at his skin. The touch was so cold and so painful that Adam yelled, doubled over. It felt as though he'd been shot with ice bullets. He staggered back and looked up again, but Neil was gone.

He remembered back to the conversation with Chrissy.

That really depends on the nature of the ghost, Adam.

This ghost certainly could hurt him. What the hell was he supposed to do? Not wanting to go back inside, to risk being trapped in a room with his revenant ex-best friend, Adam started walking instead. The day was heating up, the sun felt rejuvenating and he needed to think. Before long, he found himself heading towards the harbour again. He saw the sea witch there on the harbour wall, staring out across the water.

She knew stuff. She'd seen Neil. Without thinking, Adam took off at a run, slipping across the road and around towards the harbour to approach her from that side. If she wanted to get away from him again, she'd have to head into town and he figured she would be easier to track that way. But as he slowed to a walk and approached, she turned slowly, resignedly, entirely unsurprised by his presence.

"It's likely all too late," she said. Her voice was low, throaty, but strong despite her appearance of extreme age. She had three teeth, one top centre and two evenly spaced in the bottom of her pale gums.

"What?" Adam hadn't anticipated that and found himself wrong-footed.

"You're likely in too deep."

"You keep saying likely."

"Nothing is fixed. Everything is in flux. All things are subject to waves of possibility."

Adam frowned. Maybe talking to this crazy old lady was a mistake after all. He decided to stick to the things he thought he knew. "You saw my friend last night, didn't you? My dead friend."

"He's so angry with you, but still trying to help. Desperately hanging onto this place to warn you."

"Why is he angry with me?"

"You know why."

"It's not my fault he died!"

"You convinced him to climb over. You were too scared to go yourself."

"How do you know that?"

The old woman pointed past Adam and he turned to see Neil standing there, broken and bleeding, gasping through the sludge that seemed to be taking him over as he held his head up to stare at Adam.

Adam's stomach tightened at the fury in his friend's gaze, but in the sorrow there too. The sadness. "Neil, bro! I'm sorry, man. I didn't want you to die. I wish you hadn't died!"

"Tell him the truth," the old woman said.

Adam looked at her then back to Neil. "She's right. I was scared, bro. I was too scared and I wanted you to do it. But I didn't want you to die." He was crying now, unashamedly. Several people wandered around the harbour and along the footpath opposite, heading up to the lighthouse or maybe the fish and chip shop on the wharf. Many cast concerned glances Adam's way and he imagined what they saw. Some crazy man crying and talking to no one while the old sea witch watched, but he didn't care. There was sudden and unburdening catharsis in his admission.

Neil let go of his hair and his head slapped back down. His shoulders slumped in a kind of resignation. Maybe relief?

Adam turned back to the sea witch. "You said he was trying to help me. Warn me. I can't understand him any more. Like he can't speak. Help me how?"

"Whatever it is you're doing, that you were both doing, you're being used."

"I know. Chrissy is up to something. She's putting stuff in the weed we sell and I think it's important for a reason, but I don't know what." Adam heard the words coming out of him and knew they sounded mad. Gibberish. But how else to explain?

"The Carters have long tried to protect Gulpepper. It's more of the same. But the cost! They pay such high prices every time."

Adam frowned, remembering the night everyone in Gulpepper had suffered their mass psychosis. When so many had died or gone missing, when so many had killed or been killed. "Chrissy's dad died saving The Gulp though, right? He stopped whatever was going down? That's the consensus among locals on the rare occasions anyone talks about it."

The old woman sighed. "All that happened before was a precursor. A beginning, not an end. There are no true ends, just a series of connected beginnings, one leading to the next into eternity. Even when something is seemingly over, something else has already started."

"So what can we do about it?"

"People like the Carters and their associates try to fight. Others of us watch, bear witness. Your friend there, he wants you to go. He wants you to leave, while you still can, because if you stay much longer it'll be too late."

"What will? Too late for what?"

"For anything. You'll end here."

"I thought you said there were no endings."

"Your end will be the beginning of something else." She leaned forward, squinting at him. "Something altogether less pleasant than whatever you've endured so far."

"So I should just drop everything and run? Is that it?

Away from Gulpepper?"

"That's what your friend is trying to tell you to do. Whether it's the right thing to do... well, that depends. The right thing for you? Maybe. The right thing for this place? Maybe not. The right thing for the future? Who knows?"

Adam's mind churned. He wasn't getting any answers here, only more questions. Unless finally understanding Neil was the only answer he needed. Maybe it was. It was terrifyingly simple. Leave. He had a bunch of possessions in his flat, but did he really have anything else? Did he have any genuine reason to stay? He could put as much stuff in his car as would fit and just... leave. Why not?

"Who are you?" he asked the woman. "I don't even know your name."

"Most people don't. And those who remember my name don't remember me. Not really."

"You've been here a long time, though, right?"

The old woman laughed, but it was a bitter sound. "Longer than anyone else. Longer than Gulpepper."

Adam frowned, tried to remember his local history. He knew Charles Gulpepper founded the town in 1862. Charles Head to the north was named after him. Charles went mad and killed his four children and his wife, Jacquelin, then threw himself off the cliff beyond the lighthouse. Jacqueline Head to the south, where the cemetery was, had been named in honour of Gulpepper's murdered wife. He also remembered the stories that no Indigenous people would have anything to do with the place, one of the few parts of Australia where white people met no opposition in settling. Most agreed the Indigenous folk proved themselves a lot smarter than the whitefellas on that front. And that was largely the extent of Adam's recall of anything about Gulpepper's past. But if this woman claimed to be older than the town, that made her older than 1862, which meant she had to be well over a hundred and fifty years old and that seemed unlikely even for someone as used to the weirdness of The Gulp as Adam.

"Does it matter?" she asked.

He glanced up from his reverie. "What?"

"Who I am, what's happening, what your role might be? Does any of it matter?"

"Of course it matters. Doesn't it?"

"If it does, then you have a simple decision. Stay and play your part in it or listen to your friend and go."

"Does anyone ever really leave The Gulp though?" Adam asked. "The place has a bit of a reputation of never letting anyone leave."

"People come and go all the time. It depends what kind of person you are."

"What do you think I should do?"

"I have no opinion."

"What are you always here looking for? You spend day and night staring out across the ocean. Why?"

The old woman turned her back on him and did exactly as he'd described, watching out once more. "I told you," she said quietly, her words almost lost in the light breeze. "Some of us simply bear witness."

Adam stood for a time, wondering at her existence. Ever since he was a kid she'd been a feature of town, and clearly for a long time before that. The crazy old lady, the sea witch, any number of other insulting names. But talking to her, she was lucid and insightful and seemed anything but crazy. She obviously knew a lot more than she was prepared to let on, at least to him. And he couldn't help feeling there was a kind of importance about her. Was it as simple as being witness to events? Was that such an important role? And was she cursed, to be put in that position for so long? If she was right and there really were no true endings, Adam wondered if her vigil would ever be over. Perhaps she was doomed to bear witness forever.

"I'm sorry," he said softly.

"For what?"

"For... everything, I guess."

She nodded, still not turning back to face him. After a moment more, he sighed and walked away.

It occurred to Adam that he'd never thought more clearly. Perhaps the sea witch... He didn't want to think of her that way any more. The old woman? The harbour woman? He wished he knew her name. Regardless, perhaps she'd been more helpful than he realised. As he walked slowly up Tanning Street back towards home, his thoughts clarified.

Stay and play your part in it or listen to your friend and go.

His last homage to Neil would be to listen to his friend's warning. He was going to leave. Having managed to avoid being drawn into Carter's business for so long, the events of the last couple of days marked a turning point. Unfortunate, sure. Certainly difficult. But he wouldn't stay any longer.

He went indoors and dragged a battered old suitcase from Neil's room. His friend didn't need it any more. It took about ten minutes to pack all the clothes he thought he needed. He could leave a few old and tattered bits and pieces behind. It took maybe another twenty minutes to go through each room of the small apartment and collect everything else he wanted to take. He almost started crying again at the pathetic sight of it. So little of any real importance. So little achieved in three decades of life. And he had some of Neil's stuff too, including a laptop and Nintendo Switch that he figured he could sell. He'd need money to keep moving and get himself set up somewhere new.

He put his paltry life into a few bags and boxes and loaded them into his old Camry. Breaking a lease agreement on the apartment was a problem and might give him trouble in the future if he tried to rent somewhere new. But perhaps not if he left New South Wales. Which raised the question of where to go. The nearest state border was south, to Victoria. So maybe he'd head to Melbourne. He knew a guy down there, Pavel. He scrolled his phone and saw he still had a number for the guy. Now there was someone who had successfully left Gulpepper. Pavel had come to the town for work and he'd made friends with Adam and Neil one night in Clooney's. But Pavel had been observant and decided there was too much about The Gulp he didn't like and had quit the job and left again. Moving back to Melbourne, that's what he'd told them. He hadn't been in town more than a few months.

Adam tapped out a text message.

pavel, its adam from gulpepper. remember me? heading to melbourne, thought we might catch up for a beer or something

He stared at the phone for a moment, but no return message was immediately forthcoming, so he pocketed it and went back upstairs. He'd leave the apartment keys on the kitchen counter. When the rent failed to be paid they'd eventually come looking and find him gone, but if he left the keys maybe they'd be happy to cut their losses and simply re-let the place. The landlord would get to keep the bond money, after all. An irritating but acceptable loss for Adam and perhaps enough for the landlord to forget everything.

As he went to pull the front door closed behind him, Adam paused. Was he really doing this? He was scared, if he was honest. And so was Neil. The poor fucker.

Yes, he *was* doing this. Too many people didn't heed warnings, especially in Gulpepper. Time to cut and run. He closed the door behind him and the solid click of the latch engaging, the keys inside, was like a full stop in the chapter of his life until now. Time to write a new future.

He went downstairs and got into the battered Camry, turned the key. The engine made its most gravelly grinding sound to date.

"Ah, fuck, come on. Please!"

He turned the key again and the metal-on-metal grind became a kind of tortured squeal.

"You're a good car! Please, you're great. You've got me so far. Just one more drive, yeah? Please?"

He turned the key again and the grinding gave way to a muted rattle and then nothing. Frantically, Adam turned the key again and again but got nothing except an electric clicking.

"Well, shit."

The big, bronze Isuzu D-Max pulled up to the curb behind him, Rich Blake's face clearly visible behind the wheel. He knew Rich was due to his place later that day with the weed they wanted him to deal, but Adam thought he had hours yet.

Rich flashed his lights once and got out, came around to Adam's window carrying a sports holdall. Adam tried to roll down the glass, but the battery didn't even have the juice for that any more, so he opened the door and got out.

"Going somewhere?" Rich asked.

"Not any more. Fucking car's cactus."

Rich handed over the bag. "Guess you'll be walking around for a bit then."

"Guess so."

"Just like Ramsey used to, eh?"

Adam sighed. Only for a little while. Make enough deals to make enough dough to get the car fixed. Then he would leave Gulpepper for good. As Rich climbed back into the Isuzu and pulled away, Adam glanced up at his apartment, wondering how he would break back in to get his keys back.

Neil stood in the window, blackened, rotting, barely recognisable, but still Adam thought he saw sadness in his old friend's eyes.

Sunlight on Clear Water

Sunlight On Clear Water

Summer sun lanced through pale gum trunks, the trees in thick profusion on either side of the narrow road. Broken asphalt edges and potholes made the way treacherous and Beverly drove slowly.

"Where are you taking me?" Will asked. A slight smile twitched his lips as he asked, but he was a little concerned as well. Apart from where they were heading, there was nowhere to turn around, and Will didn't relish sitting in the small Volkswagen while Bev reversed all the way back down the steep, broken, winding road.

"Trust me."

The road got a little steeper still, then dipped through another shallow valley before rising again. They had to be nearing the top of the ridge.

"I didn't even know this road was here," Will said.

Beverly smiled. "Well, you've only lived in Gulpepper a few months, right?"

"Almost six now. But it's not a big place. I thought I'd seen all of it."

"No one has seen all of The Gulp."

"Sounds ominous."

"You'll get used to that." Bev gestured vaguely to their left, the ridge rising beside the car. "There used to be a couple of farms on top up there. Look, there's an old gate now."

A rusted metal three-metre farm gate hung crookedly from a rotten wooden fence post a little back from the road, the whole thing mostly overgrown. Probably the long grasses were all that kept the whole thing from collapsing forever. "How long since anyone lived up here?" Will asked.

"A generation or two, I guess. But it's not entirely abandoned. The last farm at the end of the road, right on top of the ridge, is still occupied."

"Hell of a place to farm, this deep in the bush."

"Oh, it's not a working farm any more. Hasn't been for decades, I don't think. Hilda, sister of Gottfried, lives up there. Children of German immigrants from after the Second World War, they were born on the farm. It's all bush down here among the valleys, but when you get on top there's a lot of cleared land."

"And this Hilda and Gottfried live up there but don't farm?"

"Only Hilda. Neither married and neither left home, and when their parents died they inherited the land. Stopped farming. So town gossip goes, anyway. They must have some kind of independent wealth, as they never worked as far as anyone around here can tell. Gottfried died a year ago, but Hilda's there. She's got to be at least seventy, I guess? Probably more."

"Must be lonely."

"Doesn't seem to bother her. I've lived here all my life and only seen her in town once in all my nineteen years. That was when Gottfried died and she came to his funeral at the cemetery north of town."

"Why were you at Gottfried's funeral? You know the family?"

"I worked hospitality in the private room upstairs at Clooney's for the wake. I do that part-time now and then, when they need extra hands. It's decent money when it comes up. Hilda came in, drank one sherry, then insisted on being taken home. Left the other dozen or so guests to carry on without her. The whole thing was over in less than an hour. So I didn't actually make much that time. And I missed out on a Blind Eye Moon gig in Enden to be there. All my friends had left before I finished and I spent the evening watching TV at home like a loser."

"I can't imagine you ever being anything like a loser, Bev."

She flashed him a smile. "Here we are."

Will looked out the window, frowning. It looked no different, just a narrow, broken road almost swallowed by bush. "Where?"

Beverly pointed as she slowly turned onto a small, grassy clearing. Once they were facing it, Will saw two more farm gates, these also crooked and rusty, not quite lining up as they hung from split, silvered posts spotted with pale green lichen. The one on the right had a sign on it, almost obscured by lichen and dirt. A red oval with 'DANGER' in the centre, then under that, black writing on a white background.

KEEP OUT!
AUTHORISED PERSONNEL ONLY

To the left side of the gates, a cement culvert was almost lost under moss and fallen leaves. Will twisted in the seat and saw the culvert's twin on the downhill side of the road, with a narrow, rocky creek descending steeply away from it through the trees. "What is this place?"

"Secret paradise." Bev gave him a wicked smile and reached behind her for the large canvas bag on the back seat. "Come on."

Will pointed to the sign on the crooked gate. "You sure? That's pretty conclusive."

"Standard stuff, Will. You know how to swim, right?"

"Of course."

"Then there's no danger. Come on!"

Swim? Will thought. *Up here?*

But he knew he would follow Beverly anywhere. She was the hottest girl he'd met in a long while and only a year younger than him. Since moving from the city half a year before, he'd found it hard to fit in with the weird harbour town in the middle of nowhere, and often wondered if he'd made a terrible mistake taking the job with Klaus Brunswick. It had been advertised as an old-fashioned apprenticeship, learning the skills of the traditional cabinetmaker, which fit extremely well with Will's passion for carpentry. And that the job included accommodation in the flat above Klaus's workshop made it particularly appealing. Learning a trade, a decent wage as there was no rent to pay, plus an easy method to get far away from his drunken father? Seemed too good to pass up. Yet still he found the town strange and hard to adjust to. More isolated than he'd expected, the population insular and, frankly, weird.

Then Klaus's daughter, Beverly, came into his life and suddenly everything seemed a lot more worthwhile. He'd met several relatively normal people around town, but only normal by Gulp standards. Beverly was a beacon of light in the strange darkness. She was funny and smart and gorgeous and, as it turned out, as starved of normality as he was. After only six months he'd wondered about quitting the apprenticeship and Gulpepper, trying his luck elsewhere. She'd put up with the place for nineteen years, her whole life. He found it hard to imagine that. So they'd been drawn together, each a moth to the other's flame. Will could easily imagine sticking around The Gulp all the time if he had Beverly to hang out with after work. That she was Klaus's daughter might prove awkward at some point, but her father knew they were seeing each other and seemed entirely okay with it so far. Will would be sure to remain respectful to them both and prove his worth on all fronts.

They'd only been actively dating a little less than a month and already he was falling for her, he knew that. Falling hard and fast, and that had turned out badly before, but Will was nothing if not a slave to his emotions. He'd always known it to be so.

"You have the heart of a gentle lion," his mother had told him, only days before breast cancer stole her away, when he was just sixteen, four years before. "Always trust that heart of yours." It was almost the last thing she said to him.

With a mental shrug, he climbed from the car into the sweltering summer humidity and followed Beverly to the gates. Standing there, he saw the rocky creek heading into the culvert and leaned against a fence post to look further into the bush. A wide cement slope, slick with moss, rose up from the creek about twenty metres in. It had barriers either side only half a metre high, and water ran down the centre of it in a gentle stream. "Is that the spillway of a dam?"

"Yep! Come on." Beverly ducked under broken fence wire next to the gate and headed up the overgrown track on the other side, her bag slung over her shoulder.

As he followed and cleared the initial screen of trees, Will saw the face of the dam above, stretching either side of the spillway. The whole thing was probably fifty metres across. Every inch of it moss-covered, dried gum leaves stuck here and there. Shreds of bark littered the ground along with the fallen leaves, all crunching underfoot in the summer heat. When they reached the top, Will stopped and let out a soft, "Wow."

Beverly grinned. "Told you."

The dam itself had a low wall all around and stretched back into the bush about another fifty metres, the whole thing as moss-coated as the rest he'd seen. It made the entire perimeter look like a comfortable bench seat. Beyond the edges was nothing but thick trees, overhanging the expanse of water. Sunlight glittered and rippled through it. The only open space was the narrow track along one side they'd used to get there. At the far end, the land rose steeply. The creek that fed the dam snaked up through the trees and the narrow track continued up alongside it. The water was crystal, almost preternaturally so. Will saw rocks and leaf litter at the bottom as clearly as if there were nothing between him and it. The only real giveaway that the dam was full was sunlight glittering where it lanced between the trees.

"Why is this even here?" Will asked.

"I guess when there were more working farms up this way, they needed the water. But since most people have moved on, the bush is slowly taking everything back. Only locals know about this place, and even then, not everyone. We've got it all to ourselves. That's usually the case. If anyone else does come along we'll hear them long before they get here." She gave him a sly grin and peeled her t-shirt up over her head. She wore nothing underneath it. Will stared, smiling. Beverly wriggled out of her shorts and underwear and stood unselfconsciously naked before him.

Will stood still, drinking her in for a moment, then pulled his clothes off as well. For the next little while they were lost in each other. At some level, Will remained concerned they might be seen, that if other locals knew about this place they would visit too, especially on a day as hot as this, and it seemed likely he and Bev wouldn't hear them, distracted as they were. But his lust largely blanked those concerns.

The ground was dry and the leaves scratchy, but they found a shaded spot that was mostly moss. Afterwards, sweat soaked and sated, Beverly said, "Now to make the most of the location." She stood, ran, and hopped over the low wall to disappear into the clear water with barely a splash.

As the sound of her entry faded, Will heard a guttural giggling from somewhere in the trees nearby and spun around. He looked, heart hammering. Maybe it had simply been water gurgling, disturbed by Beverly diving in. But it had sounded so much like laughter.

Beverly bobbed in the water, slicked her long brunette hair back with both hands. "What are you waiting for? Come in, it's deliciously cold!"

"I thought I heard..." Will frowned, looking into the trees again. Maybe it had been an animal of some kind. A bird? Probably a kookaburra, he told himself, if it wasn't the water.

He stood on the low wall and just as he launched himself into the water he heard an old, burbling woman's voice say, "Such fine flesh!"

He hit the water, the coldness taking his breath, and immediately clawed for the surface. He turned back to face the trees, pushing up on the wall for a better view.

He saw no one.

"What are you doing?" Beverly asked. She paddled over to him, put a hand on his shoulder. "Are you okay?"

"Someone's here."

"I don't think so. We'd have heard a car. No one would walk all the way up here, it's like five or six kays from town."

Will stared into the trees, a chill on his skin from more than the fresh water. "I heard someone say something."

"What?"

He was a little embarrassed to admit it. "It sounded like an old woman. She said, 'Such fine flesh.'" He gave a wry laugh, the absurdity of it apparent when he spoke the words aloud. "I think," he added.

Beverly's brows knitted. "Well, that's creepy."

"I know."

"But there's no one here." She gestured around them. "Look."

Will turned slowly in the water, scanning the trees all around. They were alone but for trees and birds, the sun dappling the water. It was a beautiful spot and they were the only ones enjoying it.

Beverly reached between his legs, squeezed playfully. "You ever made love in the water before?"

And that was the last he thought about anything for a while.

A little later, they lay on the wall of the dam. It was about half a metre thick, so plenty wide enough for comfort, and the spongy moss only added to that. Will had begun to enjoy the outdoor nudity and wasn't too bothered if other people did arrive. Let them see. There was something liberating about it and he was young and fit. He was proud of his body, gym toned and lean. There was something subversive as well as liberating about public nudity, he realised, and Beverly's utter lack of self-consciousness about her own undress seemed strangely infectious.

They lay at the right angle of the front corner of the dam, Will's feet pointing at the spillway, Bev's feet pointing at the creek rising up from the far end. Their heads were close together at the corner and they chatted quietly, amiably. Will hadn't been this comfortable with anyone for a long time. Maybe ever. Perhaps taking that apprenticeship had been the right decision for a lot of reasons.

"Want a drink?" Beverly asked after a moment of comfortable silence.

"Sure, why not. What do you have?"

She stood and moved over to her bag. Will shielded his eyes, enjoyed the view of her walking away, bending over. She was indeed beautiful, he couldn't really believe his luck. He'd been out with attractive people before, but maybe none as amazing as Beverly. And she was so much more than good looks. He honestly couldn't get enough of her company, dressed or naked. When she stood and turned back, caught him watching, she smiled crookedly and struck a pose for a moment.

"God damn," Will said, grinning. He knew he looked goofy, but couldn't help it. And didn't care.

Beverly glanced down at his crotch, which told no lies on his thoughts, and smiled. He smiled back, enjoying her scrutiny.

She hefted a bottle of Kraken Black Spiced Rum. "This okay?"

Will pushed up onto one elbow, gestured up and down at her with his free hand. "Everything about this is way more than okay."

"*sofffft flesshhh*"

Will sat up sharply. "You hear that?"

Her eyebrows rose. "Hear what?"

He turned, looked back into the trees near the crooked gates. Beverly was only five metres away in the other direction, but maybe that was enough to have missed the soft whisper. "I heard a voice again."

"Wind in the trees?"

Will shook his head. "You felt even a breeze today? It's completely still."

"True. An animal?"

"That's what I thought before, but I heard words."

"What words?"

"This time it said, 'soft flesh.'"

Beverly laughed, popped one hip. "Maybe it's your own internal monologue you're hearing?" She nodded at him. "Nothing soft about your flesh."

She came and sat beside him, opened the bottle and took a swig, then passed it over.

Will took it but didn't drink yet.

"Your hand is shaking," Bev said.

"It really startled me. That voice."

Beverly's face became more serious and she scanned the trees. "You really heard something?"

"Twice now. Maybe three times."

"Who's there?" Beverly shouted and Will jumped at the sudden shattering of the hot stillness.

They sat waiting, but there was no reply.

Beverly looked back at him, frowning. "You're kinda scaring me."

"Yeah, I'm a little spooked myself."

"Maybe we should go." She looked back into the trees. "It would be easy enough for someone to stay hidden in there, it's so dark and thick."

"Now *you're* scaring *me*."

"Didn't you say it sounded like an old woman?" she asked.

Will nodded, looking into the shadows between the pale trunks. "Yeah. So maybe not much of a threat, eh? And I'm probably just hearing things." He realised he'd said that to appease Beverly more than because he really believed it. He was pretty sure he had heard a voice.

"Maybe someone escaped from the Institute that opened a year or two back. The one at the other end of town?" Beverly said with a wry smile.

"The Gulpepper Institute of something or other? I

think that's one of those expensive spas for rich people with 'exhaustion.'" He made air quotes with his fingers as he spoke. "I mean, it's not an insane asylum, right?"

"The entirety of Gulpepper is an insane asylum." Bev grinned. "But you're right, that place is for rich losers."

Will sighed. "Maybe I'm hearing things." He took a swig of rum, passed the bottle over. Beverly drank again.

"Hey, who's going to drive back?" he asked.

She smiled. "I will. Don't worry about cops, there are never any around here. Even if you call them, they take an hour or more to arrive. If they arrive at all. So should we go?" She leaned back on one hand, passed him the bottle. The sun lit up her pale skin, every beautiful inch of her. She reached over and took hold of his cock, bringing it immediately back to attention from where it had started to falter. She slid her hand slowly up and down.

"Let's have a drink and stick around a little longer."

She allowed a soft smile. "Sure."

They passed the bottle back and forth, playing with each other's bodies the whole while. The insatiable need of the newly acquainted. After a time, Beverly went back to her bag and got some snacks. She laid out a tea towel and put down crackers, dried fruit, cheese. They ate and drank more as the sun began to lower, shade slowly laying over them like a blanket, though the heat persisted.

Will was glad to be out of the direct sun, realised he'd probably spent too long naked in it and was likely sunburned.

"One more swim?" Beverly asked.

"And then head back to town?"

"Sure. We can leave my car at my place and head to Clooney's for a few more drinks, if you like."

"Sounds good."

Beverly turned and shoved him with unexpected strength. Will cried out as his feet flew up and he tumbled backwards into the chill embrace of the water, cold enough to suck his breath away. As he spluttered back to the surface, Beverly stood on the low wall, laughing. She dipped her knees, then arched over him in a graceful dive, disappearing with barely a splash, just as she had before. Will realised the water had become inky dark without the sun overhead. From crystal clear to impenetrable murk. He looked left and right, waiting for Beverly to emerge and his heart began to quicken as the seconds passed.

"Beverly?" he said cautiously and struck out towards the place she'd entered the water, panic building in his chest.

Then she burst up from the middle of the dam, a good ten metres away. "Ah, it's *so* good!" she said. Then she caught his eye. "You okay?"

He laughed. "You were under a while there. I was worried."

"Oh. Sorry about that!"

They swam in circles for a little while, kissed and ran their hands over each other. Before long, Will realised Beverly was shivering, felt the goosebumps all over her.

"You're cold?"

"Yeah, starting to get that way. Time to go home?"

"Sure."

They swam to the edge and climbed out. Beverly pulled a towel from her voluminous bag that seemed to have everything they could ever want. Will was impressed with her preparedness. They towelled off and got dressed. The embrace of clothing even as light as shorts and t-shirt seemed strangely encumbering to Will after being naked for so long. He felt he had a better understanding of people who enjoyed nudist beaches. Naturalists, he remembered they called themselves. It wasn't something he'd ever really thought much about before, but he got it now. It was good.

"A minute," Bev said. "I need to pee."

She winked and ducked under some low branches beside the narrow track. Will waited for a moment, then realised he needed to go as well. He turned in the opposite direction, being sure to move a good few metres away from where Bev had ducked under, and stood facing the edge of the trees. As he finished up and zipped his fly, a croaking voice whispered. "Nice cock."

Will jumped back, looked left and right. He saw no one. He turned a slow circle.

Then the voice came from behind him. "I enjoyed watching you put it in her as well."

Will spun around. "Who's there?" His voice was loud, cracked with shock and nervousness.

The guttural laughter, soft and phlegmy, came from beside him, somewhere in the trees. Above him?

Will took several steps back, staring hard into the darkness, and his heel fetched up against the low dam wall, nearly toppling him in. Catching his balance, he looked left and right again, trying to see into the bush. But the lowering sun and rapidly swelling shadows made it almost completely dark under the tangled canopy. The bright, glittering dam he'd enjoyed all day was suddenly gloomy and cool, somehow oppressive.

"Bev?" he called out. "You okay?"

There was no answer.

"Beverly!"

That thick chuckling again, from somewhere in the darkness.

"Who are you? What have you done with Beverly?"

Will was a little drunk from the rum, thick-headed from too long in the sun. Fear clawed at his gut and rising panic thickened his throat. "*Beverly!*" he yelled, his voice high and strident, punching through the gloom.

He ran to the trees where she'd ducked in only moments before, yelled her name again. The darkness only a metre or two in was stygian, but he pushed through, looking all around. He called her name, forcing his way past the thick branches that whipped at his face, scratched his arms and legs. He wore thongs and the dry leaf litter dug and gouged between his toes.

"Beverly, where are you?"

He heard only the crunching of his own panicked passage and that wet, phlegm-filled laughter. It seemed to echo and travel, as though the sound were disembodied and circled like a vulture over carrion.

"What have you done with her? Who are you?"

Will heard the catch in his voice, felt tears burn and prickle at his eyes. One of the best days of his life was shattering and dissolving by the second. He pushed back out through the trees into the clearing and turned in a slow circle.

"Fucking show yourself!" he yelled.

He was answered only by laughter, fading slowly away. It seemed to retreat up the slope behind the dam. He turned to the creek across the smooth expanse of dark water. Water like a black mirror, reflecting a few clouds overhead in a sky turning rapidly indigo. It would be dark soon, the full dark of night. They had stayed much too late into the evening, should have left hours before. Already a few stars speckled the encroaching darkness to the east. And the laughter seemed to continue retreating, away up the ridge.

What should he do? Where was Beverly? He put both hands on his head, tried to suck in deep breaths to stop the panic rising, taking over.

"Wiiilllllll!"

He spun back to look up the ridge, up along the feeder creek. The voice had been faint and terrified, but surely it had been Beverly. Hadn't it? Who else could it have been? Who else would know his name?

"Okay, okay," he said, his voice high and breathy. What had Bev said? That old woman, Hilda, lived alone up there. The farm at the end of the road. At the top of the ridge. Was that who he'd heard whispering to him? That crazy old lady? Had she taken Beverly? Even if not, he could hopefully get help there. There was nothing else between him and town, five or more kilometres away back down the long and twisting, broken road. At least if he went up to this Hilda's place he'd find some kind of civilisation.

He ran over to Beverly's bag, still where she'd left it, and started rummaging around. There was the damp towel, remnants of their food, half a bottle of rum, Beverly's phone. He paused, dug in his pocket and pulled out his phone. No reception. Of course not. He had trouble getting reception anywhere in town and had kept meaning to change providers, but Wi-Fi at the flat meant he'd never worried too much about it. Who called anyone any more? Bev's phone was locked. He dug back into the bag. "Come on, come on." He heard a soft jingling and dug deeper then let out a "Yes!" of triumph as he came up with Beverly's car keys.

He grabbed up the bag and ran for the car, ducked under the wire and jumped into the driver's seat. He threw the bag onto the back seat and started the engine, then backed out onto the narrow road. He had no idea how far up Hilda lived, but Beverly had said it was at the end, so he just had to keep going.

It was less than a kilometre until the road levelled out a little and the trees thinned. The land on top of the ridge had indeed been significantly cleared compared to how dense the bush had been all the way up. Will kept going and, after another kilometre or so, the road simply ended in a farm gate. This one was a lot newer and in better repair, the fences either side strong-looking post-and-rail surrounding overgrown paddocks. Tussocks of grass marred the fields like a giant rash.

On top of the ridge, without the trees crowding in on all sides, there was more light. Dusk was deepening, but the shadows weren't as thick. Beyond the gate, a dirt track went between two overgrown paddocks. Barbed wire fences marked the boundaries of the fields either side of the track and, about a hundred metres distant, was an old sandstone farmhouse. It had sash windows with peeling paint, pale but probably not white, and a tin roof that looked like it might have been replaced not long ago. The new metal seemed incongruous with the age of the old stone walls. The place was large, two stories in a rough square with a wide, covered wooden veranda all around the ground floor. Two big, old-fashioned cement water tanks stood off to one side, a slightly leaning wooden barn beyond them.

Stone steps, the same pale yellow as the house, led up the front of the veranda to a tall front door with stained glass panels. Some lights burned inside, a pale orange glow pushing against a couple of the downstairs windows. As Will watched, a light came on upstairs.

The gate was chained shut, so he killed the engine and got out. By habit, he locked the car even though Beverly hadn't at the dam. Then he pocketed the keys, vaulted over the gate, and ran for the front door.

Will staggered as he reached the top of the steps, the old veranda flexing underfoot, nearly tipping him over. The wood was rotten in places, fallen in here and there. Closer up, the wooden frames of the sash windows were also spongy with rot, the paint flaking and missing altogether in many places. The front door seemed to be in slightly better condition, the squares of frosted, coloured glass glowing red and yellow and green from the light inside.

He stepped gingerly to the door and looked around. Seeing no doorbell, he banged on the wood beside the stained glass with the side of his fist.

"Hello? Anyone home? Hello?"

He cupped his hands to one of the small windows, but the wavy texture of the glass and the green stain in it meant he saw nothing but glow. He stepped back, checked the windows to either side, but they were opaque with drawn curtains, light from inside diffuse through the fabric.

He went back to the door, banged again. "Please, open up! I need help!"

There was no reply and no sound from inside the house. He'd seen that light come on upstairs. Perhaps it was on a timer? But Beverly had said the old woman, Hilda, hardly ever left the place. And maybe it had been her talking to him down at the dam. He shuddered, remembering the things she'd said. Had he beaten her back here, perhaps? He drove up, after all, and he'd heard that laughter disappearing along the creek.

He walked down the steps, looked through the deepening twilight across the paddock to where he'd left Beverly's car. He wasn't sure which direction the dam was, the road had twisted and turned on the way up. He walked back a way further, then turned and looked at the house.

The light in the upstairs room that he'd seen was on no longer. Why would a timer work a light for only a few minutes? That meant there had to be someone inside, surely.

He stared at the dark rectangle of glass.

"Hey!" he yelled. "I know someone's here! Please, open up."

He ran back to the front door, stepping carefully on the broken veranda, and banged again. There was an ornate brass doorknob and he grabbed it, twisted. But the door was locked.

What was happening to Beverly? Was she here, held against her will? Had she even been brought here? Surely she wasn't simply lost in the bush after going for a pee and he'd driven away and left her there. Please, not that.

Will turned in a circle, panic threatening to swallow him again. A rising tide of dread began to douse his senses, all the possibilities tumbling over each other in his mind. With a noise of fear, of desperation, he ran back to the grass, not trusting the veranda in the rapidly darkening evening, and sprinted around to the back of the house. A patch of garden marked by a rundown picket fence covered a few hundred square metres behind the building. A half-collapsed garden shed and a glasshouse with most of the panes broken stood in one corner. Shrubs and roses rambled over the fencing and more paddocks extended away from the house, overgrown like the others with long grass in random tussocks.

The back door had six small windows in it, these ones plain, clear glass. Will approached it and looked inside. He saw a kitchen, old-fashioned with a wrought iron range and scratched wooden benches. Copper pots hung from a frame in the centre and a deep, wide, cracked ceramic sink bristled with dirty dishes.

Will thought about knocking, but urgency drove him on. He tried the door. It opened.

He stood framed in the doorway for a moment, wincing against the smell of something savoury and unpleasant. "Hello?" he called out eventually. "Hello, is anyone here?"

Silence rang heavily. He stepped inside, a soft creak from floorboards beneath black and white tiles, then silence once more.

"Hello?" he said again, and it was almost a sob this time.

He moved further in and a soft burbling came to him. He realised it was emanating from a large copper pot on the range. Steam rose gently from it. Perhaps the source of the smell? And definitely an indicator that someone was here. Or had been recently.

He went over, looked cautiously in. Thick, dark gravy bubbled gently. It reminded him of the grey-brown volcanic mud pools he'd seen in Rotorua, on holiday in New Zealand as a teenager before his family disintegrated. He stared at it a moment, mesmerised. What the hell was it? Then something shifted and rose to the surface briefly and Will cried out, staggered back.

A finger.

That was a human fucking finger.

That soft, phlegmy laughter again, so similar to the sound of the pot simmering thickly. Will spun around, but no one was there.

"Such young, pliant flesh."

"Where are you?" Will screamed, fighting the almost overwhelming urge to sprint from the house. He wanted to run away, jump into Beverly's car and drive as fast as he safely could back down the hill. And then what? Tell Klaus, perhaps? Beverly's father would surely help him out. Or maybe he ought to simply keep going, right through town and out onto the only road away from Gulpepper and never look back.

But Beverly was here somewhere. He tried hard not to think about the finger simmering in the thick, grotesque soup. There was no way that could be hers, there hadn't been time to get back and dismember a person *and* get that on the boil.

So it had to be someone else's finger, which led to a whole new bunch of horrors. Why was the old lady cooking people? Did that mean Beverly would be next? Regardless, the thing that stopped him from running away was the knowledge he would be leaving Beverly if he did, and he could not countenance that. He had to save her. Assuming she had been taken by whoever he kept hearing.

One old woman, all alone up here. What challenge could that be? Then again, the disembodied laughing, the finger boiling away on the hob... This clearly wasn't any ordinary old woman.

"Beverly!" he yelled. "Bev, are you here?"

"*Wiillllll!*" Her voice was plaintive and distant.

He looked up. Had she called from upstairs? He ran from the kitchen into a hallway decorated with floral wallpaper. A grandfather clock stood against one wall, old sepia photos in ornate brass frames hung haphazardly. The front door of the place with its stained glass panes was at the other end and several doors led from the hallway into rooms on either side. A smaller door right beside him seemed to be a cupboard under the stairs, the stairway above it polished dark wood like mahogany. It had a thick, carved balustrade and the apprentice carpenter in Will couldn't help but admire the craftsmanship of it. The balusters were carved in perfect spirals, the newel post a masterpiece of leaves and vines. He realised all the woodwork in the house was similarly crafted. The doorframes and lintels, the doors themselves, all expertly worked dark wood. The decrepit outside of the house belied the beauty of the well-appointed, well-maintained interior.

He pounded up the stairs. "Beverly!"

"Wiiillll!"

How had one old woman managed to abduct and entrap a young, fit, strong woman like Beverly? She must have used something, some kind of trap or drug or… Whatever, Will was bigger, fitter, stronger.

He came out onto a landing that extended left and right, several doors all around it. At one end a door stood open with a light on inside. As he looked that way, he saw movement and a form moved into the doorway, silhouetted. It was the hunched shape of an old woman, knees bent under a long skirt, her hair a curling nimbus with the light behind her shining through it.

"Here's that delicious young flesh!"

Will took strides towards her. "Where's Beverly? What have you done with her?"

The old woman stepped away from the door, disappeared from view. Will paused, sucked in a long breath. He looked around and saw a small, occasional table up against the wall. This too was ornate and expertly made. Without a care for that, he kicked out at it and broke off one finely turned leg. He hefted it like a club, nodded once to himself. He was not above cracking an old woman upside the head if he felt in any kind of danger. He strode into the room at the end of the hall.

The first thing he noticed was the room was uncomfortably hot, overheated, and that savoury, throat-cloying smell he'd noticed in the kitchen hung in the air here stronger than ever. It was a big room, with no furniture in it and bare, polished wooden floorboards.

On the far side were two windows with a double door between them, that opened onto a small balcony. The doors were open, the night darkening outside, stars speckling the sky. The soft breeze drifting in did nothing to dissipate the close heat of the room.

"Will!"

He spun around at the sound and gasped to see Beverly high up, held against the wall near the ceiling, caught in a mass of ropes. Her clothes were ragged, underwear showing through, and she hung a little forward, suspended by her wrists and ankles, bound and held apart, pulling her legs wide, spreading her like a star. But not rope, Will realised. She was trapped in the thick strands of something fibrous and striated, like a huge spider's web that filled that upper corner of the room. The web looked deep as well as wide, almost as though Beverly had been fixed to the outside of some giant cocoon.

"Will!" she said again and sobbed.

The old woman emerged from the shadows behind the door and scuttled up the wall, onto the web, her knees and elbows bent wide. Bent the wrong way. The uncanny movement, the impossible physics of it, made Will's breath tighten in his chest. As she came close to Beverly, she turned in a circle and looked down at him.

In the light from the central fixture, Will saw her face clearly for the first time. Wrinkled skin stretched over a head that was too large, too long somehow. Her mouth hung wide and low, something moving inside it. She stretched forward, that thick, bubbling laughter. Two black mandibles, half-concealed in her cheeks, clacked together repeatedly. She reached out and ran one over-long fingernail along Beverly's neck and Beverly screamed. The fingernail was curved, jet black. The old woman's feet were bare, her toenails similar claw-like extensions of her toes, her ankles twisted so her feet stuck out at the wrong angle.

Will stared, his bladder straining, heart racing.

"So fresh!" the old woman said, her voice slurred slightly as she spoke around those glistening ebony mandibles.

"Why?" Beverly sobbed. "What *are* you?"

Will stood frozen in the middle of the tall room, staring up at them. Too high to reach, he had no idea what to do. He wanted to scream and run away from the sheer inconceivable nature of what he was looking at, but the terror and impotence of his position rooted him to the spot. He gasped in a breath, tried to get saliva moving in his suddenly dry mouth. His eyes prickled with tears.

"Are you brave?" the old woman... the creature, Hilda, whatever she was, said with more of that slopping laughter.

"Leave her alone!" Will yelled, and it sounded weak and pathetic even to his ears. His mind raced. He needed something to either get him up there or Hilda down. Was he really prepared to face her? Maybe something he could throw, sharp or heavy. He looked at the broken table leg in his hand and had never felt so useless, so pathetic.

Hilda laughed, thick and wet. "Take her place, would you? Trade your firm flesh for hers?" There was the trace of a German accent to her speech and Will remembered the story of her and her brother, their supposedly independent wealth. Did it come from this kind of thing, taking people? And would she really let him take Beverly's place?

He stared, dumbfounded. Would he do such a thing?

"Male flesh is so much sweeter to me," Hilda said. "You came to me willingly, after all. You could have left, but no, you came. Hmm? Coming for her? How I will enjoy chewing on that fine young body!" She screeched with laughter, her head tipping back, those mandibles extruding past her cheeks to clack at the air.

Beverly screamed, tried to turn her face away. "Run, Will! Get help!"

"Will you?" Hilda asked, snapping her attention back to him. "Run for help, eh? And should you find help, what then? Too late for her, oh yes. Far too late. Try to convince them sweet, old Hilda Braunschweig took your lovely girl, is that what you'd do?"

"There'll be something!" Will yelled, thinking of the pot on the stove downstairs.

"You'll be institutionalised, you young fool. I'll tell them I saw you at the dam, raping and beating a poor young girl." She cackled again. "This one missing and you trying to blame a weak and feeble old woman. As if they'll believe a word of it."

She was right. There was nothing he could do. If he ran for help, it would only be sacrificing Beverly. He could simply run, hope to get away from Hilda, but would he be able to live with himself, knowing he'd condemned Beverly to whatever horrors awaited her. Something deflated inside him. "Let her go," Will said. "Let her go and you can have me."

He had no intention of giving himself over so easily, but if he could only get Beverly released they could try to fight their way out together. The two of them stood a far better chance of overpowering or outrunning the hideous thing, whatever it was. And if not, at least it would give Beverly a chance to escape if he kept Hilda occupied.

"So gallant! So noble." Hilda reached down and slipped a claw alongside Beverly's ankle. The thick webbing parted and her leg swung free.

"Will! Save yourself. Send help!"

"She's right, Bev. It's already too late for that." *Cut her free, you bitch*, he thought. He just wanted Beverly to get away, that's all that really mattered.

Hilda scuttled around the web to Beverly's other side, let go her other leg. Beverly swung forward, let out a grunt of pain as she hung from her wrists, wincing.

"Will, no!"

He stared hard into her eyes. "As long as she lets you

go, that's all I care about!" He willed her to see his intent, his determination to fight. He desperately hoped she would turn and fight with him. Beverly was fit and strong too.

"True to your word, are you?" Hilda asked, and she slit the webbing on Beverly's right wrist.

Beverly came loose with a cry, swinging from her one restrained arm, suspended from the high ceiling a couple of metres above the polished floor. Hilda was trying to tempt him forward, he realised. Was she hoping he'd move to catch Beverly, then Hilda could drop on him from above and have them both? It was a trap, surely.

Will had to hope Beverly would be able to land safely without hurting herself. "Let her down!" he yelled, and backed up, made as much space as he could between them. Behind him were the double doors opening onto that small balcony. The night outside, hot with summer though it was, felt cool and fresh compared to the closeness and stink of the room. *Run to me, Bev*, he thought at her, willed her to perceive. *When you get free, run to me and we fight together. We* both *get away.*

"You can have me when she's free," Will said to Hilda. "No tricks!"

Hilda burbled wet laughter and cut the last bind. Beverly yelped, dropped heavily to the ground and went briefly onto one knee. She gasped in pain, looked up at Will.

"Come to me!" he shouted, raising the broken table leg. "Quickly!"

Beverly rose and sprinted across the room. Her face as she came changed, morphing from fear and pain to a kind of delight. Will started to smile back, but saw something else in her eyes, something feral. She didn't slow, raised both hands in front of herself and slammed two palms, arms straight, into his chest.

Will barked out the air in his lungs and flew backwards, stagger-stepping once, twice, three times, out the open doors, then his lower back fetched up against the balcony railing and he flipped up and over backwards. The sensation of freefall was intense and terrifying and so very brief, then impact rattled every atom of him as he bounced off the edge of the veranda roof and hit the grass below.

Will's vision swam, his body shuddered. He couldn't move, pain lanced through every part of him as he tried to gasp breath back into his burning lungs. Through tear-stained eyes he saw Beverly lean over the broken balcony and smile down at him. She gave a little wave. Then movement over her shoulder and Hilda came around under the lintel of the balcony doors and scurried down the wall to him.

Will writhed, tried to get up but that only triggered more pain. He hoped not too much was broken, but the wind had been knocked so thoroughly out of him that his vision blurred and his muscles were like wet ropes, useless.

Hilda squatted next to him and her arms and legs seemed to flicker and wave. Will began to turn against his will, to roll over and over, something hot and sticky and tight binding him up.

"I told you he was a good one, Oma." Beverly called down.

"Oh, very good, dear! Very, very good. So strong and young and fresh. Ahaha, such delicious flesh for them all!"

Will kept turning, being rolled by Hilda over and over as the thick, hot webbing wrapped him up.

"It's such fun to play with you, Oma!" Beverly called down. "But I liked him! I hope this is worth it."

"More than worth it, sweetness."

Will watched Hilda's face pass by again and again as he was turned, the grass and the sky, the grass and the sky. The webbing came up over his face, hot enough to sear his skin. He wanted to scream out, but was rigid with fear, frozen with terror. He saw through the web like it was a net curtain over a window, Hilda a blurry presence above him as he stopped turning. She shifted and raised her back end, somehow more rounded than seemed possible, something long and thin at the end of it. It drove down and he felt white hot, penetrating pain in his stomach and screamed, muted by his restricted mouth. Was she stinging him?

"I'll get Daddy to put an ad out for another apprentice, shall I?" Beverly called down.

"No, dear," Hilda said. The web covering Will's head muffled all sound, but he heard them well enough despite a sudden washing sensation of dizziness coursing through him. "This one will be enough."

The pain in his stomach radiated outwards, creeping along his limbs. Where the webbing wrapped over his bare skin, it burned. He was going to die. Restricted sobs began as Will's mind turned slushy and everything went dark.

The first thing he noticed was pain. Searing, howling agony across his skin. Every inch of him on fire with nerve-shredding pulses of agony. And then he perceived a deeper hurt, an internal throbbing like fresh bruising. And in his gut a sickening ache, and a tightness like some giant hand clenched him in its fist.

Will sobbed, the sound echoing slightly. He wasn't wrapped up in the web any longer. He wasn't dead. Weak light pressed against his closed eyelids and he reluctantly eased them open. He saw his room around him. The space he had been allowed with the apprenticeship, a small one-bedroom flat above Klaus Brunswick's workshop on Booker Street.

Brunswick Cabinetry the sign below his lounge window said, the steps up to his apartment through a separate door on the opposite side of the small, two-storey building from the shop's entrance. His curtains were half-open, his door wide. He saw a blue sky with barely a cloud through the lounge window and the leaves of the large blue gum behind the workshop from his bedroom. He was at home. At home, not dead, and in terrible pain. And he was starving.

The room was hot and close, the windows closed. Will threw back the sheet that covered him and released a funk of old sweat and piss. Appalled, he looked down to see his bed was a mess, stained and wet. He was naked, his skin red raw like he'd been sunburned all over.

He remembered the day before at the dam and thought that could explain it. He'd worried about sunburn then, before... before everything. But the feeling and the look of his skin belied more than simple overexposure to the sun.

He frowned at his stomach, ran one palm tentatively over it. He hissed, wincing at the rawness of the skin, but there were definitely bumps there, a raised rash from breastbone to pelvis. And in the centre, just above his belly button, a blackened circle with an ugly red welt in the middle. He crunched up tighter for a better look, grunting with combined hurts. The wound was a puncture, raw and weeping, the flesh around it almost necrotic-looking. That was where she had stung him.

Will fell back, crying. Tears rolled over his cheeks and his chest heaved with sorrow, with pain, with horror. What the hell had happened to him? He allowed himself several minutes of self-pity, then hauled himself to his feet. He was wobbly, dizzy. The bumps on his stomach itched interminably, but he didn't dare scratch for fear of the agony it would set off in his skin.

He staggered to the bathroom and swallowed ibuprofen and paracetamol and then stood under a cold shower. The cool water was a balm, the painkillers began to ease the worst of his agonies, and Will breathed a little easier. He realised he was thirsty as hell and tipped his face up, drinking deeply from the shower as it sluiced over him. Eventually he turned off the taps and opened all the windows to air out the stench of the place. He found his phone, but it was dead. It had been charged the day before.

He went into the lounge and plugged it in, waited while it took a moment of charge then started up. When the home screen loaded, he stared in confusion. Ten a.m. Thursday? He'd been at the dam with Beverly the day before, which was Saturday.

He turned to look into his room, the piss-stained bed. Had he been out for four days? Did they just bring him back and put him to bed and leave him there? For four days? No wonder the place was so foetid and he was so hungry. His stomach itched and he absently scratched at the field of bumps there, then yelped at the scream of raw skin. What the fuck had they done to him? He needed… what? What did he need? What could he do?

Eat first. He needed sustenance to fill the hole inside him, to get past the dizziness.

A lot of stuff in the fridge had started to go bad and his bread was stale like old cardboard, but he found enough things to start sating the hunger that clawed his guts. And once he started, he couldn't stop. Washing things down with glass after glass of cold water, he downed half the dry loaf and all the ham and cheese that was still good from the fridge along with tomatoes and cucumber. He started in on the fruit that was still mostly mould-free and eventually slowed as energy began to return. Finally full, for the time being at least, he went back to the bathroom and found a large tube of aloe vera cream from his last bout of sunburn. While he suspected his raw skin was from the burning web as much as the exposure at the dam, he figured treating it would be the same. Sure enough, slathering aloe over every inch of himself gave instant and blessed relief.

Still naked, Will stood in his bedroom and wondered

what the hell to do next. Everything to this point, since waking, had been triage. Now, though his gut still ached with a deep throbbing and his skin had reduced to a dull roar, he finally had a moment to consider. What the hell was Hilda anyway? Some hideous human-spider hybrid monster thing. How was that even possible? And was Beverly one as well? And Klaus? So many questions and so few answers. But did any of it really matter?

He should leave. Just get in his car and drive away from Gulpepper. Why they'd done what they had, hurt and tortured him then simply left him back in bed, he couldn't understand. But so what?

He didn't have much stuff, so it didn't take long to pack. Finally, he had to face pulling clothes over his searing skin, but he found the lightest t-shirt and shorts he could and slipped thongs onto his feet, then carried his bags downstairs. He put his stuff in his car and then drew a deep breath. He would leave the key on the shop step and leave. Simple.

He turned to the door of the cabinetry shop and saw the CLOSED sign in the window. Below that was a sheet of paper with a hand-written message.

Monday 14th
Away on business for a week, sorry!
Open again Monday 21st

Will stared. That seemed weird, Klaus had never mentioned anything about this to him. Was he avoiding everything that had happened with Beverly and Hilda?

He caught sight of a man across the street, thin and pale-skinned. As they made eye contact, the man smiled and held up a sheet of paper. It had a strange, bracketed design on it and seemingly nothing else, but the symbol was weirdly compelling somehow.

Will's gut stabbed with pain, sharp and sudden enough to take his breath away. He staggered, clamped his palms across his belly, and cried out as the pain kept up. It felt like someone stabbing him from the inside out in a dozen different places at once.

The man across the street stared, his smile faltering, then shook his head and hurried away.

But a young woman walking past hurried over, one hand outstretched in a gesture of aid.

"Are you okay?"

Will winced, grit his teeth. "I... I don't know."

"Here, let me help."

The woman took his arm and guided him to the big display window of *Brunswick Cabinetry*, sat him on the wide, black-painted sill there. She kept one hand against his shoulder to stop him pitching forward.

"You're really sunburned," she said. "Think you have heatstroke?"

No, Will thought. *I was captured and poisoned by a giant old lady spider monster.* But he didn't say that out loud. "Dunno," he managed. "Maybe."

"Where do you live? Can I help you home?"

Will nodded to the door on the other side of the shop. "Up there. I was just going out."

"Shall I help you back inside?"

"Thank you."

She took his keys and opened the door, then held one arm and helped him up the stairs to the apartment above. He could barely lift one leg after the other without the stabbing pains threatening his consciousness and was glad of her assistance. He'd left the windows open, but caught her expression out of the corner of his eye, her wince and wrinkled nose as they came into the funky space. After getting some fresh air outside, he realised just how awful it was.

To her credit, the young woman didn't say anything, just guided him to the couch and helped him sit.

"I should call you a doctor," she said.

"No, no. It's okay. I think I just need to rest."

"If you're sure." She looked around the small apartment. "Can I get you anything else?"

"I don't think so. Thank you, though."

"Okay. I have to get to work."

"No problem. Really, thank you."

She smiled, nodded once. "You're welcome. I hope you feel better soon. Call the doc if you don't."

"I will."

Will watched her let herself out, almost running in her haste to leave, and then laid back into the couch. He felt sick, nauseated in a way he hadn't experienced before. He lifted his t-shirt to see the rash all over his abdomen, the weeping puncture wound in the centre. Were the bumps bigger now? Standing up a little more roundly? The wound had left a greasy-looking stain on the pale blue material of his shirt. The stabbing pains persisted, but less intense as he lay back. Were they easing?

He needed to rest more. He laid his head back and closed his eyes.

When he woke again it was dark outside. He didn't feel even slightly rested, but the horrible nausea seemed to have passed. His skin had calmed a little more as well, but he still went and found the aloe again, gave himself another slathering. As he did so, he found the rash of lumps had spread further, up onto his chest and down towards his hips. The bumps were also moving around either side of his body, small and rounded they reminded him of the moguls skiers navigated in the winter Olympics. Each was about the size of a five-cent piece at the base now, firm to the touch and hot. And itchy as all hell.

"What the fuck did she do to me?" Will whispered to himself, though his mind turned over with a variety of possibilities, each one more horrifying than the last.

He pulled his phone out and tapped to use WhatsApp to voice call Beverly. He wanted to leave, but imagined being halfway along a highway doing 100 kph and having another attack of stabbing nausea like outside the shop. He would surely crash and kill himself if that happened. So maybe he needed to know what they'd done to him, if it would ease. When he would be safe to travel. And it seemed like Beverly was the only one he could ask.

The call rang and rang, but Beverly didn't answer.

He wrote out a message instead. *Beverly, what the fuck is happening? What did she do to me?!*

He sounded desperate and scared, and that pissed him off, but he *was* desperate and scared. He checked the time. Nearly 9 p.m. He rang Beverly again, then again, but still got no answer. She worked a variety of ad hoc jobs, like the event catering at Clooney's she'd talked about before. She could be working, could be anywhere, could simply be ignoring him. His anger grew.

Will's stomach stabbed with pain again, but he felt it in his chest and legs as well this time. The horrible rash was spreading and the pain with it. How much worse was it going to get? He could simply leave and go to the hospital, check in at the emergency department. But that was in Enden, a good forty-five-minute drive from The Gulp. He thought again about crashing on the way, an episode of pain while he drove to hospital killing him. Or he might survive the crash but be injured and undiscovered in the bush all night. There was no chance of a cab or anything like that from The Gulp at this time of night. And he really hadn't fitted in, hadn't made any friends who could drive him, especially after he'd hooked up with Beverly and she consumed every waking hour he wasn't working.

It had seemed so good. So real. His heart ached almost as much as his gut. And his anger grew again. Maybe rage was all that kept him going but he welcomed it. Perhaps it *would* keep him going well enough to drive to the hospital in Enden. He decided he was determined to do that much. Wasn't he? He grabbed his keys and went back down to his car, fell into the driver's seat, gasping from the exertion of it. Pain lanced through his guts again and he cried out, gripped the steering wheel as he willed the agony to pass.

The driver's door of the car opened. He jumped, turned to look into Klaus Brunswick's concerned face.

"What are you up to, Will?"

Will stared, teeth gritted against the barely easing pain. "You're not away?" he said stupidly.

"You shouldn't be up and about."

"What's happening to me?"

Klaus frowned, one side of his mouth hitching up in something close to a smile. "No, seriously. You *shouldn't* be. She said you were a tough one, but I didn't expect this. Come on, let's go."

"What?"

"Mother will have to deal with you." Klaus reached in and grabbed Will's arm. He cried out at the roughness of the man's grip on his sore skin, but Klaus ignored him and dragged him from the car.

"Please, Mr. Brunswick! What's happening?"

"Look, lad, it's a shame. You're a good kid. But bigger things are under way. Important things. Come on."

Klaus's *Brunswick Cabinetry* van was parked at the curb a little way up, a fairly new Toyota Hiace. Klaus pulled open the sliding side door. It smelled of timber and varnish inside, but was empty except for some blankets Klaus used to cushion various items for transport.

"What are you doing?" Will pulled against the man, tried to break free, but Klaus was a large man, and strong. Will was strong too, but currently weak, dizzy, in all kinds of pain. Klaus backhanded him once across the jaw and a new dizziness set in. He nearly fell, knees weak. Klaus hauled him up and threw him into the back of the van, then climbed in behind. He rolled Will into one of the blankets, rough and abrasive against his tender skin, and then tied something else around that.

"Got ourselves a Will burrito here," Klaus said with a laugh.

He picked Will up, tightly wrapped, and slung him over one shoulder. The man's shoulder pressing up into Will's gut was sickeningly painful as he was carried back up into the apartment and dumped on his fetid bed.

"Should keep you from trying to get away. Now just lie still."

"What are you doing?" Will asked.

"I need to talk to Mother, of course."

Klaus pulled out his phone and dialled. After a moment, he said, "Hello, sweetheart. Are you still with Oma? Good. I need you to bring her down to the shop. Yes, he tried to get away. I know! Okay, see you soon."

Without another word, Klaus left the apartment closing the door behind him. Will yelled until he was hoarse, but it was useless.

It was some time later when Will, through the haze of his agony, heard the door open again.

"In here." Klaus said. The man came into the bedroom, Beverly behind him and Hilda last, looking like nothing more than a small, frail old woman. The lengthened face, the mandibles pressing inside her cheeks, the large, rounded abdomen with its poisoned sting, all those monstrous mutations Will remembered were nowhere to be seen. But he hadn't imagined all that.

Will thrashed in his bonds, tears running over his cheeks. "What the fuck have you done to me?" he yelled. "What is wrong with you people?"

Beverly looked genuinely upset. "Oh, Will. This isn't how it was supposed to go."

Hilda shuffled over to look down at him. "You said he was a strong one, didn't you, dear."

Will twisted to look beseechingly as Beverly. "What the hell, Bev?"

"I'm so sorry, Will. I am. I really liked you. We were good together, weren't we? That last hurrah at the dam was pretty amazing, right?"

Why was she talking about him in the past tense?

"What changed?" he asked.

She sighed. "You do know how to make a woman feel good. I'll miss that. But things in The Gulp *are* changing, Will. Something's coming. Everyone needs to prepare." She looked up at her father and Hilda and smiled, then back at Will. "And family always comes first."

"What do you mean, 'something's coming'? What does it have to do with me?"

"Well, nothing really. Not directly, anyway. But we're an old Gulpepper family, Will. And the old families remember. We know when we have to step up. When we have to prioritise. And you were right there, a perfect candidate."

"For what?"

"Enough chatter," Hilda said, and her voice held none of the kindness Beverly displayed. "He shouldn't even be awake. Amazing he had the strength to move around before it was time."

"How much longer?" Klaus asked.

"Only a day or two, I would say."

"Can you immobilise him again?"

Hilda frowned. Her body began to morph slightly, face growing longer, her back end rounding out, tipping her forward. Then she sighed, shook her head. Her body slowly returned to its regular old lady proportions. "My venom now might destabilise the process."

"So what do we do, Oma?" Beverly asked.

"Do you still have those tablets from Beverly's mother?" Hilda asked Klaus.

"The sleeping pills?"

"Yes. They did little for Caitlin towards the end but they're strong drugs, no?"

Will remembered Beverly telling him how her mother had died of breast cancer about three years before, succumbing incredibly fast to the disease after ignoring a lump in her breast for months. They'd bonded over that shared experience, his mother going the same way.

Fear addled his thinking as they spoke over him, talked of drugging him, of venom, of 'the process', whatever the hell that meant.

"Just let me go, please!" he begged.

"No, not possible," Hilda said.

"I really am sorry, Will," Beverly's eyes betrayed genuine pain, regret. She meant it, but she'd done it anyway.

"Sorry? You allowed this!" Will snapped, her contrition somehow making him more furious.

Beverly laughed. "Of course! And I'm trying to be compassionate here. I really am sorry it had to be you, but that's just your bad luck, I suppose." She looked up at Klaus. "I know where Mum's pills are. I can go and get them."

Beverly still lived in the family home with her father, just a bit further north along Booker Street from the cabinetry shop. Will had been several times, enjoyed meals with Beverly and her dad, picked her up to go out and spend time together. She'd walked from the house down to the apartment and they'd enjoyed good times here too. It all seemed like a dream now, a kind of nightmare, compared to the position he found himself in. This entire family were monsters and psychopaths. He thrashed against his restraints but was powerless to free himself, tied tightly and weak of limb, skin searing with pain.

"You sure you've got this in hand?" Hilda asked. "We can't afford to start again, I think. Time is running out."

"It's all good, Mother" Klaus said. "We'll watch closely."

"Good. Then take me home, please."

Klaus led his mother from the room. Beverly followed them out, gave Will a little wave as she went.

Will's dizziness remained with him, his body hot, itching, aching deep inside. He felt as though his stomach were curdling and feared he would vomit, but it never quite rose up. Eventually, Klaus and Beverly returned. As the apartment door opened again, Will yelled out, "Please let me go. I don't deserve this."

Klaus appeared in the bedroom doorway. "You know, that's true. You don't. You're a good guy, and you always seemed to do right by Beverly. But this is far bigger than you and what you do or don't deserve. The world in general, and certainly the larger universe, cares little for what people do or don't deserve. Things are, and we must respond to them. My mother has little compassion and honestly, I don't have much myself any more. This hurts Beverly a lot, though. If that's any consolation. Another generation removed from the source, it's harder for her."

Will shook his head, dumbfounded. "No, that is not any fucking consolation, you fucking psychopath! Let me go!"

Klaus sighed. "Ah, well. I tried. Maybe just remember this is necessary, eh? Your role is perhaps passive, but it's important."

Beverly slipped past her dad, a soft smile on her face. "This place is gross," she said, wrinkling her nose.

"Leave the windows open," Klaus said.

"I brought these," Bev said, and held up a handful of plastic cable ties.

"Good idea."

Will tried to fight them, but it was useless. The pain through his skin and deeper in his body made any struggle an agony. His dizziness and weakness made him putty in their combined hands. Yet he fought as best he could and blacked out from the effort.

He came to some indeterminate time later and found himself spreadeagled on the bed, wrists and ankles secured to the bedframe. He tried to sit up but could barely move. He saw he'd been stripped of clothing, nakedness adding to his terrifying vulnerability, nothing like the liberation of that day at the dam.

Beverly sat on a chair beside the bed, reading a book. She smiled and put it aside when he moved.

"You're awake. A shame, because now I have to put you to sleep again. But properly this time."

"Don't do it, Bev. Please."

She drew a deep breath, then sighed it out. "Will, I am genuinely sorry but please stop begging. Nothing you can say will change this. It's happening. Try to at least retain some dignity, hmm? You're a very important piece of the plan, really. In some ways, it's an honour to be you."

"Yeah? Why don't you fucking take over whatever it is I'm doing then?"

"No, it doesn't work like that. Too late anyway, you're already it."

"I'm already what?"

She held up a couple of pills, white powder in clear plastic capsules. "Take these, yeah? Take these and it'll all become a dream. They're really good. Very strong."

"I'm not going to make this easy for you. Fuck you and your pills."

"Oh, these are not to make it easy for *me*. Really, Will, you shouldn't even have woken up at all. The fact you did is remarkable, but trust me. The best thing you can do now is accept these and let it all go."

"Fuck you!"

Will began thrashing again, using what little strength remained in him to fight against his restraints. The bed shifted, squeaking against the floor, and he yelled, ripping his throat raw with wordless screams of panic. The bedroom door burst open and Klaus ran in.

"Make him stop! We can't afford the attention if someone hears."

Beverly stood, slapped Will hard across one cheek. It didn't slow him at all. Klaus climbed atop him and sat across his hips. He planted one large, rough palm hard on Will's forehead and used the middle finger and thumb of his other hand to force Will's jaw open.

"Give him the fucking pills!"

Beverly ducked forward, jamming the capsules into

Will's mouth. He thrashed again, bit down and felt a surge of satisfaction as his teeth closed on a finger and Beverly yelped. She pulled a hand back, blood dripping from it. Will spat the pills out.

"Fucking hell," Klaus snapped, and cuffed him hard across the chin.

Dizziness whined through Will, his vision went shadowy. He felt them manipulating his face again, heard Klaus say, "Find them!" and Beverly shout, "I've got more!"

Then he felt fingers in his mouth again, tried to bite, but disorientation made even his jaw unresponsive. Klaus's rough palm pushed up under his chin, forced his mouth closed. Then fingers clamped his nostrils together.

"Swallow, damn you! Or you won't breathe again!"

Will tried to resist, thought he'd let them kill him, suffocate him, rather than comply, but panic made a mockery of bravery. His throat convulsed against his will and the pills started down. Klause roughly massaged his throat, forcing them further, and Will sucked air in through his released nose.

Klaus sat back, panting, staring down at him. Will tried to regurgitate the pills, but they were past the point of no return. The lump of them slid painfully down his gullet. Beverly stood by the bed, hair in disarray, eyes wide in something like shock.

"Fuck both of you," Will said hoarsely. "Fuck you all the way to hell."

Klaus climbed off him and walked away. "Watch him," he said, as he left the room.

Beverly slumped back into the chair beside the bed, but she didn't pick up her book. She watched with a guarded expression. "Just go to sleep, Will. Please."

"Fuck. You."

But the exertion had exhausted what little energy he had. His skin felt like it had been peeled off everywhere she or Klaus had handled him. His gut squirmed with sickening motion and stabbing pains. And slowly the pills began to work. One small blessing was the painkilling effect that settled in first, a brief respite from his myriad discomforts, but then the soporific effect came in and he slipped away.

He came to in deep darkness, felt as though he were floating. His stomach felt swollen, pain radiating outwards like it was about to burst. He gasped, winced, forced himself not to cry out. But a light came on anyway, Beverly moving to look over him. She looked ragged, had clearly just awoken. She stared a moment at his face, then her gaze tracked down his body and she winced.

Will sat up against the restraints, moving as far as they would allow, which was little more than raising his head and shoulders a few inches, but it was enough to see what Beverly watched. His stomach was swollen, more than he'd thought possible, stretched upwards like he'd been over-inflated. The surface of it covered with rounded lumps, each the size of his closed fist, that seemed to squirm and shift of their own accord.

"I can't believe you woke up again," Beverly said. "You… you shouldn't… Maybe the venom is giving you some resistance? Everyone's different, Oma says." She sighed. "There's nothing I can do about this. Unless you take more pills."

He growled at her, too docile to form words, too energised to do anything but stare at his distended gut.

"You were out for a long time," Beverly said. "Almost long enough."

Electric shards of agony pierced Will, like something stabbed him from the inside, trying to carve its way free. He yelled out, incoherent dismay.

Beverly sighed. "I'm guessing the pain is what woke you. Grit your teeth, Will. It'll be over soon. I really am sorry."

"No you're fucking not. You wouldn't be able to do this if you really cared, don't you understand that? Normal people don't do shit like whatever the fuck this is."

Beverly smiled. "That's just it, though. We're not normal people. Gulpepper is not a normal place and extreme circumstances call for extreme measures. You're important though, please remember that. If nothing else, please remember that."

Will went to say something more, but the lancing pain came again. This time it kept going and he stared in horror as the lumps on his abdomen split, the skin parting to bleed and weep, and something pushed its way through.

Will screamed in agony, as first one, then two, then more than a dozen things squirmed out of him. Black and rough, dragging at the tender skin with stiff hairs that covered their bodies, they forced their way out and began to unfurl. Many-jointed legs sprang open from where they'd been wrapped against the rough carapaces of the things and they stood atop Will's eviscerated gut, some pulling loops of intestine with them. Their pointed limbs dug into undamaged skin and fresh wounds alike as Will passed from something like unbearable pain into a fire of sensation that consumed his mind, tunnelled his vision.

More than a dozen now, spider-like and bigger than seemed possible to have emerged from the confines of Will's flesh, they opened maws with two shining black mandibles surrounded by a ring of smaller, lamprey-like teeth.

"They're so beautiful!" Beverly said, one hand moving forward like she wanted to pet them but managing to keep her distance. They ignored her and rose up as Will tried to buck them off, weakly shifting his hips left and right, trying to arch his back, but the pain stole all strength from him.

They rose on their sharp, bristled legs and then drove down, piercing him all over with those glistening mandibles, and fiery venom pumped in. Will quickly collapsed, felt the paralysis pulsing through his body, quickly spreading through his limbs. He gasped in shallow, quick agonistic breaths as the paralysis began to reach his organs too.

From the corner of his eye, he saw Beverly scurry from the room, then the last thing he felt before a final darkness descended was the things beginning to feed on his flesh.

Doc Blaney grumbled as he hauled himself out of his car. It seemed to get harder and harder to simply move himself around as the months toiled on and his rapidly advancing diabetes stole more of him away. A new complication every other week, it felt like. And he couldn't seem to sleep past 5 a.m., some bodily function or other driving him from bed earlier and earlier.

"Fuck getting old," he muttered. "Privilege my arse."

And again, he questioned the wisdom of ever returning to Gulpepper. For a while there, things had seemed calmer again, like the old days. The good old days, that was, not the bad ones. But now? Now he questioned his sanity again.

A black and tan kelpie barked at him from the back seat, bouncing up and down and wagging his tail.

"Calm your farm, Scrapper. We'll have a run after this." *You will, anyway*, he thought. *I'll sit and watch.*

He looked at the big front window of Brunswick Cabinetry and the doors either side. The one on the right led into the shop, still closed at this early hour. The other door on the left side led up to the apartment the young woman had talked about.

Blaney checked his watch, just after eight. Still too early for a house call? He remembered what the young woman had told him, late on Friday afternoon.

I saw this guy yesterday, he seemed really sick. I know it's none of my business, but I helped him back up to his apartment and the place was rank. I tried to tell myself not to get involved, but it's been bugging me since then, so I had to tell someone, and who better than a doctor, right? Are you able to check on him?

Blaney had explained it didn't really work like that. If the guy wasn't a patient, if the guy didn't seek help, there wasn't really anything he could do. But the young woman said she'd fulfilled her sense of obligation to tell someone and now it was up to him. And damn her, if it hadn't preyed on his mind all weekend. So here he was, Monday morning before seeing his scheduled patients, staring at a stranger's door. What could he really do? He'd knock, offer assistance, and see what happened. Fulfill his own sense of obligation the young woman had rather thoughtlessly dumped on him.

He approached the door and saw there was a bell with a little camera lens above it. Someone up in the apartment could see who waited downstairs that way. He pressed the button, heard the tone from somewhere above, and waited. Nothing.

He tried again. Same result.

"Well, shit." He stared, wondering if he should take that as a cue to simply leave. He could always try again later, after his appointments. Reluctantly, he reached out and tried the door handle. It was unlocked, the door shifting inwards.

He opened it a few inches and leaned forward, started to call out, "Hello? Anyone home?" then staggered back from a terrible stench. He knew death when he smelled it, and this was death with added hell mixed in.

"Ah, fuck." He should call someone. But this was The Gulp. 'Someone' would take ages to arrive. He'd have a quick look first. He took a handkerchief from his pocket and held it against his nose and mouth and slowly ascended the stairs.

He called out all the way up, in case someone was there, but the place had the stillness of somewhere uninhabited. By the living, at least. He moved into a small lounge-kitchen area and saw a bedroom door standing open. As he stepped in, Blaney cried out and gagged, then backed quickly away.

On a hideously stained bed lay the skeletal remains of someone, blackened tatters of flesh and skin and muscle hanging here and there from otherwise stark white bones. Even with all the windows open, the stench was appalling.

Blaney staggered back down the stairs and closed the apartment door behind him, gasping of the fresh salt air outside. He found his phone and dialled for the Enden police. As it rang, he muttered, "Sometimes I really hate this fucken town."

Vitulinum

Vitulinum

Connor Tucker was an expert at going unnoticed, but still copped a beating from his father on a regular basis. As the man's fist landed again, hammering already bruised stomach muscles, Connor gritted his teeth and refused to cry. Crying would only bring those fists to his face.

"Is it that fucken hard to remember?" Frank Tucker shouted, slamming another punch into Connor's stomach. "Is it?"

"Sorry, Dad. I just forgot." The last word escaped in a rush, driven up his throat by the man's knuckles in his gut. One more and he was sure he would puke, then he'd really be in trouble.

"Fucken useless!"

"Dad, he's had enough," Brendan said. At sixteen, he was the eldest, only by a year, and assumed some kind of leadership role among the siblings. But he wasn't any good at it. Not really.

"Enough?" Frank snarled. "Hardly. He's still fucken breathing."

Gasping was more like it, hunched over, clutching his stomach, desperate not to collapse though his knees shook and his vision had blurred. Connor often wondered if he was destined to die under his father's fists one day. It seemed the most likely end result of his cursed life.

He caught sight of Serena, watching through a tiny

gap in their bedroom door. Only eight years old, an unexpected third child and frequently reminded of that fact, she stared with frightened eyes. *Please shut the door*, Connor thought. *If he catches you watching, you'll be next.*

"What is it now?"

Frank looked around to see his wife enter the house, stepping over the pile of shoes in the doorway. She wore her Woolworths uniform and looked haggard, dark bags under her eyes, a cigarette hanging off her bottom lip.

"Can you believe this little cunt, Lydia?" Frank slammed a fist into Connor's shoulder, staggering him sideways, numbing his arm. "Went out for two hours and still forgot my smokes."

"He's fifteen, how can he buy smokes, fuck's sake?"

"That prick Wong at the newsagency knows they're for me. I told him to make sure he serves our kids or I'll have him deported back to fucken China."

"He's an Australian citizen, Dad," Brendan said with an incredulous laugh.

"Was he fucken born here?"

"Well, no, but he's been here like forty—"

"Then he's not fucken Australian, is he! Fuck it, I'll get 'em myself." Frank snatched up his wallet from the side table near the door and walked out. "I'm going to Clooney's."

The door slammed behind him and silence sank over the house for a moment.

Lydia went to Connor, rested a hand on his shoulder. "You all right, love?"

"Will be." Connor still had his teeth clamped together, waiting for the pain and nausea to subside.

Serena emerged from their room, came and gave Connor a hug.

Lydia sniffed. "Shouldn't have forgotten his smokes, eh."

She went through into the kitchen and started clattering around.

Brendan headed for the front door. "Don't worry about me for dinner, Mum. I'll be out till late."

"Fucking around with those stoned losers like usual?" she called from the kitchen.

"Something like that." Brendan paused, looked at Connor. "You gotta try harder, gay boy. When you make him mad, we all suffer. You're lucky Mum came home so he could go to the pub."

"Don't call me that."

"Why not?" Brendan slammed the door behind him.

Serena hugged Connor more tightly and he was grateful for her, even though he feared every day for her safety. He'd take her away from this place. He *would*, as soon as he figured out how. Brendan thought he was protecting the two of them by hardening them up somehow, but the truth was Brendan became more like their dad every day. Connor knew the answer wasn't to find a way to survive their family, that was an impossibility. He'd have to die or become like them, and that wasn't an option, for him or Serena. Or for Brendan, really, but perhaps that ship had already sailed. Escaping the family was the only option. Their mum was as bad their dad, or aggressively passive at best. Connor would protect Serena. He had promised himself and he'd promised her.

"He shouldn't call you that," she said in a small voice, looking up at him with wet brown eyes.

"It's okay." The accusation was true, though he'd never actually admitted it. His whole family assumed he was gay, constantly gave him shit about it, and he was, but letting them think it true was a world away from ever confessing it. That would be the last excuse his dad needed to beat him to death. If there was one group of people Frank Tucker hated more than non-white people, it was queer people. The man was hate wrapped in nicotine-stained skin.

"It's not okay."

Connor smiled at Serena, returned the hug.

Thankfully the pain had begun to recede. "No, you're right. But I'll be okay."

"How did you forget dad's smokes, though?"

Connor laughed, then winced at the aggravation in his new bruises. "I didn't. He never asked for any."

Serena rolled her eyes. "About right."

"Oven pizza tonight, you two," Lydia called from the kitchen. "It's just the three of us now, so I've only put one in."

"Thanks, Mum," Connor said. One between three instead of two between five was actually a decent feed by Tucker family standards, given Frank would have most of one to himself if he'd stayed home. He just hoped his stomach would cope with food. He was hungry enough without skipping whatever meagre dinner was offered.

Connor heard his dad come home late, well after midnight. A tiny sound of distress from the bunk above told him Serena had heard as well. Brendan snored in the single bed on the other side of the room, oblivious. Connor hadn't heard Bren come home. His brain was wired for other triggers.

They listened as Frank stomped about the house, heedless of anyone who might be sleeping. The fridge door opened and closed, a muffled curse as something crashed but didn't shatter. Then a shaft of light burst into the room. Connor willed himself invisible and, through slitted eyes, watched the silhouette of his father standing there, looking in. *Please leave her alone*, he thought. *Please.*

After a moment, the man came into the room, up to the bunk beds. "Hi, little one." His voice was low, slurred.

Predatory. "You sleepin'?"

Connor knew Serena was an expert at feigning sleep. He heard his father's hand running over her covers, a condensing beer bottle held in his other, resting against his thigh.

"Are you sleepin', little mistake? Huh? Are you good for anything? You will be before long, won't you. Any time now."

Connor pictured himself holding a knife. His father stood inches away, visible from knees to chest. Connor refused to look at the tenting of the man's loose jeans at the groin and imagined using the knife, stabbing repeatedly at every possible organ.

"I should wake you up. Make you touch me the way I like. Shouldn't I?" Frank crooned.

Please, no, Connor mentally begged. *Please leave her alone.*

Their father often talked this way and Connor knew it was only a matter of time before he started acting more on his perversities. If he hadn't already. Serena assured her brothers the man had done nothing but talk so far, except sometimes hug her too tight and rub himself against her. She told them he'd sit her on his lap now and then and shift her around until she made him cough. But always fully clothed, she assured them. She didn't like it, but it was okay. Connor and Brendan had shared a pained glance at that, realising Serena may not get it entirely, but understood enough. It was so far from okay.

They insisted she sleep in the top bunk in some tiny effort at keeping Frank off her, but it wouldn't last. She wasn't safe. Connor needed to get her away from all this. He and Brendan often took beatings, as did their mother. And whatever happened in his parents' bedroom was their business, his mum needed to look after herself. She certainly did next to nothing to look after the three of them. But despite avoiding anything but the most cursory slaps so far, Serena was subject to far more dangerous abuses. Connor would kill the fucker if he had to. If he couldn't get away first.

Frank spat a noise of annoyance, staggered a little sideways, then turned to leave. "Kids sleep too fucking deeply," he muttered as he left and closed the door again.

Serena let out a long-held whimper and Connor stood on the edge of his bunk, reached up to hug her. "You okay?"

She nodded in the weak light from the street lamp coming through their thin curtains, but he saw tears on her cheeks.

"I won't let him hurt you, okay? I promise."

"I know."

"He'll pass out now. We can get some sleep."

Serena reached out, put a small hand on his cheek. "Will you wait until I'm asleep first?"

"Sure I will."

Connor stood there, one hand holding the bed frame to balance, the other stroking her wavy dark blonde hair. It wasn't long before she slowed, her breathing getting longer and deeper. In sleep she was angelic, perfect and untroubled. She deserved that all the time. They all did.

Connor quietly slipped back into his own bed, but it was a long time before he slept.

When Connor woke Sunday morning, Brendan still snored, covers wrapped around his legs, but Serena was up and gone. He went into the kitchen to find his mother at the table, smoking a cigarette and nursing a mug of coffee. She had a fresh bruise below her left eye, but Connor ignored that. He'd long since given up caring what happened to his mother. As far as he was concerned, every bruise she gained was one less for him or Brendan or Serena. It was pretty much all she ever did for them and even that was inadvertent rather than deliberate.

"Where's Serena?"

Lydia looked up, expression blank. "The fuck should I know?"

"You're her mother and she's eight."

"Lucky she got that far."

Connor frowned. "What?"

Lydia huffed a sound something like a laugh. "She only just made it into this world, did you know that?" At Connor's confused expression, she rolled her eyes. "Your dad beat the shit out of me when I was about six months pregnant, blaming me for the imminent arrival of a new mouth to feed. Like it was only my fucken fault. Pretty sure he was trying to abort her."

Connor swallowed down bile. "What the fuck?"

His mother sighed. "Shame it didn't work, really. Would have been better for all of us. Even Serena."

"I can't believe you just said that."

Lydia shrugged. "The world's fucked, Connor, you know that by now. Shouldn't have brought her into it."

Was that some twisted, poisoned kind of love on his mother's part? Connor didn't even know any more. Or care, if he was honest. He walked away, tears running over his cheeks, not sure what to do.

"She went out the back earlier," Lydia said resignedly. "Probably still there."

Connor went to the kitchen sink and looked out the window. Serena was there, in the grubby, broken plastic cubby house they'd inherited from somewhere. She was moving dolls around and had some plastic teacups on the table. She spent a lot of time in the garden, never in the house unless she had to be. He went around to the back door and leaned out.

"You want to come for a walk? It's Sunday so the market is on at Carlton Beach."

"Nah, I'm good. Dad went fishing, so he'll be gone

all day."

Which meant Serena could stay at home and feel safe. Connor was surprised his dad was up and gone already. Probably meant he was still drunk, no way would he be moving around this early with a hangover. Regardless, it meant Connor could go out too, knowing Serena was safe. He would have some hours to himself. For all her faults, his mother usually only damaged the kids by inattention and absence, rarely by direct harm.

"Okay, have fun." He ducked back inside. "Dad say where he was going fishing?"

Lydia looked up, shook her head. "Matty picked him up about half an hour ago."

"So probably Enden then?"

"Maybe. He'll be out till late, you're good."

Connor stared. She knew why he was asking. She knew he wanted to be in the house when his father got home and she knew why. But still, she did nothing about it. Her vapid disengagement infuriated him. On one hand, he knew she'd been broken down by the man, had nothing left to give. He'd overheard a conversation once, when she was on the phone in their small front yard, talking to a friend when Connor came home from school. He'd paused behind a ragged bush next door to listen and only caught one bit, but it was telling.

"...haven't got a single fucken dollar of my own. How would I leave? Where would I go?"

Connor had some sympathy for that. It was a simple and powerful trap that his father controlled all the money. Even his mother's wages from Woollies were paid into Frank's account, not a joint one. He had an iron grip on his family. But Connor's sympathy only went so far, because she was a grown-up. A parent. Supposed to protect her children above all other concerns. She *should* do something about it. But she didn't. She smoked and drank and sat staring at the walls like some answer might come out of them. More likely a solution would come from his father's fists one day and it would be a very final answer at that. Connor often wondered if that's what his mother hoped for, she was such a fucking coward.

He would get himself and Serena out, at least. He had to. But fear was a kind of inertia that made him plan and plan and never act. He knew it would be preferable in some ways to simply leave, be homeless, thumb their way up the coast or something. But he also knew the streets were more dangerous than his home, that starvation was a real possibility there if violence and robbery didn't end them first. Sometimes the sensation of entrapment was suffocating, sapping all energy to resist it, to escape. But that's what his father relied on. Connor had to find a way. He had been seven when Serena was born and realised even then he would need to be responsible for her. But time was surely running out.

Without another word to Lydia, he left via the front door. As he walked, he pulled his cheap, crappy phone out and called Lauren Hart, his only friend. Connor had largely avoided making friends throughout his life, partly because he was ashamed of his family, partly because he'd learned to exist alone and trust no one.

And while he'd kept a low profile before Serena was born, he'd doubled down on that since she came along. His little sister was his only focus, his only concern and responsibility. The only one, that was, other than Lauren, the one friend he'd allowed into his life. They had a lot in common, despite the fact that Lauren was an only child to loving parents who supported and nurtured her in every way. She dealt with her own issues and they had enough shared experience to be close, not least that they were both gay. She liked girls and he liked boys, so they could relax with each other, safe in the knowledge there was no subtext anywhere. Not that he'd ever acted on his desires. Maybe one day, when he was free of... everything. That was something else on the long list of things other people enjoyed, not the Tuckers.

Lauren answered on the second ring. "Con-man. What's up?"

"It's Sunday. Markets?"

"Yeah, why not. Meet you at the end of Massey in ten?"

"I'm nearly there now. I'll wait for you."

"Cool."

Connor lived on Anthill Street, which he'd thought was cool when he was little. But home life was so shitty, he'd come to even hate ants. Which he knew was irrational, but so what? Lauren lived on the almost parallel Grip Street, one block north. Massey Street was a block south and they could turn right onto Booker Street and head into town that way, past Brunswick Cabinetry. They would go via the Gulpepper Bookshop, too, which was something they never openly discussed but always just assumed would be a feature of any outing. One of the many things they shared was a love of books and trawling through the secondhand shelves was a kind of therapy for them both.

He'd only been standing on the corner of Massey and Booker for a couple of minutes when Lauren called out and waved. She wore her signature baggy shorts, these ones bright yellow, and long t-shirt that almost covered the shorts, this one with a design on the front of a cat using chopsticks to eat sushi. Her hair was a shoulder-length brown bob cut, and small, gold-coloured hoop earrings swung underneath it. She had on pink and yellow sneakers that had seen better days. She made Connor feel drab in his threadbare board shorts and slightly too small plain t-shirt.

His dad had only met Lauren once, and then briefly when they'd inadvertently bumped into each other on the street one weekend. Afterwards Frank had said, "Would it hurt her to wear a dress?"

"She doesn't like dresses, or even skirts," Connor said, annoyed he needed to defend his friend in any way.

"She's bloody pretty, would look much better in a

dress."

Like the man's opinion of a teenage girl was relevant in any way at all. She *was* pretty though, even Connor knew that. If only his dad knew the truth, he'd lose his shit. Another reason Connor never took her to his place, just in case awkward conversations arose. Frank and Lydia both had no qualms about voicing their various bigotries.

"How's things?" Lauren asked.

"Shit as ever," Connor said with a shrug. "You?"

"Yeah, I'm good. My parents just told me they've booked a trip to Bali for the Easter holidays. We're going for a week."

"That's something good to look forward to. Only a couple of months away."

"Yeah, I guess. Wish you could come too."

"Yeah, in my dreams. Wouldn't leave Serena for that long anyway."

"Nah, course. So what's up today? Just the markets?"

"I've got the day, pretty much. We can hang as long as you want. Hey, look." He pointed to a lamppost on the corner of Gulpepper Street as they reached it. A few different black and white posters had been taped or pasted to it, the usual array of missing people, cars for sale, bullshit antivax conspiracy theories and the like. But he pointed to one higher up that showed only a strange symbol on an otherwise blank A4 sheet.

The symbol was like a pair of thick offset parentheses, the right one lower than the left, with a shape in the centre that reminded Connor a little bit of Gulpepper lighthouse, only upside down. There was something strangely compelling about the design, and he stared at it, wondering what it meant.

"Connor?"

He startled, looked around. Lauren's expression was concerned, brow knitted. "You back with me?"

He swallowed, cleared his throat. "Sorry, what?"

"You went blank for a good thirty seconds there,

bruh. You had me worried."

Surely it had only been a moment. "Really?"

"I was calling your name and you were just staring at that thing. You know what it is?"

Connor looked up at it again, its draw no less strong but he was able to resist it this time and realised how mesmerised he'd been by it before. Though it still disquieted him somehow. "No, I don't. I've been seeing it around a bit lately."

"Posters like this?" Lauren asked.

"Yeah, but there's one spray-painted on the side of the old surf club at Carlton Beach too. And a small one above the door at Suzy's Café, like done with a Sharpie or something."

"That's weird. Some loser with a new tag maybe?"

"Sure, for the spray ones. But what graffiti artist prints posters?"

Lauren laughed. "Point. Come on, let's check the bookshop."

Connor tore himself away from staring at the weird design and followed her across the road. They spent a good half hour in the bookshop, idly browsing, chatting to Maisie McConnell who owned the place. At one point, Lauren called his name and, when he looked over, she held a copy of *If I Was Your Girl* by Meredith Russo beside her face and pouted at him, then laughed. He grinned, shook his head. She'd got him to read that book early in their friendship, a move he thought was brave as hell, and it had cemented everything for them. Her family were entirely supportive, but in a town like Gulpepper, no one else knew everything about Lauren Hart except Connor himself, and he was honoured by her trust. She was also the only person he'd ever actually told about being gay, and she'd just laughed and said, "Well, duh. But thanks for trusting me." That reciprocal confidence was probably the most valuable thing they shared, and Connor knew it kept them both a little saner than they might otherwise be.

In the end, they both bought one secondhand book—*Insomnia* by Sarah Pinborough for him and *Incidents Around the House* by Josh Malerman for her—and then carried on towards the market.

As they strolled up Tanning Street, cars filling every space on both sides, Lauren pointed. "Look, the bug guy is unloading his van."

Connor frowned. "The bug guy?"

"You know the bloke at the market who always sells Gulpepper Bugs? He once told me one of the members of Blind Eye Moon loves to cook with them. Buys from him frequently. Weird to think such a famous band lives right here in The Gulp."

"You ever tried those bugs?"

"Yeah, they're delicious. Hard work, it's a lot of shell for not much meat, and you have to know how to prepare them, but worth the effort. You?"

"Nah, we've never been able to afford them."

Lauren paused, looked up at him with pursed lips. "They are pricey. Would you come to my house for dinner one night if I invited you? I'll get Mum to make something with bugs."

Connor smiled, but his heart was heavy. "I'd love to, but it's not that simple. For one, I wouldn't want to leave Serena at home—"

"Bring her! And Brendan, if you want. You're all invited. I mean, not your parents, obviously, that would be super awkward. But you can all come over to hang out if you want?"

Lauren's eyes were wide, pleading. She had really pretty eyes, Connor thought, open and trusting and largely untroubled. Which he knew wasn't true, because she had so much to deal with. He wondered if his eyes gave him away or if he was as good as Lauren at hiding behind them.

"I don't know. Not sure how I'd sell it to my parents. Let me think about it?"

"It's a standing invitation. You decide how and I'll

make it happen."

"Thanks."

They went into the markets and started wandering among the various stalls. It was fun to look at all the various crafts and produce on display without any real intention of buying anything. Connor didn't have the money and Lauren usually respected his position and never showed off any wealth on her part. It was enough to be together and laugh and joke about the things people sold.

"Hey, look." Connor pointed to a man standing on his own on one edge of the park behind the beach. He had a wheeled shopping trolley with him, green and black tartan like old ladies used for their weekly groceries, and held out a sheaf of papers. He was handing a page to anyone who showed an interest, but most people ignored him. Connor saw the papers he handed out were the same as the sign on the lamppost. Blank but for that strangely bracketed design. Maybe it said something on the other side.

"Let's get one," Lauren said.

They went over and the man grinned as he handed over a sheet. His teeth were broken and yellowed, his fingernails the same. He was cadaverously thin, his skin almost grey. He said nothing, but simply nodded vigorously as Connor took a sheet. Lauren dragged on his arm, pulling him away.

"Creepy fucker!" she said, wide-eyed, still moving away from the man. "I wasn't expecting that."

"Yeah, seriously." Connor turned the page over but it was blank on the other side. Nothing but the symbol, no explanation at all. He held it out for Lauren to see.

She took it, looked it over, then screwed it up and threw it into a bin as they passed one. "Yet another Gulp weirdo."

Connor laughed, agreed with her, but he glanced back as they walked away and the strange, thin man met his eye, staring hard and nodding slowly. Then he took hold of his trolley and turned, walking slowly away from the markets, heading south.

Connor spent a good day with Lauren and almost forgot most of his troubles. At least, he was able to push them to the back of his mind for a little while, which was like an emotional rest, and he needed that. Lauren got a call from her mother late in the afternoon, reminding her they had a dinner reservation at Hanoi Nights, the Vietnamese place on Shellhaven Street, and she agreed she would meet them.

"My cousins' family are coming down from Enden," she said, miming a yawn.

"You like your cousins, right?"

"Sure, the twins are good fun, even if they are a bit young. Although, they're eleven now, so starting to seem more like people. But my aunt and uncle are so boring. Like, it's unfathomable just how boring they are. There's literally nothing interesting about them, they might as well be rocks or something. It'll be tedious."

"Nice food though?"

Lauren gave him that sympathetic look again. He appreciated it, but sometimes resented it too. "You've never been, huh?"

"Nah. Can't afford to eat in places like that. All our food is whatever's on special at Woollies this week. Plus, of course, my dad is a fucking racist."

"Even about food?"

Connor laughed. "Absolutely. He wouldn't set foot in any place that sold foreign food. You know, once my mum was yelling at him about never having anything nice and she said, 'Would it hurt to have a Chinese takeaway once in a while or something?' and my dad said, 'You want to eat shit that'll give you slanty eyes, be my guest.'"

Lauren frowned. "The fuck?"

"Yeah. Don't expect racism to make any kind of logical sense. It's just hate in a cloak of stupid."

Lauren stepped closer and gave Connor a hug, warm

and tight. He stiffened just briefly, always nervous of any kind of physical contact, then reminded himself who it was and relaxed, returned the gesture. They stood like that for a moment and Connor had never been more grateful to have Lauren as his friend.

"I'm sorry," she said quietly into his shoulder.

"It's okay."

"It's not."

"No. No, it's not. But thanks."

Lauren stepped back from the hug, one hand lingering on his arm a moment before dropping away. "You want me to stick around? If not, I should probably head off. We're meeting in Blumenthal Park beforehand, let the twins burn off some energy before they have to sit still for an hour or something."

Connor checked the time and all his worries sank back onto his shoulders. "Nah, I should get back. Dad might be home at midnight or any minute now. Just in case, I want to be there for Serena."

He'd talked to Lauren about his concerns before, about his determination to get away, and take Serena with him, somewhere safe. He saw the understanding in her eyes as she nodded. She leaned in and planted a quick kiss on his cheek. "It's been fun. Let's catch up again soon."

"For sure."

"And my house isn't far away. If you need somewhere to run to, with Serena..."

"I know. Thanks."

"Maybe you'll get lucky and your dad's been washed off the rocks into the depths."

"Eaten by a shark!"

"Then spat out because he tastes like bile."

They both laughed and Lauren gave Connor one last, quick hug then headed off towards the park. He watched her go a moment, more grateful than ever to have one good person in his life, outside his siblings. He didn't know what he'd do without her. Then he sucked in a deep breath and turned towards home.

As he reached the end of Tanning Street, he saw the old woman on the low harbour wall, staring out across the ocean. The sea witch. She seemed to always be there and he'd often wondered about her. He was used to his father being hateful or disdainful about pretty much everything—the man had an absolutely mystifyingly high opinion of himself and managed to think he was better than just about everyone—but the one time Connor had seen his father sobered by talk of another was once when Brendan had brought up the sea witch.

They'd been sat around the table, one of the rare occasions when the whole family was present for a meal. It had been frozen chicken nuggets and frozen chips, all baked dry as hell in the oven. Frank had looked up from his plate, eyes hooded, and said to Lydia, "Would it hurt you to include some fucken vegetables with a meal once in a while? Where are the kids supposed to get their fucken vitamins?"

Like he cared about vitamins or his kids' well-being. It was just one of his standard random belittling attacks, the kind of thing he constantly chipped away at Lydia with, wearing down any self-esteem or resistance she might be developing.

"Chips are potatoes," Lydia spat back. "That's a fucking vegetable, isn't it?"

Frank had curled his lip, his mood accelerating towards anger. "Reconstituted shit!"

And Lydia grabbed the red plastic Woollies own brand sauce bottle, waved it in his face. "They've all got fucken sauce! Tomatoes are a fucken vegetable, Frank!"

And there it was, about to explode into yelling and the inevitable beating that would follow. Almost like Connor's mother directly provoked Frank into a rage, like she wanted the slaps and punches. She could have headed it off, just agreed to make some vegetables next time, whether she intended to or not. But their animosity to each other had a life of its own, a perpetual, insatiable energy. Serena had started to cry and Connor was ready to pull her from the table and hurry to their room, was contemplating the possibility of bringing their remaining food too so they didn't go hungry, when Brendan said a little too loudly, "Saw that sea witch doing something weird today!"

His voice was nervous, a blatant attempt to interrupt the rapidly brewing storm, which Connor knew would never work. Except it did.

"What?" Frank asked, his attention swinging to Brendan like the Eye of Sauron.

Brendan quailed momentarily, but persevered. Connor appreciated his older brother in that moment. Brendan often did his best to manage the family, to head off the worst of the violence, even if that often meant bringing it down on himself instead. He hadn't told his parents or Serena that he couldn't see properly out of his left eye after one particularly severe beating he'd copped for breaking a plate. It had been Serena, in fact, who broke it, but Brendan had claimed responsibility and his father had beaten him across the kitchen for it. He'd admitted to Connor that his left eye never really recovered after Connor caught him covering it with one had while trying to read something for school.

"That sea witch," Brendan said. "Always on the harbour wall, looking out. She was doing this weird sort of dance today."

"Dance?" Frank's face was still red with burgeoning rage, but his attention had been neatly drawn. Connor feared for where it might lead, but Brendan continued bravely.

"She's always standing there, yeah? Just looking out? But today she was making all these weird hand gestures and kinda bobbing up and down. You know how deaf people use sign language? It was a bit like that, only like she did it with her whole body."

"The fuck are you talking about?" Lydia asked.

"Best you let her be." All eyes turned to Frank. He

glanced around his family, lips pursed. "She's been here since I was a kid and my dad said she was around when *he* was a kid. Always old like she is now." He raised a hand to silence any dissent. "I know how it sounds, but fucken accept it. She's something else and you'd do well to show her respect and keep your distance."

The anger of moments before had dissipated and Frank turned back to his meal, eating with the aggressive speed that was his signature. The rest looked at each other and shrugged. Connor nodded to Serena's plate and the two of them hurriedly finished their meal and excused themselves, rinsed their dishes and retreated to their bedroom. That had been about a week before everything in Gulpepper went crazy that time, a couple of years before. The time most people seemed to avoid talking about, or even remembering. The whole thing was a blur even to Connor himself, and sometimes he told himself he'd dreamed the huge, bottomless hole that had appeared in Anthill Street, right outside their house. Except, it couldn't have been a dream, because the hole swallowed half the garage of the place opposite. The garage remained ruined for a year or more even though the hole had vanished like it was never there. They'd finally repaired it after sorting out issues with the home insurance or something. There were stories like that from all over town after that horrendous night.

As Connor recalled that strange evening around the dinner table while watching the sea witch on the harbour wall, she turned and looked directly at him. He jumped slightly and was about to look away, carry on home, when she reached out, crooked one finger at him.

Stupidly, he pointed at his chest in a classic, *Who me?* gesture. He almost looked back over his shoulder like she might mean someone behind him, but he knew better. He crossed the road and approached her cautiously.

She squinted up at him, saying nothing. Connor wasn't a big youth, only about 170 centimetres and probably fifty kilos dripping wet, skinny from malnourishment and stress, but he still stood head and shoulders taller than the tiny old lady. He began to feel distinctly uncomfortable under her scrutiny.

As he opened his mouth to say something, anything, to break the weird tension, she put one hand on his forearm. Her palm was warm, dry as paper and strangely strong. "You've seen," she said, her voice wet, phlegmy.

"Seen what?"

She looked around for a moment, as if hoping to spot someone else nearby, then back at him. "Too many are noticing. Their influence, yes? That stranger..." She looked off again, gazing west along Gulpepper Street that ultimately led to the road out of town.

"Noticing what? Ma'am?" He added the honorific at the end and felt immediately foolish, but he remembered his father's admonition to show respect.

"Ma'am," she said, with a bark of guttural laughter. "Good grief, no." Her face immediately sobered again. "The signs. There are many and there is one, and the one is gathering the many and something... something new, eh? Or old, perhaps. Same thing, really, of course. Always."

"I'm sorry, I don't understand."

"No. Not enough do." She dropped her hand from his arm and turned back to face the ocean. The cement wall that lined the footpath all around the harbour was only half a metre high and about as wide, dropping down to the water on the other side. The old lady put one knee and both hands onto the wall and pushed herself up to stand there and stare out.

"I think they're leaving," she said, and her voice held such sadness that Connor felt it in his chest. "They never did that before, not even when..." She glanced towards Charles Head, where the manor house had collapsed into the sea that fateful night a couple of years before, then stared back out over the ocean again.

She fell silent and Connor stood awkwardly for a moment, unsure what to do, what to say. Should he even say anything?

"All those years ago I gave up the best of myself, eh?" the sea witch said, almost too quietly to hear. "And for what? Love? Pah! What a fool."

Connor waited, a flurry of questions in his mind but finding voice for none of them.

"I thought at least they'd always be nearby. But if even they're leaving... Really alone now, eh?"

"Do you... have family or anything?" Connor knew the question was absurd, given the circumstances, but he felt the need to say something.

The sea witch jumped, glanced around like she'd forgotten he was there. "Not here. Only there, given up." She turned back to look out over the small, calm waves. "But it's coming around, isn't it? The beginning and the end, again and again."

After a few seconds, Connor decided to simply extricate himself. Her muttering made him uncomfortable. He wanted to ask questions but wasn't sure he really wanted any answers.

"Have a good evening," he said weakly and started to walk away.

"Beware the bearer of the sign," she said when he was almost out of earshot.

He paused, glanced back, but she was still looking at the sea. Was she talking about the weirdly bracketed design he kept seeing? How could she know?

"Allegiances are still being drawn," she said. "So much in flux, but nothing good. No, nothing good is coming."

She fell silent once more and, after a moment longer, Connor slipped quietly away.

He dreamed of the fall again that night.

He had got home and his mother was working the late shift, so Brendan made food for the three of them, which they ate quickly before Frank came in. Serena and Connor were in bed, Serena already asleep, Connor reading and Brendan gone out again, when he heard his father come home. Within a minute or two of Frank's return, Lydia had got home from work and there had been some noise and grunts and suppressed cries of pain from their bedroom, then the house had fallen silent. Connor had been grateful for the relative peace of a night like that and allowed himself to sleep. And he dreamed of the fall.

He stood on a slick, black beach, his footing unsteady on cold ichor. The sky above was thick, heavy with low clouds in deep reds and purples. A rain fell, icy cold and slantwise, driving into him, making him squint. Then those clouds began to tear and rent, deep crimson inside, swirling and somehow endless. Connor staggered with the vertigo of sudden exposure to an abyss and he watched the things fall. Creatures of all sizes, many-limbed and misshapen. Some limp and clearly dead, others writhing in the agony of their terrifying descent. He watched them landing among the churning waves, then the ocean itself seemed to heave, to lift in a vast bulge as if something unfathomable began to rise.

Connor screamed but the sound was the screech of tormented gulls. He gasped for breath as he watched the heaving sea and then cried out, some incoherent warning, but only made the hoarse bark of a seal. Somewhere, a bell rang, deafening and sonorous, but distant too. Any proximity to that sound would instantly destroy any creature's hearing, he was sure. The swelling ocean pushed further, the waves beginning to sluice in cascades down the sides of whatever rose up, and the centre opened. A vast, yawning chasm, a circular pit that somehow Connor knew led into an endless void like the bleeding wounds in the sky above. And the things that fell were swallowed by it, vanished into its endless depths. Then something inconceivably bigger still seemed to roll up and curl out of the thing, bending Connor's mind as he tried to perceive the physics of it, but there was nowhere for his brain to land.

Connor screamed again and snapped awake, sweating and panting, tangled in the sheets of his bed at home. Serena leaned over from above, eyes concerned, hair hanging in disarray.

"Connor? You okay?"

"Yeah, sorry. Just a nightmare."

"Sure?"

He reached up, put a hand on her cheek. It was soft and warm. "Really. Sorry. You go back to sleep."

"'kay."

She vanished again and her breathing went back to the slow cadence of sleep almost immediately. Brendan was home and had slept through the whole thing, as usual. Connor's older brother could sleep through a hurricane.

It had been a long time since he'd had the dream all residents of The Gulp shared. Or at least, seemed to share some version of when they were young even if most grew out of it eventually. He remembered the first time he'd woken from it, terrified, yelling out for his parents, back when he'd thought they cared, that they might protect him. He'd only been four or five years old. His dad had looked in, beer in hand.

"What are you screaming about?"

"A big storm at the sea," young Connor had said, tears on his cheeks. "Things were falling from red clouds."

"Oh, that." His dad barked a humourless laugh.

"Everyone dreams that sometimes. It goes away as you get older."

"Everyone? You too?"

"When I was a kid, yeah. Not for years now. Just a dream. Don't be a baby. Go to sleep."

And he'd left and shut the door. Connor had lain there for hours afterwards, afraid to even shut his eyes for fear of seeing those hellish images again. After the third or fourth time he'd had some version of the dream it began to scare him a little less, but he never felt rested following those disturbances.

"The dream steals a night every now and then," Lauren had said when he'd shared the experience with her years later. "But I don't think I get it any more. Not for ages, anyway."

And Connor couldn't remember the last time he'd had the dream. Maybe not since he was eleven or twelve years old. So why again now? And he'd never seen that thing rising before, whatever that was. Had it even been rising? Or opening? His mind slipped and slid around the memory of it, unable to find purchase, to even remember quite what he'd seen. Or thought he'd seen.

For some reason it got him thinking about the weird sign he'd noticed around town, the strange fellow handing out sheets with the symbol on them. He couldn't explain why, but for some reason the symbol, which he found weirdly disquieting, and the dream were somehow linked. Then again, like many things in The Gulp, interconnections were not unusual, but rarely made any sense.

It took quite a while for him to fall asleep again, but he eventually did.

The next morning found the family struggling through the start of the week routine. Monday morning was a hectic time in a household of five, especially when there were only two bedrooms and one bathroom. Lydia needed to be at Woollies by 8 a.m. and Frank worked at Gulpepper Tyres, right on the western side of town near the first roundabout. It was only a five- or ten-minute walk from their house, but he needed to be there by 8.30 a.m. and was invariably hungover and foul-tempered. The three kids always kept a low profile on weekday mornings.

Serena had developed the habit of getting up much earlier than everyone else, often before 5.30 a.m., and slipping away. She'd get her school uniform on and creep from the house under cover of darkness. If Connor managed to wake in time, he'd make sure she took at least something to eat with her, but often he'd go to her school later in the day instead and give her a sandwich he'd brought with him, much to her embarrassment in front of her friends. But he knew she secretly appreciated it. What she did in those hours between leaving and the start of school, he didn't know, but assumed she was simply enjoying time alone. She was smart enough to know safe places around The Gulp and certainly smart enough to never talk to strangers.

This Monday was no different. Serena was already gone when Connor woke. Frank and Lydia circled each other angrily in the kitchen. Connor and Brendan quickly dressed and grabbed a moment in the bathroom when the risk seemed lowest. Connor used his special skill of going unnoticed to avoid too much attention.

"I swear you literally go invisible sometimes," Brendan had said once. "Like, you're nowhere to be seen, then you just appear."

"Coping mechanism," Connor had replied, refusing to look too closely at what might really be happening. Since he was small, he'd had an ability to will himself unseen. He knew he was still there, but he would watch people look directly at him, then their gaze slide away, a brief furrowing of the brow, and then nothing. He used the skill all the time to move around the house, and sometimes around town and school as well, unmolested. But he never questioned it or tried to understand it, for fear it would somehow stop working.

He let his family move around him, worrying about themselves, not noticing him, as he put together a ragged lunch box for himself and one for Serena, then slipped from the house. Sometimes he walked to school with Brendan, but most days he walked alone or with Lauren.

She waited at the corner of Booker and Massey when he got there and Connor was happy to see her. They fell into step together and walked for a good while without saying anything, enjoying a companionable silence. Booker Street was one of only three roads, Shellhaven and Tanning being the other two, that ran in a more or less straight line north to south through almost the entire length of Gulpepper. They could follow Booker, up and down through the shallow hills of town, all the way to Cowpasture Road, then make a left turn there and head across to Shellhaven. Turning right when they reached Shellhaven put them right outside Gulpepper High. It was a journey Connor had enjoyed for years, one of the few carefree parts of life, out on his own recognizance, away from family and before or after the obligation of school.

School itself was a blessed relief from home life, six hours a day where he had somewhere to be, things to do, relieved in the knowledge Serena was safe too at her primary school. But school had its own trials, boredoms, bullies, among the student body and the teachers. It was a good place compared to home, but not a great place otherwise. The walk to and from school however, about thirty minutes each way if he took his time, was a kind of freedom. Connor usually walked home with Serena, meeting her outside St Augustine's Primary where she would wait for him, the two of them getting increasingly more nervous as they neared the house, wondering what might await. Brendan rarely joined them, finding his own escapes with his mates in who knew what private bolt holes around town. But as Serena always left early, Connor got to walk to school alone or with Lauren almost every day and it was one of his favourite things.

The mid-February day was hot and humid, the two of them wearing only shorts and school uniform polo shirts, and Connor's bag made his back sweat. Something felt heavier in the air and he wondered if a storm was brewing. He looked up and frowned at the clouds, a strange arrangement of two long curves with a familiar shape in the middle. He jumped as the image came into a kind of focus, the vast skyscape resolving into the sign he'd seen all around town.

Beware the bearer of the sign, the sea witch had said.

How could he beware the sky?

"Do you see that?" he asked Lauren.

"See what?"

He glanced down to see her frowning at him. He pointed, looked back up, "There, in the clouds—" But it had gone, dissipated into the high, striped cirrostratus common to the coast. "Oh."

"What, you see an elephant up there?"

He laughed, casting Lauren a confused glance. "An elephant?"

"Isn't that what people usually see in the clouds? Or a dragon?"

"I didn't know there was a hierarchy of subjects."

"Pareidolia."

"Bless you."

She flipped him the bird. "You know what that is?"

"Seeing faces in tree bark and shit, right?"

"Well, yeah, faces in things is the most common version, I suppose. But specifically, it's seeing something meaningful in an inanimate thing where there actually is no meaning."

"All right, professor."

She laughed. "So, is that it? Did you see something meaningful in the clouds?"

"Yeah, I thought so. But it's gone."

"What was it?"

He wanted to say, *It was that sign I've seen all over town the last few weeks, but it covered the entire sky,* except that seemed absurd. Instead, he managed, "Ah, I don't know. Just tired."

"Didn't sleep so well?"

"Nah. Had the dream. First time in years."

"Oh, wow. I can't remember the last time I did."

"Same."

"We have that biology test today. You study for it?"

And the mundane world came crashing back in, forcing disquieting thoughts of uncomfortable signs from Connor's mind. "Fuck! I completely forgot."

"You're a swot, you'll do okay."

"I hope so. Did you study?"

"Crammed a couple of hours last night after that dinner. Who gives a shit anyway, it's only fucking school."

"I hear that."

They walked on, but Connor kept surreptitiously glancing up and around, unsure why he was so reluctant to see the sign again, but compelled to look for it.

At lunchtime, he walked the three blocks to St Augustine's Primary and found Serena taking a drink from one of the water fountains. He gave her the lunch he'd made. She smiled, gave him a quick hug as her friends weren't around, and said, "I'm going to Ivy's after school. She said I could have dinner with them."

"Great! Don't be too late back though, okay?"

"Eight o'clock?"

"Sure, but no later."

"'kay."

She scurried off and he watched after her, wondering again why he was the parent in their dynamic. Not that he resented her for it, but he certainly resented Frank and Lydia. As he went to turn away, he noticed a darkening of the asphalt where the water from Serena's drinking had splashed. It made the sign, offset thick parentheses and an inverted lighthouse silhouette.

Connor frowned at it. "What the fuck?"

As he watched, the small puddle spread a little further and the shape vanished like it had never been. He left without another glance at it and went back to Gulpepper High to make his afternoon classes.

With Serena hanging out at Ivy's and Lauren doing music club after school on Mondays, Connor got to walk home alone. When he left school, instead of turning left onto Cowpasture Road, to head through the middle of town, he turned right. It was a longer way around, the route he would usually take to meet Serena, but he wanted to be nearer the ocean, and wanted an even longer walk than usual. Cowpasture would eventually lead all the way up to Jacquelin Head and the cemetery but he didn't go that far. He turned north again before the road started to rise steeply and followed a couple of backstreets to get down to Carlton Beach. He had a mind to carry his shoes and socks and walk knee deep in the surf, feel the gravelly black sand between his toes.

As he crossed a small street not far past the Ocean Blue Motel, he paused, frowning at the hedges that made a rough boundary on the north side of the property opposite. They were unkempt and ragged, half-dead, dry leaves scattered forlornly around the footpath. But from just the right angle, he saw the sign. Move a little left or right and it was lost as if it had never been. But if he stilled in just the right spot, the branches and leaves still attached were exactly the sign he'd seen everywhere. He stared at it a moment, unsure whether it was exciting or frightening. Everyone knew weird shit happened in The Gulp and the vast majority of the time, people ignored it. A bit like an angry animal, if you avoided making eye contact, it would probably leave you alone. Paying too much attention to the strangeness in Gulpepper might bring its attention too much to bear. But Connor sensed something powerful happening. He remembered the weirdly cryptic conversation with the sea witch.

He looked up from staring at the sign and jumped. The scrawny, yellow-toothed fellow who had handed him the sheet with the sign at the Sunday market stood across the road, watching intently. When Connor met his gaze, the man nodded vigorously and grinned, gave him a thumbs up.

Connor returned a quick smile, then tried to do his disappearing act, to be unseen, and hurried on. He turned left on Burly Road, that ran down directly onto the south end of Carlton Beach and tried not to think about the sign or the strange man. His desire to get his feet wet had faded and he courted the idea of simply going home, but his dad might be there. Maybe he'd sit in the park and wait for Lauren to finish. Perhaps she'd be keen to hang out as Serena would be safe at Ivy's.

As he slowed his pace, looking down the hill and out over Carlton Beach ahead of him, he had the disquieting feeling of being watched, despite his desire to go unnoticed. He looked right and there, among the houses and garages, was one place larger than the rest. Like a kind of old community hall, maybe an ancient Scout hut. It seemed incongruous among the regular houses and Connor wondered if it had been there first, then the land around it got slowly sub-divided and sold off, other dwellings popping up like mushrooms. But the hall itself, weatherboard walls and steep metal roof on a footing of old sandstone, had stone steps leading up to double doors that were closed. On those doors, in bold black paint standing out against the peeling white, was the sign. And while he couldn't explain it, Connor knew it was the sign that he'd felt watching him. So much for his disappearing act.

He stared at the building, knew there was something inside that would answer all his questions about the symbol. And he knew too that perhaps he didn't want those answers. It felt like a tipping point. If he was to go into that place, it might be an irreversible course of action.

"These are the hardest decisions, aren't they?"

Connor jumped and spun around. A tall, thin man stood behind him, smiling. But it was a smile like a shark. The man wore a dark grey three-piece suit with a crimson cravat, despite the heat, and highly polished black leather shoes. A gold watch chain hung from the pocket of his waistcoat. His face was smooth, his age hard to determine, but perhaps more than middle-age. Although far from old. The fact that his hair was white as porcelain confused the perception, the man's teeth as white as his hair.

"Sorry?" Connor said, concerned again that he had been seen.

"To delve deeper or turn away, yes? Quite a decision."

Connor looked from the man to the old hall and back again. "You mean...?"

The man's smile faded. "You're too smart to play dumb, young man."

"Right. I just... well, I don't really know what's happening."

"Of course." The man reached out his hand to shake. "Winterbourne's the name."

Connor shook, surprised at how cool and dry the man's touch was. "Nice to meet you Mr Winterbourne. I'm Connor."

"Just Winterbourne, no need for honorifics."

"Right." Connor wasn't sure 'Mr' qualified as an honorific, but decided to let it go.

"There are many answers, if you ask the right questions."

Connor shook his head. "I kinda have a particular responsibility in my life. I don't need to complicate things."

"She's ever more in danger the older she gets, hmm?"

Connor's heart seemed to pulse an extra beat. "What? How do you know...?"

"I have many answers, Connor Tucker. They start in there, if you're really willing to go all the way to save her."

Connor turned to look at the old hall again, brow furrowed. "I don't know," he said, turning back, but Winterbourne was nowhere to be seen. Connor turned a full circle, scanning everywhere. How could the man possibly have vanished in so short a time?

He heard footsteps approaching behind and turned again to see the scrawny, grey-skinned man from the market. The man gave his rapid nods again, face split in a manic grin, and hurried past Connor and into the hall. As he opened the door, Connor saw a wash of blue-green light inside, then the door closed. He stood alone on the footpath, chilled even though the day was hot. If anything, it was getting hotter, building in humidity.

Connor looked up over the buildings, out to sea and south a little, familiar with the weather patterns around Gulpepper. There were thunderheads building up far out on the horizon. A big storm coming.

He shook his head. Too much going on, even by Gulp standards. But one thing he was certain about was getting away from the hall and the sign on the door that was still somehow staring at him. He looked around once more for Winterbourne, but the man was nowhere to be seen.

Connor walked on down Burly Road and onto the beach to put his feet in the water after all. Something natural and grounding. He would enjoy some quiet time there, then perhaps try to find a way to get a bite to eat somewhere away from home, or just go hungry, then meet Serena when she headed back. He'd wait outside the house and go in with her, as he expected their dad to be home. But until then, he would be alone and he refused to think further about the sign.

When he walked back up Anthill Street towards his house a few hours later, marginally less hungry thanks to some dim sum he'd bought with a couple of dollars he'd found in his bag, the first thing he heard was yelling. He wondered often what the neighbours must think, but most Gulpepper residents had long since grown used to minding their own business.

Connor sighed and waited a couple of houses down, watching out for Serena. Movement caught his eye and he saw a couple of large, dark shapes scurry over the roof of a house opposite, then down behind it. He shuddered, sure the things had been some kind of spider, but that wasn't possible. They'd have been some half a metre across if that were true.

"Must have been ravens or something," he muttered, but wasn't convinced. Perhaps best not to know what they were.

It wasn't long before Serena turned the corner and approached him. His heart ached as her expression switched from apprehension to joy at seeing him. She'd clearly been trepidatious about coming home and then saw him waiting. He would always protect her.

"He home?" she asked.

"Yeah. Yelling at mum earlier but it's gone a bit quiet now."

Serena sucked in a long breath, then nodded. "Here we go then."

"You eaten well?"

"Yeah, Ivy's mum made spaghetti bolognese. I'm stuffed."

"Great!" He was a little jealous, but genuinely happy for her.

They went in through the front door and Brendan immediately leaned his head out of their bedroom and whispered, "Brace yourselves!" He gestured for them to quickly come into the room.

Frank's voice boomed from the lounge. "That my gayboy so-called fucken son coming home?"

Brendan winced, Connor and Serena froze.

"Go easy, love," Lydia said, but Connor heard the wine saturating her voice.

"Or fucken what?"

"Just try not to be mean, eh?"

Frank stumbled out into the hallway, glass in hand, a couple of inches of whisky in the bottom. If he was on spirits this early, that was a bad sign. "You know what I had to do today?" he asked. Connor wisely said nothing, knew it was rhetorical. "Had to leave my own fucken pub!"

Frank meant Clooney's. Claiming ownership of things was a frequent quirk of the man, from his family to his job to the place he drank. He owned nothing except the house they lived in, and that only by inheritance, but it made him feel better to think he owned things and was owed things and the family allowed him his delusions.

"Ask me fucken why, son!"

"Why, Dad?"

Frank took a few steps forward, straining as though on an invisible leash. "Because there at the fucken bar, shameless as all fuck, were two blokes kissing each other. Fucken gross, disgusting scum, like it was no big deal."

Connor bristled inside, terrified and outraged at the same time. "Why did you have to leave?"

"Because we're not allowed to put down animals like that, why do you fucken think?"

Connor saw where this was going. Frank, personally insulted by the existence of gay men, wasn't allowed to hurt them, so he'd come home to drink and stew and wait to take it out on his gay son instead. Connor had another beating coming, his stomach still bruised and sore from the last one. But if it was coming anyway, he'd say his piece too.

"Of course you can't kill gay people, Dad. Because it *is* no big deal. There's nothing wrong with it!"

Frank closed the last few steps between them and backhanded Connor hard across the cheek. His vision crossed and bouncing his shoulder off the wall was all that stopped him from falling. He pushed Serena towards the bedroom and hissed, "Go!"

Brendan stepped out and pulled Serena into the room, then stood between his dad and the door.

"You fucken talk back to me?" Frank yelled. "You think you can defend that fucken awful shit?"

"It's not awful, it's natural!"

Frank hit him again, sent him sideways once more.

"Connor," Brendan said, low, a warning.

"It *is* natural!" Connor yelled.

Frank grabbed Connor by the throat, not spilling a drop from the glass in his other hand. He slammed his son hard against the hallway wall. Lydia appeared in the loungeroom doorway, called Frank's name, but weakly, like she hoped he wouldn't hear.

"Of course you'd fucken say that!" Frank said, spittle flying. "Like all these fucken blokes saying they're women now, the fucking perverts! You gonna say that's natural too?"

"It *is* natural! And it's not perverted!" Connor cried, voice restricted as he fought for breath, but something had snapped inside him. He would not take this bigotry any more. "It's not about sex. It's gender!"

"It's fucken disgusting!" Frank yelled, pulling Connor away from the wall only to slam him back again. His head cracked against the plasterboard, vision swimming.

Serena was crying, calling Connor's name. Lydia stood frozen in the doorway. Brendan stepped up, put a hand on his father's arm where it braced Connor against the wall. "Dad, please."

"Why do you care?" Connor yelled, voice rasping and weak as his father's fingers gripped tighter and tighter. *He's going to kill me*, Connor thought. *He'll choke the life out of me.* But he couldn't stop. If this was his last chance, he would go out fighting, even if he only had ideas to hit with. "How does it affect your life *at all*? How do gay people or trans people simply existing affect you *at all*? Why do you care?"

"You fucken faggot piece of shit waste of fucken

space!" Frank punctuated the words by slamming Connor into the wall again. He blacked out a moment, felt as though his neck were about to snap.

"Dad, please!" Brendan begged. "You're going to kill him!"

"I should fucken kill him!" Frank yelled.

"Daaaad!" Serena screamed from the bedroom.

"Frank, please calm down!" Lydia said, actually stepping out into the hallway.

Brendan dragged at his dad's arm again as Connor began to make restricted gags. His eyes felt like they would burst, his vision closed to two grainy tunnels, his father's twisted, furious face seeming to retreat down them. His lungs burned, he desperately wanted to suck in a breath he couldn't have. *Serena, I'm sorry. Run away. Just run away!*

"DAD!" Brendan yelled and Frank barked an incoherent noise of rage.

The grip at Connor's throat vanished and he hit the hallway floor on his butt, gasping, as Frank turned and punched Brendan hard. Brendan yelped, falling backwards, but snatching at their bedroom doorframe to stay upright. Serena scurried out and grabbed Connor's arm, hauling him back with her. Brendan took the other arm, the three of them retreating into the room as Connor fought for breath.

"You're all fucked!" Frank shouted and there was a crash as his glass smashed against the door as Brendan kicked it shut.

The three of them sat on the floor, listening as Lydia said, "I'll get you a new glass. Come on, have another drink. This way."

Connor imagined her tugging weakly, nervously, at Frank's arm, trying to convince the man to drink more, and quickly, to subdue him into unconsciousness. It was the most she ever did to stand up to Frank and even that was a risk. He might turn on her, beat her, or worse. Or he might allow himself to be led away, plied with more booze.

Their voices faded and Connor sucked in rapid, shallow breaths, his vision starting to come back. Serena clung to him, crying, her face pressed into his chest. He looked at Brendan, whose eye was already swollen and blackening.

"Thanks."

"Why the fuck did you back chat him like that?" Brendan's eyebrows were high. "I thought he was really going to kill you that time."

Connor shook his head. "So did I. So did he, I think."

"Shit, Connor." Brendan was on the verge of tears. He looked away. "Why can't you just like girls?"

Connor was aghast. "Why can't you just like boys, Brendan?"

Brendan sat back, face scrunched. "I'm not gay, bro!"

Connor nodded. "See how that feels? I *am* gay. And there's nothing wrong with it."

They sat in silence for a minute, but for Serena's muffled sobs.

"You're right," Brendan said eventually. "Of course, you're right. There isn't anything wrong with it." He grinned crookedly. "First time you've ever actually admitted it though."

"Geez, I fucking wonder why?"

They both began to laugh, softly for fear of Frank hearing. Serena looked up, first at Connor, then Brendan, her face twitching up into a smile.

"You two are weird," she said. "And I love you both."

All three gathered each other in a group hug. "We love you too, sis," Connor said.

"I love you both" Brendan said. "We need to take care of each other. I've got your backs, you two."

Connor nodded. "Me too." He frowned at Brendan's still swelling eye. It was almost closed. "When he passes out, I'll get you some ice for that."

"Thanks. Your neck is bruised as fuck too."

Connor sighed. "I'll have to dig out that old skivvy.

Hope it still fits."

They stayed on the floor, holding each other, for a long time, until the house sank into the kind of quiet that meant both their parents had finally passed out.

Tuesday morning dawned hot and humid, the sky closed over with heavy cloud. It would only get hotter and more close until eventually a storm broke through. Connor hoped it would be soon, the high neck of the slightly too tight shirt he had on under his school uniform was itchy and sweaty as hell.

All three kids had risen early and slipped away before Frank or Lydia emerged. They didn't talk about it, the unspoken agreement well-established after Frank's bigger blow-outs. Everybody kept their distance in the hope things would calm down again. Serena hurried off to wherever she went in the early mornings and Connor was tempted to follow, or ask to go with her. But he knew she needed something of her own. She would invite him one day, maybe. Brendan said goodbye at the gate and headed in the opposite direction from school, and Connor knew he was going to pull some early bongs with his mates. *Whatever gets you through the day, bro.*

So Connor found himself alone again on the streets of The Gulp, at a little after 7 a.m., wondering what to do with his time. Instead of heading south across town in the general direction of school he went east, thinking he'd sit and look out over the harbour. His walk took him to the end of Massey Street and the small harbourside park there. As he went to cross over to it, he saw the proprietor of Gulpepper Curios on the polished wooden bench outside the shop just down the road. A couple of years before, the man had taken over from old Stanley Frost. Connor heard Frost had retired. But this guy had seemed to show up out of nowhere.

The man saw him looking and raised a hand in a wave. Connor waved back.

"You're out early," the shopkeeper called.

Connor turned to walk closer. "Not as early as you."

"Good point. Honestly, I've never been one for lying in, but since coming here I rarely sleep much past dawn."

"I see you sitting here a lot."

"I like this spot." There was something melancholy in the man's eyes as he said that. Then he smiled. "Andrew McDermott. I've seen you around."

"Connor Tucker. I live just up that way. Quite often like to come down here."

"And what do you see when you do?"

It was a strange question and Connor felt like it meant more than the words conveyed. He wasn't sure how to answer. "It's just a lot better than being at home."

McDermott nodded. "Ah. I'm sorry to hear that. Tough being a teenager at the best of times, but for some it's a lot worse, eh?"

"I guess."

"If you don't mind my saying so, I would venture you have some tough decisions coming up."

"Why do you say that?"

"Since I... arrived here in Gulpepper, my life has changed a bit and one of those changes seems to be an increased awareness of people's internal struggles. I often sense what they need or what they're burdened with." McDermott gestured back over his shoulder at the shop. "It's partly this place. It fulfills a role, you know? Supplies people with just what they need, when they need it. Seems I'm something of a facilitator there." He smiled. "Sorry, I'm rambling. I guess what I'm saying is that if you find you need something, perhaps I have it in stock."

Connor nodded, a little nonplussed by the turn of the

conversation. "I'll bear that in mind."

McDermott pointed. "Look! On the fishing boat."

Connor turned, surprised at the man's sudden animation. The harbour jetties were a decent distance away from them, across the small park and the width of the harbour itself, but several boats were moored there, among them a few fishing vessels. "Which one?" he asked.

"The Eclipse, far left. See it?"

"Yes. What about it?"

"On the cabin."

Connor squinted, shaded his eyes, and saw a shape scurry over the roof McDermott indicated. Then a second one, then a third. They split up and moved across the deck of that boat and then others, zigging and zagging side to side. Connor couldn't deny it this time, they were definitely large, spider-like creatures. Black, many-limbed, maybe the size of a big cat, but rounded where a cat would be long.

"What the hell?" he whispered.

"I keep seeing them recently," McDermott said. "Usually at night or around dawn, but once or twice later in the day."

"I saw them too, I think. In my street yesterday."

"Ah! So it's not just me. They're all over town?"

"I guess so. You seen them anywhere else?"

"No, I don't get out much. But you're the first person I've spoken to who's seen them as well."

"Others must have noticed, they're quite big," Connor said, gesturing, but realised they weren't there any longer. "Where did they go?"

"Fast, curious things, aren't they? I wonder what they're looking for?"

"Looking for?"

"I get the distinct impression they're searching for something. Or someone."

Connor frowned, looked down at McDermott still relaxed on his bench. "Why?"

"That's exactly what I'd like to know. Something is up in town, don't you think?"

"Up?" *I've kinda got my own stresses going on,* Connor thought, echoing what he'd said to Winterbourne the day before. He realised he paid little attention to anything else these days, but he *had* been seeing those signs everywhere. It did feel like things were shifting in The Gulp.

McDermott nodded. "Yes. Up. And nothing good, I fear."

Connor saw the sea witch on the side of the harbour some hundred metres away, watching them both intently. McDermott followed his gaze and nodded.

"She's aware of it too, I think."

"I reckon she knows a lot more than anyone gives her credit for," Connor said.

McDermott laughed. "You are certainly right there."

Connor had the sudden strong urge to talk to her again. "I'll see you later," he said and started walking away.

"Have a good day, son. And remember, if you ever need anything..."

"Sure. Thanks."

Connor made his way around the harbour, the sea witch watching him the whole way. When she saw he was making his way to her, she stepped down off the wall and came to meet him. When he opened his mouth to speak, she held up one hand to forestall him.

"The one or the many," she said.

"What?"

"That's all there is to consider. That's all you have to think on. The one or the many."

"I don't understand."

She stared up at him a moment, then shook her head. "Already too late, I think."

She turned and walked away. Connor fought a dozen questions that fluttered around his mind, trying to think of something to say, something to ask, but no one point would land. He was untethered in a way he hadn't experienced before and unsure what to do. He needed to get away, to get Serena and Brendan and himself away. Whatever other weirdness might be going on in The Gulp, his single focus remained.

His phone buzzed in his pocket and he took it out, saw a message from Lauren.

walk with me today?

He messaged back, *i'm already at the harbour. wait for you here?*

early bird! see you in 10

Connor started to reply, then another message came in.

or 15. it's really early con-man

He smiled, typed, *no rush i'll be here*, then went to a bench overlooking the water. McDermott still sat in his spot and Connor did his best to avoid eye contact. The man was nice enough, but there was something unsettling about him. And the sea witch had wandered off towards the lighthouse and disappeared. Connor enjoyed the solitude but for the few passing joggers and dog walkers, and the scavenging seagulls.

It was over twenty minutes before he saw Lauren walking around the harbourside towards him and he lifted one hand in a wave. She waved back, then frowned. Her face was stern as she reached him.

"What happened?"

Connor raised his eyebrows. "What do you mean?"

"It's me, Connor, don't play dumb. Out of the house at the crack of dawn, wearing that stupid skivvy."

Before he could stop her, she reached out and pulled the high neck down. Her face crumpled. The bruises were pretty bad, black and purple in the obvious shape of fingers.

"Connor!"

She sat beside him and gathered him in a hug and some dam he hadn't been aware was cracking finally failed. He buried his face in Lauren's hair and sobbed. She said nothing, just held him tight and he wrapped his arms around her and had never been more grateful for anyone in his life. Lauren, he realised, was the only anchor in the world. The only person who genuinely cared about him and was there for him. Serena loved him, of course, but he had to take care of her, it wasn't his little sister's job to look after him. Brendan loved him, but Bren was about toughening up and bearing the load. Brendan didn't so much look after Connor as force Connor to look after himself. But Lauren? Well, she loved him and was there for him and was the only person in the world he could be one hundred per cent honest with about everything.

After crying for several minutes, the act cathartic and unburdening, he said, "Really thought it was over last night." He made a sound that was like a laugh, but the furthest thing in the world from humour. "I almost welcomed it. But there's Serena."

"Connor, please don't even think that. The world is better with you in it, I promise."

"Sometimes feels like it's either me or him."

She sat back, met his gaze with serious eyes. "I'm there, bro. A good friend will help you hide a corpse. A real friend will help you make the corpse first."

He smiled. "I have no idea how to even start something like that. He's like a planet with its own gravity, Loz. We just can't seem to escape him."

"But you must! And I'll help. There has to be a way."

He nodded, wiped his eyes.

"Hey, have you eaten?"

Connor shook his head. "Left early. Don't think there's anything in the house, anyway."

"It's still early. We'll go by Suzy's and I'll buy you a pie or something." She held up a hand. "No argument, it's not charity. I didn't eat either because you dragged me out, so I'm getting breakfast and I refuse to eat alone. It's unseemly."

Connor laughed, genuine this time. "Unseemly?"

"For a woman to eat alone. Yes!"

"Okay, then. Who am I to argue against such propriety?"

"Exactly. Let's go."

By the time they were walking down Shellhaven Street and nearing school, finishing off their pies, Connor felt immeasurably better. He certainly needed to escape his father, who seemed to be spiralling into bigger and more frequent rages as time went on, but he could think more clearly with food in his belly and Lauren's friendship on hand. He needed to keep his head and get a plan happening.

As they crossed Freemantle Street, Connor looked up and saw the white-haired fellow, Winterbourne, on the opposite corner. Winterbourne smiled, then gestured with one thumb to his right and gave a little knowing nod. Connor frowned, confused, then realised the man was indicating the way to where Shellhaven Street met Burly Street down near Carlton Beach. And just by that junction, the old community hall with the strange sign on the doors.

"Who's that?" Lauren asked.

Connor caught himself, looked back to her. "Just this weird dude I met yesterday. Not really sure what his deal is."

"Weird people in The Gulp? You don't say?"

"Right?"

They carried on to school, but Connor couldn't stop thinking about the man and what he represented. What he clearly suggested. He remembered looking at that building and feeling as though it held answers.

These are the hardest decisions, aren't they?

Winterbourne had said. *To delve deeper or turn away.*

There are many answers, if you ask the right questions.

She's ever more in danger the older she gets, hmm?

I have many answers, Connor Tucker. They start in there, if you're really willing to go all the way to save her.

What did that mean? What could any of it mean?

The first thing Connor noticed when he came out of school that afternoon was the sign. It had been sprayed in black paint on the grey asphalt in the middle of the road right outside the school gates. Connor stood staring at it a moment, then someone behind him said, "What is that, oil?"

"Probably leaked from one of the shitty busses," someone else said.

"Probably leaked from your mum," another said and they all laughed and walked away.

Connor looked around and realised only a few people seemed to be noticing the sign and those people didn't give it a second glance. He looked up and saw it again, carved into a wooden garden fence across the road from the school. No one seemed to notice that one. He started to think about the old hall again and what answers might lie in there. Without thinking too hard, he headed east along Cowpasture Road. After a block or so, he saw Winterbourne, still in his suit and cravat and polished shoes. The storm had yet to break and the heat was oppressive, but Winterbourne seemed unbothered by it. He smiled and waved to Connor, then slipped away between buildings.

Connor kept on, knowing he was going to that old hall while refusing to consciously admit it to himself. He needed whatever answers might lie there. When he reached Burly Road and turned left, he saw movement on a roof opposite. Another of those weird, big spidery things. He shuddered, imagining one up close. No one lived in Australia for long without becoming at least somewhat used to spiders, but not things the size of the family dog. Would they bite? He hoped to never see one any closer than a rooftop across the street. It had gone already, only ever glimpsed briefly, always on the move. Had they always been around? Surely he would have noticed before. No one had ever mentioned them that he recalled, other than Andrew McDermott that morning, so they had to be a new phenomenon in town. Why?

The rangy, grey-skinned man stood on the footpath in front of the old hall. When Connor caught his eye, he grinned broadly and gestured inside.

Connor stared, indecision clawing at him. On some primal level he knew this was a pivot point in his life. He would learn things here, but would they change him? Would they save him? Or at least save Serena? Surely, he thought to himself, he could learn what there might be to know and then still take time to decide what it all might mean.

The man gestured inside again. With a sigh, Connor turned off the footpath and walked the short distance to the hall doors.

Up close, he realised the sign wasn't painted. It seemed somehow projected onto the old wood. It shimmered slightly, seemed almost three-dimensional, as if he could reach out and put his hand in it rather than on it. Before he realised it, he was reaching forwards, fingers outstretched.

The thin man caught his wrist, his grip cool and dry. "Not yet. Don't touch yet." His voice was as dry as his grip, and rasping. He reached past Connor and opened one side of the double doors.

Immediately, Connor was overwhelmed by an oceanic stench, old kelp and dead fish, salty and wet. The light inside undulated in shades of green, as though the deep ocean was somehow trapped in there, unable to pour out through the door.

"Okay, okay," the thin man said reassuringly, nodding and gesturing inside. "Safe!"

Connor wasn't so sure, but was compelled

nonetheless and he stepped into pelagic depths. As soon as he crossed the threshold, he felt immense pressure, like he was being crushed to a fraction of his size, his lungs tightened, his eyes bulged. Panic set in and he went to turn around, run away, but a voice said, "Breathe, Connor! One breath to acclimatise."

Still determined to run away, Connor sucked in a breath anyway and his desire to escape eased immediately as his senses equalised with his surroundings. He staggered slightly, but stayed where he was and took in the room. It was large, high-ceiled in an old-fashioned A-frame, all the joists visible. The floor was dark, glossy boards. All the windows had been blocked, plywood or something similar nailed over them. On the far side was a door leading into a back room of some kind, but the place was otherwise one big space, open and empty, except for about a dozen people. They all looked at him, smiling.

"Well done," said the voice again, from beside him.

Connor turned to see Winterbourne there, smiling like the others.

"A brave step," Winterbourne said. "Most would have run before risking a breath. But you have strength, hmm?"

"I dunno," Connor managed. "I still feel like pissing my pants."

Winterbourne let out a soft laugh. "Bravery isn't a lack of fear, Connor. It's doing the right thing despite the fear."

"What is this place?"

"The centre. The alpha and omega. The end and the new beginning. It's all here, but not here. Now and past and not yet."

"Well, glad you cleared that up for me." Connor turned, suddenly wanting nothing else but to be outside in the hot, close day, to feel humidity and light and a normal breeze instead of this heavy, oppressive stillness.

Winterbourne put a hand gently on his shoulder.

"Give me a minute, hmm? Hear me out?"

Connor looked at the man, uncertain. "Why?"

"Because I can save Serena."

Connor's heart thumped. "How do you know about her? About us?"

"Because I've been looking for you. Studying you. Because you, Connor, could very well be the key to unlocking the future." Winterbourne looked up to the group in the middle of the hall. "Show him."

The small crowd parted and Connor saw there was one other thing in the big space other than people. A kind of lectern stood in the middle of the room, carved with strange shapes that seemed somehow more than three-dimensional. They shifted, he realised, a little like the sign on the doors. On the lectern was a large book.

"Take a closer look," Winterbourne said.

Connor went to it, the sensation of ocean depths, the marine stench, stronger than ever, and looked while keeping his hands behind his back. He had a strong desire to not touch the thing. It was about the size of a ring binder, but much thicker, its covers heavy and solid. He thought maybe they were made of wood or something like it. On the front cover was the sign, rippling and pulsing like a heartbeat. Vertigo swept over him as he saw it, a sensation like he might fall into it and never stop. He staggered, stepped back and cast a horrified glance at Winterbourne.

The man smiled again. "Its presence is powerful, isn't it? Look inside."

"I don't want to touch it."

Winterbourne gestured to one of the people nearby and she nodded, stepped up to the lectern and lifted open the cover.

Connor moved back a little closer to see. The pages were heavy and uneven. He remembered learning in school a year or two before about vellum, prepared animal skin used for writing on, and immediately thought this was an example of it. But this was thicker and had some marks and blemishes. The page was covered in a script Connor couldn't recognise, a kind of pictographic that made him think of Egyptian hieroglyphics but with an entirely alien design. The writing, if that's indeed what it was, seemed to be a dark brown in colour. The woman turned the page and Connor saw a spray of freckles across one corner of the next page. She turned again and this page was two separate pieces of skin stitched together, the stitches tiny and neat. Human skin, Connor knew, without a doubt. A book of human skin pages, written in blood. He shook his head, backed away.

"That's wrong," he muttered. "That shouldn't be..."

"Right, wrong," Winterbourne said softly, right behind him. "That's always a matter of perspective."

"No, it's not! Some things are objectively wrong."

"Like murder?"

"Yes!"

"What if you knew beyond a shadow of a doubt that someone was going to kill you. Or kill Serena, maybe? Hmm? So you killed them first. That's murder. Still wrong?"

"Fuck you. Why are you playing these games?"

"This is the Void Atlas, Connor. Though the name does little to truly explain what it is. What it's capable of. This atlas is the past and the future, and also the present. Things are shifting and time is coming around again. A time that was before and has never been and is always now, and the Void Atlas is a focus for those energies. And a catalyst."

"You're a fucking maniac. I need to go!" Connor turned, tried to push past Winterbourne.

The man moved aside, let him go. As Connor neared the doors, Winterbourne called out, "You can free Serena. I can make that happen. And Brendan, if that's what you want."

Connor stopped, still with his back to the man and the profane book. "I don't believe you."

"Listen to my offer. I will be one hundred percent honest about it."

Connor slowly turned back, but stayed where he was near the door. "Make it quick."

Winterbourne nodded. "You will die. You have already discerned, in part at least, how this book was made. The nature of its construction. You're a smart person. The Void Atlas has everything except the last page. The page that will complete it and create the conditions required. I can give you more details of what those conditions allow, but I feel like you only need to hear the details of your part in all this. So here it is. All the pages were made without the consent of the person supplying the skin, obviously. But the last page must be given willingly. However, it's not only the skin that's required, but the life of the person donating. Every page was made from skin removed at the moment of death. That's the power imbued, you see. So the last page must be given willingly and that person's life along with it. There is great power in sacrifice. People have known this for millennia."

"You're mad. Who would do that? Why would I do that?"

"Because you're desperate, Connor. Because you know Serena has very little time before she's broken beyond her ability to endure. Because you and your brother are likely to die under your father's rage. And where will that leave her, hmm? You're also, importantly, old town blood. Which is why I know you're a perfect candidate for what I need. If you're going to die soon anyway, why not free Serena first. And Brendan."

"How would that happen?"

Winterbourne smiled. "For all the mysteries of the numinous, some things are entirely mundane. Money, Connor." He reached into the inside pocket of his jacket and pulled out a wad of green one hundred dollar bills about a centimetre thick. "This is ten thousand dollars. I have ten of these for you. One hundred thousand dollars,

Connor. The money will go to your sister and brother. They can escape, start a new life. That kind of money is life-changing, after all. Still not easy, of course, for children. But money like that... I can perhaps offer some advice regarding safe places too."

"So you picked me because I'm desperate?"

"And because of who you are. Events are often anchored in space as much as they're loose in time. This place is a powerful nexus, so I need someone intrinsically linked to here. A generations-old Gulpepper family like yours is powerful. You're a rare commodity, Connor Tucker."

"That's the value of my life? A hundred K?"

"That's the value of your siblings' freedom. You know it'll free them. And all you have to do is give yourself for it to happen."

"How do I know you'll hold up your end of the bargain?"

"Bring them here. I'll give them the money, even arrange a ride for them out of town. Once you know they're safely away, you fulfill your role. How's that?"

Connor shook his head. Why was he even considering this? It was madness. He would willingly die for Serena if necessary, but surely this was plain lunacy. "You're crazy!" he yelled and ran for the door.

Winterbourne and the others made no move to stop him. "Think on it," Winterbourne called out as Connor crashed through the doors and into the humid day outside.

He staggered to the footpath and stopped, hands on his knees, gasping for breath, close to vomiting. The day was solidly overcast still, but the brightness of the clouds made him squint after the subdued interior of the hall. A strong breeze pushed in from the south and he knew the storm was coming. He turned and ran home as large raindrops splatted into the pavement. By the time he reached the harbour, the storm broke in full and he was drenched, the rain cold, chilling him to the bone, but so welcome after the crushing confines of the old hall.

The sea witch stood on the harbour wall and stared at him but said nothing. As he ran past on the other side of the road, she shook her head and turned away.

When he got home, Connor's mind spun with all that had happened. Not only Winterbourne's insane offer, but the place itself, the hideous book. The hall had felt somehow removed, like it didn't really exist in Gulpepper. Or not all in Gulpepper. Connor felt besmirched by it, infected by the knowledge he carried. Not least in as much as Winterbourne had admitted to murder. Multiple murders and stealing his victim's skin to make what he called the Void Atlas.

Connor took a deep breath and went inside, bracing himself for what might be happening in the house. How much of last night's rage would still be evident? Serena ran over and gave him a hug as he entered.

"You're late! You didn't meet me."

"Sorry, got distracted by something. You okay?"

"Yeah, I'm just on my own here. Weird when I'm the only one in the house. Peaceful, kinda, but frightening too."

"In case Dad comes home."

"When you're not here, yeah. Or Brendan."

"Mum still at work?"

"I guess."

"Let's find some food."

They managed to scrape together a small feed from stuff in the cupboards and were watching TV together when Lydia came home from her Woollies shift.

"Any word from your father?" she asked.

"Nah. Why would he tell us anything?"

"Doesn't tell any of us anything any more." Lydia frowned, looked at the front door like she might see through it and discern something of her husband's whereabouts.

Connor saw something in his mother's eyes that was maybe new. The woman was always downtrodden, resigned, all the stuff he was used to, but there seemed to be a new level of fear in her demeanour he hadn't seen before. Something more specific bothered her. Living in the eye of the storm for so long had given Connor an almost sixth sense for changes in his family's weather and there seemed to be a new low pressure system building.

"Hey, Mum." He was speaking before he'd consciously made the decision to ask and realised the question had been nagging at his hindbrain since he'd got home.

"What?"

"How long has our family been in Gulpepper?"

Lydia frowned at him. "What do you mean? We've always lived here."

"Like, our ancestors, I mean."

"Oh, shit. Forever. The Tuckers were here when Charles Gulpepper settled the town. The Covingtons too, my father's people."

"And before that?"

"Fuck knows. Criminals, I expect, same as most people in this country."

"White people," Serena said quietly.

Lydia gave her a scathing look. "Obviously. We're talking about civilisation here, aren't we?"

Connor chose to let that appalling remark slide. "So there have been people of our bloodline here as long as there's been a Gulpepper?"

"Yep. And we've got exactly fuck all to show for it. We only have somewhere to live because your father's great-grandfather built this house and it's been handed down. We've always been in Gulpepper, and no doubt we'll stay here, assuming you lot have kids. Well, not you, obviously, but maybe Brendan and Serena will have normal lives. Why all the history questions?"

"Just curious. Something someone said." How could Winterbourne know so much about them? Then again, it seemed Winterbourne knew plenty about a lot of things. The man was far from anything resembling normal.

Frank remained thankfully absent for the evening and Brendan messaged Connor to say he'd be back late. When he and Serena headed for bed, Connor cracked the bedroom window open so his brother could slip in that way and not have to risk moving through the house too late at night. One of many survival tactics the siblings had developed.

Connor woke in the depths of the darkness and took a moment to orient himself. He startled as he realised he'd been roused by his father's voice, the man standing beside their bunk beds again. He usually woke long before the man got this close.

"Come on, little mistake. Up you get. Come with Daddy." Frank's words were slurred.

Serena made noises of confusion and Connor saw the mattress above him shift and flex as she sat up. Brendan had slipped in at some point and was awake too, sitting in his bed across the room.

"What are you doing, Dad?" Connor asked, chest fluttering with nerves.

"Shut the fuck up and go back to sleep, gay boy." Frank grunted as he braced and lifted Serena from her bed.

"What are you doing?" she asked, voice rapidly changing from sleepy to panicked.

"You and me are going somewhere quiet. Time to start earning the food you eat. You think everything is free in this fucken world?"

Serena tried to get free of him as Frank crossed the room, but he held her tight.

"If you struggle it'll only hurt. Which is fine by me, just by the way!"

Connor stood from bed, Brendan kneeling up on his.

"Dad, don't!" Connor said.

Frank rounded on him, Serena clutched hard against his chest, her eyes wide. "You really wanna do this, fucker?" Frank snarled.

Connor and Brendan moved to stand either side of their father. Connor's knees shook, but he knew he couldn't let Frank leave the room with Serena. "Dad, it's not right! You can't do this!"

"I *can't?* You, of all fucken people, gonna lecture me on what's *right?*"

"He *is* right, Dad!" Brendan said, voice high with pleading. "Don't."

Serena struggled again and Frank growled, crushed her tighter against him. She yelped with pain.

"This fucken mistake," Frank hissed. "This waste of space and money! She has to do something to earn her place. Your mother is saggy and fucked from you lot already, and like a fucken corpse in bed. I deserve better. I deserve something for everything you've all taken from me! A man owns his fucken family and will do with them as he pleases."

He went to stride from the room, but Connor ran to put himself in front of the door.

"Leave her alone!" Connor shouted.

Frank kept Serena against his body with one arm, lashed out with the other to backhand Connor across the face. Connor fell sideways into a chest of drawers, driving a whining pain into his hip. He staggered back to block the way again. Serena cried out and grabbed her father's forearm with both hands and leaned down to bite him, her small teeth clamping into the skin just above the wrist. Frank howled and let her go, went to follow her to ground with a punch but Brendan threw himself in the way and collected his father's bunched knuckles across the top of his head. Brendan took two stutter-steps, legs jellied and sat down hard against the doorframe, blinking rapidly.

Connor put both hands into his dad's chest and shoved the man back, away from Serena, then grabbed his sister and ran from the room. He wasn't sure where he was going, but needed to be out of there, out of a room that suddenly felt like a trap, a prison cell.

Brendan pulled himself up and came after them as Frank roared, hot on his heels. Then Lydia was there, hair in disarray, all five of them stumbling into the lounge room, almost circling each other. Frank snarled, an animal sound of fury.

"What's happening?" Lydia cried. "Stop this!"

"These fucken shits think they can tell me what I can and can't do!" Frank yelled. He lunged for Serena again and she danced sideways, clinging so tightly to Connor's hand that the small bones in it ground together. But he wouldn't let her go, tried to keep himself between her and Frank.

"Do as he asks!" Lydia said, and Connor was appalled at the sorrowful pleading of her tone. "Maybe you need to make him happy, love. Easier for us all."

"Are you fucking kidding?" Brendan said, one hand pressed to his skull, eyes half-winced as he tried to focus.

"Your father might lose his job," Lydia said.

"Don't tell 'em my private fucken business!" Frank yelled and slapped Lydia this time. The sound was high and sharp, like a whip crack.

Lydia made an "Oh!" of surprised pain and sat back heavily into the sofa, dazed.

"We have to go, Mum!" Connor said. "He'll kill us!"

"We'd be on the streets!" Lydia said, sounding drunk herself now. "There's no money. Nowhere to go!"

"And I'd find you and fucken kill you. All of you ungrateful shits!"

"Just be nice to him, please? It'll be all right."

"All right? You think any of this is all right?" Connor said.

"There's nowhere to go!" Lydia sobbed. "We have to survive and survival means doing things we might not like. All of us!"

"You won't like this beating!" Frank said to Connor. "And then I'll have my time with her!" He jabbed one finger at Serena.

Serena cried out. Connor braced himself, then

something rang out, high and hollow-sounding, and Frank staggered forward, eyes glazing. He went down onto one knee, almost in slow motion. Brendan stood behind him, a heavy glass vase in hand. Connor stared. How hadn't that broken?

"Go!" Brendan shouted at him. "Grab some things and take Serena. Go!"

"Bren..."

"I'll follow! Now, while you can."

Frank groaned, swaying as he sank to both knees and dragged a palm over his face. Brendan raised the vase again, ready. Lydia looked on, mouth and eyes wide.

"Come with us!" Connor said. "Quickly. Come on!"

Brendan looked down at their father, then their mother immobile on the couch. He dropped the vase and it bounced, still not breaking, and all three siblings ran back to their room. It took moments to pull on clothes, grab phones and wallets. Serena clutched Ted to her chest, the only plushy toy she'd ever owned, staring at her brothers in terror.

"Where do we go?" she asked in a tiny voice.

"I know somewhere," Connor said, and knew he would never see the dawn. But he would see Serena and Brendan free.

He grabbed her hand and they ran from the house as Frank staggered back into the hallway, roaring in incoherent rage. Brendan slammed the front door behind them as their father's shouts rose in volume, then Lydia started screaming.

"What do we do?" Brendan asked.

"You have to trust me," Connor said. "This is the only way and it's horrible and insane but you and Serena will be free of him."

"What about you?" Serena asked.

"I'll save you. Wait, I need to make a call."

They ran along the street, frequently glancing back but it seemed Frank wasn't giving chase. Connor hoped his mother was taking all the wrath they'd left behind, she deserved nothing less. He tapped on his phone, pleading with her to answer.

"Connor? It's like three in the morning. What's happening?"

"Lauren, thank fuck you answered."

"You're on my emergency call list, even when my phone's on silent. Are you okay?"

"No. We need your help. I have no one else to call."

"Anything, you know that."

"Can you meet us at Carlton Beach? With a car?"

"A car?"

"You told me you sometimes drive your uncle's car on their property. You know how to, right?"

"Well, yeah. But not on the street. And it's illegal. I'm fifteen, Con!"

"I know, but this is really serious. Can you please sneak your dad's car and meet us? I wouldn't ask if it wasn't... well, it's life and death, Loz."

"Fuck. Okay. Okay, I'll be there. Now?"

"We're on our way."

"I'll be there."

They were still running, halfway to Carlton Beach already.

"Slow down," Brendan said, pulling on Connor's arm. "Walk. He's not coming."

They slowed, panting from exertion, three abreast across the footpath with Serena in the middle. She held Connor's left hand and Brendan's right, Ted tucked under her arm.

"What's the plan?" Brendan asked. "This feels... I mean, it feels kinda final. I don't know if we can go back."

"We're not going back. Ever. Any of us."

"You're scaring me," Serena said.

Connor looked down at her, smiled. She was so beautiful and still had so much life to live. He would get her out. "Don't be scared, okay? For the first time ever we can make our own decisions. Please believe me when I say I *want* to do this."

"Do what, bro?" Brendan said.

They reached Tanning Street and turned towards the beach just as a fairly new Subaru Outback slowed alongside them. The passenger window rolled down and Lauren leaned over. "Guys? You getting in?"

Connor had a strange sensation of utter relief and complete finality. He pulled open the back door and ushered Brendan and Serena in, then got in the front passenger seat. "Thank you, Lauren."

"Ride or die, Con-man. Where are we going? What's happened?"

"Burly Road first. There's something I need to do."

"Burly…? Okay. Connor, what's happening."

"Please, I'll explain, but we need to go." He knew Winterbourne would be there. He didn't know how he knew, but it was a certainty.

Lauren drove around the beach and onto Burly Road, her control of the car not exactly smooth, but fairly confident. Sure enough, Winterbourne stood outside the double doors of the old hall. The sign behind him seemed to pulse like an excited heart. He smiled widely.

"Pull up here. I'll be one sec."

"That's the guy we saw," Lauren said.

Brendan leaned forward. "Connor, who's that? What are you doing?"

"Please, trust me. Promise me you'll stay in the car."

"Conn—"

"Promise me!" Connor shouted.

"Shit, okay, okay!"

Connor jumped out and went to Winterbourne.

"Arranged your own lift, I see," the man said, still smiling.

"I give them the money and watch them drive away before we go inside."

"Certainly. Seems eminently sensible." Winterbourne leaned down to see across to the driver's side of the

Subaru. "Got a good friend there, huh?"

"The best."

Winterbourne reached down beside the door and came up with a paper grocery bag, held it out. Connor took it and looked inside. Wads of cash, one hundred dollar bills strapped in bundles of ten thousand. He thumbed through, checking.

"It's all there and it's all legitimate tender," Winterbourne said.

Connor nodded. "Wait there."

"As long as you need."

Connor went back to the car and opened the back door, crouched beside it. He handed the bag over Serena to Brendan. "There's one hundred thousand dollars in there—"

"What the fuck?"

"Bro, shut up and listen, please. I made a deal. You don't need to know the details, but it's worth a hundred K. That's free money. That's get out money. It won't be easy, but you can get far away with that. Safe from Dad."

"What do you mean we can? What about you?"

"I'm not coming." Connor knew they wouldn't go if he told them the truth and quickly added. "Not right away. I have to hold up my end of the bargain here. I'll follow, okay? Lauren, please drive these guys somewhere safe. Enden or even further. Maybe somewhere they can get a train? And Brendan, message me and tell me where you've gone, yeah? And I'll catch up."

"There has to be another way," Lauren said, twisted around in the seat to see them.

"There isn't." Connor pinned Brendan with his gaze. "You think we'll survive another night at home? You think Serena will be even slightly safe? There's no more time. It has to be now."

Brendan nodded, tears on his lower lids. "You're right. But you'll follow!"

"Please," Serena said, shooting forward to grab him in a fierce hug. Her voice was muffled against his shoulder. "Please follow as soon as you can."

"I will." He swallowed, hating the lie. "I promise."

He closed the back door and went around to the driver's side. He opened Lauren's door and gathered her in a hug. "Please see them somewhere safe."

"I will. Then I'm coming back for you, Connor. Do not fuck me around."

"I love you, Lauren. You're a better friend than anyone deserves."

"That's not true. Everyone deserves good friends. I'm lucky to have you." She pushed back, looked him in the eye. "I am coming back for you."

"Okay." He stood, closed her door.

She put down her window. "I'll call, let you know where I drop them."

"Me too," Brendan called from the back.

Connor crouched to look in. "Good. Thanks."

Serena's eyes were wide in the dark, desperate. He smiled at her and felt his lips quivering, but steeled himself to be strong.

"Go!"

Lauren nodded and pulled away as Connor stepped back to let her pass. He watched her make the turn onto Cowpasture Road then sighed, turned back to Winterbourne.

"Brave and smart," Winterbourne said. "Well played."

Played? Like this was a game. Connor felt empty inside, as though his entire being had been scooped out leaving him an ambulatory husk. But he'd done it. Serena and Brendan had money, plenty of money, and were leaving. They had a chance now. As good a chance as possible at a life away from Frank Tucker. Away from Gulpepper.

"Come on then." He walked past Winterbourne, shoved open the hall door and stepped into the abyssal interior, gasping in an acclimatising breath.

The people who had been gathered there before were still present, perhaps even more of them than previously. They sat on their knees in a circle around the profane lectern, the book open to the last page. Behind the lectern was a construction of wooden beams, like a weird bedframe standing at a forty-five-degree angle. Leather straps hung from each corner, and another from the centre.

"You knew I was coming?" Connor asked, not particularly surprised.

"I anticipated it would be tonight. I read the energies, Connor. They tell much."

"So what do I do?" Connor felt strangely unmoved. Not frightened, not even nervous. Simply numb, as though his whole life had been leading inevitably to this. Serena was away, that was all that mattered. With Brendan to take care of her. They would be okay.

Winterbourne gestured to the framework. "Remove your clothes, lie against there and we'll do the rest."

Connor nodded. He took out his phone and sent a message to Lauren, then copied and pasted it to Brendan. It said, *I love you.*

He put the phone back in the pocket of his shorts and started to remove his shirt when the hall door banged open. They spun to see Brendan standing there, face scrunched in discomfort as he squinted into the confusing interior.

Before Connor could say anything, Brendan strode in, gasped, and closed the door behind him. "I'm not stupid, bro. I know you're doing something fucking mad in here. Something final. I could see it in your eyes. It should be me."

"What?"

Winterbourne laughed. "Well, isn't this delicious! Just for the record, either of you will do as you both have the old family blood. That's the key. As long as the sacrifice is willing, that is."

Brendan nodded. "Sacrifice? I knew it. This fucking town, Connor."

"Bren, please. This is something I need to do."

"No, it's not. I need to do it. I'm the oldest."

"Don't pull that shit with me—"

"And Serena needs you more than me. I made her and Lauren promise to wait in the car. You and Serena, you've got something special. Something I never had. And what the fuck would I ever amount to, huh? I'm destined to be no better than fucking Frank. But you! And Serena. You both have potential. And you have Lauren. I have a gang of stoned fuck ups who won't even notice if I stop showing up. Please, Connor."

Connor stared at his brother, confused, conflicted. Brendan walked up and grabbed him in a crushing hug. "This way I make something of my life, Con. I make a future for you and Serena. That's more than I can ever do otherwise."

"But—"

"But nothing. Isn't that what you thought you were doing for us? But I'm no good at anything else."

"You could be!"

"But you already *are*. Serena has her best chance with you. You know that. Please."

Without waiting for a reply, he let go and walked around the book, heading for the frame. "I don't know what the fuck is going on here, but I'm guessing it's this thing?"

Winterbourne gestured with one upraised palm. "Indeed. Please, remove your clothes and lay back. So you understand, I need to take a section of your skin and kill you. Do you consent?"

Brendan barked a laugh. "Fucking hell, mate. This is more fucked up than I thought. I consent, but only if you let him leave first."

"He'll be allowed to leave whenever he likes."

"Connor, please. Go."

Connor licked his lips, shook his head. He hated it, but Brendan was right. Connor and Serena had always been close. They would never make her choose, but if they forced the issue, she would likely pick Connor. He was furious that Brendan was right about it. "I'll go," he said, voice cracking. "But not yet. If you're doing this, I stay. I need to witness."

Brendan nodded, then stripped off his shorts and shirt, stood barefoot in nothing but threadbare boxer shorts.

"Please," Winterbourne said, gesturing again.

Brendan laid back against the frame and Winterbourne strapped his wrists and ankles to the corners, splaying the young man like a star, then cinched the central strap tight across Brendan's hips. He held out a short length of wood. "Bite down on this?"

Brendan took it in his teeth, breathing shallow and rapid through his nose.

"This will hurt," Winterbourne said. "It will hurt a lot. But I will be as quick as I can. Ready?"

Brendan nodded, then locked eyes with Connor.

"I love you, Brendan," Connor said, tears running over his cheeks. "Thank you."

Brendan held his brother's eye as Winterbourne produced a shining silver blade with a black stone handle and made a rapid incision across Brendan's chest, just below the collar bones. Brendan screamed around the wooden gag in his teeth, eyes scrunching shut. Connor gasped, crying harder. Winterbourne made three more rapid cuts, two vertical and then another across the belly, a blood-soaked rectangle marked out on Brendan's chest.

Winterbourne turned to one side and slipped the point of his knife under the upper left corner of the marked section and began expertly flaying it away from the muscle beneath, muscle that gleamed, shiny and almost black under the undulating green light filling the hall.

Brendan's screams came in waves and he stared, his gaze drilling into Connor's mind. "I love you! I love you!" Connor said over and over again.

Winterbourne worked rapidly, lifting the skin from

top left to bottom right, the large flap held taut as he worked along underneath it. Brendan's chest pumped in rapid gasps, but he didn't faint, even as his blood flooded his legs. When there was only an inch or so of the skin rectangle still connected, Winterbourne shouted a series of staccato, evil-sounding words and in one quick motion plunged the knife directly down into Brendan's heart. As Brendan howled and arched up against his bonds, Winterbourne severed the last connecting section of skin, the flap of it coming free as Brendan collapsed and lay still.

Connor sobbed. "You evil piece of shit! You fucking evil son of a bitch. Believe this! I will come back for you. One day you will pay dearly for what you've done. What you've made us do."

He stared one moment longer at his dead brother, then ran from the hall. Lauren and Serena were in the car outside, faces masks of worry in the dark. They both smiled when they saw him, then frowned when they realised he was alone. Connor jumped into the car, doing nothing to wipe the tears from his face.

"Drive."

"It's just you?" Lauren said.

"Just me. Brendan saved us. Please, drive."

Serena cried quietly in the back but reached through between the seats to take his hand. Connor gripped her small, warm fingers tightly.

"He saved us," he said again. "Brendan saved us."

"Where to?" Lauren asked.

"Anywhere out of The Gulp."

The Gulpepper Institute of Health and Wellbeing

The Gulpepper Institute of Health and Wellbeing

Elise Griffin, known to the world as Eevie Chill, looked up at the façade of the Gulpepper Institute of Health and Wellbeing and wondered what the hell she was doing. She'd never heard of the place before Michael booked her in. Shit, she'd never even heard of Gulpepper, the weirdly isolated harbour town that had seemed to birth itself from thick bush as the hired limo emerged from a tunnel of old growth forest and the ocean suddenly sparkled ahead of them, the surprisingly large town spread out before it.

She'd been up and down the coast of New South Wales and Victoria dozens of times since she was a kid, passed Enden and Monkton frequently enough, but had no idea this place existed. Of course, she'd spent less and less time in Australia since her meteoric rise, but still... Weird she'd never heard of the place.

"The Institute is brand new," Michael assured her effusively two days before. "State of the art, amazing facilities. It was only opened a little over eighteen months ago, exclusive clientele. It wasn't easy to get you a spot, I can tell you that. Or cheap! But money is no object with our girl, right? We need to make sure we do all we can to get you rested and back to firing on all cylinders."

It was her money her manager had spent, of course, the amount of which had become embarrassingly hard to imagine in recent years. One thing she never needed to worry about again, at least. The man garbled on, talking about exhaustion and overwork, but Eevie wasn't fooled. She was falling apart. Michael was terrified because it was clear she was in the throes of a significant mental health breakdown, an unstoppable downward spiral, and he saw profits potentially going down with her. But, to his credit, he'd found this place and perhaps what she needed *was* some isolation and pampering. Some rehabilitation. Fuck, she just needed to be *off* for a while. Michael was her manager because she made him a shit ton of cash, so even if he was only protecting his own income, it still benefitted her. Didn't it?

Did she really want to keep doing this stuff? It was all so removed from the love of music that motivated her originally. That got her noticed. Now the stadiums, the interviews, the blockbuster movies. It was all so artificial. Ten years ago, eighteen-year-old Eevie Chill would have laughed and derided the person she'd become. Perhaps that was part of what she might figure out in this place. Who the fuck she really was. She didn't *need* to do anything ever again, but what might she *want* to do? Could she go back to the source of her love, the music without the superstardom? The goth and metal chick she'd been? Well, that was uncertain. Crawl into a hole and never come out was all she wanted right now, so maybe this fancy new institute could be that. For a little while.

"You sure it's not just another over-expensive clinic for rich junkies?" she'd asked Michael.

He'd laughed, wobbled a level hand back and forth a little. "Look, it's not *not* that. But it's not *only* that! There are some wealthy recovering addicts among the residents, sure. I was able to get that much out of them, past all their confidentiality bullshit. But no absolute losers. All functioning people in need of space. In need of a break, some therapy, some healthy living and recuperation. Just the same as you! And this place being new and in such an out of the way place? Well, that's fortuitous, right? A good find. You're guaranteed anonymity. No paparazzi anywhere near you."

Eevie sighed. She really wanted a drink already, but of course it was a dry institution. The booze was one of her problems. One of her crutches. She'd managed to stay largely away from anything worse, notwithstanding a fair amount of weed, a line of coke here and there.

Nothing too heavy, nothing injected and nothing regular. Except the booze. That had become a habit.

She'd be okay. This would be good. She'd keep telling herself that and maybe, possibly, perhaps it might turn out to be true.

"Fucking Michael," she muttered.

There was a crunch of gravel as the limo that had delivered her turned on the wide driveway and headed back out of town. Back to civilisation, she couldn't help thinking. Talking of civilised… She pulled out her phone and tapped the screen alive. No signal. Of course there was no fucking signal here at the arse end of nowhere. Getting on the institute's Wi-Fi would be a priority. Social media was another crutch, though her social media team had managed that mostly for her in recent months. Eighteen-year-old Eevie would have laughed aloud at that too, a social media *team*. A whole fucking team, creating "content". It was so gross. But she needed to keep on top of her personal email at least, and stay connected to the few genuine friends she had. Not the fucking parasites like Michael, riding her like a show pony. But the handful of actual friends, who cared about her. She would stay connected with them. Well, some of them. A couple, maybe? Fuck it, Sonja, at least. If she had no one else, she would always have her little sister, and Sonja would always have her back.

"What a fuck up you are, Eevie," she said, voice gravelly with emotion. "What a waste of fucking space. All that talent and nothing but heartache."

She stepped back from the building to look around, get her bearings. The Institute was on the southernmost end of the town, she knew that. Thick bush rose up behind it, only neatly manicured lawns between the building and wilderness that continued who knew how far south. All the way to Monkton, presumably. The Institute occupied a pretty desirable block of land, overlooking most of the town to the north. A couple of blocks west was one of the main roads through town, that they'd driven up to get here. To the east the land rose up a little more and Eevie knew it went past some houses and a small sports oval and eventually to Jacquelin Head and the town's cemetery. She'd looked up that much on the way down from Sydney, to get some idea of where she was going. She would enjoy a walk up there at some point. For all her mainstream success, Eevie was a goth chick at heart and always would be. Hanging out in cemeteries was her jam. Jet black hair, always wearing tight-fitting black clothes, her signature black leather fingerless gloves. She knew she was a cliché, but she owned that. Embraced it. She felt a little naked without her gloves on now, but needed to be more Elise and less Eevie for a little while. Black jeans and t-shirts were non-negotiable, though. Those things were Elise since well before Elise became Eevie.

She quite liked the idea of a walk now. No matter how luxurious the limo had been, spending hours cooped up in a car always made her feel seedy. The hint of a sea breeze reached her as she stood among small rose gardens and the thought of standing on cliffs overlooking the vastness of the ocean appealed. She could check in later, right?

"Ms Chill! Welcome! Or would you prefer Ms Griffin?"

Ah, fuck it. Always rely on people to interrupt a good thought. She turned back to the Institute and saw a man standing there, tall and dapper in a three-piece grey suit and red cravat. His hair was bone white, but he didn't seem old. The phrase "indeterminate middle-age" fluttered around her mind for a moment. "Hello. Eevie is fine, thanks." She hated Ms anything. More than one expensive therapist had told her Eevie was a mask she wore to protect herself but so what if it was? Had recent years not proven that masks were fucking effective. Perhaps she would drop it during her stay, but old habits and all that. More to think about while she "rested" here at the Institute.

"Eevie. So glad you could join us. I'm sure we'll be everything you hoped for and more. I'm Winterbourne."

"Right. You run this place?"

Winterbourne laughed, but she had no idea why what she'd asked was funny. "No, no. I'm more a silent partner in things here. I set up the institute, financed and organised it, if you like. I leave the running of it to people eminently more qualified for the task."

"Okay. Why would you finance something like this?"

"Call it a public service. Giving something back."

Eevie frowned, not buying it. "You have some massive wealth and want to give back to the people who helped make you rich, so you set up an exclusive clinic only the extremely wealthy could ever afford?" She was always going to be a working-class girl at heart, embarrassed by her success.

Winterbourne laughed again. "So cynical! Yes, our fees reflect our service, but we also take certain pro bono residents and people admitted through various reciprocal agreements. It's not all about profit, I assure you. Although profit is, of course, also a strong motivator."

Assure me all you like, I don't fucking believe you. Whatever. Eevie was used to this kind of bullshit. Spend enough time around music, film and TV like she had and peoples' justifications for their atrocities started coming thick and fast. It appalled her just how many people in the world were selfish and greedy. She refused to become like them. Perhaps that's partly what made her so crazy these last few months. Well, look at that. Little insights already and she hadn't even entered the building yet.

Winterbourne stepped back and gestured inside. Her single suitcase stood on the cement footpath beside her and she sighed, pulled up the extendable handle, and headed for the double glass sliding doors with *Gulpepper Institute* written across them in swirling gold calligraphic script.

She entered a space like the lobby of a high-end hotel, all velvet sofas and armchairs, glittering chandeliers, walls painted in muted pastels. More double sliding doors like the main entrance led away from the back of the space. A desk sat in one corner and a well-presented young woman sat behind it. She had blonde hair cut in a neat bob and plastered on a huge smile, cheeks rounding out like rosy apples, as Eevie entered. "Welcome! It's so good to have you here. I can't tell a lie, I'm a huge fan."

Eevie sucked in a breath. Fans were the last thing she needed. Absolute anonymity would be ideal, but she thought perhaps she'd never know that again.

"But let me assure you, that won't affect your stay," the young woman went on quickly. "I'm Adele."

Wearing your alt text on your face again, Eevie.

"Nice to meet you, Adele. You need me to sign in or anything?"

Adele swept around her desk carrying a clipboard and pen. No cheap biro, either, but an expensive-looking metal Parker. "All the paperwork has been taken care of by..." She paused, looked at the papers clipped to the board.

"Michael?"

"That's right! I just need a signature at the bottom here, legal name, to confirm your arrival and adherence to the terms of residency. Of course, if you'd like to read through everything before signing, please choose a comfortable spot. I'll be at my desk." She handed Eevie the clipboard and pen.

Eevie took it, shook her head. "Whatever, it's all good." She signed Elise Griffin on the dotted line and handed it back.

Adele smiled, put the clipboard on her desk and gestured to a hallway. "Then I'll show you to your room."

"An absolute pleasure to meet you, Eevie," Winterbourne said. "I'll leave you in Adele's capable hands, but I wanted to welcome you personally."

"Right. Thanks." Eevie paused, saw something flash behind Winterbourne's eyes. Not actual movement, but the sensation of something deeper and altogether unpleasant. She sensed a malevolence briefly, like a bad smell wafting off the man, then it passed.

Winterbourne smiled, gave a slight bow, and left through the sliding front doors. Eevie watched him walk out across the driveway and head west. When she looked back, Adele was waiting patiently.

"Weird dude," Eevie said, jabbing a thumb back over her shoulder.

"We don't see him very often. Interesting he came to meet you personally." Adele paused, thinking. "You know, it's only the third time I've ever seen him in person and I've worked here since the Institute opened."

"Well, that's not very long, is it?"

"A little over a year and a half. So no, not long. This way?"

Adele led Eevie through the double glass doors at the back of the reception area into a wide corridor running left and right, quiet with plush carpet and tasteful sconced lighting. Directly opposite were another pair of doors.

"Communal lounge and dining area through there," Adele said.

It reminded Eevie again of a fancy hotel, fine furniture everywhere. One end was all tables and chairs, with neat white tablecloths and silver cutlery already laid out. The other end was velvet and leather, armchairs and sofas. No bar, Eevie noted.

"Everyone eats together?" she asked.

"Your choice. You're welcome to take your meals in your room or here with whoever else might feel like socialising."

"Right." Eevie saw doors on the far side of the room leading outside. "The gardens are that way?"

"That's right. Lovely and peaceful."

"Right."

"This way."

Adele went to one end of the corridor where it opened into a T-junction. She turned right. At the end of the short passage was what seemed like another, much smaller communal area with easy chairs and occasional tables. Off this were three doors. The entire institute was a single storey, Eevie realised, symmetrical with the lobby front and centre, everywhere with high ceilings and lots of open spaces.

"This is you," Adele said, indicating a door on the right marked with a shiny brass number three.

Eevie paused, looked around. "How many rooms are there?"

"In total? Just twelve. Three here, and three more that way." Adele pointed to the other end of the T-junction. "And the same on the other side of the institute."

"Exclusive."

"The Institute is about the quality of its services, not the volume."

"Right. We passed other doors coming here that weren't marked with numbers."

"Treatment or consultation rooms. And there's a gym, lap pool and spa baths, sauna."

"Treatment?"

"We cater to all kinds of needs here, so yes, sometimes treatments from in-house or freelance professionals. Therapy, massage, exercise and so on."

"Right."

Adele held a pass card to a metal plate on the door marked *3* and a green light pinged on. She opened the door and held it for Eevie. The room inside was opulent, they were certainly getting their money's worth. A huge king size bed stood in the middle of one wall. There were bedside tables with lamps, ivory-coloured shades and heavy, square porcelain bases. A desk and chair, built-in wardrobe, big screen TV mounted on the wall with a bar fridge beneath. Tea and coffee making things sat on top of the fridge. A couple of big armchairs to one side.

Another door led into a bathroom with a decent-sized spa bath as well as shower stall, toilet and sink. On one side of the room a tall window gave a view out onto the gardens and the thick bush beyond.

"Nice," Eevie said, feeling like it was an insulting understatement.

"Hopefully you'll be comfortable here." Adele pointed to one bedside table where a landline phone sat. "Dial nine for the front desk. There's someone there twenty-four seven and they'll organise anything you need."

Eevie waved a finger left and right. "Who are my neighbours?"

Adele smiled, pointed right. "That's the kitchen, but don't worry. The walls are thick and you won't hear a thing through them. All the rooms are soundproofed for your comfort." She gestured left. "Room two is currently unoccupied."

"Right." Was it annoying Adele as much as her that she kept saying *Right* in response to everything? But what else was there to say? Everything seemed so... organised.

"It's just after four, so you have a little under an hour until dinner. It's available from five until eight every evening. Just come on through to the dining room after five or dial nine and order for your room here. Look in the bedside drawer for a menu. Breakfast is available between six and nine, again, in the dining room or you can order room service. Then there's a general menu available all day and night for simpler things. You know sandwiches, stuff like that. Anything else you need?"

"No, I'm good, thanks." More than good, really. This place was something else. Eevie wondered if her embarrassing wealth was enough to stay forever. She could get used to this combination of comfort and isolation.

Adele nodded, then handed Eevie the pass card and slipped quietly out, closing the door behind her. Eevie parked her suitcase in one corner and sat on the end of the bed. "Well, bitch. Now what?"

Her mind went into a kind of fugue state for a little while. What Eevie had come to refer to as her shutdowns. Sometimes the world and its demands on her got too much and her thoughts flatlined. It was deliberate and she welcomed the ability at first, used it as a way to disconnect. To find some mental peace in otherwise hectic environments. When it started happening without her conscious consent, during recording sessions or a on a movie set, well, then it was less welcome.

Her therapist had been concerned when Eevie explained she deliberately dissociated as a survival mechanism. The woman had frowned, said, "Dissociation can be anything from mild emotional detachment to a more harsh disconnection from both physical and emotional experiences. Eventually a complete detachment from reality if you're not careful."

"And what's so special about reality?" Eevie had asked. "It's a pretty fucked up place a lot of the time." She was keenly aware of her privilege, her insane levels of success with platinum records and movies alongside Hollywood's hottest stars. She *was* one of Hollywood's hottest stars, for fuck's sake, her fee was eye-watering. Embarrassing. But it was all so fucking puerile. So vapid and empty. Why not disconnect from it?

"The thing is," her therapist had said. "You risk disconnecting not only from your thoughts and feelings, but from your sense of identity. Who you really are."

"And who the hell am I really?"

And wasn't that the root of it all? Who the hell was Eevie Chill? Who was Elise Griffin? Did either of them really exist? Eevie was a creation, a concept, a fucking product. But had Eevie swallowed Elise whole?

Eevie blinked, realised she'd had a shutdown for a fair while there. Glancing at the bedside clock she saw it was nearly six. She was hungry, but the last thing she wanted was company. Who here might recognise her? What other residents might there be in the dining room with their own problems? She grabbed the phone and dialled nine.

"Hello, Eevie. How can I help?"

"Hey, Adele, I need some food."

"It's Icelynn actually. Adele's finished for today."

"Oh, right, sorry. Wait, you sound exactly like her. And you know my name."

"The desk shows the name and room number of whoever is calling. And do we really sound so alike?"

Eevie's ear was never wrong. She'd started her professional career at sixteen but had been a musician since she was three, picking out songs on the piano no one else touched. Her parents had been amazed, started testing her ability by playing records and asking her to repeat them. Which she did. It quickly became apparent she was a musical prodigy. She could hear and recreate any tune with a single listen, had absolute pitch and a singing voice her first vocal tutor had called "beyond angelic". In all honesty, all that had been the start of her problems. She would give it all up, the voice, the money, the movies, the fame, for a normal life. Whatever the fuck a normal life might be. Maybe there was no such thing. Then again, would she really give it up? Singing used to bring her such joy. She wanted that simplicity back. She wanted that joy again.

"Eevie, are you still there?"

"Yeah, sorry. And yeah, you have the exact same pitch and timbre. Are you fucking with me, Adele?"

The woman on the other end laughed. "No, I promise I'm Icelynn."

What sort of name was that anyway? "Right. Okay. Well, I'd like to order dinner. Can I get a burger and chips? I feel like junk food."

"Of course, no problem. Any special requests for the burger?"

"Cheeseburger, salad, no bacon or egg. And no beetroot."

No beetroot was un-Australian, her Irish-heritage

Australian father had proclaimed, appalled that she wouldn't have it. But screw that, it was just weird. She'd never understood that about Australians and their burgers, and her Japanese-born mother agreed. Maybe she was more her mother's child than her father's but it was his wonderful voice she'd inherited. Her mother's singing was like cats fucking.

"No problem," Icelynn said. "Someone will bring it by shortly."

"Thanks."

While she waited, Eevie got undressed and took a shower, washing off the journey and the day so far. She was in a robe and drying her shoulder-length straight black hair—a goth affectation requiring no effort thanks to her mother's heritage—when there came a knock at the door. She opened it and found a trolley outside with a covered silver dish on it, but no one in sight. Did they leave it and literally run away?

Eevie shrugged and wheeled it inside, the aroma hitting her instantly. She realised she was ravenous and tucked in with abandon. It was one of the best burgers she'd ever had, and not only because she was so hungry. As she ate, she realised she still hadn't hooked up with the local Wi-Fi. She needed to tell Sonja about this place, let her sister know she'd arrived safely.

She finished up, put the trolley back just outside her door and went to the bedside phone again, dialled nine.

"Hello, Eevie. Was your dinner okay?"

"Brilliant, thanks. Really good."

"Great. How can I help?"

"Couple of things. I need the Wi-Fi password and my phone has no reception here. What do I dial from this phone for an outside line?"

"Oh, I'm sorry. There isn't any Wi-Fi here. And the phones are in-house only."

Eevie stopped, stunned for a moment. Then, "Wait, what? There's no Wi-Fi?"

"No, there's not, sorry. Contact with the outside

world while undergoing a stay at the Institute isn't allowed."

"Isn't *allowed*? What the fuck is that supposed to mean?"

"Please don't shout. Aggression against staff isn't tolerated under Institute policy."

Eevie gasped a breath, physically biting back a sharp response. She hadn't even been shouting. Okay, take a second here. She breathed once more then tried again. "Contact with the outside world?" she asked, modulating her tone as much as she was able.

"That's right. When you signed in, you agreed to the Institute's policy of complete immersion in your treatment."

Eevie's mind flashed back to the clipboard Adele had handed her.

I just need a signature at the bottom here, legal name, to confirm your arrival and adherence to the terms of residency.

"So you're saying I can't call anyone or use the internet in any way while I'm here?"

"That's correct. It's Institute—"

"Institute policy, right. Okay, thanks."

"You're welcome. Call any time for anything."

"Will do." Eevie hung up. How about I call and ask to use your cell phone, Icelynn? How about I punch your stupid, super polite face? No contact at all with the outside world? That was insane, and unacceptable.

Well, Eevie Chill hadn't been successful by following rules. She was the metal chick who got super mainstream popular. She was the Japanese-Australian who bombarded Hollywood's blonde-haired, blue-eyed stereotype and took all their awards. She would go into town in the morning and get a new sim card for her phone, simple as that. Ask around for the best service provider for this arsehole of Australia and get fucking connected.

They would let her outside, right? A shiver passed

through her, the opulent room suddenly felt oppressive. Malevolent. No, they would have to let her out, surely. Screw waiting until morning, she would go now.

She got dressed again and left her room, carrying only her phone, wallet and the pass card for her door. She went back along the corridor to where the two sets of sliding glass double-doors faced each other. The ones to her left led into the dining and lounge area. She noticed a couple of people in there, one big guy with his back to her, someone else further in, obscured by shadow, but paid them no further mind. She walked to the doors opposite, that led into the main reception lobby. She stopped in front of them when they didn't slide open.

She stepped back then forward again, looking above for the sensor, but there was nothing there. No buttons on the walls either, just a metal panel like beside her room door. She swiped her pass card at it. It beeped but the small light remained red.

Eevie's heart rate ticked up, a mix of fear and rage starting to roil inside her. If she went close to the doors and looked sidelong, she could just make out the reception desk tucked into one corner, but couldn't see the person behind it. She knew Icelynn was there, though. She banged the side of one fist against the glass, called out, "Hey! Hey, you there?"

There was a moment of movement as whoever was behind the desk stood to look over it at the doors, just a glimpse of brunette hair, then gone again.

Eevie banged again, harder. "Hey! I saw you! Open this door, please!"

"The doors can't be opened from your side."

Eevie jumped back, looked around for the source of the voice, but no one was there.

"Please return to your room or make use of the lounge facilities. To your left at the end of the corridor is a fully equipped gym, spa and sauna if you have a desire for exercise or relaxation."

Eevie realised the voice was coming from speakers somewhere in the corridor ceiling. Maybe built in around the concealed lighting somehow? "Can you hear me, Icelynn?"

"Yes, of course."

"I need you to open this door right now."

"I'm afraid that's not possible, I—"

"Open this fucking door, Icelynn!"

"Please don't shout. Aggression against staff isn't tolerated under Institute policy."

"Fuck Institute policy! I need to go outside!"

"Contact with the outside world while undergoing a stay at the Institute isn't allowed, as agreed when you signed the Institute's policy of complete immersion in your treatment."

Eevie paused, taking a moment to draw a few long, deep breaths before the dizziness creeping in at the edges of her vision took over. "Icelynn, I need to go outside right now."

"Someone is coming to help you calm down."

"What?"

From the other end of the corridor, two men rounded the corner and walked towards her. They both wore dark blue pants and white shirts with *Gulpepper Institute* embroidered over the breast pocket. One of them had a thick seventies porn-style moustache. They were both quite large and they smiled. But Eevie knew smiles like that and they meant nothing good.

Eevie backed away, palms held out in front of her. "Stay the fuck away from me!"

"It's okay, Ms," the one with the moustache said. "We're here to help."

"You stay the fuck away! I don't need any help."

"You're agitated and we can assist with that."

They moved slightly apart, clearly intending to come at her from each side. The wide corridor would make it easy for them to surround her. The one with moustache moved his hand and she saw he held a syringe. Her heart lurched. Should she run for her room? She pictured it, the big window leading out to the neat gardens.

"I'm going, okay? I'm going back to my room, so keep your fucking distance!"

"Please don't shout. Aggression against staff isn't tolerated under Institute policy."

Rage blossomed behind Eevie's eyes, but she forced it down.

Icelynn's voice came over the hidden speakers again. "Emil, do you require further assistance?"

The man who'd spoken, who carried the syringe, smiled more widely. "No, everything is in hand."

They got closer and he reached forward, like he planned to grasp Eevie's upper arm with his free hand.

She turned and ran, around the corner and back to her door. Her hand shook as she held the pass card against the lock and it seemed to take far too long for the green light to ping on, but it finally did. She ran inside and slammed the door behind her, glimpsing the two orderlies only a couple of metres behind. She turned, planning to turn the deadlock, to hook up the security chain. All hotels had that stuff. But of course, there wasn't anything like it. Because this wasn't a hotel.

Eevie stilled, heard footsteps outside approach the door and stop. Were the men just standing there? She backed away, looking for something heavy, anything she might use to defend herself if they opened the door. There was nothing to stop them having a duplicate pass card, or some kind of master card. And no way for her to prevent their entry.

She grabbed the back of a heavy armchair and hauled it over, wedged it hard against the door. It wouldn't stop them for long, but it would slow them. After a few moments more she heard a soft scuffing as they moved away.

Eevie dragged a hand over her face, took more long breaths. What the actual fuck? She went over to the window, but knew before she got there it wouldn't open.

It was solid, fixed in the frame. Because of course it was.

"Fuck this."

She took the straight-backed chair from the desk and swung it with all the strength she could muster into the glass. It rang with a bassy, resonant sound but didn't even flex. Two of the chair's legs snapped though.

Eevie threw the chair to the floor and sat on the end of her bed. Her mind raced, but she felt the shutdown coming. Unbidden, unrequired, but she was powerless to stop it. Whenever Eevie Chill's life began to slip from her control, a shutdown came. Wasn't that a large part of why she was here in the first place?

Eevie stood on a beach looking out over a churning ocean. Heavy clouds occluded the sky, deep grey and purples swirling. A strong wind brought with it the screech of gulls and the sonorous tolling of some distant bell. The waves increased, began to whip and spray. She slipped, the beach rocky and covered in some thick, black slime that made footing treacherous. A cry rang out, deafening and everywhere at once as the clouds split open. Eevie screamed at those fathomless rents in the sky, but her voice was the howl of the wind. Then things began to fall, many-limbed, writhing, tumbling. Something in the depths below the falling creatures heaved up, like a giant maw opening to receive all that fell. Eevie screamed again, formless fear chewing at her insides, and woke with a start.

The room lights were still on and she'd fallen back onto the bed. She shook, from the memory of the dream and what had happened before it. She crawled back more fully onto the bed, terrified, and dragged the covers over her. As she began to slip back to sleep, she saw the armchair she'd moved to block the door had been returned to its spot in the corner.

She woke again with a ringing in her ears and realised it was the bedside phone. She picked it up, groggy. "What?"

"Good morning, Eevie. I trust you slept well."

"Adele?"

"That's right. I wanted to let you know—"

"I want to leave. I'm done here. I'm going."

"I'm afraid that's not possible. By the terms of the agreement you signed—"

"Fuck the agreement!"

"Please try to remain calm. Aggression against staff isn't tolerated under Institute policy."

Eevie ground her teeth. If she heard that phrase just once more... "Look, Adele, I know you're only doing your job, right? I get it. But surely you can see this isn't okay. You're holding me against my will."

"Not at all. We have the signed agreement consenting to the Institute's methodology. That's why I'm calling. You're late for your session."

"My... what?"

"You have a nine a.m. with Doctor Sleeson. It's ten past nine. Someone will be there to collect you momentarily."

"What session?"

"Your first therapy session. As per the agreement. I see you're already dressed, so you're good to go."

"What? You can fucking see me?"

"The desk chair will be replaced while you're in therapy."

"What?"

A knock at the door startled Eevie and she missed the click of Adele hanging up, but the dial tone left no doubt the call was over. She scanned the room, looking for cameras or anything that might conceal a lens. Watching her in her room surely had to be illegal. Just what the fuck had she signed?

The knocking came again, more insistent. She went to the door, side-eyeing the armchair. Who had been in her room while she slept? Was it that moustachioed arsehole? Emil, Icelynn had called him. She knew a predatory piece of shit when she saw one. She'd had to work around them her entire life. Every industry she touched was lousy with the fuckers. The knock came again.

"I'm coming, shit!"

She opened the door and Emil stood there. She took a couple of quick strides back, heart racing, but he remained where he was, smiling.

"If you'd like to come with me, Ms Griffin."

Using her legal name felt somehow like an insult. An assault. It was a power play, Emil pointing out he knew her personal details. Could he watch her room at night too? What about the bathroom, were there cameras there? She decided to assume she was always on display, like some fucked up Big Brother house. She needed to escape.

She looked around the room, decided her case could stay there, but she she'd take her handbag with wallet, phone, a few essentials.

"You won't need that, Elise."

First names now, huh? "You can call me Eevie and I'll take what the fuck I want."

"Your name is Elise and you will leave that behind."

"The fuck I will, you don't get to—"

Emil strode into the room so fast she barely barked a noise of shock before he'd grabbed her, turned her back against his chest and locked one arm around her neck. The crook of his elbow crushed into her throat, made her gasp. With his free hand he snatched the bag from her and threw it onto the bed, then marched her forward. "You'll do as you're fucking told, bitch," he snarled in her ear. His stubble rasped her cheek, his breath a mix of tobacco and something savoury, cloying.

"Fuck offa me!" Eevie yelled, scrabbling at his arm. She braced, drove an elbow back into his ribs and stamped back onto his foot at the same time. It was ineffective against the big bastard, he had been ready for it.

Emil grunted, laughed, and grabbed around her waist with his other arm. One at her neck and one around her middle, he hoisted her off her feet and carried her forward.

"Stop struggling or I'll ram your head into the fucking wall!"

Despite the threat, she still had her arms free and reached out, bracing against either side of the doorframe as he tried to carry her through it. She thrashed in his grasp, did anything to make it harder for him to hold on. With a noise of frustration, Emil dropped her legs down, then let go of her neck and shoved her forward. As she clipped against the door jamb, just managing to move her head aside from an impact, he slapped her. Hard.

She tasted blood from her lower lip as stars burst through her vision. She stumbled, knees weakening, but refused to go down. Emil grabbed her again, around her ribs, pinning her arms against her body, and lifted her. He was much larger and her feet cycled uselessly in the air as he walked down the corridor to one of the doors Adele had said was a treatment room. He used his foot to knock and the door was opened by a man who appeared to be in late middle age wearing a tweed suit. He wore round, wire-rimmed glasses and was bald on top, with a ragged, grey ponytail behind. He smiled, completely unbothered by the method of Eevie's delivery.

"Ah, Ms Griffin. Do come in."

"Let me fucking go!"

Emil dumped her into the room and stepped back, closing the door quickly behind him. Eevie immediately ran for it, grabbed the handle just as something clicked on the other side. She rattled the door, but it was locked.

"Let me out of here!"

"Please calm yourself."

"Fuck calm! I want out."

"There's only one way out, Ms Griffin, and that's through."

"Through what?"

"The process. The treatment. Please, sit. We have a lot to discuss."

Eevie turned, stared at the man. "You're a man of what? Science? Medicine? Can't you see what's happening here? You can't possibly approve of this."

"I'm Doctor Sleeson. I have opinions about some of the Institute's methods, but I only control what happens in this room. So, shall we?"

Eevie swallowed, tried to calm her ragged breathing and hammering heart. "Shall we fucking what?"

"You've been in therapy before, yes? Let's just start by having a seat. Calm down. Let's talk."

"Tell me to calm down once more and I'll rip your fucking face off." She jabbed a thumb back over her shoulder. "He's a big, dumb brute, but what are you? Sixty kilos soaking wet? I'll tear that stupid fucking ponytail off and make you eat it, cunt."

Sleeson's hand lifted almost involuntarily towards his hair and he winced slightly. Eevie had a pang of sorrow for the man's obvious hurt. Was he really so easy to wound? She narrowed her eyes. Was he as much a prisoner here as she was? "Please," the doctor said. "Take a seat. I have green tea, would you like some? Let's talk."

The room had no window, just a desk and two chairs. The chairs were white leather armchairs, but small and angular, not especially comfortable-looking. Knowing she had little choice, confused, scared, Eevie sat. She needed time to think. "Sure. I like green tea."

Sleeson smiled, genuine and warm. "Excellent! I get some very good stuff from a Chinese friend of mine. Geoffrey Wong, he runs the newsagency here in town. Still has family in China and they send stuff over. None of your Australian supermarket rubbish here, eh?"

"Are you for fucking real?"

"Oh, very real indeed." Sleeson poured two cups of tea from a terracotta pot. It had a stylised Asian dragon of some kind carved into it and the cups were handleless white porcelain, brushworked cherry trees on the sides. He handed her one, almost reverentially.

Eevie took the cup and the aroma rose to meet her.

It was good, something floral and clean about it. Sleeson smiled as she sipped. It was delicious. He took a sip or two of his own, then set it aside and picked up a tablet, tapped the screen alive.

"I know the conditions under which you've entered therapy here, Ms Griffin. But why don't you tell me, in your own words, what's going on for you right now?"

"Eevie."

"Excuse me?"

"My name is Eevie Chill." The tea was really good.

"Your stage name is Eevie Chill. That's what it says on your album covers and movie credits. But your *name* is Elise Griffin. Hmm? There's great power in names."

"Which is why I want you to use my chosen name, not the one my parents gave me."

"Ah, exercising your power that way, hmm? But isn't it dangerous to deny the truth of who you are?"

"The fuck do you know about who I truly am?" Eevie licked her lips. They tingled. Her tongue felt a little swollen. And was she slurring slightly? She looked in horror at the teacup she held, then threw it aside. It bounced on the pale carpet without breaking. "You fucking... You drank it too!"

"Oh, the tea is perfectly fine. The drug was already in the cup before I poured."

"You piece of shit." Her words slurred further and dizziness crept around the edges of her mind. Her legs were leaden and she knew she wouldn't be able to stand if she tried.

"There's no hiding here, Elise. No artifice, no Hollywood special effects, no remix from the producer. Here is only unvarnished, stark truth."

"Fuck you."

"Who are you?"

"Fuck. You."

"Who *are* you, hmm?"

"Stop fucking humming, you shitstain. Fuck you." She was dizzy and numb, slurring and blurred at the edges, but seemed to have plateaued. Instead of going unconscious like she'd expected, it seemed the effect had reached its desired stage. Docile, helpless, but communicative. She tried to raise a hand, if nothing else to flip this arsehole off, but her arm only moved slightly then flopped back onto the arm of the chair.

"Why are you here, Elise?"

"You know what? Because the world is a fucking parasite. Because this bullshit industry I'm in is a parasite. Because I chased my dreams and I caught them and they were a fucking lie."

Sleeson smiled. "Now we're getting somewhere." He leaned forward and something about his face changed. Like soft clay, it shifted, chin elongating, eyes widening. He opened his mouth, now larger than it had any business being, and sucked in a long rasping breath. Was she hallucinating? She had to be, surely.

"All that doubt," Sleeson said. "All that disappointment!"

Eevie had the sensation that something was being drawn from her, sucked out of her soul. She tried to speak but only heaved.

"Tell me how it makes you feel, Elise. *Think* about how you *feel!*" Sleeson's words were slushing and wet now, articulated poorly with his oversized lips and questing tongue, so close to her face. His body, arms and legs seemed longer too, overly articulated.

Eevie tried to scream, but her breath had been stolen and she only wheezed in abject horror, in total desolation, thoroughly impotent.

"Yesssss!" Sleeson sucked again, drawing more from her. His wet lips rippled over her cheeks, his tongue explored her mouth, his inbreath unceasing, drawing, drawing, drawing, extracting the essence from somewhere deep inside her.

Blackness swirled in from the edges of her vision and she fell, mercifully, into an abyss.

Eevie woke on the bed in her room and the first thing she noticed was a ravening hunger and desperate thirst clawing at her insides. She gasped, rolled over, but dizziness swept through her. She slipped from the side of the bed onto hands and knees and crawled to the bathroom. As she gulped water directly from the tap, her mind began to equalise. She shuddered at the memory of Sleeson and his office. What had he become? Was it some hallucinatory effect of the drug he'd given her? But no, she'd felt him too. And more than that, felt him take something from her.

Fuck, she was so hungry.

It was dark outside, she realised. She'd been dragged into Sleeson's office first thing in the morning.

She needed food. Weakness from hunger made her limbs shake. She thought about using the phone, asking for food to be delivered to her room like before, then thought again. Perhaps she needed to explore her prison a little more. She pulled herself to her feet and took a moment to straighten herself out, brush her teeth, brush her hair.

She stared at herself in the mirror, looking for evidence of Sleeson's gross attack. But she looked normal, no marks on her skin. With a shudder she remembered a casting call with one of the biggest Hollywood directors, right as her acting career began to take off after music raised her to the awareness of millions.

"You got that real wasian thing going on, kid."

She'd been confused at the time. "What thing?"

"Wasian. You know, like white Asian. Caucasian and Asian mixed together? You haven't heard that term before? It's all over TikTok."

At the time, she wasn't sure if she was more offended by the term or by this guy using TikTok for research. "No, I never heard it before."

"Ah, whatever, doesn't matter. You got the real genetic jackpot of looks, great voice and acting chops. You're gonna go far, kiddo!"

She thought maybe kiddo was more offensive than wasian, but the man had not been wrong. Her rise off the back of that movie had lifted her music and acting careers to stratospheric heights.

"A shame that genetic jackpot didn't include a properly functioning fucking brain," she growled at her reflection. "Because all it did was lead me here."

With a noise of frustration, she grabbed her phone and left the room, heading for the common area. Her phone was likely a brick everywhere, but she planned to check around for any hint of a signal. It said the time was 9.30 p.m. She'd been out cold for twelve hours? And dinner was officially finished, Adele had said it was available until eight. Maybe there were vending machines.

Walking the quiet, carpeted hallway she felt more alone than she ever had in her life. For someone who could feel alone at the biggest Hollywood parties, surrounded by the kind of stars most people would give a limb to hang out with, it was a strange sensation. As she passed one door she heard sobbing from inside the room and paused. A part of her wanted to knock, to ask after the person inside. But it was impossible to know why anyone was here or what they were going through. She needed to learn more and help herself before she tried to look out for anyone else. Like they said on aeroplanes, in case of emergency, put on your own oxygen mask before helping others. Like an oxygen mask or bracing against the seat in front would do anything when a plane was falling from thousands of metres in the air. So much of life was placatory bullshit. She often thought the oxygen masks in planes might actually pump some kind of anaesthetic into panicking passengers.

She moved on and reached the dining and lounge area. The doors slid open as she approached and she went inside. There were a couple of other people in the big room. One sat in the corner on a sofa, curled into a foetal ball, but the other looked up as she entered. She saw the range of expressions cross the man's face and knew she'd been recognised.

He raised one hand, pointed. "You're…"

"Eevie. Hi. How are you?"

"Wow. Hi. I'm Pete. And honestly, I'm fucking awful."

She laughed. "Yeah, stupid question. Sorry."

"Why are you here? You're, like, a superstar."

"Even superstars get anxiety, Pete. And honestly, that's among the least of my problems. But why I'm here in particular, as opposed to literally any other facility in the world, is a mystery that's gonna cost my manager his fucking job. I'm starving. Are there machines or anything."

Pete gestured to one end of the room. "Ring at the hatch. You'll get something."

Eevie saw a serving counter built into the end wall with a shutter pulled down to close it off. Stencilled lettering said, *Ring For After Hours Service.*

"Thanks."

She went over and found a small button at one end of the counter, pressed it. After a moment, she tried again, held it a little longer, then jumped as the shutter shot up.

"How can I help?"

Eevie frowned. It was Adele, but her blonde hair had gone brunette. A dye job? "Adele?"

"No, Adele does days. I'm Icelynn."

"You're..? Are you guys twins?"

"Sure, if you like."

"If I like?"

"Are you hungry, is that it?"

Eevie shook herself. Everything about this place was

messed up. "Yeah, ravenous since I was drugged and assaulted this morning. What is there?"

Icelynn smiled, ignoring everything but the request. "Most of the kitchen stuff is off and dinner is long finished, but I can make you a sandwich, toasted or not, or put together a salad? Bowl of cereal?"

"A sandwich is fine, maybe cheese and tomato?"

"No problem."

Before Eevie could say anything, Icelynn pulled the shutter down again.

"They act like it's good service, but it's actually just another kind of abuse," Pete said.

She turned. "Seems like everything here is."

"They call it therapy, but it's not. Before long everyone ends up like that." He pointed to the thin woman curled up on the couch. "Then they're gone."

"Gone?"

"Therapy completed!" Pete said, in a high-pitched mockery of Adele and Icelynn's tone. "Not long for you now!"

Eevie grimaced. "Not long for you? Sounds final."

"Oh yeah, they're all dead. I'm sure everyone who comes through here gets sucked dry and then killed eventually. No one leaves. No one gets any kind of actual therapy. It's a farm."

"And they're farming what? Despair?"

Pete wagged one index finger at her. "You've got it. Already on the ball, you're smarter than most."

"I don't know about that. How did you end up here? I got booked in by someone else, so missed the process."

"We live in Enden. My wife saw it advertised and suggested I check it out when I had a bit of a breakdown over work."

"What do you do?"

"Financial adviser. I made good money, but started getting overworked, overwhelmed, made some bad calls for clients and lost them money. Kinda got to me and I had a bit of a collapse about it."

Eevie went and sat in an armchair across from him. "Sorry to hear that."

Pete shrugged. "Checked myself in here thinking it would help. I could afford the exorbitant fees. It charges so much, it has to be good, right? Turns out I made one final mistake there. Kind of fits the pattern really. At least I won't have to worry about letting anyone down any more."

"Hey, everyone makes mistakes. Sounds like you were doing well, just had a bit of a downturn. Nothing a rest and reset won't fix." *Listen to you, Eevie Chill. Take your own advice once in a fucking while.*

"Yeah, there was a time I thought so."

"Cheese sandwich!"

They both jumped, turned to see Icelynn had entered unnoticed. She handed Eevie a plate. The sandwich looked good, thick fresh bread and plenty of filling.

"Thanks."

"No problem. Just leave the plate on the counter when you're done." Without another word, Icelynn turned and left.

When she'd gone, Eevie said to Pete, "Twins, right? Her and Adele?"

He shrugged again. Seemed he did that a lot. "Hard to say. Looks like it, but I'm starting to think nothing is really real in this place."

Hunger overrode discomfort and Eevie started in on the sandwich. It was surprisingly good for something so simple. After chewing down a couple of large bites, she said, "You ever had a session with Sleeson?"

Pete nodded. "Everyone does. He's the only therapist." He made air quotes with his fingers on the last word.

"The only one?"

"For all their talk of facilities, it's the plastic twins, Emil and Chinner, the orderlies, and Sleeson."

"Emil is the fucker with the porn tash?"

"Yeah, he's fucked. Chinner is no better, really, but

somehow creepier. Never heard him say a word. No one else is ever here, except us lot. The residents." He made air quotes again. "Victims, more like."

"I saw some weird guy when I first got here. Winterbourne?"

"Oh yeah, I've heard about him. Never seen him."

"He owns the place, apparently. Financed the whole thing."

Pete made a noise of surprise. "I always assumed Sleeson did that. He's the one feeding off us all."

"So it's not just me. That really happened?"

Pete made his mouth all wide and wriggled his fingers at her, sucked in a breath. "Tell me how you feeeel!"

"Jesus."

"Yeah."

"What the fuck is happening here, Pete?"

"I don't know. Honestly, I've lived in Enden my whole life. Should have known better than to ever come to anything in fucking Gulpepper. What was I thinking?"

"How many residents are there?"

"Right now? No idea. I've seen three go through the process and they're not here any more. So dead, I guess. Then there's me, Debbie over there, and one other guy I know about. Big bloke. He's really not okay, violence just, like, clouding off him. He only turned up a few days ago and I've been avoiding him. Now there's you as well."

"So that's four of us and five of them?"

Pete frowned. "Us and them? Are you thinking of taking them on?"

"Why not? Adele and Icelynn are a pair of fucking Barbie dolls. I could snap both of them in half, at the same time if necessary. Sleeson is something fucking weird, but he's an old man, isn't he?"

"I mean, he looks like he's in his sixties or something, but that's just... I don't know. A mask or something? He is not a normal guy, Eevie."

"But he drugged me, so I think maybe he's weak."

Pete laughed, shook his head. "Man, I can tell you're new here. Sure, maybe the Barbie twins and Sleeson are easily overpowered or whatever. That still leaves Emil and Chinner, and those two are big, mean fuckers who will happily beat the shit out of you. And on our side? You certainly can't rely on Debbie, she's pretty much catatonic now. Two, three days tops and she'll be gone. I'm about as athletic as a wet paper bag. You could smash the crap out of me easier than Adele or Icelynn." He raised a hand to forestall her protest. "I've been a desk jockey my whole life, I know my limitations. I used to think I was at least good at the desk jockey stuff. Turns out I'm actually shit at literally everything. Pretty sure my wife was happy to get rid of me. She'll be glad I'm gone. Our two kids will be delighted to never see me again, too. At best I'm an embarrassment to them."

"Dude, you have issues."

He grinned crookedly. "You think? You too, superstar. Look, what I'm saying is, if you think you can bust out of here, you're on your own. Unless you maybe manage to recruit that weird, violent new guy. But even then... Fuck that. There's no escape."

"How long have you been here?"

"Hard to tell for sure. I think about three weeks. Bit more. I lose track of time because of the drugs and Sleeson's 'therapy' sessions."

Eevie finished her sandwich, thankful for the easing of the ache in her belly and a bit of strength returning. But it brought with it a desolation at all Pete had imparted. Surely it wasn't as hopeless as he suggested. How could something like this place exist? How could they cover up the disappearances of all these people, if Pete was right about them being killed?

Well, they'd fucked up this time, because the world would notice if Eevie Chill disappeared. She had a new album being remixed and scheduled for a June release to hit the northern hemisphere summer and she was due on set at the end of April in New Zealand for principal photography on the next Peter Jackson flick. People would fucking notice.

But she couldn't wait for people to notice she was missing. She needed to get the fuck out, and quickly.

"I see you thinking," Pete said. "I thought the same way at first. I tried busting windows, ripping out doors. I attacked Adele one day, intending to hold her hostage to force them to let me out. But Emil snuck in behind me and..." Pete lifted his shirt to show a huge bruise on his ribs, blue and purple, yellowing around the edges. "Pretty sure he busted at least three of my ribs. It's why I'm sitting so still, even breathing hurts. This was about a week ago. And then they injected me with something and it was like a horrible acid trip. I thought I was dead then. Dying, at least. I was like that for two days straight. When it passed, they said there was nothing to stop them keeping me in that state twenty-four seven. They'd still be able to conduct my therapy sessions." He barked a vicious laugh, and winced. "Even now they're still keeping up the façade that all this is treatment for my benefit. It's fucking psychotic!"

He dropped his shirt, pressed one palm against his injury and rose, wincing again, to his feet.

"I'm going to bed. I'm sorry you're caught up here. I'm honest, I've never really vibed with your music, but my sixteen-year-old daughter loves your stuff. She's always been into that angsty, heavy kind of thing. You know, she told me there would never be a band better than Evanescence, then she saw you in Wollongong and said you were a hundred times better."

"Huh. That's really nice of her. You can tell her I said thanks when you get out."

"Nah, not gonna happen. But she'd lose her mind to know I was just hanging out and chatting with the real Eevie Chill. And just by the way, I thought you were incredible in Silent Partners. I know you got the Oscar nomination for that, and well-deserved. It's a crime you didn't win."

"Thanks."

"You should do more of that drama stuff and less blockbuster shit. I guess that's where the money is, though, right?" He gave her a sad smile. "Irrelevant now. You've sung your last song and made your last picture. End of the road here." He gestured around with the hand not pressed to his ribs. "This place? You, here, now? I'm sorry. It's all over. We're done for."

"Fuck that, Pete."

"I'm a realist."

"You're really fucking depressing."

"My wife and kids would agree."

He gave her a sad smile and walked slowly from the room, turning down the corridor in the opposite direction to her room. Eevie watched him go and sighed. This couldn't be happening. There was no way this could be real. And if it was, there was no way she would let it win.

It was late and, despite being unconscious for the day, Eevie was exhausted. KOd by drugs wasn't the same as sleep, after all. With food in her belly, she felt marginally more human and decided to go back to her room and think for a while before sleeping.

The hallways of the Institute were still and quiet as she padded along. She let herself into her room and stripped off, heading first for a shower. As she stood under the steaming hot water, she thought about what Pete had said. The real threat were those two goons, Emil and Chinner. She didn't really know what Sleeson was, and maybe he was more dangerous than she anticipated, but was he even here all the time? Presumably he came into the place to conduct his bullshit therapy sessions. Surely he didn't live here. How could she get the better of Emil and Chinner?

Pete had mentioned a new resident, what he called the 'weird new, violent guy'. Someone like that would be a good ally, potentially more able to stand up the goons.

Perhaps in the morning she'd try to find him for a chat, get a feel for what was what. Pete was damaged and kind of chickenshit, so maybe he had a skewed perspective of the new guy. In her career, Eevie had met all kinds and her music frequently played well with the metal and nu-metal crowds, so she was used to big, weird, violent-looking people. In her experience, about the safest place in the world was a metal gig. Everyone way more balanced and compassionate than 'regular' people. The most trouble she'd ever seen at gigs was always at the big festivals where most of the crowd were the pastel polo shirt, popped collar arsehole crew. Those guys were a nightmare.

Clean, full, tired, she put on fresh sleeping shorts and a baggy t-shirt and crawled into bed. She was terrified and thoroughly lost in this awful place, but she refused to let it beat her. One thing she would need is sleep. The trouble was, insomnia had plagued her for years. Often, she would fight it off with booze and drugs, prescription or weed usually, she wasn't bothered. And she knew that was a significant contribution to her overall mental state. Which was why she'd been sent to this hellhole in the first place. And now those things weren't available anyway. The irony was ridiculous.

She lay staring up at the dark ceiling, wondering if she should get up and read. A previous therapist had pointed out that it was important to make sure her bed didn't become a place of added anxiety. When insomnia struck, give it some time and, if it didn't pass, get up, sit somewhere else and read a book. Avoid screens as they were too stimulating, but a book and soft lighting was a good way to fill time and not obsess over the sleeplessness. Then, after a while, try going back to bed. Maybe sleep would come.

With a sigh, she pulled herself out of the bed and retrieved a book from her bag, slumped into the armchair. With everything going on, escaping into a book seemed faintly ridiculous. It had always been her safe place, a quiet corner and a good book. Maybe she could find that again, even if just for a little while. In the end, she read quietly for hours, doing her best to think of nothing else except the story. Thankfully, it was a good novel and made that mental transportation easier. It was close to dawn again before she even began to feel sleepy. Knowing she needed to attempt at least a few hours of proper rest, she tucked the book away and slipped back into the bed, pulled the covers over herself. She was close to dozing when a sound caught her attention, made her look up across the room.

The silhouette framed in the doorway was unmistakably Emil.

Eevie scrambled back to sit up in the bed, hauling the covers up to her chin. "Get the fuck out of here!" The door had been locked, but she'd neglected to drag something in front to block it.

"Hello, there. I can't wait to fuck a genuine megastar."

"What? Fuck off! Get out!"

Emil closed the door behind him and the room sank back into gloom, the only light from the soft glow of the moon through thin curtains, making everything muted, the shadows black holes.

Then Eevie blinked as Emil flicked on the lights and everything burst into stark brightness. He moved across the room towards her.

"Stay away from me!"

Emil laughed. "No. Not a chance. You're gorgeous, you know that? I can't wait to add you to my trophy shelf."

He undid his belt and dropped his trousers. His cock, short but fat and standing, pointed at her. He reefed the covers back, snatching them from her grasp. Eevie was only too aware of how flimsy her shorts and t-shirt were. She went to roll off the other side of the bed as he moved up to her, but he grabbed an ankle, his hand hot and rough, grip like a vice. She rolled over, kicked back with her free leg but he batted it aside and dragged her over.

"This can be easy or rough, Eevie. And I fucking love it rough, so your choice!"

He grabbed her arm and pulled her over, put one knee painfully across her thigh to pin that leg as he swung the other over her and pressed one big palm into her chest, pinning her.

The sight of him, his appalling nudity, the stench of his sweat and foul breath, made her gasp. She thrashed at him with both hands, tried to claw his face with her nails, but he seemed an expert at dodging and blocking with his shoulder. He used the hand not holding her down to grope at her shorts, hard fingers questing for the waistband.

Eevie sobbed, cried out incoherent noises of refusal.

"I saw you talking to Peter earlier," Emil said. "I fucked him last night. He didn't tell you that, did he? He just laid there and took it, like a wet fucking rag. Useless. But I love a bit of fight like this!"

He found the waistband and hauled at her shorts, half-tore them off, half dragged them down. He jammed the knee of his free leg against her inside thigh and shoved, forced her legs apart.

"No no no!" Eevie hammered at his face and chest as he ducked left and right, avoiding the worst of the blows.

"The harder you fight, the more it'll hurt, bitch!"

He drove forward again, trying to line up his hips. Eevie knew she only had two choices, to keep fighting or give in, and it seemed both would result in the same outcome. She was powerless otherwise and that drove a rage behind her eyes, a fury of injustice. But were those really her only choices?

She stilled a moment, considering, wondering if she could see through what might be necessary.

Emil paused, grinning. "That's it. Accept the inevitable."

He leaned forward, sucked like he was breathing her in as he shifted his hips again, and she surged up, clamped her teeth into his cheek. He roared and she bit down hard, felt the flesh give then pop and blood flooded her mouth, metallic and foul. At the same time, she grabbed his face and found his eyes with her thumbs, drove her hard nails into the orbits.

Emil howled and bucked up, pushing hard with the hand on her chest, but she refused to give up her grip even as his face tore further between her teeth. Her thumbnails dug in, all her rage forced into the strength of the act, and his eyeballs burst, showering her face with blood and viscous gel. Emil screamed, batting at her with both hands, knocking her free. She fell back hard against the bed, gagging as she spat out blood and tried to wipe the gore from her eyes. Emil howled, slamming his bunched fists downwards and it was her turn to squirm left and right, trying to avoid the worst of the blows. One knuckled clipped just above her ear and sound whined into a high-pitched burr as dizziness swept through her.

"No fucking way," she growled, refusing to pass out, and closed her fingers into a flattened fist, bracing with her thumb against the side of her index finger.

This is a panther fist, she remembered her sister, Sonja, telling her, demonstrating it once after she'd taken a few months of kung fu lessons. *Superb for punching a motherfucker right in the throat.*

At the time, Eevie had laughed, but even then she'd thought maybe it wasn't such a bad call. Now she would try it. She drove the ridge of her aligned middle knuckles up with all the force she could muster, aiming directly for Emil's Adam's apple. There was a sickening crunch as her strike connected and Emil made a strangled choking, then started gasping, scrabbling at his throat as blood poured from his face.

That still leaves Emil and Chinner, she remembered Pete saying. *And those two are big, mean fuckers who will happily beat the shit out of you.*

Yeah, well, guess what, Pete, you fucking loser? One down, one to go.

She shoved up and sideways with her hips, tipping Emil off the bed. As he hit the floor, still gasping, she jumped up and swung a soccer kick under his chin. It hurt her foot, but his head snapped back and he fell, rolled onto his side and tried to rise. Eevie grabbed the bedside lamp and raised it high over her head and brought it down with all the strength she could muster, slamming the porcelain base of it into the side of Emil's head. It smashed and he slumped, fell, rolled onto his back, gagging, crying, legs kicking.

"Fucking die, you cunt!" Eevie yelled, and jammed the ragged, broken remains of the lamp into Emil's throat. She stirred it around, dragged it left and right, ruining the flesh there as the man's heels drummed the ground and his arms flexed out to either side, fingers grabbing at the air. Eevie staggered back, staring, disbelieving as the big bastard continued to thrash and make wet, choked, restricted noises of distress, his face and neck a mess of ragged skin and blood.

"Fucking die!" she said again, weaker this time.

Finally, Emil fell still.

Eevie stood gasping, looking at what she'd done. She was equal parts appalled and elated, terrified and electrified.

She realised a strange hissing noise was coming from somewhere and looked around, each corner, then finally up. Doctor Sleeson hung there, braced upside down against the walls and ceiling in one corner of the room, sucking in a long, endless breath through his distended mouth.

How long had that fucking... thing been up there? Eevie grabbed the remains of the lamp and threw it, then started picking up anything that came to hand, throwing everything at the creature. "Get out, you fuck! Get out!"

Sleeson slushed a wet, ululating laugh. "Delicious!" he managed to get out past it. "Delightful!" And he dropped to the ground and scurried away, moving on twisted hands and feet the whole way, then grabbed the door and let himself out.

Eevie ran to the door, saw him flex back up into some semblance of human dimensions and arrangement as he rounded the corner of the corridor, still laughing.

She'd done it now. Emil had forced the issue. No time to plan, to discover allies. There were cameras in her room. She needed to act. Emil had worn a kind of utility belt and she ran back to check it. She found a metal extendable baton in a short case and a kind of penknife multi-tool. She dug in his pockets, looking for a working phone, but he seemed not to carry one. She did discover his pass card on a lanyard tucked into his back pocket. If that had opened her door, would it open all the doors?

She looked down at Emil. "Do not fuck with Eevie Chill, you fucking chode."

She needed to get the others. Pete, Debbie, even the weird new violent guy, and get everyone out. And quickly. She ran into the bathroom and rinsed as much of Emil's blood off as she could manage. The taste of it remained, so she squeezed a worm of toothpaste directly onto her tongue and swished it around her mouth, then gulped water from the tap. It would have to do. She tried not to think about what diseases she may have ingested. Back in her room, she put on jeans, t-shirt and boots, grabbed her phone and wallet and jammed them into her pockets, then flicked open Emil's telescopic baton. It felt heavy and solid in her hand. She whipped it left and right a couple of times and felt powerful. Good. Anyone coming anywhere near her would get this across the head and face without a second's hesitation.

Eevie grinned. "Time to go!"

Baton in one hand, Emil's pass card in the other, she stalked from her room into the quiet corridors. She remembered Adele telling her the room next door was unoccupied, but did she trust anything any more? There were three rooms on her end of the building, so she started at number one and swiped the card. The door clicked, the green light went on, and she pushed the door open. The bed was neatly made, just the bedside lights on, and clearly no one there. The same turned out to be true for room two.

She went to the other end of the wing, past the room where Sleeson had abused her, and found three more rooms, a mirror image of the area she'd been in before. Rooms four and five, were as empty as the others, but room six immediately assaulted her senses. As she pushed the door open, a stench of old sweat and urine wafted out to make her take a stagger-step back. Was this where she'd heard the sobbing from before? Shaking herself, Eevie held her breath and stepped forward again, reached in to flick on the light.

On the bed was a cadaverous man, ancient-looking. He had a single sheet pulled up over him that bloomed with stains. His head tipped towards her, rheumy eyes searching but clearly seeing nothing. His mouth opened and closed a couple of times with a sticky clicking sound and one bone-thin arm raised to weave uselessly in the air.

Eevie gasped and moved away, shaking her head. How was such an emaciated person still alive? He looked like he was a thousand years old. While she knew it was a mercenary thought, she was aware that trying to help him would only slow her down. If she got out, she would absolutely report everything here and make sure people checked room six. No, not *if* she got out. *When* she got out.

She ran past the dining and reception areas in the centre of the building, heading for the rooms on the opposite side. As she went to turn left at the end of the corridor, a voice said, "Eevie, what's happening?"

She turned to see Icelynn standing by the doors to the reception area, eyes wide in fear. This bitch knew what was happening. They could see everything in her room, couldn't they?

"I suggest you fuck off," Eevie said, raising the baton. Her mind raced. Would the woman raise an alarm? Did she have an emergency button to put the building into some kind of lockdown? Despite her suggestion that Icelynn fuck off, Eevie decided that wasn't such a good idea after all and started back towards her.

Icelynn's eyes went wider still and she turned to duck back through to reception. Eevie doubled her pace and caught up just as Icelynn stepped through the open doors. She grabbed the night receptionist's collar and yanked her back. Icelynn cried out, staggered and fell, sitting hard on her butt as the doors slid closed. She yelped with pain and squirmed, pressed one hand to her lower back.

"You hurt me!" she wailed and her free hand rose holding some kind of device. It was the size of a cigarette packet and had nothing but one large red button in the centre. Without waiting, Eevie brought the baton down on Icelynn's wrist. A sound like a dry stick snapping and Icelynn yowled, the device spinning free. Eevie brought the baton around again and cracked it across the side of Icelynn's head. The woman slumped like her bones had been removed and lay still.

"I hope I haven't killed you," Eevie muttered, "but there's no way you're unaware of what goes on around here, so fuck you too, I guess."

She hung Emil's pass card around her neck from its lanyard and grabbed Icelynn's unbroken wrist. The other was already swollen to twice its size, bent at an incredibly unpleasant angle. She dragged the woman along and around to room seven and opened the door. No one again. She ripped the bedside lamp out of the wall and used the cable to tie Icelynn's wrists and ankles, baulking at the further damage she might be doing to the broken bones, but also not really caring. She left the room, letting the door click locked behind her.

Room eight was also empty but room six was not.

When she pushed open the door she saw the blood first. So much blood, spreading in a pool across the floor. She tracked up from the scarlet stain to see Pete sitting in a chair, his elbows resting on its arms, palms up. His skin gaped open from wrist to elbow on both sides. His head had tipped back, his mouth a grimace, eyes staring blankly at the ceiling. A steak knife, no doubt stolen at dinner, lay at his feet.

Eevie ran in. "Oh no! You fuck, Pete, I said I'd get us out! You stupid, poor fuck."

"I almost missed it!"

Eevie spun around, baton raised. Sleeson stood between her and the door. His body was distended, arms and legs too long with too many joints each. His face swung left and right on a neck seemingly too long and thin to support it, his mouth stretched open. His tongue snaked out, pointed and blackened, to lick at the air.

"What a night!" he said, almost singing it. "What a glorious night!"

Eevie raced forward, planning to bring her baton down on that oversized, leering head, but Sleeson flexed and looped out of the way, her blow swishing through the air. Eevie staggered with the force of it, took a step to right herself and turned for another go, but Sleeson was already on his way, a tumbling mass of limbs that somehow reminded her of an octopus racing across the sea floor.

She glanced back at Pete. "Fuck!"

There were only three more rooms to check. Debbie and the weird guy Peter had talked about had to be in them. She raced from the room, bracing in case Sleeson was waiting for her, but of course, he was long gone.

Rooms ten, eleven and twelve awaited. She used the pass card and opened ten to find Debbie curled in a ball on her bed. As Eevie stepped inside, someone said, "What's happening?"

She spun, baton high, and a tall, broad man with buzz cut blond hair and piercing blue eyes stood behind her in t-shirt and boxers. The door to room eleven was open behind him. He raised his palms and said, "Woah, easy! What's happening?"

"Who are you?" It had to be the weird, violent guy Pete had mentioned, but other than being large, he seemed pretty normal. He was damned large though. With thick muscle banding his limbs he looked like he could lift a car.

"Olaf. I'm Olaf. Is everything okay?"

"Very fucking much not, no. You been here long?"

"Long enough to know it's not what the brochure said." Olaf had the name and looks of someone Scandinavian but spoke with a normal Aussie accent. "We getting out?"

"Yes, we are. You with me?"

"Fuck, yeah. I'd been making a plan, but I guess we're going with yours. Wanna share?"

"I killed Emil and incapacitated Icelynn. Sleeson is some kind of weird monster. I've got a pass card and I'm leaving." She grinned. "That's the fucking plan, Olaf."

"Then let's go."

"Not without Debbie."

Olaf nodded once and pursed his lips, looked down at himself. "I'll dress. Back in one minute. You try to wake her?"

"Yep."

Eevie ran to Debbie's bedside and crouched down. The woman was young, maybe still in her twenties. Despite being curled up tight, she was alert, staring hard at Eevie.

"Come on, I'm getting us out of here."

Debbie just stared, deep green eyes intense under a fringe of brown hair. She was thin, emaciated to the point of anorexia, and hugged herself tightly.

"Debbie, right? I know you've been through some shit. I mean, I don't know what, but something to get you here in the first place then the stuff that happens here? It's a nightmare, I know. But I can get us out. I killed Emil."

Debbie reacted for the first time, eyebrows twitching up.

"He tried to rape me. I bet he's been at you too, right?"

Debbie stared.

"Well, I managed to gouge his fucking eyes out and then shredded his throat with broken porcelain. He's dead as fuck, Debbie. It can't fix what he did, but it's vengeance of a kind. Don't let these cunts win, okay? Let's go."

Debbie twitched but didn't rise. She looked away from Eevie, moving only her eyes, and tears started over her cheeks.

"It's never too late, Debbie. You know who I am?"

Debbie nodded, almost imperceptibly.

"Good. Then you also know I'm richer than fucking god. I'll get you help, I promise. Not like this place, real help. You're my buddy now, if you come with me. We leave together and I will not let you down. I'll see you cared for. Please?"

Debbie still didn't move to stand but her chest hitched with sobs. Eevie reached down and gently took one thin, bony hand. She eased it away from the girl's chest and coaxed her to sit up. Debbie wore baggy track pants and a t-shirt. There was a pair of thongs on the floor beside the bed. Eevie gently, ever so gently though her hands shook and she was desperate to rush, eased Debbie's legs around and put her feet into the thongs.

"Come on, please. Let's go."

Olaf appeared in the doorway. "We're leaving?"

"You see there?" Eevie said to Debbie. "That's Olaf. He can bench press a pregnant cow. And he's going first to clear the way."

"I am?"

"Yes, you fucking are."

Olaf shrugged. "Okay. Let's go."

Debbie allowed Eevie to lead her and they went along the corridor following Olaf. As they turned into the main passage, Olaf paused. Chinner stood in their way. He held a baton like Eevie had in one hand and some chunky, square, pistol-looking thing in the other. Eevie realised it was a taser.

"You all need to be back in your rooms right away," Chinner said, but Eevie heard the tremor of nerves in his voice.

"Let us pass," she said. "Just turn around."

"I can't do that."

"You can. It's a choice."

Olaf took a couple of steps forwards. "Do as she says!"

Chinner raised the taser. "Stay back!"

Olaf roared and strode forward. Chinner baulked, backpedalled fast, and fired. The electrified barbs on their wires snaked out and slammed into Olaf's chest. He stiffened, arms out at forty-five-degree angles, legs driven straight as he vibrated under the shock, fists clenched. But he didn't go down. His roar rose in volume and he slowly raised one arm, hand curled into a claw, and raked it across the wires, ripping the barbs from his skin.

He staggered forward, then found his footing and advanced on Chinner. The guard brought his metal telescopic baton around hard, but Olaf put up one hand to block it against his forearm. There was a crack and Eevie wondered if Olaf's arm had just been broken but he didn't seem to care. The man's pain threshold was unnatural. He grabbed Chinner around the throat with his other hand.

The two men were similar in size and bulk, but where Chinner was soft and heavy, Olaf was raw power and strength. Chinner wailed, a strangely high and feminine sound, as Olaf walked him backwards, lifting as he went, and slammed Chinner into the wall. The orderly's head made a sickening thwack as it hit, his feet half a metre off the ground, and he went limp, head lolling. Olaf used his other hand to grab the man's utility belt and, with another roar of effort, he lifted, tipping Chinner first horizontal, then continuing that momentum to raise the man up, flip his legs high, and drive his head vertically into the hard floor. Chinner's head and neck made a rapid series of snaps and cracks and blood burst out.

Olaf dropped the corpse and turned a smile to Eevie and Debbie. "Tasers are quite a rush!"

Eevie gaped. "So it would seem. Let's go!"

She swiped the pass card at the double sliding doors leading into the reception area. Nothing happened. With a low curse, she swiped again, but the light on the panel remained red.

"Stand back," Olaf said. He moved back to the other side of the passage and ran hard at the lefthand door near the centre, leaning his shoulder in. The entire thing seemed to flex and bulge, but it didn't give. Olaf grunted, rubbed at his shoulder, but backed up for another run. He went further this time, so the doors to the lounge and dining area opened and he went into the room. "Stand there to keep those doors open."

Eevie moved in front of the sensor, still with one arm around Debbie, and waved her free hand to prevent the doors closing.

Olaf came through them like a bull aiming for the matador he hated most. He dipped his shoulder at the last and hit the reception door full-tilt. The thick glass flexed, bowed, then suddenly shattered in a rain of glittering cubes. Olaf stumbled through, fell, and rose to his feet without stopping, one hand pressed to his shoulder. His face twisted in an expression of pain but he still somehow managed to grin.

"Weak as paper!"

"You're a fucking maniac!" Eevie said.

"Well, yeah. Anger issues, apparently. Among many other things."

"Massive glass door therapy seems to be working for you."

"Painful, but effective."

"Let's get the fuck out of here."

Sleeson dropped from above and landed on Olaf. The doctor's huge, overstretched mouth engulfed Olaf's head. Olaf howled, muffled by the restriction, and scrabbled for freedom, but Sleeson wrapped overly jointed limbs all around the big man. Eevie was reminded again of an octopus. Sleeson's body began to pulse, convulsing as he sucked and sucked, Olaf's howls and struggles growing weaker as he staggered around in random circles. Then he fell and lay still, Sleeson locked in place, gulping.

Debbie moaned and Eevie snapped her gaze away from the atrocity. Poor Olaf, he seemed like a decent guy. "Okay, we have to go." She nudged Debbie forward. "We're out of here."

She gently guided Debbie through the front doors of the building and into the warm, fragrant, pre-dawn light. She thought nothing had ever felt so good.

Winterbourne arrived later that morning to be met by Doctor Sleeson, back in his more or less human shape. Sleeson appeared quite self-satisfied.

"I think I missed a lot of action here," Winterbourne said. "Interesting night?"

"Yes. Quite something."

"I was busy preparing a space." He smiled. "Decorating, in a way. A shame. Events here were perhaps too long ago..."

"Two wandered off," Sleeson said. "Difficult to manage them all when things accelerated. Elise Griffin and Debbie Eckersley."

Winterbourne shrugged. "So be it. One can only juggle so many balls at once."

"I'm sure your plans are resilient enough, no?"

"Oh, certainly. This is all a little sooner than ideal, but nothing I can't account for. Things are moving apace." He turned to look Sleeson up and down. "You fed well, hmm?"

"Yes, it's been a wonderful time. And this past night in particular, my goodness! A shame it couldn't have continued for longer. Thanks for bringing me in. It is over, I assume?"

"This stage is over, yes. Other things, bigger things, are only just beginning."

"Hmm. So what now?"

"What now? Well, thank *you* for collecting all that delicious energy for me."

"For... for you?"

"You didn't think I was supplying you with such sustenance at such vast expense through some kind of altruism, did you?"

"I don't understand."

Winterbourne turned, fast as a striking snake, and grasped Sleeson's cheeks. He slammed his mouth over Sleeson's and opened himself, consumed everything Sleeson had ever collected. Everything he had to offer. Despite Sleeson's thrashing, Winterbourne's strength and power were barely tested. It took time, but eventually Sleeson's form was emptied, a wineskin drunk dry. Winterbourne dropped the flaccid remains to the ground and turned, looking out into the brightening day, buzzing and alive like never before. His power was reaching previously unknown peaks. He drew in a long breath and strode from the building, heading down into Gulpepper.

"Well," he said as he went. "No rest for the wicked, eh?"

The
Rise

The Rise

Chrissy Carter stood in her kitchen at 6.15 a.m. and wondered if she'd ever sleep again. The energies were chaotic. Gulp mist her father had called it, the miasma around certain people and places in Gulpepper. A kind of aura they gave off. She'd learned to recognise it as well, to read it, and in truth saw it more clearly than her father ever did. But she'd never before seen it on such a scale, drifting across the landscape itself. Fundamental shifts were underway.

She sensed Rich stir in the bedroom at the other end of the house, smiled as she felt him notice her absence. She gently put the thought of the kitchen in his mind and went back to staring out at the dawn light, bright over the ocean, still indigo to the west. She had become more powerful than her father at a young age and was always more subtle in her abilities too. *You've got more Carter in you than me or my dad before me,* her father had said when Chrissy was still a teen. But she wondered how much any of that might help in the coming days. She would be tested, that was beyond doubt. The Gulp itself would be sorely tested.

"Couldn't sleep again?" Rich asked as he slumped into the room.

"Coffee's made. Pour me another, will you?"

"Sure."

When he handed her a steaming mug a moment later, he asked, "You think it's nearly time for... whatever you're anticipating?"

Chrissy drew in a long breath before answering. "Things have been shifting more and more rapidly. I can't figure it out but it feels like all kinds of cogs are dropping into place, like some great machine is about to start working. I can see the changes happening, I can see some of the cogs, sense others, but I can't see the whole machine or its purpose. Just glimpses of its parts. It's infuriating."

"I know your dad never liked it when he wasn't fully informed."

"And I am my father's daughter. We're running out of time." She took a few sips of coffee, then, "Fetch Hilda for me, please? If she'll come. If not, ask if I can go to see her. And see if you can shake up that fucking band. We're going to need them again."

"So soon. I thought we'd put a kind of lid on things for a while back when... Before. Is it going to be like a couple of years ago?"

Chrissy sighed. "Worse. Much worse."

Bob Sackett pushed his bicycle uphill past the Ocean Blue Motel. He'd ridden to Turner's Manufacturing every workday for forty years, but the last few months had seen this incline start to beat him. He'd ride again when it levelled off a bit after the next block. Another five years and he could stop coming to work five days a week. He didn't have much to retire on, but what he did have, he'd earned and he planned to enjoy it. He didn't want or expect much from life, just a bit of peace and quiet and enough money for a few drinks now and then.

A thin man approached along the footpath holding a sheet of paper, a confused expression on his narrow face.

"You lost?" Bob called out.

The man hurried up and held out the sheet of paper. It was almost blank except for a strange bracketed symbol in the centre.

"What's this?" Bob looked from the paper to the man's wet eyes. "Not any kind of map I've ever seen."

The strange man's other hand rose and Bob caught

a whiff of something caustic just before he noticed the small glass bottle gripped in the thin fist. Its cap was off.

"The hell is that?"

The man waved the bottle left and right, the acrid aroma stronger. Bob took a step back but the smell seemed to be drawn back with him. He coughed, eyes watering.

"What are you doin..?" His voice trailed off as dizziness swept over his mind. He blinked, tried to focus, but his vision blurred and he heard his bicycle clatter to the pavement and then nothing but darkness.

The thin man gestured and a small car pulled up to the curb. Bob was bundled into the back seat and the car pulled away again, driving slowly towards Carlton Beach.

Rich was at his desk in the back room working on a small landscape when Chrissy returned from a walk around the paddocks. She'd needed time to think, to feel the energies moving ever more chaotically around Gulpepper. The exercise had done little to reassure her. If anything, she was more unsettled than ever.

She watched Rich for a moment as he added wisps of clouds over the miniature pastoral scene with deft brushstrokes of white oil paint.

"That's really beautiful," Chrissy said.

Rich looked up with a smile. "You think so?"

"Yeah. It's a real talent you've got."

"I organised a table at the next markets. Gonna see if I can sell a few. I've got a couple of dozen now, ready to go." He nodded to a side table where several of the small oil paintings were laid out. Some of the town, some seascapes, some farms and bush, a few of the lighthouse from various angles.

"You know, my dad left me a ton of cash as well as this farm, right? We don't need the money."

"Yeah, I know. And I have no problem with you supporting me. I get it, I work hard around the farm and… the other stuff we do. But this is mine, yeah? Something I had before I came to Gulpepper and something that's not somehow entangled with anyone or anything else."

Chrissy nodded, kissed the top of his head. "I get it. It's healthy. You talk to Hilda and the band?"

"I couldn't reach Hilda, but I talked to Beverly."

Chrissy frowned a moment in thought, then, "The granddaughter, right? Worked for us a few times."

"Yep. She said Hilda is completely tied up at her place. Like, can't leave. But that you'd be welcome to go up. Beverly said to just go on up and let yourself in, if you want. She said she'd go with you if you prefer."

"You have her number?"

"Yeah, I can text or whatever."

"Ask if she can meet me at the pub in an hour. We'll go up together. I'm not keen to surprise the old lady, whatever Beverly suggests."

Rich laughed. "Yeah, don't blame you." He pulled out his phone and started tapping a message. "As for the band, they're on tour."

"Fuck's sake."

"But I kept a contact for Edgar after the last thing that went down and I messaged him. They're playing the final gig of the tour tonight in Sydney and they're due back tomorrow or the next day. I asked him to come and see you as soon as they get in. He asked if it was serious."

"What did you tell him?"

"I said it was worse than last time."

"What did he say to that?"

"Just sent back an angry face emoji."

Chrissy nodded. "Good. That should put a fire under

his unnatural arse. You let me know as soon as you hear anything?"

"Of course."

"We're running out of time. Whatever is going down, it's accelerating. I'm heading down to the pub and then to see Hilda, assuming Beverly is amenable. Then later today, we need to go to Enden. Someone else I want to talk to."

"Okay. You want me to come with you now?"

"Nah, enjoy your painting. Head down to meet me back at Clooney's about one or so."

"Will do." Rich's phone pinged. He looked, then smiled, held it up. "Beverly says she'll see you in one hour."

Shirley Patel walked home from a short shift at Woollies, wondering if her request for more overtime would be approved. Since Kuresh left, feeding her three kids, even with the employee discount, had become difficult. The other bills stacking up could only be ignored for so long. Her supervisor had said all the right things, but budget cuts made it fairly obvious he was paying lip service to her desperation and nothing more.

She sighed. She'd already made tentative enquiries with a local real estate agent about the possible value of the house. Loathe though she was to pull the kids out of school, they would have to sell and move somewhere cheaper. Unless she managed to find something smaller in town. Perhaps it was a good excuse to get out of The Gulp. Just because she'd grown up in the godsforsaken harbour town didn't mean she needed to stay.

When she'd been awarded the house in the

acrimonious divorce three years before she'd thought the future was secured for her and the kids. But a single Woollies income, part-time at that, simply couldn't cut it.

Shirley let out a rueful laugh, a sudden lifting of the weight off her shoulders as she realised she'd just made a decision. Why had she been so determined to keep the house? Simple pride? Maybe. She already had the paperwork organised to switch back to her maiden name, the last vestige of Kuresh expunged from her life. The kids would remain Patels, but they could decide their directions as they grew up. Barely even teenagers yet, the youngest only just out of primary school, they had their whole lives to decide. But along with shaking off the name, Shirley *would* sell the house. Make a bit of equity to actually secure their future and find a small townhouse or apartment, in The Gulp or elsewhere. Maybe they could go to Monkton or Enden, stay relatively nearby for the sake of her kids' friends.

She would talk to them tonight, tell them selling the house was the only option and let them decide where to go next. If they wanted to stay in The Gulp, she would find somewhere cheaper in town. It would be difficult regardless, but not as hard as starving to death or having debt collectors start knocking on the door.

She checked her watch. Still a couple of hours until school let out. She'd go home, change, then visit the real estate and organise to get the house on the market right away.

An old Holden Commodore pulled up to the curb and the front passenger window rolled down. A man looked out, smiling awkwardly. He had a thin face and held a sheet of paper in his hand.

"Excuse me, sorry! Can you help?" He gestured with the paper.

"You lost?" Shirley asked.

She went up to the window and leaned down. The man held the paper up and it showed a weirdly bracketed design and nothing else.

"I don't understand," Shirley said.

The back door opened behind her and something sharp scratched her neck. Shirley yelped, slapped a palm against the stinging hurt. Another man stood behind her, slipping a syringe into his pocket as he moved around the door and caught her.

She couldn't feel her legs, her hands tingled. She tried to cry out, but only drool escaped her lips. In blurred, staccato images she saw the man who had caught her looking around as he dragged her into the back seat beside him.

Was no one on the street paying attention? Shirley tried to scream but only managed a choked exhalation. Then the car was moving.

Two teenagers across the road exchanged a glance.

"Did that lady just faint?" one asked.

The other shrugged. "Maybe. Good her friends were there, I guess."

"I guess."

They carried on towards the skate park at the leisure centre on the outskirts of town, boards tucked under their arms.

Chrissy took her mind off things by serving behind the bar for a while. Clooney's wasn't busy, but a decent lunchtime crowd kept her distracted. So many residents going about their day, oblivious to most of what went down where they lived. Her dad had told her more than once to hold some empathy for these people. Even while he turned himself inside out to protect them and hold the various malevolences at bay. And sure, he exploited them plenty too, but there had to be some perks to this stupid position that he'd held and passed on to her.

"Don't begrudge people their ignorance," he'd said once. "The majority of people can't function under the kind of pressure we endure. And besides, most people simply don't have the capability to see and feel what we can. We carry this burden so the rest of the town gets to have something close to a normal life. Normal by Gulp standards, anyway."

And there they all were, having a beer, maybe a counter lunch. Some on their days off, some on a lunch break, some retired. Living their lives. There existed a low-level anxiety in Gulpepper, Chrissy knew that. Everyone had some sense that where they lived and worked and played wasn't quite like other places. But most managed by ignoring it. It was remarkable what people could grow used to if that's what they wanted. And most knew it wasn't so easy to slip away from this depraved corner of Australia. Many did, of course, but pretty much all knew that attempting to leave The Gulp was a bit like playing Russian Roulette. Some got away, but plenty who tried found a bullet when they pulled that trigger, only the bullet wasn't lead. It was simply Gulpepper.

Beverly Brunswick stepped in through the doors and looked over at the bar. Chrissy raised a hand in greeting. Time was passing fast, she thought, noticing Beverly had become a good-looking young woman now, no longer the gangly teenager Chrissy remembered.

The young woman came over to the bar. "Hey."

"Hey yourself. Want a drink before we go?" Chrissy paused. "I mean, you're old enough now, right?"

"Sure, I'm nineteen. Been drinking a lot longer than a year though."

"Same as it ever was. So, you want something?"

"Nah, I'm good. You want to go talk to Oma? My grandma, I mean."

"Hilda, yeah. She's okay?"

"She's tied up. Busy searching the web."

The two women stared at each other for a moment, then Beverly smiled. Chrissy shook her head. "Come on, then, let's go. I'll drive us."

Ten minutes later, Chrissy's Mercedes jounced along the rough road leading up into the bush north of town. Beverly seemed a little subdued and Chrissy wondered if it was the weight of the woman's connection to the place. Gulp mist swirled thickly around her, so she was clearly keyed into things more than most people. Certainly more than the people Chrissy had been watching in the pub. Beverly's family, particularly her grandmother, certainly made that inevitable. Old Gulpepper blood. As old as the Carters and some other families.

"She's worried," Beverly said suddenly, quietly.

"Hilda?"

"Yeah. She's always been... I don't know, she just doesn't give a fuck about anything much, you know? Happy to live her own life. Me or dad bring her a treat now and then, usually someone from out of town, of course." Beverly glanced over, a question in her eyes.

"I have no idea what your grandmother is exactly, but I know a fair bit about what she does. Her and my father were allies, so I'm hoping she and I will be too. Although she didn't get much involved last time."

"That was... it was a hard time for her. Complicated. Besides, she said you lot would handle it."

"Fair enough. But she's worried now?" *And so she should be*, Chrissy thought.

Beverly nodded. "Yeah. I haven't ever seen her like this before."

"Has she told you what she's worried about exactly?"

"No, she hasn't even told me she *is* worried. I can just tell. What's going on, Chrissy?"

"That's what I'm trying to find out."

"She's been on the web for days now, not going anywhere, not eating, just... watching, I guess?"

"I did send a message a couple of months ago, asking

her if she could help me look out for things. I know she has a way of surveilling the town if necessary."

Beverly gave a soft laugh. "Yeah, thanks for that. She did as you asked. Cost me a good guy."

Chrissy glanced over, not sure she wanted to know exactly what that meant. "Sorry about that. I've noticed her little minions or whatever they're called around town a bit. Assumed that was it?"

"She calls them spyders. But with a Y, yeah? Spiders who spy. She thinks that's hilarious. She says English can be funny sometimes."

"Like German isn't?"

Beverly laughed. "German is the barbed wire of languages. But the pun only works like that in English."

"Okay. Well, let her have her fun. I appreciate the help. Do you know if her spyders found much?"

Beverly shrugged. "I don't think so, which is maybe why she's worried. Pull up there, I'll get the gate."

Chrissy drove through and Beverly waved her on to the house while she closed the gate again and walked to catch up. Chrissy got out of the car to wait, scanning the view from the high, cleared ground. It was mostly bush all around and quite calming for all that. Easy to think the world was at peace and life would go on quietly and normally. Which was the illusion most people lived under. Which was the reason folks like Chrissy had to exist. She resented it sometimes despite the perks that came with it.

"Come on in." Beverly opened the unlocked front door and held it for her. As Chrissy entered, Beverly called out, "Oma, Chrissy Carter ist hier, um dich zu sehen!" Then she turned to Chrissy. "Let's go on up. It'll be hot."

Chrissy chose not to question that, as the day was pretty warm already despite being into the start of autumn. She followed Beverly up the stairs. When they entered a room at the end of the hall, it became clear. It was like stepping into a sauna, the heat oppressive and humid. The far corner of the large room was full of thick, entangled spider web, spreading across two walls and half the ceiling. Suspended in the middle of it was Hilda, but not like Chrissy had ever seen her. On the few occasions they'd met in person, Hilda had appeared to be an elderly but vibrant woman with a shock of grey hair. The creature hanging above them bore only the most cursory resemblance. Her face was elongated, dark, shining mandibles protruding from stretched cheeks. Her arms and legs had too many joints and bent back to cling to strands of webbing. Her back end had swollen out into a rounded abdomen that ended with a sharp point. Chrissy swallowed, determined not to be deterred by the sight.

"Hilda, thanks for seeing me. When Beverly said you were searching the web, I didn't think she meant Google. But this is quite something."

"I've done as you asked, but I can't find him." Hilda's voice was strained, talking around the mutation of her face, but her frustration was evident. "He's oily."

"You can't find him at all?"

"Oh, I see him. Glimpses here and there. But he slips away somehow. One moment there, the next, gone. He is highly sensitive, highly reactive. My spyders have caught sightings all over town, but never more than a second or two. Infuriating bastard."

"Is he human?"

"Was, maybe. Once. Mostly. But he's become something more, I think. The tiny observations I get reveal little, but he's powerful. Very powerful. And getting stronger fast." Hilda's hands and feet danced around the webbing, plucking at strands like she was playing some profane instrument only she could hear. "My spyders are everywhere, they see so much, but he always slips away. There! I see him, near the beach… and gone. The moment my attention lands on him, he vanishes."

"You see him vanish? Does he leave any trace?"

Hilda concentrated a moment. Eventually she let out a frustrated sigh. "No. I see him clearly, his infuriatingly calm smile, then nothing. People can't expend the amount of power to move like that without leaving something behind, can they? Some energetic residue?"

"Not that I would imagine, no."

"Then how does he do it?"

Chrissy shook her head, sharing the old woman's annoyance. "I don't know. But maybe we need to ignore that for now. Ideally, we would look at him, but perhaps we should refocus. Look instead for what he's doing. See if you can pin down the influence rather than the man himself?"

"But what will I look for?"

"He must have some kind of base of operations, no?"

"If he has, I can't find it!"

"Are there places he's been hanging around more than others? When you catch a glimpse, instead of focussing on the bastard himself, look at where he was. Maybe a pattern will emerge and we can figure out what he's doing. Sort of triangulate his movements? Can you expand your awareness like that?"

"I don't know, but I can try. I have spyders everywhere. Much as it pains me, perhaps I'll ignore the white-haired bastard for now and try as you say."

"He can't be working alone. There must be some thread we can follow and start to unravel this."

"Things are in flux, Chrissy. This isn't like anything I've ever felt before and I've been in Gulpepper a long time."

"Beverly said you were concerned. Me too." Chrissy turned to Beverly. "Can you stay here and pass on anything your grandmother discovers? Call me or text or whatever? If you'll be missing work, I can recompense you. Pay you for your help."

"You don't need to pay me, I'm happy to help. We're heading into trouble, aren't we? Like a couple of years ago?"

"And then some. Thank you, Beverly. And you, Hilda."

"This place needs to come together," Hilda said. "Face down this threat."

"What about the band?" Beverly asked. "I heard they were a bit late to the party last time."

Chrissy laughed. "They were. But they came through in the end and gave my dad the chance he needed, even though it killed him. He bought us time to end the threat. But they won't be late this time. I'll be talking to them soon. Meanwhile, I have to head out of town for a few hours. Call me with anything, yeah? However seemingly trivial?"

"Of course."

The last thing Eric Dixie felt like doing was going to work. Thursdays were always the worst of the school week because there was double maths—which Eric had always hated—in the morning, then sports in the afternoon. He didn't hate sports. He was pretty good at most physical activity, especially compared to a lot of his cohort. But it was draining. Mental drain in the morning, physical exhaustion in the afternoon, *then* his part-time job at Clooney's. He wasn't quite eighteen yet, so couldn't even work the bar, and had to bust his arse shifting stock, working in the basement, washing dishes. All the shitty drudgery.

But, he reminded himself, he was *nearly* eighteen. This was the last year of school and he needed to keep his part-time work and save dollars, because he was out of The Gulp the moment he was out of school.

His home life wasn't so bad. His parents were fine.

They loved him well enough, provided for him, but were disengaged most of the time. The trouble when two people began to grow tired of each other, he supposed. His older brother was already off at university in Tamworth and loving it. Eric felt like maybe his parents were simply waiting for him to leave so they could accelerate the dissolution of everything the Dixie family had been. All four off on their separate ways. Well, so be it. He'd do all he could to help.

He knew his parents wanted him to go to uni as well, but he didn't have it in him. He was saving up enough to head to Tamworth once school finished, regardless of his HSC results. He'd hang with his brother, see what Tamworth was like. Get a job to keep the dollars coming in and save up enough to go somewhere else. And then somewhere else and somewhere else and somewhere else until he found a place he fitted. Anywhere except Gulpepper, really.

He sighed. That meant the job at the pub now. A means to an end. His shift started at three-thirty, so he had half an hour to kill after school. He walked the long way, following Cowpasture Road all the way to Burly Road, then turned north planning to check out the beach. Maybe get some chips from the fish and chip shop on Tanning Street at the other end of the sand.

As he passed a large white hall on Burly Road, one side of the double doors opened. He briefly noticed a weird symbol on the doors, like off-centre parentheses around another shape, but the opening door had cut it in half. A strange, rippling green-blue light seemed to be on inside. A woman leaned out. She had long brown hair and bad teeth, obviously yellowed even from this distance.

Eric immediately thought of his aunt, his mother's sister, who smoked a pack a day and smelled awful. Her teeth were like that too. The woman waved at him. Ever polite, good manners costing nothing, after all, Eric waved back.

"Could you lend me a hand, please?" the woman asked. She gestured back over her shoulder. "I'm trying to get organised for later and need a hand shifting this thing."

Eric frowned. "What thing?"

"Heavy furniture. Please, it'll only take thirty seconds of your day."

Eric frowned, uncertain of going near her. The shifting light in the room behind her was disquieting. She held up a sheet of paper with a symbol like he'd seen on the doors and Eric felt the need to have a closer look. The strange compulsion had him crossing the road before he realised he'd started moving.

Well, it was no skin off his nose. And being helpful was its own reward, right?

He went up to the doors as the woman smiled gratefully. A strange aroma wafted out at him as he got close, like when seaweed gets washed up by a storm then starts to dry on the sand. Salty, acrid, almost rotten but not quite yet. The kind of smell a person could taste against the back of their throat.

The woman stepped aside and put a hand on Eric's back like she wanted to help him inside, pushing a little too hard. He took an involuntarily bigger step than he'd planned then gasped against sudden pressure. The first thing he noticed was a kind of lectern in the centre of the room with a large book on it. But his eye was distracted from that almost immediately by the sight of several people around the room, dozens of them, seemingly suspended on the walls. The hall was large, empty, with wooden floors. The windows had all been boarded over on the inside and the people hanging from the walls were naked. That green-blue scintillation made it difficult to see and Eric couldn't figure out how they were held up, feet dangling a good half metre above the floorboards. Some were skinny and drawn like the woman at the door, pale and cadaverous. But others were full and healthy-seeming. Some he even recognised from around town. Except they all appeared to be unconscious. Were they dead?

"What the fuck?" Eric started to turn, planning to run right back out again, but a strong hand clamped over his face from behind, a folded rag of some kind in the palm was pressed hard over his nose and mouth.

He'd once broken his arm at the skate park and the paramedics had given him a green plastic tube to suck on for the pain. It had immediately eased the pain and made him feel wasted and stupid, made him say dumb things that had the paramedics laughing. For a moment he was reminded of that by the smell of whatever was soaking the rag pressed into his face, then everything went dark.

When Chrissy got back to Clooney's, Rich was already there, a half-finished beer in hand. He raised it in greeting and stood as she walked in.

"Sit, finish your drink." Chrissy sat across from him at the stained table and frowned. She called over to the bar. "Greg, these tables are a state. Can we get some cleaning up done?"

"Bloody Eric hasn't shown up, so I'm short-handed. He should be here by now."

Chrissy checked the time. 3.30 p.m. Where the hell was the day going? "You call him?"

"Yeah, no answer."

Chrissy paused as a sensation washed through her stomach. Rich reached over, put his hand over hers in concern. "You okay?"

"Shit is moving too fast." She looked up to Greg. "Call someone else in. Eric isn't coming."

"Really?"

"I think so. Call someone else anyway. I have to go out." She grabbed Rich's hand and stood. "Come on."

Rich slugged the rest of his beer and followed her out. "Where are we going?"

"To see a survivor."

Rich was smart enough to keep quiet on the drive, let her think. That was one of the things she'd come to appreciate most about him. His arrival in The Gulp a few years before had been unusual, but he'd slotted into the life well. At first a kind of grim acceptance, but he'd really blossomed, especially over the past year or so, and she'd come to rely on him. Her father had always warned her not to let anyone get too close. "You can only rely on yourself, when the shit really hits the fan," he'd said. But then hadn't he always leaned on her anyway? So who else did she have now he was gone? She had Rich, and he was a powerful ally. Mundane in numinous ways, but a rock of normalcy in the maelstrom of weirdness that was The Gulp. She needed him, his normality, and she hoped he'd be up to the tasks at hand, whatever they turned out to be. Hell, she hoped she would be too.

She drove fast, too fast, but cops were rare on these highways, and they pulled into the hospital in Enden about forty minutes after leaving Gulpepper.

"Who's here?" Rich asked, frowning.

"Remember that whole thing with the fishing crew a couple of years back?"

"Colley's crew. Went missing out by Cathedral Stack?"

"Yep. One made it back. My dad talked to her before. I feel like there's more she knows. Come on."

At the front desk of the psychiatric unit, Chrissy switched on what her dad had called her "pretty charm", when she ramped up the politeness and relied on her good looks to disarm people. And perhaps a little pressure somewhat less mundane that most folks found hard to resist. "Hi there, how are you doing?"

"Just fine, thanks." The nurse at the desk was tall, lean, maybe late forties, with her brunette hair pulled severely back into a tight bun. She wore a name badge that said Martha. "What can I do for you?"

"I need to see Kate Cuthbert, please."

Martha glanced up at the clock. "It's a little late for visiting hours."

Chrissy reached across the desk, touched her fingertips to the woman's arm and let a little energy surge. "I need to see Kate Cuthbert, please."

Martha gasped softly, her eyes tightening in a moment of discomfort, then, "This way."

She walked out from the desk and along a corridor, then turned to follow another and eventually reached a room at the end. The door had a number on it, 14, and the name *Cuthbert* underneath. Chrissy knew her dad's money, her money now, was paying for this, keeping Kate Cuthbert safe and cared for. She didn't mind. The Carters had all kinds of altruistic arrangements like this one. And every now and then, like today, hopefully, they paid a little back.

She turned to the nurse and smiled. "Thanks."

Martha smiled back, a frown beginning to form, then nodded and turned away.

"She'll leave us be?" Rich asked.

"Already forgotten we're even here. Come on." Chrissy tapped on the door and opened it a crack. "Kate?"

"Who is it?"

Chrissy was relieved to hear the young woman's voice, after the report from her father a couple of years ago. Maybe Kate had become less unresponsive over time. She stepped into the room and Rich followed, closed the door behind them. "I'm Chrissy Carter, from Gulpepper. Do you know who I am?"

Kate narrowed her eyes at them and Chrissy suppressed her surprise. Those eyes were all black, the pupil, iris and sclera alike, like a storm cloud filled the woman's vision. Kate sat on a bed by the window, but the blinds were drawn closed. "You're the daughter?"

"That's right." There was an armchair beside the bed and a small desk and chair to one side. Chrissy pulled up the desk chair and sat. Rich remained standing by the door.

"Your father visited once. Haven't seen him since."

Chrissy nodded. "He's not around any more."

"Ah. It got him after all."

Chrissy let out a soft, rueful laugh. "I think it gets us all in the end, one way or another. It's what we do with the time it allows us that matters."

Kate Cuthbert looked well, given what she'd been through. Her dark blonde hair was shiny, cut shoulder-length, her eyes, for all their strange darkness, were alert and bright. "I'm not going back. I'm not going anywhere."

"I know, you can rest easy there. You can stay here as long as you want. My dad made that arrangement ironclad. And if you ever want to go anywhere else, just let me know, okay? I'm taking care of everything my dad left behind, including your wellbeing. So, if you want a change of scene—"

"I'm not going anywhere!" Kate's tone sharpened. "I got this far, and that's far enough. I don't plan to risk going anywhere else. This is safe enough, I think. Far enough."

"Okay, then here you stay. No worries. But can I talk to you about some stuff, please?"

"You were always coming to see me," Kate said, and Chrissy looked away from the woman's dark eyes, frightened by the void she saw swirling there. "As was your dad. It's all happening, has happened, will happen."

"But what is it?" Chrissy asked. "It's all so big. I can see parts of it, I can see influences, but it's too much to see all of it. So I don't know how to battle it. What do you know?"

Kate laughed, but it was a brittle sound. "I know

nothing and more than I want to at the same time."

"Is it like what happened before?" Rich asked, and Chrissy shot him an acid look. He usually knew better than to interrupt.

"Oh no," Kate said. "Not really. Before was something trying to grow here. To find its place here. Now? I suspect this is different. I can see in you that it's bigger, less obvious."

"I can't fix what I can't see," Chrissy said. "Can you help me see?"

"No. You don't want to see. I saw too much and I saw hardly anything at all. Our minds aren't built to perceive so much, you understand?"

"But something is building and there's not much time," Chrissy said, doing her best to keep the growing frustration from her voice. Kate clearly had an understanding of sorts, but teasing it from the woman was like untangling a knot that had been pulled too tight.

"Oh, there's all the time there is." Kate turned her dark gaze on Chrissy, the void there threatening to swallow. "That's exactly the problem. Time is not how we perceive it, don't you see? It's spread wide. I tried to tell your father this, but he didn't get it either. Then, now, tomorrow, next year, a thousand years ago and ten thousand years from now, ever and ever onwards in all directions, it's all right now. And not now at all." Kate made a noise of frustration and turned away. "How am I supposed to explain something even I don't understand."

"But you do understand. More than me, at least. I need to do something."

"What's the point? It's happened, is happening, will happen anyway."

"I don't accept that."

Kate laughed suddenly, loud and brash. "Your acceptance has no bearing on anything!"

"I know my dad asked you if Cathedral Stack was central to things. But you didn't answer, not really. Is it? Is that place relevant?"

"All of it is." Kate returned her abyssal gaze to Chrissy and Chrissy's grip tightened involuntarily on the hard plastic arms of the chair for fear of falling. "You've had the dream. Everyone dreams of the fall. It's across the land and sea, isn't it?"

Chrissy hadn't dreamed of the fall since she was a teenager, but she remembered it well enough. Everyone did. "That really is Gulpepper in the dream?"

"Gulpepper grew in the middle of the dream," Kate said. "The fall spreads far and wide, but Gulpepper grew like a tumour at its centre. The place, you see. That's more fixed than time can ever be. But the place is only part of it. The event is what's always happening, happened, will happen." Kate gasped like she was suddenly out of breath and ground the heels of her hands into her eyes. "I don't want this! I don't need to be here again!"

Chrissy reached out, put a hand on Kate's knee. "It's okay. I'm sorry. I don't mean to cause you distress. I'm just trying to understand."

Kate pulled her hands away and her shoulders slumped a little. She stared at the wall behind Chrissy, the deep void in her eyes somehow blanked.

"Kate?" Chrissy glanced at Rich, then back to the young woman.

"I think she's gone," Rich said quietly.

Chrissy nodded, feeling awful. "I think she made a lot of progress over the last couple of years here and perhaps I've just set her right back again. Kate?" The woman didn't answer, didn't move, just stared at the wall. "Fuck. I'm sorry, Kate."

Chrissy stood and leaned forward, gently kissed the top of Kate Cuthbert's head. She tried to push a little peace and calmness through, but felt like perhaps it didn't make any difference. Like a breath into a cavern, not even stirring the dust. She would do all she could to help this woman, assuming she survived whatever was happening.

"Was it worth it?" Rich asked.

Chrissy nodded softly, thoughts and ideas beginning to coalesce. "Maybe. Drive us home, please. I need to think."

Adam Campbell walked across town, drawing surreptitiously on a joint cupped into the palm of his hand. He wasn't too bothered about smoking weed in public—he couldn't remember the last time he saw a cop in The Gulp—but it seemed like the right way to do things.

One more deal to sort out, then he could grab a couple of drinks in Clooney's and see who was there to hang out with. After all, he'd be leaving on the weekend. Only a couple more days and then he was finally out. He'd made enough to fix the car a few weeks before and the repairs had been done, but he was still dragging his feet for some reason. Reluctant to leave Gulpepper? He laughed. What the fuck was he thinking? He'd been so close to leaving before, then got held up. But this weekend for sure. He had the car fixed, had some extra cash tucked away, and Rich hadn't come to him with the next delivery yet. They'd got into the habit of Rich dropping off the stuff every Sunday. So, he'd make this last sale now and leave on Saturday. Slip away unencumbered, owing nothing, and leave Gulpepper behind. Finally.

A thin, pale woman came along the street towards him. So pale her skin seemed almost grey in the early evening light. She had greasy long hair and he saw rotten teeth when she grinned at him. He hadn't seen Neil's ghost for a long time now. He assumed his friend had finally gone wherever dead people go. But this woman gave him a strange kind of déjà vu that he could only associate with Neil.

He started to move aside, meaning to give the woman a wide berth, but she held his eye. "Excuse me," she said.

"Yeah, sorry. Busy. I'm running late."

"Oh, it won't take a moment." She lifted a sheet of paper into view. It had a weird design on it, brackets around an upside down lighthouse.

"The fuck is that supposed to be?" Adam said, and hurried past. He glanced back as he went and saw the woman watching after him, a frustrated expression on her face. "Fucking weirdo," he muttered, and took a long draw on the spliff.

As darkness settled over Gulpepper, the streets became quiet. There were always some people around, at any time of day or night, but very few after dark. Sometimes a dog walker would move between pools of streetlight, revellers would turn out of a pub at closing time and stagger home, people on night shift might come and go. But, in a general sense, The Gulp slept after dark. So it was unusual to see a small crowd gathering in Blumenthal Park, on the open grass to one side of the play equipment. A strange mix of the population, young and old alike, moving cautiously around each other.

Furtive glances were cast, but slowly the group seemed to come to some kind of comfort with each other, especially when they saw they each held a sheet of paper with the weirdly bracketed symbol on it.

In quiet voices, some began to discuss it. "Do you remember where you got it?"

"I picked it up off the street."

"I found it on a table in Suzi's Café."

"Why did it bring us here? It doesn't say anything?"

"But you knew to come, right? At this time?"

"I'm not sure why."

"It's persuasive, isn't it?"

Some people grinned and giggled, like teenagers doing something subversive. Others were more nervous, but no less compelled to stay. By the time some forty or fifty people had gathered, the mood was one of nervous excitement.

Then a man approached across the grass, impeccably dressed in a grey three-piece suit and red cravat. His bone-white hair almost glowed in the darkness. He raised his hands as he drew close.

"Friends, thank you so much for coming! My name is Winterbourne."

A few other people waited a few metres behind the man, eyes alert though they seemed pale, thin and unwell to a cursory glance.

"I'm sure you're all wondering why you're here, but fear not. All will be revealed and you will be richly rewarded for your bravery in stepping up. This is indeed a time of great import and you can be integral to it. Let me take your invites, please."

Winterbourne moved among the crowd, collecting the sheets of paper. He held the gathered sheaf in one hand and gestured with it. "Please, follow me."

Like the Pied Piper leading rats, Winterbourne turned and headed south out of the park. The gathering moved en mass to follow. In the trees, large, spiderlike creatures scuttled from branch to branch, watching. Winterbourne looked up and grimaced, noticing first one, then another.

He moved to the few sick-looking people who had come with him and whispered some instructions, then turned back to the crowd. "Please, follow my friends here. I will catch up shortly!"

Winterbourne started in the other direction, glancing back as he went to ensure the spidery creatures followed him and not the crowd. He appeared a little uncertain, but persisted as the large gathering moved out onto Tanning Street and kept going south. As Winterbourne reached the far side of Blumenthal Park, he vanished.

When they'd got back to the farm, Chrissy had gone into her father's study, saying she needed more time, more quiet. She'd spent hours trying to figure things out. To feel her way into events. Eventually, she emerged and poured a couple of generous measures of the good scotch, handed one to Rich.

"Did you get anything from her?" Rich asked tentatively. "Kate Cuthbert, I mean."

He'd remained silent the whole drive home, giving her the space she'd asked for, and hadn't complained when she went off on her own when they got back. She appreciated it, but wasn't sure it had helped.

"Kate kept talking about time. I'm trying to understand what she meant about everything happening and not happening."

"Yeah, that was twisting my brain a bit too."

Chrissy slumped into her favourite armchair, sipped scotch. "My dad used to talk about this stuff too. About how we perceive time so we don't go mad."

"We do what now?"

"It's a theory that's gone around a lot over the years. That time is something we construct to survive reality. When people experience too much at once, they start to lose their mind. Can't cope with it. So we perceive things as separate. My dad thought perhaps Kate and her crew were exposed to something out at Cathedral Stack that broke down the linear nature of how we perceive time. He never did decide what he really thought about it, and then... well, you know what happened. But he said to me that perhaps Cathedral Stack has broken through our reality somehow. That it exists here in geography, but maybe somewhere else in time. Maybe lots of somewhere elses in time. And Kate and her crew experienced that. Most of them died, but Kate survived, even though it unhinged her."

Rich frowned, clearly doing his best to understand. "But Kate seemed to suggest today that all of Gulpepper is like that, right?"

"Yeah. Maybe to varying degrees? My dad always said that real power could be found in manipulating time, but of course, he never had the chance to pursue that much. He was of the opinion that people in general would never be able to manage it. I can't help wondering if this is somehow tied in to what Kate was trying to say."

"You think this white-haired guy is trying to do something like that?"

Chrissy sighed, shrugged. "I don't know, man."

She looked up, senses alert to someone approaching along their winding driveway.

"Everything all right?" Rich asked.

Chrissy stood, heading for the kitchen. "Beverly's coming."

Rich stood to follow as Chrissy headed out the kitchen door to the driveway and raised a hand in greeting. Beverly pulled up into the car port. The young woman didn't seem surprised that Chrissy had anticipated her arrival. Then again, it could be as simple as a camera somewhere on the driveway, which reminded Chrissy she needed to overhaul her father's home security arrangements. Something else that would have to wait while this current situation played out.

"Sorry to come by so late," Beverly called, stepping out of her car.

Chrissy shrugged. "Only a little after nine and we're always up late anyway. What is it?"

"Something Oma asked me to tell you about, but I figured it might be easier to chat in person."

"Cool. Come in. Want a drink?"

Beverly smiled, a little ruefully. "Yeah, actually. I think I do."

Settled in the lounge, Chrissy kept silent, waiting for Beverly to broach whatever was on her mind. Rich sipped quietly, looking from one woman to the next and back again. Chrissy sensed his tension, but recognised it as more concern for her personally than the bigger issues around Gulpepper. In some ways, that was Rich's strength. He had the ability to focus on smaller stuff, things close to him, and deal with those without the stress of the big picture. Chrissy envied him that sometimes.

"So," Beverly said eventually. "Oma saw a gathering at Blumenthal Park earlier and her spyders were all sent to pay attention. They saw people coming from all over town, each holding a sheet of paper. The papers were all the same, just this one symbol on them. Oma said the people themselves appeared confused about their presence there. Almost, she said, like they'd been led there against their will or as if they were sleepwalking. Then the white-haired man arrived with a few others in tow. He announced himself as Winterbourne."

Chrissy nodded. "Before everything went down last time, my father warned me about him. They had a brief run-in and my dad said he wasn't a problem now, but would be at some point. So this is it."

"Okay."

"And what did this group do?"

"Oma said Winterbourne collected all the sheets of paper they held and was about to lead them somewhere when he noticed her spyders. Most people don't notice them, even if they see them, if you know what I mean."

"Yeah, they have a kind of psychic shield. I've seen

that."

"It's part of what they are. Folks with a better attunement to things tend to spot them though, so no surprise this Winterbourne does. Anyway, when he saw them, he sent his people off with the crowd and tried to lead the spyders away, assuming they were there only to watch him, I guess. Two things happened. Firstly, the spyders who followed Winterbourne got across the park and then he just vanished."

"They didn't see any energies?"

Beverly held up one finger. "I'll get back to that in a sec. Oma wasn't foolish enough to send them all after Winterbourne, of course, after your talk earlier. She had two follow the group. But despite their usual sharp attention, they got as far as Carlton Beach, heading along Tanning Street, and then the spyders kind of paused. Like they stopped paying attention despite Oma's attention. And the crowd moved on and the spyders lost them. Oma couldn't understand it until she realised there's an area of town her spyders never go. Like a kind of null space, she said, that she hadn't even realised was there until now."

Chrissy narrowed her eyes. "He's warded it off somehow. Has she figured out where it covers? How much of town?"

"She's still checking and will let me know, but at least between Tanning Street, near St. Augustine's Primary, and Cowpasture Road. Presumably from there all the way to the ocean, from the south end of Carlton Beach."

"That's quite a chunk of town." Chrissy turned to Rich. "We need to go and have a physical look around that area."

"Sure. Maybe we can get some help too?"

"Maybe." She turned back to Beverly. "So, Winterbourne?"

"Right. Well, here's the weird thing. She said that when he vanished, he just blinked out. No particular residue or anything left behind that she could recognise.

But she realised something else. One of her spyders had noticed Winterbourne about an hour before all this happened, walking from the western side of Blumenthal Park up along Booker Street. She didn't watch too closely at the time because she was doing as you asked, paying more attention to others around town than Winterbourne himself. But after the gathering she realised Winterbourne was carrying the sheaf of papers he'd collected from the people in the park."

"She saw him carrying the papers an hour before he'd collected them?"

"Exactly."

"Definitely the same papers?"

"Oma said there was a stain on the top one, like someone had put a coffee cup on it. A kind of brown ring, you know? Same stain both times."

"Sharp eye, your grandma."

"She's a predator." Beverly gave a soft smile and Chrissy wondered, not for the first time, just what Hilda was and how similar Beverly might be to her grandmother.

"You said maybe Winterbourne is doing something with time," Rich said.

Chrissy looked over to him, nodded. "That's how he keeps disappearing. He doesn't go somewhere else. He goes some*when* else."

"You think there's less of that weird leaf stuff in this deal?" Jackson asked Dan.

Dan held the baggie up to a streetlight, peered at it. "Yeah, I think so. There was more in the last one."

"As long as the bud is good, right?"

"Carter's bud is always good. Not sure what that other stuff was that's been in it recently, but there's hardly any this time."

"Good. Well, there aren't usually cops in The Gulp but maybe stop flashing it around quite so blatantly."

Dan tucked the baggie into his pocket, then pointed. "Who's that?"

Jackson followed the gesture and saw a thin, sick-looking man standing on the footpath just ahead of them. As he caught their eye, the thin man held up a sheet of paper, with a strange, bracketed design on it.

Jackson laughed. "Just another Gulp weirdo, I guess."

The thin man made some complicated gestures with his hands and both Dan and Jackson subconsciously lifted a hand to their chests, rubbed like something was bothering them there. Another man emerged from the shadows to their left.

Jackson stepped sideways and nudged Dan over too. "Back the fuck up, man!" he said to the stranger.

The two men looked to each other and some unheard communication seemed to pass between them. They both turned away and melted into the darkness.

"Why do I feel like we just avoided something nasty?" Dan asked.

Jackson watched where the men had gone, then shrugged. "Shall we head on to the lighthouse and have a spliff?"

"Nah, let's get back to your place and get stoned. I don't much feel like being outside any more tonight."

Chrissy woke to an insistent ringing just as Rich sat up beside her and scrabbled for his phone.

"The fuck is that?" Chrissy asked, squinting at the clock. Barely after 5 a.m., dawn light a pale glow against the bedroom curtains.

"Edgar."

"Edgar who?"

"Blind Eye Moon." Rich tapped the phone open and put the call on speaker. "Hey, man."

"Sorry to wake you."

"S'cool. What's up? You coming back?"

"We're here. Drove all night because it sounded kinda important."

"No fucking kidding," Chrissy said, fully awake. "Something big is building."

"You're not wrong. We felt it before we even got close to town. We need to make plans. Okay to come directly there? We're just dropping gear off at the Manor now."

Chrissy sat up and rubbed her eyes. "Yeah, do that. I'll get the coffee on."

"Cool. See you in ten."

Lauren Hart couldn't sleep. She was worried about how Connor and Serena were getting on. She was glad to have got them out of Gulpepper and knew they were currently safe enough, but what did their future hold? Lauren's mother had a cousin up in Brisbane, and that cousin had been more than kind and taken Connor and Serena in. They'd even got a place in school up there. Connor planned to apply for guardianship of Serena when he turned eighteen, but that was nearly two years away and Lauren wasn't sure they'd be able to stay with her mother's cousin that long. Regardless, she planned a trip up to see them soon. And, in the meantime, she'd been getting ever more restless, often unable to lie in. Connor still wouldn't tell her what had happened to Brendan, and that preyed on her mind.

She'd left the house that morning before dawn, anxious as ever, deciding fresh air and exercise was better than tossing and turning in bed or disturbing her parents by moving around the house.

As she headed up Tanning Street, not really sure where she was going other than vaguely in the direction of school, she saw two people walking towards her. Immediately, Lauren's senses were on alert. One of the women was supporting the other a little, talking quietly all the time. As they got nearer, Lauren's heart skipped a beat. The woman doing all the supporting looked just like the rock star, Eevie Chill. She was a movie star too, but Lauren was all about the music. Surely not.

She moved a little quicker to close the distance and, just as the woman looked up and saw Lauren watching them, Lauren came to the conclusion this actually *was* the megastar, not simply some lookalike. Lauren had posters of this woman on her bedroom wall, had all her albums. What the hell was Eevie Chill doing in Gulpepper? The other person seemed weak and drawn, wearing only thongs, shorts and a t-shirt. Lauren ran up to them.

"You're—"

"Yes, I am. It's me in the flesh, Eevie fucking Chill. I'm sorry, don't mean to be rude, but we need help. We've had a hell of a night and just got away from a bad situation and I have no idea where I am."

Lauren nodded. "Okay, sure. No problem. What do you need exactly?"

"Mainly a way out of this freaky fucking town."

Lauren laughed. "Yeah, there's a lot of that about lately. I can help."

A dark van drove by, then braked hard and stopped before backing up again. Lauren saw the logo on the side, a blood red eye superimposed over a full moon.

"You're fucking kidding," she whispered.

The van stopped beside them and a beautiful woman with fire engine red hair, equally red irises and heavily kohled eyes leaned out of the front passenger side window. "Eevie?"

Eevie shook her head, a wry smile twisting her mouth. "What brings you guys here?"

"We live here," Shirley said, idly twirling a drumstick. "What's your excuse?"

"A long fucking story. Can you get me outta here? And my friend Debbie here? She needs medical attention."

"We've got a pretty important meeting we have to get to right now, but come with us. Chrissy has people who can look after your friend there and we'll see you out of here once we've talked to Chrissy."

Eevie nodded. "That's better than staggering around these fucking streets wondering where the hell to go."

The van's side door slid open, revealing a couple of bench seats behind the front seats and an empty cargo area behind them. Howard, the Blind Eye Moon bassist, leaned out, offered a hand to help Eevie and Debbie in. Edgar was driving and Clarke sat in the back, watching impassively. All the band members wore black and all had their signature crimson eyes and heavy dark make-up that Shirley sported.

Lauren looked around the group in stunned amazement. "Eevie Chill and Blind Eye Moon just hanging out before dawn. This place has all kinds of weird."

Howard gave her a half-smile. "You wanna come along?"

Edgar twisted in the front seat to look back. "Dude, she's a fucking child!"

"I'm nearly sixteen!"

"Like I said, a child!"

Howard threw Edgar a look. "Mate, you know me better than that. I'm not suggesting anything untoward.

Just seems rude to turn up like this and then leave her behind."

"We kinda have more important things to take care of."

"I know Chrissy Carter," Lauren said quickly, determined to somehow extend this bizarre moment, imagining hanging out with this lot for a while longer. "I worked for her a couple of times. Doing events at Clooney's, you know?"

"See?" Howard said to Edgar. "She's part of the team already. Could be useful..." he added, in a more sombre tone.

A moment of tension suddenly hung between the two men and Edgar narrowed his eyes in thought. He sighed, shook his head and turned back to face the road ahead.

Howard extended a hand towards Lauren. "So, you wanna come with us?"

"Fuck, yeah!"

Chrissy and Rich were drinking coffee when the Blind Eye Moon van pulled up beside Chrissy's Merc. She was surprised to see more than the four band members get out. She was even more surprised when Rich yelled, "That's Eevie fucking Chill!"

Eevie was helping another woman out, who looked scared and somehow weakened, and a kid climbed out behind them. Chrissy frowned, searching her memory because she knew the kid from somewhere. "Lauren Hart," she said quietly after a moment.

"With the brown hair?" Rich asked.

"Yeah. She lives here in town. Works events sometimes. Good kid."

"Why is she here?"

"Good question."

Chrissy opened the door and let everyone in. Edgar gestured to the unexpected guests and said, "Long story, but we're just helping these folks out. Debbie there needs some medical help, I think."

"She mainly needs somewhere safe for a little while," Eevie said. "And some decent food and drink. But I would like a doctor to check her out."

Chrissy nodded. "We can do that."

"I plan to stay with her, just FYI. I mean, thanks a fucktonne for your hospitality, especially unannounced like this, but I made Debbie a promise. I'm taking care of her."

"That's fine. You're welcome here. Are you, like, touring or something?"

Eevie laughed, but it was bitter. "Nah. Like he said, long story."

Chrissy cast her mind over the woman and saw Gulp mist swirling thickly, and a familiar presence lurking at the edges of the rock star's psyche. That esoteric connection warped and shifted around all of them. Even young Lauren Hart was connected. But Eevie was thick with it. "You've had... a less than natural run-in lately?"

"To say the fucking least. What are you, psychic?"

"Kinda."

The two women stared at each other for a moment, and Chrissy was impressed with Eevie's strength.

"Let's just say if I see that white-haired fuck again I'm going to feed him his balls."

Chrissy smiled. "Synchronicity. He's the reason we're meeting here. So I'm guessing this is all falling into place."

"White hair and grey suit?" Lauren asked. "Red cravat?"

"That's him," Eevie said.

Tears stood out on Lauren's lower eyelids. "That cunt killed Brendan, I'm pretty sure. My best friend's brother.

I still don't know exactly what happened. I got Connor and Serena away, they're safe. But I'm sure Brendan died for it somehow. Connor has promised to come back and finish him, and I plan to help."

Chrissy pointed to the large kitchen table that could comfortably seat a dozen people. "Well, it seems we've all got a reason to be here. Take a seat, everyone. If you can, Lauren, warn your friend Connor against coming back. It's too dangerous right now and we plan to deal with Winterbourne anyway. Rich, coffee all around?"

"On it."

Chrissy sat with the rest and leaned her elbows on the table, face in her palms. This was all too much. Too much and too soon. But what choice did they have? At least it seemed she had some direct allies, but sometimes too many people could be a hindrance. She drew a deep breath and looked up. "Okay. This Winterbourne is working towards something. It's huge and it will almost certainly be bad for us, for Gulpepper. We've been trying to get a handle on what he's doing, but he's fucking elusive. We've established two things so far. One is that he keeps avoiding our scrutiny by manipulating time. Seems he can slip back in time at will."

"That's not an easy thing," Shirley said. "I mean, that's more-than-human power."

"Right. I think he is human. At least, he was. But he's clearly become something more. I'm guessing he's been working up to this for a long time. We're not sure how much power he has, but he can move back at least an hour or two. I mean, it's pretty useful, right? You want to disappear, so you stay in the same place but go back to an hour before?"

"The implications of that are massive," Eevie said. "Are you serious, he can do that?"

"Yep."

"Far out."

Chrissy gave a soft, rueful laugh. "Yeah. But I think that's the least of it. Probably just one of many powers he's developed."

"You said two things?" Edgar asked.

Chrissy nodded. She paused while Rich handed coffees around, then said, "The other is that he's warded off a section of town. For all our looking and trying to figure this shit out, there's at least a whole block of Gulpepper we can't see properly with the methods open to us. I can only assume that whatever he's doing, it's centralised there. So we need to go and have an actual look. In the flesh, as it were."

"Where is it?" Edgar asked.

"As far as we can tell, from somewhere around the south end of Carlton Beach, near the primary school, as least as far as Cowpasture Road."

Edgar nodded. "Okay, hang on." He looked to the other band members and gave one lift of the chin.

"Right here?" Clarke asked.

"I think these people are all pretty aware there's more than meets the eye in Gulpepper. And if not, they soon will be."

The four members of Blind Eye Moon stood from the table and moved to one side, took each other's hands in a rough circle.

"Don't be alarmed," Edgar said. "And don't touch us."

Without waiting for a response, the four hung their heads and a rapid change came over them. At first, the dark make-up around their eyes spread, branching out in dozens of tiny capillaries that spread over their cheeks. Their pale skin grew chalk white and their faces elongated along with their limbs and torsos until they'd gained at least a foot in height.

"What the fuck?" Eevie and Lauren said in unison. Debbie stared out the kitchen window, seeming to pay no attention to anything happening around her.

Chrissy watched the power pulse out from the group and tried to follow, but it moved quicker than she could. Within moments, the band resumed their previous form and broke contact, returned to sit at the table.

"You're right," Edgar said. "Can't get close. Honestly, I don't think we could even dream our way past that. I've never seen such powerful warding."

"Makes our security at the Manor look like a wet paper bag," Howard said, brow furrowed.

"Is that…" Eevie licked her lips, gestured vaguely in the band's direction. "Like, are you now in your real shape or are you really whatever the fuck that was just now?"

Edgar laughed. "Big question, difficult to answer."

"I know where you're talking about," Lauren said. "It's where Brendan died."

"Go on," Chrissy said.

"There's an old hall on Burly Road. Like, used to be a community hall or something, I guess."

"I think I know the one you mean," Edgar said. "Used to be the scout hall back in the day. Like, a long time ago. It got all painted white when the scouts moved. Hasn't been used for much in decades, as far as I know."

"Well, that's where this Winterbourne was when Connor tried to… When Brendan… It was in there."

"We need to go down there and have a look," Chrissy said. "Rich, can you come with me and the band?"

"Sure thing."

"Eevie, you're welcome to stay here with your friend. I'll call a doc on our way. Should be here in an hour or so. Lauren, maybe you should head off?"

Lauren cast a crooked smile at the gathering and shook her head. "I am certainly not going to fucking school today. If it's all the same to you, can I stay?"

Chrissy pursed her lips, wondering if she was endangering the young girl more by letting her stay or insisting she leave. The kid was already embroiled somehow, but did she need to stay that way?

"Please?" Lauren asked.

"Enough with the puppy dog eyes, kid. That might work on your daddy, but not on me."

Lauren laughed. "Yeah, fair enough. But I really want

to stay."

"You are connected somehow, I can't deny that. Okay, but you don't leave the house. Stay here and make yourself useful if necessary."

"Just hang out here with Eevie Chill? I can do that." Lauren turned to Eevie, an apologetic look on her face. "Sorry, I know you've been through some shit. I won't fangirl all over you, I promise."

"You're all right, Lauren. I'll appreciate the company." Eevie looked to Chrissy. "Can we go somewhere more comfortable?"

"Through there. Debbie can lay on the couch. Help yourself to anything. Mi casa, su casa." Chrissy strode to the door. "Come on, let's go."

The six of them crammed into Rich's crew cab ute. Chrissy drove, Rich and Edgar on the front seat with her, Shirley, Clarke and Howard behind. As she backed out and headed down the long Carter's Farm driveway, Chrissy said, "I'm guessing these wards might be more obvious now we know we're looking for them, but let's keep an eye on each other. This Winterbourne fucker clearly has some real power."

"We trawl this town almost every night we're home," Howard said. "Amazing we haven't noticed it."

"Yeah," Edgar agreed. "I mean, it's one thing to ward off somewhere. To make it inaccessible to us astrally or whatever. But to make it so we don't even know that's been done? That's next level."

Chrissy pulled out from the driveway gate and past Turner's Manufacturing, following the road that led past the new Gulpepper Institute and eventually on to the cemetery on Jacquelin Head. But before long she turned left onto Tanning Street, heading north. They passed the Ocean Blue Motel and Chrissy kept driving.

"Hey, you missed it," Rich said.

Chrissy glanced at him. "What?"

"You should have turned back there on Cowpasture, right? To get to Burly Road, yeah?"

"Oh fuck, what was I thinking?"

"Take the next right and we'll go back around the block the other way."

"Yeah."

After a moment, Rich said. "Pull over."

"What?"

"You just did it again."

"Did what?"

"You missed the turning!"

"What the actual fuck?"

"This is some powerful shit," Howard said, twisting around to look out the back window. "Did any of you notice?"

The other band members shook their heads.

Chrissy pulled up to the curb and Rich said, "Scooch across, let me drive."

They clumsily switched places and Rich did a three-point turn in a house driveway and headed back along Tanning Street. Just after the primary school, he indicated left and made the turn. Chrissy and all four members of Blind Eye Moon cried out, hands flying up to grip their heads.

"Turn around!" Chrissy yelled. Then through gritted, "Turn the fuck around!"

Rich hit the brakes and made a fast, messy turn, pulling back onto Tanning Street then over to the curb. He stopped and looked around the vehicle, watched the others slowly come back to themselves, gasping.

"That really fucking hurt," Shirley said.

Chrissy noticed all four band members' eyes had

gone a much brighter red, the dark filaments spreading wide across their cheeks and the orbits of their eyes. As they began to regain their breath, the darkness slowly retreated again.

"Did you feel anything then, Rich?" Chrissy asked. "At all?"

He shook his head. "Not really. Nothing I noticed. But you guys reacted so strongly, I don't know…"

"What do we do if we can't get close?" Edgar asked.

"There must be a way to mitigate it," Chrissy said. "Rich, do you reckon you could walk in there and see what's what? Maybe see if you can get close to the hall? Don't get spotted though, okay? Bail the moment you feel uncomfortable."

"Sure, I can try." He opened the door and hopped out. "How about I call you and keep the line open?" He rang Chrissy's mobile and then dropped his phone into the top pocket of his work shirt. He closed the door and walked a few paces away. "Hear me okay?" he asked, then took the phone out again to listen.

He came through loud and clear on Chrissy's phone. She tapped it onto loudspeaker. "Yep, all good."

"Okay, wish me luck!"

"Tell us what you're feeling all the way. I want a running commentary."

"Sure."

Chrissy watched him slip the phone back into his shirt pocket and trot across the street to head up the side road, glancing casually around as he did so. She didn't want to voice the concern, but had a bad feeling about it.

As Rich headed towards Burly Road he tried to stay as aware as possible of how he felt. Of course, that only made him paranoid that every sensation was something malevolent. Living with Chrissy Carter often led to feelings that things were off. It would be ninety per cent normal life, nine percent weird crime stuff, then one per cent absolute unexplainable bonkers nonsense. Strangely, he'd grown incredibly used to it. After everything that went down a couple of years before when Chrissy's dad had died and he'd brought down the manor with Chrissy and the others, nothing had even come close in terms of weirdness. Now though? Things were clearly ramping up again. Worse than before, Chrissy said. And the way they'd all reacted in the ute just then, the way Blind Eye Moon so casually revealed themselves in the farmhouse earlier? Things were spiralling fast.

"Okay, just turning onto Burly now," he said, trusting the phone to pick up his words. "Everything seems fine. Can't feel anything untoward."

He walked the full length of the street, glancing across at the old white hall as he went but not slowing. The weird symbol painted on the double doors gave him pause, like it was shifting slightly, as if the doors themselves were rippling. He said as much and wondered what Chrissy might say in response. Did she need to give him instructions?

Before he turned around for another pass, he slipped his phone out and put it on speaker, put it back in his pocket. "I can hear you now. Should have done that before."

"Finally! Can you describe the symbol?"

He did so and there was muted muttering in the car. After a moment, he asked, "Mean anything?"

"Not really. Keep going."

"Okay. I'm turning back and going for another walk past. Should I go up to the hall?"

"Can you see through the windows?"

"No. Looks like they're boarded up on the inside."

A small group of people walked towards him along Burly Road, on the other side of the street. The same side as the hall. They looked strange, which was not uncommon in The Gulp, but something about these three put Rich on edge.

"Two men and a woman," he said. "Skinny and kinda pale, coming the other way." He paused, crouched to pretend to tie his shoe, side-eyeing the group as he did so. "They're going to the hall, I think. I really want to go in there."

"Don't! Can you see in the door from where you are? Get a look if they go in!"

He stood quickly and walked again, trying to time his passing on the far side of the road with them pushing the doors open. He caught a glimpse of the interior as they went in. "It's weird in there. Looks kinda green and washy, don't know how to describe it. Like it's underwater inside. There's a nude guy standing behind a big book on a lectern in the middle... Wait, that's Winterbourne. Bone white hair, yeah? And all around the walls are... fuck, they're people. Dozens of people all hanging off the walls, naked. I can't tell if they're alive or—one moved. They're alive!"

Winterbourne's head snapped up and he pinned Rich with a penetrating gaze.

"Fuck! He saw me."

"Run!" Chrissy barked. "Get away!"

As Rich crouched to pretend to tie his shoe, side-eyeing the group heading towards the hall, he heard footsteps approaching behind and turned. A white-haired man in a grey three-piece suit with a red cravat walked up to him. "Good morning."

Rich stood and turned, backed up a couple of steps. The three people approaching the hall across the street paused to watch. "Morning." Rich's voice was tight in his throat. He willed Chrissy to keep quiet, trusting she would understand that need. This had to be

Winterbourne.

"Lovely day coming, I think," Winterbourne said with a smile. His eyes were dark, predatory.

"I think so. Aren't you hot in that suit?"

"No, I'm always just right. Where are you headed today?"

Rich felt the urge to come completely clean with this man, to tell him everything, but he'd known Chrissy long enough to remember one of her golden rules: Never tell anyone your business. "Just out for a walk. Exercise, you know, before the day gets too hot."

"Probably best you choose a different route in future, yes?"

The compulsion to obey was overpowering. "Absolutely. Of course. You know, I'll go back this way and walk somewhere else."

"Marvellous."

Rich felt Winterbourne's eyes on him all the way, hoping against hope the man wouldn't follow and see Chrissy in the ute, waiting. As he turned the corner, he let out a sigh of relief at the empty curb. Chrissy was smart enough to have driven away when she heard the conversation. Before buildings got in the way, Rich glanced back and saw Winterbourne in the same spot, watching him go.

"Chrissy, I'll walk up to the high school. Come and pick me up there."

"Will do. You didn't see anything else?"

"Didn't even get close on the second pass. How did he know I was there?"

"This is infuriating!" Chrissy snapped. "We have no idea if there's even anything in that hall. Let's get back to the farm. We need to decide on a better approach."

Back around the kitchen table, Chrissy did her best to swallow her rage. She wasn't used to being so out of control, especially of events directly affecting The Gulp.

"Nothing at all?" Eevie asked.

"Couldn't even get close. Winterbourne knew we were there before Rich saw more than the outside of the building." She looked up, half-turned towards the door. "Beverly's coming. Rich, let her in?"

"Sure."

Beverly took a spot at the table and her eyes widened when she saw Eevie. Chrissy was impressed with how quickly the young woman processed the presence of Blind Eye Moon and one of the world's most recognisable superstars without a word of question. Lauren Hart sat with them, also surprisingly calm. Chrissy had to admit there was something about this gathering, at this time. She felt the influence of her father and thought maybe she was imagining that rather than truly feeling it, but she accepted the comfort it brought her. All eyes were on her, waiting for guidance. But she didn't know what to do.

"Oma says more people than ever have gone missing in recent weeks," Beverly said, and Chrissy was thankful the girl had something for them.

"People missing in this town in nothing new," Edgar said.

Chrissy huffed something resembling a laugh. "You lot would know!"

Beverly raised a hand. "No, this is different. That group Oma's spyders followed and lost? She recognised a couple of them and checked. Their families have just reported them missing. When I double-checked, it seems more people than usual have been going AWOL lately."

"If they were heading towards the warded area," Chrissy said, "it can only mean Winterbourne is collecting them somehow, for something."

"Collecting them?" Eevie asked.

Chrissy dragged a palm over her face. "Okay, quick history lesson. Last time something like this happened, an ancient entity from the fall tried to manifest itself here. It used the populace to power itself, their combined wills and life energies. People and place, yeah? They're always connected." She gestured at the band. "These guys put everyone in town to sleep for a little while and gave my father the time to interrupt its growth, then me, Rich and Stephen blew the place sky high. Stephen mostly. He gave his life for it, like Dad did."

"Blew it down into the ocean and buried it in rubble, in fact," Rich said. He raised his coffee mug in a toast. "To Stephen."

Chrissy smiled sadly. "To Stephen. But Winterbourne was aware of that situation beforehand and went away again. My dad said he'd be back. Told me to watch for him. And after all that shit went down, I've been trying to make sure nothing like it happens again. I've been working to inoculate people from that kind of influence. Like this plant I developed. I've been mixing it with the weed half this town smokes and it makes people a lot less pliable to arcane forces."

"How the fuck did you do that?" Howard asked.

"Long story. Lot of research. Beside the point right now. The point is that with that leaf, and with some stuff I've been doing in the pub to cover patrons there, some other things, I've been working to make the people of this town less susceptible. But it's not something that can happen fast. It takes months. Years. I've been partially successful, but this Winterbourne fucker has moved fast. He's obviously collecting up the people in town I haven't protected."

"Okay, I know some mad shit goes on around here,"

Eevie said. "I've seen plenty the last few days. Enough for a lifetime, actually. But I don't get this. Why is he collecting people? What's he doing with them?"

"Nothing good, I'm sure. Look at it like this. Imagine you're trying to power a big machine. It takes a lot of energy, right? Loads of fuel or batteries or whatever? Now imagine that machine is your mind. Your numinous energies. One person, however powerful they've become, can only embody so much. But if you use other people to power yourself, use them up like extra batteries, you can exponentially increase your power."

"Like those pricks who hack into other peoples' PCs and use them to mine crypto?" Lauren asked. At the confused expressions around the table, she shrugged. "Don't worry. But it is like that. Kinda."

"And all these people he's collecting up must be in that hall we can't get to?" Shirley said. "He's using them for whatever he's up to. And using them to energise such powerful wards to stop us getting near him."

Chrissy nodded. "I think so."

"So what can we do about it?"

"Whatever he's using, the fact remains that Winterbourne himself is the focus of that power. He needs to be confronted directly."

"Can you do that?" Lauren asked.

Chrissy shook her head. "I don't know. I mean, yeah, theoretically. So could any of these bastards." She swept a hand towards Blind Eye Moon.

Edgar nodded, but raised his hands. "Yeah, theoretically, like you say. But I don't know that any of us are powerful enough to confront him. Not if he's dug in like he seems to be. And we don't know what end game he's pursuing."

"The why of it doesn't matter," Chrissy said. "Whatever he's doing, it needs to stop. It won't be good for Gulpepper."

"Maybe it's not something we *can* stop?" Edgar said.

"Fuck that! You lot might be able to just move on, set

up somewhere else and still be a big famous band. But for us, we're Gulpepper and Gulpepper is us. I'll do it. I need to face him."

Edgar frowned. "Why?"

Chrissy sighed. "So many people thought my dad was just a thug. They still think so. But everything he ever did, and his father before him and his father, and way back for generations, was to protect Gulpepper. They all sacrificed so much because this place and the people here matter. And sure, that meant hard decisions. And sure, maybe they all went a little off the rails here and there. Huge responsibility will do that to a person. It'll probably happen to me too. But he had power, my dad. He could have left with that power, like you're suggesting, and been something special somewhere else. But he didn't. He stayed and stood up for The Gulp. You know what my dad taught me, above all else? To take a stand. Stand up for what's right, *because* it's right. Stand up without hope if you have to, but stand. Stand without reward. Stand without witness. Above all else, stand up."

"But if none of us are powerful enough to even get close to this cunt, how do we begin to stop him?" Edgar asked.

"Can't you do what he's doing?" Lauren asked.

Chrissy turned a questioning eye to the girl.

Lauren squirmed slightly. "I mean, in a good way? You said you'd been protecting a lot of the population from his influence. Can you use *those* people to power yourself?"

Chrissy pursed her lips in thought. "Are there enough people still here not under his effect to grant me the power to face him? And if so, how do we harness that? How do we draw enough energy from enough people to even give me a chance?"

Eevie laughed. "Are you kidding?"

"What?"

"By the power of metal, baby!"

"Seriously?"

"If there was a load of people gathered in one place, like a shit-tonne of people, do you have a way to harness that energy or not?"

Edgar leaned forward, the rest of Blind Eye Moon grinning along with him. "We could do that. A gathered crowd, focussed on us? We could manipulate that energy. Big party time, right?"

Lauren stood up, unable to contain her excitement. "You serious? Together?"

"Yes!" Edgar said. "Blind Eye Moon featuring Eevie Chill!"

"If we saturate our socials with news of an impromptu free gig, this place will seethe with people," Eevie said. "They'll flood in from all around."

"You know our songs?" Edgar asked.

"Of course. Some of them, anyway."

"And we can play a bunch of yours. Give me a chance to concentrate while you sing."

"This has to be soon," Chrissy said. "We can't delay. How quickly can you arrange this?"

"Fucking tonight," Edgar said. "It's not even ten am yet. We put the word out and anyone within eight or ten hour's drive can get here. We announce it as a free gig, one night only. Can you get a stage and all the PA and lights and shit to the Gulpepper showground before, say, six? We can soundcheck and be live by eight. There will be thousands of people here by then."

Rich patted the air, brow knitted. "Hang on, hang on. It will be fucking chaos! Traffic jams and people fighting to get close and whatever."

Edgar laughed. "Oh yeah. It's absolutely fucking irresponsible. Some people will certainly get hurt. But if you want a lot of people in one place quickly, this is how you do it."

"I can talk to some folks," Chrissy said. "It won't be anything spectacular, but I can get a stage set up."

"We don't need especially fancy lights and pyro," Shirley said. "The spectacle will be us."

"I can talk to the Desert Ghosts," Rich said. "Remember they did security for us at that thing last year? They can do it again, maybe?"

"The biker gang?" Lauren asked.

"Sometimes you can't pick and choose your allies."

"It'll cost," Chrissy said. "But throwing money at this is the easy part."

"Once in a lifetime event," Howard said with a grin.

Edgar stood, spread his hands wide. "We'll call it the One Immortal Day Special Event." He turned to Chrissy. "If you want power, this will do it. We'll pump you into a god. But then it's down to you to face this Winterbourne. If we're doing the gig, being your batteries, you'll be on your own."

Chrissy looked around the group, the hopeful faces, the excitement. "Fucking hell. Okay then. We have a lot of work to do."

Chrissy had expected the announcement of the gig to raise hell, but she was stunned at just how quickly things started moving. By the time she'd got off the phone to her contacts to arrange the stage set-up, Eevie, Shirley and Edgar were gathered around a laptop with a BEM logo sticker on it.

"It's going off!" Edgar said with a laugh. "Holy shit, Eevie, you've got some fans."

"What can I say, I'm blessed."

Shirley pointed. "That post just passed one million impressions already. One million!"

"Loads of questions, too," Eevie said. "We need to rehearse and get some kind of show organised. I can have my social media team manage this, but they're already freaking out. Michael, my manager, is losing his fucking mind, but so far I'm ignoring all his messages."

"Any way we can keep this in house?" Chrissy asked. "If your corporate reps get involved, we might have more problems to deal with."

Eevie gestured at the laptop. "I can't manage this and get ready to perform."

Lauren stood and raised a hand tentatively. "I knew I was here for a reason. I kinda want to be a social media manager or events manager or something and I'm already good at this stuff. Let me do it?"

Eevie smiled. "I knew I liked you."

Lauren blushed scarlet.

Chrissy nodded, vindicated in keeping the young girl around. It had felt right at the time and now she was convinced. "You gotta be careful though. Don't say too much."

"Here's the trick," Eevie said. "Never rise to trolling and only answer direct questions that you can answer with one hundred per cent certainty. Engage, but don't converse. Never answer a follow-up question. Just because someone has access to us via social media doesn't mean we owe them anything. So, answer direct questions, block trolls, and contact me or Edgar here if anything comes up that has you concerned. Sound okay?"

Lauren nodded. "Absolutely."

Eevie concentrated a moment as she tapped out a message and hit return, then grinned. "I've just told my media team to ignore all socials for twenty-four hours on pain of losing their jobs. This is all yours, Lauren."

Lauren licked her lips, sucking in a nervous breath and taking a seat as Edgar moved aside. "I've got this."

Edgar squeezed her shoulder. "Nice job, thanks." He turned to the others. "Let's get back to the Manor. Our rehearsal studio's set up in the attic. We can plan our set there."

"Stage set-up is coming right now from Enden and

will be in place by four p.m.," Chrissy said. "At least, that's what I just agreed to pay an eye-watering sum for anyway. Rich will help coordinate that."

"Don't worry about money," Eevie said. "Honestly, I have more than I could ever spend."

"We'll need gear in place too," Edgar said. "We'll bring our guitars, but we're going to need to treat this like a rolling tour. The streets will be impassable and we won't be able to get gear close, I expect." He grabbed a pad and pen from the kitchen counter. "Here's the number of a hire shop in Enden. And a list of the amps and drum kit we'll need in place. Make sure everything's lined in for us? Pay these guys enough and they'll sort it."

Chrissy nodded. "I'll get Rich onto it now."

"We'll be at the oval by five," Edgar said.

Edgar, Eevie, Chrissy and Lauren all exchanged numbers and set up a group chat. Lauren returned her focus to her task and Chrissy gave a nod as Eevie and the band headed out of the kitchen. It looked like maybe they could pull this off. All that remained to be seen was whether or not it would raise enough power for Chrissy to confront Winterbourne and, if so, if she stood a chance in hell of doing anything about whatever the bastard was planning.

By two that afternoon there wasn't a parking space left anywhere in Gulpepper. Cars were lined up all along Gulpepper Road, almost as far as the T-junction at the end some ten or eleven kilometres away, and people were covering the remaining distance on foot. Reports were coming in of mayhem in both Monkton and Enden.

Locals and those who had arrived early enough were camped on the grounds of the oval, a festival atmosphere growing already. Rich ended up arranging boats from Enden and Monkton to bring the stage gear, stagehands and a few dozen more Desert Ghosts in by sea to avoid the jams. Hi-vis vests were handed around to the bikers, who immediately set to making sure the rapidly growing crowds remained peaceful. Sometimes they employed their fists as enforcement, but after a few such outbursts the public became much more compliant. The general air was one of growing excitement.

Rich was impressed with the swift arrival of food vans and other vendors who had arrived with the first concert goers, but he was concerned about the lack of toilet facilities. That was going to be a real problem. He'd booked every portaloo in the area, but there weren't many to be had. He was reminded of the old stories about Woodstock in the 1960s, and the impromptu party that had grown up around that. He only hoped they ended up with something half as positive out of all this. He couldn't help feeling like a disaster of some kind was just around the corner. But a far bigger disaster was certain otherwise, if Chrissy was correct.

Trusting the bikers to manage the public, he turned his attention to the stage and made sure it was the best it could be given the short notice. It didn't need to be huge, but they had PA stacks like small buildings either side and Rich knew that, if nothing else, the sound was going to be massive. He'd been on the phone to another provider to see if they could arrange big screens for people further away to get some kind of view but wasn't sure that was going to happen, so he made sure maximum volume was guaranteed. The sound mixing desk and lighting operator were set up in the middle of the showground oval, the biggest open space Gulpepper had to offer, protected by a ring of scowling Desert Ghosts.

Most of the professionals involved were excited to be

working this event, not only for the huge and unexpected payday, but because they got to work with one of the biggest names in popular culture and the biggest local band, in an unprecedented event that would undoubtedly live on. It was one of those things, Rich realised, that people would claim to have attended whether they really did or not. For the people who were there, it would be unforgettable. Edgar had been prescient suggesting they call it One Immortal Day. One way or another, it would be.

Chrissy sat in her father's study in the house on Carter's Farm. She'd left the room as a kind of shrine to the man, a way to remember him and be close to him, surrounded by the things he held dear. Some of those things were unsavoury, to say the least, but his big leather wingback reading chair, off to one side of his huge mahogany writing desk, was still one of her favourite places to be. With the door closed and only the standing lamps in the corners turned on, it was a dim and peaceful place to rest. To meditate.

"Dad, I don't know if I can do this," she whispered to the gloom.

For all their skills, Chrissy had no idea if there was anything like a life beyond this one for people who had died. There were certainly other realms and energies in existence that could be manipulated, but once someone had lost their lifeforce, she knew no more than anyone else about where that might go, or even if it went anywhere. But right now, she would give a lot to talk with her father's ghost. To get some kind of guidance.

Instead, she'd done the only thing she could, which

was prepare herself. She gathered mental fortitude, stored up whatever energy she could manifest, and waited. Without any idea what Winterbourne was doing, she would have to react on the fly. Nothing to plan for other than being ready for anything. It felt like only minutes had passed, but it turned out to be hours when she was disturbed by the loud thrum of a helicopter. A moment after she noticed that drawing close, her phone pinged. Rich.

time to go

Chrissy sucked in a long breath and nodded to herself. "Okay. Dad, if you're anywhere nearby, give me your strength."

She walked outside and saw the chopper coming in to land in the paddock directly behind the house. Edgar jumped out once it landed and ran over.

"Just as well I know people, eh?" he shouted over the rotors. "Town is gridlocked. This is gonna go off!"

"Good to hear. We ready?"

"Yep."

Lauren appeared at the fence, laptop under her arm. Edgar waved her over. "Come on, you're the official assistant for all of this. Hey, maybe you can MC the gig. You want to introduce us?"

"Are you serious?"

"Fuck yeah. Come on, hop in."

The helicopter lifted off again. The band, Eevie Chill, Lauren Hart and Chrissy Carter all looking at each other in something like amazement.

"This is absolutely fucking mental," Shirley said.

"Kinda fun though, right?" Eevie asked. "I haven't been this excited about something in years. Takes me back to why we do this shit in the first place."

It took less than a minute for the chopper to cruise across town, every road, every inch of open space absolutely packed with people. They hovered over the headland between Spiny Point and Carlton Beach that held the large pavilion building and showground. Every part of that space was packed with people too, and crowds filled the beach itself. Dozens of boats bobbed offshore, people partying on board, with more coming from north and south.

The stage itself was pretty simple, a raised rectangle with one light gantry arcing across the front and a second gantry behind holding a big black curtain as a backdrop. A drum kit glittered on a riser at the back of the stage and amps with leads running out of them stood waiting. The speaker stacks either side were huge, but no big screens. Given that was the only thing Rich had mentioned that Chrissy couldn't see, she thought he'd done amazingly well.

The only place not packed with people was directly behind the stage, which had been fenced off and a marquee set up. There was just enough room beside it for the helicopter to set down, the tent sides billowing with the downdraft.

They all piled out and the chopper left again, promising to stay as close by as possible to come back and airlift everyone out whenever needed. Rich ran to meet them and led the way into the large marquee.

"Not sure how you're going to manage the sound check," he said. "All of this is pretty grass roots."

"Like the small pub gigs of old," Howard said. "Only fucking huge. No problem."

"Chrissy, I've got a boat standing by just off the rocks. It's a bit of a clamber down to it, but once you're ready to go, we can bypass all the crowds by going on the water and get up to Burly Road via the coastal walking track. Again, a bit of a climb, but should be okay."

"That's great, thanks."

"There are a lot of other boats gathering out there. Hopefully we can get through them."

"Yeah, we saw."

"Good spot to be, really," Eevie said. "They'll hear us easily. You see those stacks as we flew in?"

Edgar laughed. "They'll hear us in Enden, probably."

Chrissy checked the time. "Nearly five-thirty. Plenty of time to get—"

She felt the wave coming a moment before it hit, like barbed wire tearing through her mind. She cried out, staggering back. The band members around her howled in pain of their own, their forms flexing briefly. She saw Rich and Lauren, otherwise as mundane as possible, flinch and loose their footing for a moment, looking confused.

"What's happening?" Lauren cried.

"It's Winterbourne!" Chrissy sucked in a breath, desperately recentering her energy. "He's started whatever he's planning. Sound check be fucked, we have to go now!" She dragged at Rich's arm. "Get me over there! Edgar, Eevie, I need everything you can give as quickly as possible. Can you do it?"

Edgar grinned. "Guess we'll fucken have to!"

Raised voices from the crowd on the other side of the stage reached them, a combination of excitement and alarm, mostly confusion.

"We can't let the crowd panic!" Chrissy yelled. "Hold them in place. We need them!"

Lauren looked around the group and then ran for the stage. "I'll hold them! Grab your shit! Let's do this!"

Chrissy ran for the boat.

Lauren shook all over, her hands tingled, her breath ran short. As she climbed the steps behind the stage and emerged behind Shirley's drum kit, she forced herself to take a deep breath. How could so much have happened in a single day? How could she possibly be about to do this?

The aftershock of whatever Winterbourne had done hung in the air, like static before a storm, only amplified. As she walked across the stage towards two mics side by side at the front centre, she was briefly overwhelmed by the sea of people before her. They milled, spooked like cattle not sure where to run.

Another pulse of Winterbourne's energy rocked through the crowd and people began to cry out, look around, eyes wide, panic setting in.

Lauren staggered, but kept moving. She grabbed the mic and said, "Hello, Gulpepper!" But nothing came from the speakers. She tapped the mic, saw it was switched on, but nothing. The crowd before her shifted like a tide, trying to move away.

She gestured frantically to the sound booth far across the oval, waving her hands and pointing at the mic. "Come on, come on, come on!" A static noise washed out and the final "on!" boomed across the crowd.

Thousands of eyes turned towards her.

For a moment, she froze. Her mouth dried up, her heart raced, she thought her knees would give out.

You got this, kid. That was Edgar, right there in her mind. She felt his smile.

She glanced back and saw the band and Eevie waiting just out of sight at the back edge of the stage. Eevie smiled, gave a thumbs up.

Lauren sucked in a breath and yelled, "Are you ready, Gulpepper?"

Thousands of hands shot into the air as the crowd roared, confusion and discomfort momentarily forgotten.

Lauren grinned, the thrill of the moment electrifying her. "You are the luckiest people in the world right now! In a matter of seconds, the music event of the century is going to be rocking your world. They're right behind me! Are you ready for One... Immortal... Day?!"

She stared hard at the sound booth, saw the distant faces of the engineers as they realised what she was saying. They started moving around frantically. Stage lights flicked on, red and blue strafing the stage despite the late afternoon sunlight and a spotlight hit her.

The crowd roared louder still, pushing forward again. The volume, impossibly, shifted even higher and Lauren realised Shirley had taken her seat at the kit, twirling one drum stick over her head.

"Gentlemen and ladies!" Lauren yelled, raising her fist. "Gentlethem and theydies! Let's go wild for Blind Eye Moon featuring Eevie Chill!"

Shirley fired off machine-gun double kicks and the crowd went wild. The drum sound fluctuated up and down slightly as the engineers worked frantically for volume balance. The crowd screamed as Edgar, Clarke and Howard walked onto the stage. Edgar put an arm around Lauren and kissed the top of her head as the crowd chanted his name. He took the mic from her and growled, "Gulpepper!"

The crowd howled. Lauren grinned and scurried off to one side of the stage.

Shirley matched her double kicks with rapid snare and tom combos, then Howard played a bass run. Clarke and Edgar took turns with guitar runs and a few quick power chords, clearly all hoping the sound engineers had something to work with and would balance the rest on the run. The crowd screamed louder still and changed the chant. "Blind Eye Moon! Blind Eye Moon!"

"Hello, Gulpepper!" Edgar said, a cheeky edge to his voice. He delivered the next line in powerful song. "Bet you didn't expect this today!" He drew out the last word into a long, high metal scream.

Another wave of Winterbourne's power swept across and Lauren watched the band grimace. But the crowd seemed to think it was all part of the show now and they were here for it. The sky above darkened, as if storm clouds had simply lowered into place where there had been clear skies moments before. As the eyes of the crowd turned up, some combination of wonder and confusion, Edgar nodded quickly to Shirley and they launched into a blistering riff, galloping along at a furious BPM. Howard joined them, Clarke played a lead fill, then Edgar yelled, "Say hello to our friend, Eevie Chill!"

Eevie stalked out across the stage and grabbed her mic off the stand beside Edgar's. "What's happening, Gulpepper?"

As the crowd roared, Shirley dropped her rhythm to a single kick double, like a heartbeat. The bass and guitars fell silent. Eevie walked to the front of the stage, leaning out towards the crowd, and waited, lifting the expectation. Shirley's heartbeat got louder, faster, then Eevie sang the opening line to her song, *Vengeance*, "You thought I was a weak one..."

Edgar joined in, "But I will watch you burrrrrrn!"

And a Blind Eye Moon version of the song's riff kicked in, faster than usual and heavy as hell. The gathered thousands began to bounce and pulse in place. Lauren marvelled at people's ability to accept the worst kinds of weirdness. The sky had literally changed above them and yet, with Eevie and Edgar acting like it was nothing to worry about, all somehow part of the show, no one seemed to be worrying.

As they reached the end of the first verse, Eevie and Edgar walked away from each other along the front of the stage, delivering the catchy four-line chorus in harmony. Then Edgar chopped out the rhythm guitar line while Clarke launched into a face-melting solo. Eevie started headbanging from the waist, whipping her hair. Impossibly, the crowd went even more crazy.

Lauren looked up, saw dark shapes writhing in the purple and black clouds.

Edgar stepped back, still playing, but his eyes were completely black and his lips moved like he was muttering a litany. A shimmering dome, like oil on water, almost too faint to see, spread over the entire stage and showground.

The Eevie Chill song morphed into Blind Eye Moon's track, *Midnight Meat*, with Eevie taking all the vocals. She marched back and forth across the stage, owning the Blind Eye Moon classic like she'd always been the one to sing it. The energy off the stage, off the crowd, was thunderous.

"Come on, Chrissy," Lauren whispered to herself. "You can do this."

As Rich powered the small launch away from the rocks heading south, Chrissy heard Lauren yell, "Are you ready, Gulpepper?"

She smiled, despite her fears. The young girl had really stepped up. They all had. Despite everything, Chrissy had to tell herself they had a chance at this. Drums and guitars played rapid tests, then Edgar started talking. Another wave from Winterbourne pulsed out, sent them rocking as Rich desperately motored left and right between other boats filling the bay. Chanting from the crowd rose up in volume, then Shirley's bass drum started marking out a heartbeat. Somehow that steadied Chrissy and she set to breathing deeply, keeping her focus. When the driving riff kicked in, the volume was staggering, rolling out over the ocean. Gulpepper residents would be either celebrating or complaining about the impromptu gig for years, assuming there was a Gulpepper left.

The sky darkened as more waves of Winterbourne's power swept out. Things writhed and twisted in the clouds. Chrissy braced herself in the boat, teeth gritted. Already Winterbourne was affecting reality. They had no time and she felt—

She gasped as energy like she'd never known before surged into her. Edgar had begun to do his thing. She glanced back and saw a kind of shimmering dome appear over the entire showground and realised Edgar was not only giving her strength, but he and the band were somehow isolating themselves and the majority of the crowd, at least partially, from Winterbourne's effects. Smart. She hoped it was enough.

The pounding music from the stage kept on, shifting into Blind Eye Moon's anthem, *Kindness Is Never Guaranteed*, as Rich steered the boat towards rocks at the southern end of the beach. Winterbourne's wards tore at Chrissy as they approached, like red hot needles sliding along her bones. She cried out and Rich looked back, concerned, slowed down, but Chrissy waved him on. Eevie Chill's vocals rang out and Chrissy felt something more. She had no idea quite how he was doing it, but Edgar's emotional manipulation of the seething crowd on the Gulpepper showground reached her in pulsing bursts and the pain of Winterbourne's wards began to ease.

Rich got the boat near, threw a rope and jumped onto the rocks to haul them close as the Eevie Chill track, *Fall Into Darkness*, started with Eevie's signature rising note, and the full force of Edgar's work hit her.

It was as though someone had injected every vein with crackling electricity. She was engorged with it, empowered by something so far beyond the human experience she nearly passed out. As she staggered, Rich grabbed her arm with one hand, pulling her up onto the rocks.

As Chrissy breathed down the surge of power Edgar channelled to her, her vision cleared. Clearer than it had ever been. The dark shapes twisting and moving in the thick clouds above began to fall.

"It's the dream!" Rich shouted. "The dream, for real. How is it happening now?"

Chrissy grinned. "It's always happening. Always was, never was, always will. It's what Winterbourne is planning to use. That's what I have to stop. Take cover here, okay? This is all me now."

Rich paused, eyebrows high. "I can protect you!"

"No. You can't. No one can. Wait for me."

Chrissy kissed him, hard and resolute, then turned and started clambering up the rocks towards the coast path and Burly Road.

Part of Lauren absolutely rocked out, disbelieving of the position she found herself in. Blind Eye Moon and Eevie Chill, right there. She knew BEM were a band that was huge in Australia but largely unknown elsewhere. She'd read somewhere they never toured outside the country. But Eevie was a global phenomenon, and there she was, absolutely tearing up the stage with the local rockers.

Another part of Lauren, though, couldn't help notice the effort on the part of the band members. While Eevie was in her element, carrying the vocal load of the gig as *Fall Into Darkness* ended and Clarke began the melodic intro to Blind Eye Moon's *The Way to Wolf Creek*, Lauren watched the effort on the faces of Clarke, Howard, Shirley and Edgar. Consummate professionals, they didn't miss a beat, but they grimaced and braced against some unseen onslaught that was clearly taking a massive toll on them.

Lauren looked up, saw the things falling from the roiling sky were reaching the shimmery dome and blinking out, like they'd never been. It gave the strange effect that everything outside the area was somehow projected up there, even though she knew it was all real.

For the first time in her life, she knew without a shadow of doubt that the dream of the fall was true. And outside the dome was mayhem. Giant creatures crashed into the ocean, capsizing boats. They plummeted into houses and roads, people crushed under their thrashing limbs.

And all the while, the thousands crammed onto the showground bounced and shouted and waved phones and sang along, eyes only for the gig, oblivious to the impossible carnage outside. Edgar, sweating, eyes black, had them in the palm of his hand.

But for how long?

Rich felt powerless, left on the rocks to wait. The pounding music of the gig continued, almost as loud as it had been when they left. The stacks he'd insisted on were more than living up to the task. But Chrissy was on her own and he had trouble believing what he saw. The sky churned, red and purple and black, and all those impossible things were falling, just like the dream. Except he wasn't dreaming.

Thousands of them hit the water and he heard them crashing into the land up behind him. Breaking timbers, smashing glass, people screaming. Hell was falling on Gulpepper while rock and metal rang through the air. The iridescent dome over the showground seemed like the only oasis of sanity in the world.

The creatures that fell were hard to understand, even as he watched them. Some were no bigger than he was while others seemed as big as buildings. All colours and some in colours he had never seen before. Colours and shapes that couldn't exist, phasing in and out of recognition as they fell. Rich's mind stretched as he tried to understand.

With a yelp, he scrambled back as something huge slammed into the rocks nearby and slid into the water, barely missing their boat. It had dozens of flailing limbs, somehow slick and smooth like tentacles, but also jointed like insect legs. Hundreds of eyes swarmed across its surface and its mouth stretched in a scream like electronic static that tore into Rich's ears like knives.

It was surely the end of the world. The end of many worlds, all colliding. Something far out in the depths towards Cathedral Stack began rising. A giant upswell as if to receive everything that fell, almost as though the ocean itself was ravenous to feed.

Sobbing, Rich could bear it no longer and crammed himself back under an overhang of rock, fingers jammed into his ears, eyes squeezed shut. And he waited to die.

Chrissy sprinted towards the white community hall charged with power unlike anything she'd ever thought possible. With her enhanced vision, the place glowed like every board of its construction was filled with light. She felt as though she was glowing the same way. Whatever Edgar was giving her, it was incredible and dangerous. She knew she would suffer for feeling like this. Already she was aware she would spend the rest of her life chasing the feeling, should she survive, and likely never get even close to it again. But that was the price she would have to pay. The alternative was unthinkable.

"You challenge me?" Winterbourne's voice cracked into her mind and collapsed her to one knee. Hard asphalt tore her jeans, then her skin. She pushed up and ran on. Winterbourne's laughter rang all around, inside and outside her mind. "You're already too late! It has begun!"

Chrissy kicked open the doors of the hall and gasped at the sight before her.

All around the large space, people were hung from the walls, two or three deep in places. Naked and blood-soaked, their bodies sliced open, entrails all snaking out, dripping, towards the centre of the room. And in the centre, Winterbourne hung suspended by that massed web of viscera, arms outstretched, cruciform. Before him was a kind of lectern and on it, a large book, open to the last page.

Winterbourne's eyes were bright white lights, his bone-white hair on end, swimming in the static of his energies. The book glowed.

"Your father stopped something before," Winterbourne said, his words echoing as if in some deep cavern. "So I understand why you think you can stop this. But you can't."

"I won't let you succeed!"

"You can't stop me! Your father simply interrupted an entity trying to manifest itself here. That was easy. I'm looking to go the other way."

Chrissy frowned, tried to understand. "Go where?"

"There are vast intelligences in the galaxy, child," Winterbourne said. "Things exist without even the concept of what humans call gods, paying no more mind to us than we pay to the bacteria in the soil at our feet. Sometimes their influence manifests in our reality, like we might leave a footprint in that soil, and it means nothing to them. But that's the gateway, you see. Why not go the other way? Why not take someone already manifest in this reality, someone with power, someone like *me*, and expand into an entity like *them*?"

"You're trying to become a god?"

"Are you listening? Far greater than any god! I will manifest *galactically!*"

"That can't be possible." Chrissy gathered everything

Edgar was pumping into her, tried to see how she might use it, but it seemed inconsequential already in the face of what Winterbourne was doing. Was it all pointless?

"Gulpepper has always been a thin point," Winterbourne said, rising higher, glowing brighter. "A footprint in the soil of reality trodden by things beyond our comprehension. The perfect place to force a tear that someone with the power and the will can step through and become vast themselves. I've spent a lifetime, many lifetimes, gathering that power, and you think you can stop me now?" Winterbourne tipped his head back and laughed. The people around the walls howled and moaned, alive and recognising their agony.

Chrissy began to panic. No amount of power given to her could interrupt this. Winterbourne was already underway, already gaining strength at an exponential rate, already transcending. His laughter was like psychic bombs raining into her mind, battering her ability to think, to plan. She cried out, bereft.

Edgar's voice cut through from somewhere far away and right beside her too. "Don't you fucking dare, Carter. Would your dad have given up here?"

Chrissy screamed, drove herself up and forward. Outside, the fall continued. Uncanny twisted forms, bigger than any living thing had any right to be, hit the ocean and the land. Buildings and people were crushed, wails of pain and anguish rang out. But over it all, the driving music of Blind Eye Moon, the angelic power of Eevie Chill. Edgar had the throng of thousands in his thrall, had their collective psyche to control. Chrissy felt Winterbourne notice and smiled.

"Yeah, we're a bit bigger than you thought, huh?"

Winterbourne's power pulsed again, growing stronger still. "It doesn't matter. You're too late. All time is now and now is all time."

And she knew he was right. He had set something in motion that seemed impossible to slow, let alone stop. But she needed to try. She needed more help. She sent her will out to Hilda, begged for assistance. And it turned out Hilda was ready, had been waiting. Dozens of her huge spyders swarmed into the hall.

"I'm sorry!" Chrissy said to the unwitting victims hanging around the walls, and the spyders fell upon them, mandibles clacking, tearing them to pieces and consuming them in chunks. The slick network of viscera holding Winterbourne up began to collapse, to go slack. Winterbourne faltered, his light and power fluctuating, but he didn't fall.

"You're too late!" he yelled again. "They've given all they can already."

But Chrissy saw a moment of uncertainty cross his expression. Could she do this?

Music pulsed across the landscape. People screamed, some in ecstasy at the experience, some in fear and pain as madness fell from the churning skies and crushed them or snapped their minds. The fall that had happened aeons ago and was yet to happen and was always happening had been focussed to one moment. This moment.

And Winterbourne was trying to use it, forcing people to experience time all at once, to cause a kind of mass psychosis that would empower his desire to step outside of time and space as people reckoned it. To become something greater than the human mind could even countenance.

Whether he was able to do that or not didn't really matter. What ultimately became of the thing that was Winterbourne was irrelevant, as he would certainly destroy Gulpepper in the process. He would tear reality apart, leave a crater in time and space where Gulpepper had once existed. And maybe far further afield than simply The Gulp. Maybe the country. Perhaps this entire world. Already people were dying by the hundreds, but before this was over? They would all be dead. Tens of thousands, extending who knew how far.

And Chrissy realised that was her chance. She could

beat him because she wasn't trying to manipulate something so massive. She wasn't fighting to control this event and exploit it like Winterbourne was. She just needed to prevent Winterbourne from controlling it.

But how?

Winterbourne's form began to expand, as if the light inside pushed every atom of him outwards. Reality began to split around him and Chrissy turned her gaze away from the incomprehensible things beyond those rips lest her mind be swept away into them.

What even was the man? What had he become? It didn't really matter, but he had clearly worked for years, decades, building his skills, his tolerance, his abilities. How could she use that against him?

Edgar's voice came into her mind. *Focus not on what he's trying to become, but on what he was.*

Oma said there was a stain on the top one, like someone had put a coffee cup on it.

That's how he keeps disappearing. He doesn't go somewhere else. He goes somewhen else.

Chrissy's eyes widened and she looked up as Winterbourne rose. He could only manifest this amount of power for so long before it destroyed the physical vessel of Winterbourne himself. He planned to transcend that physical presence and use the energies he created to expand his consciousness into something more, with no more need of what he had been. What if she prevented that transcendence while the energies continued to build? What if she held him here, now?

Edgar, I need everything you've got.

You fucking kidding? This is already agony. I can't hold on much longer.

Give me all you can. All or nothing, now.

Rock'n'roll, baby.

Chrissy gasped with the surge through her veins and knew Edgar had taken her at her word. This couldn't last long and it was the only chance she'd have. She drove her consciousness into Winterbourne's mind, merged with him. His reaction was sudden and violent, agony as he tried to cast her out, but she gripped and held on. She searched for his abilities, scoured his memories and found the park. The papers. The coffee stain. The power he'd used to step back.

"Let's go, fucker!"

Chrissy forced Winterbourne's ability, dragging the physical body he was trying to transcend with her to the past. Just a few seconds would do it.

"No! What are you doing?"

As the spyders tore apart the people giving Winterbourne his physical strength, she dragged him away. His focus faltered while surging energies continued to build.

"Turn on him!" Chrissy ordered them, and the spyders raced towards Winterbourne's suspended form.

Through his eyes, Chrissy saw her body, standing rigid in front of the lectern and Winterbourne's book. Her lips moved.

Give me all you can. All or nothing, now.

She heard Edgar's psychic response.

Rock'n'roll, baby.

Chrissy forced Winterbourne's ability again, dragged them both back a few seconds, using causality to shatter everything he was trying to become.

Winterbourne thrashed against the mental grip she had over him, but his attention was stretched in too many places at once. Part of him already outside his physical form, part of him trapped in it, part of him manipulating the power of his profane book even as the physical presence of all those poor Gulpepper residents he'd captured began to fade.

Give me all you can. All or nothing, now.

Rock'n'roll, baby.

She dragged him back again, a little less each time. The spyders got a little closer each time. Then they began to tear at Winterbourne's flesh. He screamed, tried to rip Chrissy's mind to pieces, to fragment everything in a desperate last attempt to break free. A psychic wrestling match with his power against her and the gathered masses at the showground. As a blistering riff rang out over the screams outside, she held on.

Winterbourne's window was passing. She forced linear time to repeat into the moment he'd created, knowing this much energy could only be contained for so long. The concentrated focus he'd put onto that book to manifest all times at once, to create a flat circle, to give him his route beyond their reality, faltered.

Give me all you can. All or nothing, now.

Rock'n'roll, baby.

She ripped him back one last time and Winterbourne's howl broke the sky. Everything exploded in light and dark. Chrissy saw the galaxy whole and in pieces, she saw time all at once, she perceived existence, but she held Winterbourne back long enough that it tore him apart. The last thing she saw before all consciousness fled was Winterbourne's essence explode and scatter through time and space like smoke blown apart by wind, leaving a devastated Gulpepper behind.

From the other end of Carlton Beach, over a kilometre away, Blind Eye Moon's driving music and Eevie Chill's scorching vocals, were still deafening. Rich cowered under the overhang of rock refusing to watch impossible things fall from the roiling dark sky. He'd had the dream often enough, but never thought he would see it for real. Or was he dreaming now?

From somewhere above, a howling crescendo built. He heard screams of agony and fear as well as cheers from the showground. The music pulsed, the sky thundered.

Then the sky cleared.

A great roar rose up from the gig behind him and the band launched into a new song. Rich sensed a huge pressure lift. He scrambled out from cover, up over the rocks and ran for the hall.

All around was devastation. Cars and buildings crushed, but nothing apparent to have crushed them. Bodies lay in the streets and other people stumbled around, checking the wounded or grieving over the dead.

Rich ran into the old hall. He was faced with a scene of slaughter, body parts scattered all over. Feeding on the bodies were giant, spider-like beasts. Winterbourne was nowhere to be seen, but a large book sat on a lectern and Chrissy lay facedown before it, unmoving. Rich rushed over and fell to his knees, turned her to face him. She was breathing, her eyes were open, but they were blank. She stared right through him.

"Chrissy!" He rained kisses on her lips and cheeks, called her name again, but she didn't respond. She was warm, breathing, and limp.

Rich lifted her up. The band would know how to help, he just needed to get her back there. He carried her from the hall, heading for the boat as rock music hammered the air. He laid Chrissy in the back and motored out across the waves as Blind Eye Moon and Eevie Chill continued to rock the crowd.

Chrissy lay in bed at the farmhouse, unresponsive. Rich sat at the big kitchen table with the band, Eevie Chill and Lauren Hart. Edgar was paler than usual, his expression drawn. He breathed shallow, sometimes almost half-conscious. Whatever he'd done had obviously cost him dearly. Rich wondered how long it might take the man to recover. *Man?* Whatever Edgar and the rest of this weird band really were.

Shirley, Clarke and Howard were also drained, lacking the buzz Rich would expect after a performance. They'd all given a lot. Eevie, by contrast, was clearly energised, as was Lauren. The benefit of normality, he thought, whatever that meant, but they were sombre at the news of events outside the gig. Already there were reports of a strange earthquake, possibly triggered by the unprecedented volume of the impromptu rock concert. How quickly people looked for a mundane explanation. Hundreds had died, supposedly under falling buildings even though some were crushed in the middle of the street with nothing around them. While the effects of the fall remained, the things that had fallen were nowhere. As if they'd never been.

It was close to midnight, the legions of people who had arrived for the unprecedented event slowly drifting away. Rich wondered how many had suffered, had died. How many corpses would daylight reveal in the morning? How many minds had been stretched so far they'd snapped by what had happened? And yet, at the same time, there was little evidence anything other than an epic gig had occurred. There would be repercussions, that was inevitable.

"Will she be okay?" Rich asked. He directed the question generally, but Edgar looked up, assuming it was him being asked.

"Honestly, mate, I dunno. I only felt by association what she went through but it nearly tore me apart." He huffed a soft laugh. "Her strength, man. She's tougher than her dad ever was. The power she contained and manipulated tonight was outstanding."

"But what has it done to her?"

"We can't know. It's a shame Bram's not still around,

he might have been able to tell. Perhaps we can find someone. I'll ask around. We'll get her help, don't worry."

"That was pretty fucking epic," Eevie said. "Honestly, I still don't really know what we did, but it felt incredible."

Edgar smiled. "That fucker who gave you such a hard time was absolutely wrecked. That's what we did."

"Awesome."

"Thanks for including me," Lauren said. "I'm so glad I could help."

"You were amazing," Rich told her. "You're something else, you know that? An honour to know you."

Lauren blushed and glanced away. Eevie squeezed her hand.

"Gonna be some tidying up and damage control," Howard said. "Chrissy is usually pretty good at managing that stuff. Guess we'll step in this time?"

"Yeah, we'll manage," Shirley said. "Gulpepper has a way of shaking this shit off, after all."

"Reminds me of something Chrissy said after her dad died," Rich said. "She told me how he used to always warn her she'd have to step up one day, that he wouldn't be around forever. And he said Gulpepper would always be a nexus for the inexplicable. There isn't anything they can do about it, an unchangeable fact of reality. But he said she needed to be ready because two things would always be true. One, any time something tried to exploit Gulpepper, someone would be there, standing in the way. And two, don't worry about the residents, because they've grown used to it. He said as long as there was someone taking care of The Gulp, The Gulp would take care of its own."

Edgar smiled. "Yeah, this place is a trip, that's for sure. Let's just hope it's at least a little while before anything comes up again. I could really use a nice, long rest."

A young girl walked through the night, not quite able to believe she'd been to the most amazing gig the world was ever likely to see. And it had happened right here in her hometown of Gulpepper. She was only fourteen and wondered if perhaps life had just peaked for her. Regardless, she would be riding the high for weeks.

And the quake that had caused such mayhem didn't seem to have touched the showground. She laughed. Quake! So many people had suggested that already and she thought perhaps it was a little stupid. Gulp weirdness is what it was, just like the unexpected gig. The good and the bad, as always.

The damage around town was extensive. So many broken buildings, people lying everywhere. She kept heading for home, doing her best to ignore the destruction and hoping her home was still there. A man ran past her, gibbering something rapidly about the stars, his eyes wide. She looked away, kept walking.

As she passed the old community hall on Burly Road, she saw the doors were open. Curious, she went up the short path and looked inside. There were dark stains all over the walls and floor, though no evidence of anything that might have made them. Clearly something brutal had gone down here. She thought she caught movement at the back, something spindly slipping out where a boarded-up window had been broken through. She paused, nervous, but nothing else moved. Slowly, her eyes adjusted to the gloom.

In the middle of the room was a strangely carved wooden lectern holding a large book. The girl walked up to it. The book had thick, hard covers and heavy pages of some kind of stiffened leather. She turned the pages slowly. Each was inscribed with writing she didn't recognise, a language she had never seen before, but that somehow appealed to her. As she progressed through the book, she felt an affinity for the writing, like it might reveal itself to her if she studied it hard enough. She closed the book and stared at the symbol on the front. That appealed to her as well.

"It's the Void Atlas," she said quietly, then frowned. "How the hell do I know that?"

But she did know it. Intrinsically, like she'd always known it.

"Classic Gulp," she said with a soft laugh, and left the old hall, the heavy book tucked under her arm.

Read more from Alan Baxter
www.alanbaxter.com.au

Afterword

I wasn't sure for a long time whether I'd write a third *Tales From The Gulp*. After *The Gulp* and *The Fall* were both so well-received, I was worried about spoiling that by writing another volume. You know the old adage: Always leave them wanting more.

I've written Gulpepper Mythos things in the meantime, like the novella, *The Leaves Forget*, and the novel, *Blood Covenant*. Those things exist in the Gulpepper Mythos universe and there are others and will be many more. But another actual *Tales From The Gulp* volume? I was cautious. But I also knew the love I have for this town meant I couldn't resist going back just once more. While I will continue to return to this mythos in novels and stories for as long as I keep writing, I decided one more official volume of *Tales* was needed.

I hope you enjoyed this third collection of dark weirdness as much as the first two. I hope it's answered some of your questions about the place and its denizens. I hope it's raised a few more questions too. It's boring to have all the answers, after all.

I did say I would tell you what the story is with Winterbourne. That, at least, should be settled by now. Mostly. The Mythos will continue and you can find out all you need to know about that at my website at alanbaxter.com.au

So thank you for coming along with me this far, and I hope you'll join me again in the future. Like I've said before, I get the feeling no one can stay away from The Gulp for too long...

Alan Baxter, October 2025

Acknowledgements

Huge thanks to Joanne Anderton and John Durgin for reading early drafts of this volume. Your feedback is invaluable. Also massive thanks to the amazing people who help put the actual book together: Mallory Wiper for excellent editing, David Wood for layout. You guys rock.

Extra special thanks to my amazingly talented wife, Halinka Orszulok, whose oil painting once again provides the powerful artwork for the cover of *The Rise*, as it did for both *The Gulp* and *The Fall*.

And finally, thank *you*. Thank you for reading and being a part of this journey. That people read these weird stories I drag out of my twisted psyche—that they, in fact, keep asking for more—is truly staggering to me. I appreciate you more than I can say.

*Throughout this book, I've used Australian English spelling, and a bit of Aussie slang. For a **Glossary** of all that, have a look at https://alanbaxter.com.au/a-glossary-of-aussie-slang/*

About

Alan Baxter is a multi-award-winning British-Australian author of horror and weird fiction. *This Is Horror* podcast calls him "Australia's master of literary darkness" and the *Talking Scared* podcast dubbed him "The Lord of Weird Australia." He's also a martial artist, whisky-soaked swear monkey, metalhead and dog lover. He writes his darkly strange tales deep in the valleys of southern Tasmania. Find him online at:

www.alanbaxter.com.au